RUNNING FROM THE LAW

Brides on the Run, Book 3

JAMI ALBRIGHT

Running From the Law

One night of passion. Two second chances. Three little texts . . .

Former child star, Charlie Klein, is in a world of trouble. She's broke, jobless, and no longer famous—except with the IRS. She's ready to run, so an emergency call from Texas is all the excuse she needs to get out of Hollywood. But she doesn't expect to crash into the sheriff of her hometown, the boy she loved and lost. One look at Hank Odom confirms what her heart has always known . . . She never stopped loving him.

Unlike the men in his family, Hank's a do-the-right-thing kind of guy. When his cheating, soon-to-be ex-wife texts him wanting a second chance – or a *twentieth* chance – he's determined to honor his vows. One problem? His traitorous heart has never forgotten the woman who just blew back into town.

One night of passion. Two second chances. Three little texts.
And nine months of OMG!

To Nathan and Stephanie, thank you for the lock and key idea. I'm so happy you two found the key to your Happily Ever After.

To Miranda Lambert & Eric Church, your music inspired every emotional word of this book. Thank you for carrying me through the writing of Running From the Law .

Chapter One

It wasn't every day that a Hollywood star lost their shit.

Oh, wait, that did happen every day, but not to Charlie Klein.
As the child star of the Carousel Network's *Charlie Takes the Town*
for the last eight years she'd learned to keep her freak-outs on the
down low.

Until today.

"What do you mean it's all gone? Like, define *all*." She held her
phone in a death grip.

"Every penny in the account you set up for your grandfather is
gone, Ms. Klein. You didn't know?" Jerry Lattimore, the president of
Zachsville National Bank, sounded almost as worried as she did.

Crazy clawed up her throat like a Kardashian with a broken phone
camera. "No, I didn't know. Why the hell would I call you to try to
transfer money for my grandfather if I knew?"

"Ms. Klein, please calm down." The tremor in the man's voice indicated to dial it back or she wouldn't get the answers she needed.

"I apologize." *Breathe in. Breathe out.* "Mr. Lattimore." She paced her
Austin, Texas hotel room. "Are you telling me that my grandfather has
withdrawn more than a million dollars from that account?"

"No."

"No?" Now she was confused on top of being freaked out. She knew she hadn't taken the money and there was no one else left who could've wiped her out.

"There were automatic monthly withdrawals that went to your mother, then six months ago she emptied the account. She was a co-signer on the account." The man's logical tone while he flipped her life on its ass made her want to hurt someone.

"My mother was never on that account." She knew this because it was the one financial thing she'd done on her own as soon as she'd turned eighteen. She'd never given her mother access to the money she'd set up for her grandfather's retirement. There had to be a mistake.

Computer keys clicked on the other end of the line. "Ms. Klein, I have a document signed by your grandfather putting her name on the account. It's dated and notarized."

Silence. Her words were jammed behind a wall of fury. This explained so much, but left so many questions unanswered. Why had she done it? It didn't matter. All that mattered now was that her grandfather was recovering from a car accident that should've taken his life but blessedly hadn't. If he hadn't been airlifted from Zachsville to Memorial Hospital in Austin, then that might not be the case.

Holy hell. If all the money was gone from the account she'd set up for him, then she couldn't give her Pops the care he needed. The pitiful truth was she was broke. Her grandfather hadn't been the only victim of her mother's crimes. She'd stolen from Charlie too, and left her in trouble with the IRS.

Six months ago, she'd woken up to find millions had disappeared. According to her accountant, every account had been cleaned out. And, yes, she had needed someone to tell her she was broke. One more thing she'd let others run for her. She was such an idiot. She'd trusted her mother and been burned in the worst way.

Two weeks later her mother was dead in Italy. The money she took, never recovered. And Charlie was slapped with a huge bill from the Internal Revenue Service with no way to pay it. The betrayal still had the power to take her to her knees.

Thankfully, she'd always followed her grandmother's advice to tuck away a little cash for a rainy day or she'd have nothing. Now every cent of her residuals from *Charlie Takes the Town* were going to pay back her taxes. If she was careful, lived modestly, and there were no emergencies, like her grandfather's retirement account being empty, she could stretch her small nest egg another six months.

"Ms. Klein?" Mr. Lattimore's voice cut through her misery. "Is there anything else I can do for you?"

"No." She disconnected the call and stared out the window of the hotel room she'd rented to be close to her grandfather. The rays of an early autumn sunset shone off the hospital's sign and mocked her.

This is what she'd given up her childhood for? Given up...well, *everything* for. Sitting broke and alone in a strange hotel room wondering how she'd care for the only family she had in the world?

She slid her finger gingerly over the phone screen and went to her voicemail to listen to the message again. Two clicks and she put the phone to her ear.

"Um...Charlie, this is Hank Odom. I'm the Sheriff of Blister County now."

At the sound of his voice her frazzled nerves stopped vibrating with pent-up tension.

"I need you to return my call as soon as possible. It concerns your grandfather. He's been in an accident. You can reach me on this number."

The way he said her name was so foreign and yet achingly familiar.

Hank Odom.

The boy who'd loved her, who she'd loved, and left. They'd never been able to be a real couple. They'd had to sneak around because he was three years older, and her mother hadn't approved. Then a few months before her sixteenth birthday, unbeknownst to her, her mother sent a tape of her singing to an open audition the Carousel Network was having, and within months she was moving to LA.

Away from Hank. Away from her dreams of a life with him.

She hadn't heard from him or about him for eight years. First it had been her mother blocking all communication with anyone from Zachsville, including her grandparents. After a while simple self-preservation forced her to put aside thoughts of those she'd left behind, including her best friend Hailey and saddest of all, Hank. She hadn't even looked them up on social media. What would that have accomplished? Nothing. She'd just be picking at the scar of an old wound.

Once she and her grandfather reconnected at her mother's funeral, the only request she had was that he not talk about her old life in Zachsville. Some memories were better left ripped to shreds.

Dramatic much, Charlie? That was all in the past. You've got bigger problems in the present.

Right. An injured grandfather, a lying, stealing dead mother, an enormous tax bill, and no money. She glanced at her phone again. Her options were slim to none except for the one horrible thing she absolutely did not want to do.

Damn it.

Her finger hovered above the phone screen. Fire burned in her belly. She'd been so close to freedom, and for a short time she'd had it. Free of the Carousel Network, free of bad writing and canned laughter, just free to do whatever the hell she wanted to do, whatever that was. But now, she'd have to take the ridiculous offer Carousel had made her before she left LA—a new show on a kid's network, at the age of twenty-four. The leash that she'd slipped only two short months ago looped tight around her throat.

Before she could think too long about it, she punched the familiar name on her phone.

"Charlie, you brat, when are you coming back to LA? Not that there's really any reason to since you turned down Carousel. FYI, nobody else is banging on your door."

There was always something so comforting and yet distasteful about hearing her manager's voice. "My grandfather's well, thanks for asking, Ron."

"Of course he's well. He's too mean to die."

Her Pops wasn't mean. He just didn't like Ron. "The Carousel deal is what I'm calling about."

"Really?" His tone immediately changed from disinterested to sweet and cordial. "What about it?"

"You can tell them I'm willing to negotiate."

"Are you serious? Don't yank my chain."

"I'm serious. But there are a few things I want. I'll text them to you." She pretended the pain in her heart wasn't really there. Just like she'd been taught to do. Smiling for the camera and hiding her true feelings was as natural as breathing.

"That's fantastic. They're offering you a shit-ton of money, Charlie, enough to get you out of hock with the IRS, and then some. This is the big time. I'm going to call them right now. You've made the right decision, sweetheart. Talk soon." The call disconnected.

Sweetheart. Now she was his sweetheart. Wasn't that just the Hollywood way. You're only as good as the last thing you did, and everything, including love, was conditional.

She briefly considered listening to Hank's voicemail again, but decided that on a scale of one to pitiful that would be a solid pathetic.

I've got to get out of here.

Anywhere was preferable to being stuck in these four walls with only her thoughts to keep her company. She grabbed her purse and headed for the elevator. On the ride to the lobby, she tried to talk herself into a better frame of mind. It was a trick her grandmother had taught her when she was little.

This situation will be fine.

It will work out.

I'm grateful I have the means to earn more money.

So what if I have to play a teenager for another couple of years. Surely that shit has a fucking expiration date on it.

Okay, that last part wasn't part of grandma's process. In fact, the woman would wash her mouth out with soap for that outburst.

She examined herself in the mirrored doors and tried again.

I'm lucky to look so young.

One day I'll be grateful for the fact that I looked way younger than twenty-four years old. Hey, maybe I can keep playing crappy teenaged roles for the rest of my miserable fucking life?

She should probably try this little exercise later. Clearly, she wasn't in the right frame of mind for positive Pollyanna thoughts. In fact, she'd happily punch Pollyanna in the vagina right about now.

She needed a drink.

The doors opened, and with her head down—the last thing she needed was to be recognized—she exited the elevator and ran straight into a wall of solid male. "Oh, excuse me." She addressed his boots because she couldn't deal with a fan right now, or having to be girl-next-door Charlie Kay.

He grabbed her upper arms to steady her. "No problem."

That voice. She knew that voice. She should, because she'd just listened to it five minutes ago, but it had also played center stage in her dreams for the last eight years. It represented all that was good with the world.

It couldn't be. Slowly, she raised her head and...sweet baby Jesus. He still stole every molecule of air from her lungs.

"Charlie?" The timbre of his Texas accent snuggled around her heart.

She swallowed twice, trying to make her vocal chords work. "Hank?"

He maneuvered them out of the way of another couple trying to enter the elevator. "I... It's good to see you."

"Hank?" Dogs three miles away probably heard her high-pitched question.

"Yep, it's me." His lips slid up on one side. "You okay, Charlie?"

Had she conjured him? How awesome if she'd developed that talent. Maybe she could conjure a buttload of money. She shook her head. "Yeah, sorry. I'm fine."

His golden bangs hung over his forehead. "Are you staying here?"

She got lost in the shape of his lips for a moment and had to refocus. "Yes, to be close to Pops in the hospital."

He nodded. "How is he?"

Tears she hadn't realized she needed to shed tried to spill over her lids. "He's good. It was touch and go for a few hours, but he's going to be fine. His leg is pretty messed up, so he'll need some ongoing care for a while, but he's good. What are you doing here?"

"Just getting out of Zachsville for a few days." His eyes never left hers and an old familiar heat blazed in his green irises.

An electric current sparked between his hands and her arms, then raced through her body. It had always been this way, even though all they'd ever done was some serious kissing. Not because she hadn't wanted more, but he'd always been careful with her. "I better—"

"Where are you headed?"

His mouth was nice. Was he saying something? "I'm sorry?"

The way his eyes crinkled at the corners when he grinned made her girly parts beg for mercy. Teenaged Hank had made her quiver with excitement, but grown-up Hank cut the ribbon on the Grand Opening of Lady Land.

He was just so...much. So much bigger, so much better looking, just so much more. Tall, golden, and a little rough around the edges. The manicured, pampered, and coiffed men in Hollywood couldn't hold a candle to his raw masculinity.

The width of his shoulders cast a shadow that invited her to hide from the world. He was the one she'd run to when her mother's demands overwhelmed her. His strong arms had held her when she'd bawled like a baby when she found out they were moving to Los Angeles. He'd been her defender, her shelter, and she ached to sink into that protection once again.

"I said, where are you going? Are you headed back to the hospital?"

She shook her head. "No. Pops told the nurse not to let me back in his room until I've had a night's rest. You know how he can be."

The smile deepened. "Yes, I do. Every time I see him he reminds me of that time he caught me climbing in your window."

If she closed her eyes, she could still see eighteen-year-old Hank standing outside her window. His heart in his eyes, and his blond bangs stuck to his sweaty forehead. The thrilling beat of butterfly wings against her heart as she'd raised the window, trying her hardest to not make a sound.

"How did you get up here, Hank Odom?"

His cocky mouth kicked up on one side. "I climbed."

"You climbed?" She grabbed his shirt. "Get in here before somebody sees you."

He gently disentangled himself from her grip. "No."

"No?"

He braced both hands on the window frame. "I didn't come here to get in your room, Charlie. I just wanted to see you."

She tried to appear unaffected, but it was hard with a marching band of happiness stomping through her chest. "You could've waited to see me at school tomorrow."

"Naw, I couldn't wait." *Two fingers went to his front shirt pocket, and he withdrew a slightly wilted daisy.* "This is for you. Sorry it got a little crumpled."

"Thank you." *She was mesmerized by how his laughing eyes crinkled at the corners when he smiled. A great, bright flame of promise flashed inside her when his white teeth bit into his lower lip. It was impossible to control the trembling in her hand as she took the flower, especially when her skin brushed his. From that first touch, she'd belonged to him.*

Unfortunately, her grandfather had interrupted their moment by pointing a shotgun at Hank and telling him to get his sorry tail off the roof.

Now Hank cleared his throat. "Where did you say you were going?"

He was still holding her and she still loved it. "I didn't really have any specific place in mind, just wanted to get out of my room." The scar he got when he ran into a low branch while chasing her at the river crossed his eyebrow. It had been hard explaining whose blood she had on her when her mother thought she was with her friend Hailey that day, not Hank. "I guess I should eat dinner. Want to join me?"

Where had that come from? But after the words were out, she wanted it more than anything in her life.

Please say yes.

He glanced away and sucked air through his nose. A shadow of regret drifted across his face when he met her gaze again. "I better not."

A wave of grief hit her when he released her arms and took a step away from her. "I understand." Could a person die from disappointment? If it was possible, she was about to drop dead on the spot.

He jabbed the button for the elevator. A frown marred his handsome face as he continued to stare at her, but his fingers skimmed lightly up her arm. "I should..."

"Oh, yeah." She shook her head to try to gain some composure, and stepped back. If he touched her again, she'd do something humiliating like beg. "I get it."

The elevator dinged. He stuck his hand in to keep it open. "It was good to see you, Charlie."

With all of the dignity and every ounce of talent she possessed, she smiled. "It was great to see you too. Take care, Hank." With each inch the doors slid shut, a piece of her heart peeled away and disintegrated. But she kept smiling and waving like a demented beauty queen.

Her ridiculous heart sank like the worthless organ it was. So much for the childhood fantasy of a knight in shining armor. The doors closed. She turned and searched for a place to hide and fall apart. This was dumb. She didn't still love him or anything, just her world falling apart made her want absurd things. They weren't a couple and never would be. So why the crushing sense of loss?

Because somewhere in the recess of her soul she'd always hoped for this reunion, though she'd never have admitted it to herself. But her fantasies hadn't included him walking away from her. In her dreams he'd swept her into his arms, taken her to bed, and made love to her, erasing all the years that stood between them and giving them both a brand-new start. A new beginning that she desperately needed right about now.

Suddenly, it wasn't oxygen that moved through her lungs but the shards of her miserable life. She turned and frantically scanned the lobby for the closest exit. Air, she needed air and a drink.

But before she could take a step to leave, the elevator dinged again behind her.

"Charlie."

Chapter Two

Hank's ragged voice ripped through her soul. She spun to face him, and the beats of her heart kicked against her ribs. He stood with his arms outstretched, holding the doors open. His face was a mask of longing, agony. "I need..."

Without thinking, she moved to him. She didn't give a damn who saw. All that mattered was getting to him. To Hank. To her safe place. As soon as she was in front of him, his arms went around her waist, and he pulled her into the elevator. His lips crushed hers. She clung to his neck and welcomed the desperate kiss. With every wet, slick swipe of his tongue the elevator became a time machine, hurtling her back to another place. She hadn't been kissed like this in eight years.

This was crazy, but she hadn't had near enough. She drank from his mouth. Every kiss was water from heaven on the cracked, dry landscape of her life.

He backed her against the panel and pushed a button, then went back to her mouth. Years fell away, and they were Hank and Charlie sneaking around, stealing long, lingering kisses that would have to last until the next time they could be together. But now, there was nothing to stop his hands from roaming every inch of her body.

Nothing but the couple that got on the elevator at the sixth floor.

They broke apart and he covered her body with his. She wiped her wet eyes on his shirt. Emotions roared through her like a locomotive without a conductor. Sanity screamed that this whole thing was pointless. Her life was in a different time zone and might always be. But her reckless heart was riding shotgun in a rocket ship of excitement and desire.

For eight years, everyone from her mother to the guy who ran errands for the production crew had owned a piece of her. She wasn't a person, she was a meal ticket. But Hank didn't care if she was a big-shot Hollywood star or Charlie down the block. And she wanted to be wanted like that. Needed it more than her next breath.

Just Charlie.

He'd never use her. He was good and honorable, everything that was missing in her life.

The whole reason she'd been able to play a girl from a small town with a white picket fence and the perfect family was because once upon a time, on a blanket under the stars, they'd dreamed and planned that kind of life for themselves.

Charlie and Hank forever.

Tears clogged in her throat when her mind repeated what they used to say to each other. Words she hadn't allowed herself to think, let alone speak, since she left Zachsville.

She burrowed into his body and held on tighter as she acknowledged all they had lost. Robbed. She'd been robbed of all the goodness that being with him brought. Her mother not only took her money, but had taken away her chance at love. She was his. She always had been. And he was hers.

They exited the elevator on what she assumed was his floor. He stepped off first and glanced down the hallway, then reached his hand out to her. The warmth of his palm pressed into hers wasn't enough. Her arm around his arm, she molded herself to his side as they made their way to his room. They leaned into each other, their steps measured and in sync like they'd always been. She tried to OD on his leather and rosewood scent, dragging one delicious breath after another into her lungs, until they stood before his room. Neither spoke, and the silence was its own aphrodisiac.

He slid the keycard into the slot and turned the handle. He didn't enter but straddled the threshold and held the door open with his hand. He was giving her a chance to walk away because there was no doubt what was about to happen. It was predestined, forever coming, and they both knew it. The moment dangled between them like the gold ring on a merry-go-round. There was no way she was letting this chance pass her by. She'd grab ahold of that prize and hang on for dear life.

To make sure he understood she was all in, she inclined her body against his, pressed an open-mouthed kiss to his throat, then sauntered into the room.

He followed her.

The door closed.

He leaned against it but made no move to come to her. He was going too slow. She knew why, but her body was at the starting line with its engine revving, while it appeared he was still making leisurely laps around the track. That wouldn't do.

"Charlie, I need to tell—"

"I don't want to talk, Hank."

"But you need..."

Her fingers went to the hem of her top. Whatever he was going to say died before it escaped his lips. Fine with her. Words weren't necessary anyway—his eyes communicated everything he wanted as they hungrily followed the path of her shirt as she slowly slid it up her body and over her head.

He scrubbed his hand over his mouth. "Fuuuck." The moaned oath made her bold enough to reach behind her and unhook her bra. The lacy cups fell to the ground, and she gave him what she'd wanted to give him since the first time he'd kissed her, when she was fifteen and crazy in love with him.

In some far-off corner of her head, her brain whispered *too fast,* but she ignored it. Her heart screamed, *faster, faster, faster.*

"You're so damn beautiful." His whispered adoration nearly took her knees out from under her.

She couldn't help how her lips curled into a smile. "Really?" The sway of her hips was deliberate as she made her way to him and unbuttoned his shirt. "Tell me more." Cheesy, she knew. It was a line from one of her favorite movies, but it sounded better than *I don't know what I'm doing.* She may talk a big talk, but the tremble that ran from the top of her head to her toes told a different story.

Hank was the only man she'd willingly allow to see her this vulnerable. The only other time she'd been intimate with someone was with a boy from the network. Carousel thought a relationship would be good for ratings. Her mother had sanctioned the whole thing, everything but the sex. That had been her idea. A way to make a point. A lot of alcohol and a crapload of regret later, she'd shown her mother that she couldn't control every aspect of her life. Sad that her first sexual encounter had been a big F-you to her mom.

"Tell you more?" He laughed, picked her up, and threw her on the bed. "I'd rather show you instead." Her squeal of laughter was cut off when his hot, wet mouth covered hers. His tongue glided over hers, licking like she was the best dessert he'd ever had. She wasn't much better. With every swipe and taste of him, the cautious side of her slipped farther and farther away, until she was writhing beneath him.

He broke the kiss and pulled back, his warm, minty breath fanning across her face. "Wait. Slow down." He sat back on his knees. "We need to slow down. There's something you should know."

The dilation of his wild green eyes didn't look like he really wanted to slow down. She slid her fingers over the tops of his hands resting on his thighs. "I know, Hank."

Three little lines slashed across his brow. "You do?"

"Yes." She yanked on his shirt and pulled him to her. Her mouth went to his ear and licked the outer rim. Once. Twice. Three times. "I know we've always belonged together." She teased a moan from him when she nipped the skin below the lobe, then smoothed her tongue over the spot. "And now that *we are* together, it's so much more than we thought it would be."

When his lips touched hers this time they were soft and reverent. Each disappointment from the last eight years, each night she'd cried herself to sleep missing him, each dashed hope fell away as he licked and sipped at her mouth then trailed kisses down her neck. "Hank."

He raised his head and his green eyes pinned her to the bed. "It's always been you, Charlie. Always."

She took his face in her hands. "For me too. Charlie and Hank forever."

For a brief second sadness passed across his handsome face. She knew how he felt. Too much time had been stolen from them. No more.

How will that work?

They'd figure something out. Besides, the only thing that mattered right now was the feel of his mouth and hands as he explored her body. Fire flashed everywhere he touched. It burned away the bad and left promises of hope in its wake.

All rational thought flew out the window when he sat back on his knees. His shirt hung open and his gorgeous chest glowed in the soft light from the small lamp on the desk. She sucked in a breath when his fingers tickled her stomach as he unbuttoned her jeans. The slide of her zipper freed something inside her.

Her hands went to his belt and greediness made her clumsy. His laughter irritated her. "It's not funny. I want to see all of you. I deserve that."

The soft kiss he planted between her breasts cooled her irritation. "I promise you can see anything you want, baby. I just need to get you out of these jeans." His hands went to the waistband of her pants. "Shit."

"What?"

"I don't have a condom." He rested his hands on his knees and dropped his head. "Damn it."

"It's okay. I'm on the pill."

He squeezed her legs. "I had to be test—I mean, I was just tested, and I'm clean. But you shouldn't just assume that, Charlie."

"Don't lecture me, Hank." The fact that he was still protecting her shifted the caustic bands constricting her vocal chords, leaching any annoyance from the words. "I'm a grown woman. I know about safe sex." Not that she'd had much of a chance to use the knowledge. "And for your information, I'm clean too." She raised her hips from the bed. "Now get these jeans off me."

Slow, sexy amusement kicked up one side of his mouth. "Yes, ma'am." He did as she directed and shimmied her pants and underwear down her legs until he was standing at the foot of the bed.

His raspy breaths filled the room.

What if I don't measure up to the hype?

Heat burned up her neck to her face and she raised her arm to cover her breasts. He didn't say anything, just stared, until she couldn't take it. "I know I'm too thin. I don't eat when I'm stressed, and I was sick last week."

"Shut up. Just...shut up." The emotion in his voice cut off the next words she would've uttered. "You're perfect."

Her muscles relaxed. She let her arm fall to her side. He still wanted her, imperfections and all. She waved her hand at his jeans. "You have too many clothes on."

He complied in record time. Beautiful. The word played over and over in her head. He was everything that was beautiful in the world. She lifted her arms. "Come here." His body over hers was where he belonged. "Make love to me, Hank. Please."

With the grace of a big cat, he crawled onto the bed to join her. His finger started at the hollow of her neck and slowly made its way down to one breast. Time hung suspended somewhere between heaven and hell while she waited for it to slide over the tip. Round and round he traced, coming close but never giving her what she desperately wanted. With each swipe around he wound her up tighter and tighter, until she teetered on the edge of sanity. He chuckled watching her squirm beneath him. Finally, he brushed across the sensitive tip. An electrical surge burned through her core, obliterating any rational thought. There was only him. She gripped at the sheets and arched her back.

"You like that?"

Words were beyond her. Her response was an exhale followed by a deep throaty moan when he closed his mouth over her nipple and circled the nub with his tongue. Ribbons of pleasure crisscrossed her body, lacing and tying her to this man. She clawed at his back and whimpered as his hand slid between them and found the place that longed for his touch. "Yes."

"I've got you." He gave her other breast the same attention. All the while he continued teasing pleasure from between her legs. Higher. Higher. Higher. The wave crested, and she was flying.

"Ahhhh." Where had her ability to speak gone? Who the hell cared? She just wanted more of him, more of this for the rest of her life.

Soft, sweet, kisses brought her back to the here and now.

"Hey."

The look of triumph in his eyes made her smile. "Hey."

"You ready for me, baby?"

"Way past ready." And she was. This should've been their reality, would've been their life if her mother hadn't pulled them apart.

He entered her in one smooth motion and the pleasure of it caused sparks to flash behind her closed eyes. Perfect wasn't a big enough word. He filled her. He covered her. He possessed all her parts, seen and unseen.

"Open your eyes. I want to see you while we're together." The tension in his command made it impossible to ignore.

Her lids slowly raised, and she was swept up in the green fire of his eyes.

He thrust, then withdrew, then thrust again, over and over until they both were slick with sweat and she was drunk on him, over the legal limit of pleasure one person could stand. And still she wanted more.

His mouth covered hers in a kiss that made her forget her name. His big hand slid to her calf and he wrapped it around his back. He surged in deeper, thrust harder, coiling her tighter and tighter.

The rhythm changed to a frantic, desperate pace. Never once did he take his eyes off her. Faster they went, until she was sure she couldn't take the intensity of him. She came undone again with a cry. Unlike the slow winding release from before, the orgasm detonated, ripping her apart and reconfiguring her, changing her very essence.

His hips continued to piston in and out several more times, until he lost himself with her name on his lips. A long, low moan escaped his mouth as he poured himself into her waiting body. "Charlie."

If eyes were truly the window of the soul, he'd laid his bare. Then the moment passed and he collapsed on her spent body. Happiness washed through her as her hands went to the back of his head when he buried his face in the crook of her neck. It was everything she knew sex should be, but would only ever be with him.

He pulled back and rested his forehead on hers. "Are you alright?"

"Perfect." She kissed him slow and deep. Making a promise with her lips and sealing it with her tongue.

He rolled to the side, snuggled her to him, and pulled the blanket over them. "I've missed you, Charlie."

"I've missed you, Hank. So much."

"We should talk." Sleep was thick in his voice.

She ran her fingers over the hand resting on her stomach, then interlaced their fingers. "In the morning." They did need to talk. She wanted him to know that she was all in, no matter what. "Sleep and dream of me."

He pulled her closer. "Always." The whispered word was the last thing she heard before sleep claimed her.

Chapter Three

The morning sun teased open Charlie's lids. She stretched her well-loved body and remembered that she was in Hank's bed. Blissful sparks fired through her and, if it were possible, she was happier than she had been last night and more hopeful than she'd been in years.

Hank was singing in the shower. Badly. And it was the most beautiful sound in the world. She gathered the sheet around her and made her way to the bathroom. "Hey, good-looking. You sing real pretty."

He pulled the curtain back and grinned. "Liar. You're the one who sings pretty. I sound like a dying goat."

She shrugged. "True, but I like waking up to it anyway."

"Why don't you get in here and show me how much you like it?"

Lust raced through her belly and pooled between her legs. "I'll do that, but let me call the hospital first and check on Pops. Save me some hot water."

"No promises, but I'm pretty sure we can make our own heat. Hurry up."

She laughed and went to find her phone. The call to the hospital was quick with no extra bad news. "I'll be there later this morning," she told Pops' nurse.

"No problem," the nurse replied. "He'll be here when you get here."

"Thanks for taking such good care of him. See you in a bit." She sat for a moment and enjoyed the happy, hopeful glow she was floating in. Hank's phone pinged with several messages one right after the other. Dang, she hoped it wasn't the sheriff's office calling him back home. She checked the screen in case she needed to pass a message to him, and her empty stomach seized.

On the screen were three messages. The display read, *Wife*.

Hey baby, it's me.

Surprise!

I'm in the lobby.

Wife, baby, lobby? The words slammed into her and beat the hell out of her. Her hopeful heart shattered with each vicious blow.

He. Was. Married.

He'd said they needed to talk. Now she knew why. While she'd been planning a future, he'd been married.

"Oh, my..." Her skin burned from the inside out when she thought of all the ridiculous, immature assumptions she'd made. They were nothing but pathetic teenaged romanticizing. She was too stupid to live.

"Charlie. I'm waiting."

The words floated through the steam to where she sat, paralyzed. Nauseous bile burned her throat. She'd slept with a married man. Hank was married. Married. Married. Married. The words were on a warped playback loop like the soundtrack from some screwed-up carnival fun house.

Panic drove her to dress in record time but also made her movements uncoordinated and jerky. She ripped the blankets aside and the sheets smelled like sex. Their sex. It smothered the last flicker of hope in her chest. None of it had been real. Hank was just one more person in a long line of people who'd used her for what they wanted. You'd think she'd have learned by now.

She caught a glimpse of herself in the mirror above the desk. Devastation etched every curve and hollow of her face. The last vestige of the trusting young girl she'd been before those three texts evaporated before her eyes. Another tear slid down her already wet cheeks. "I'm so stupid."

"Charlie?"

The urge to run, to flee from him, her miserable life, and most of all her stupid self, burned her gut. Where could she go? With her last speck of dignity, she made her way to the bathroom. "Hank." The word wobbled and barely stood on its own.

His head popped out of the shower curtain. The expectant smile he wore broke her heart all over again and another tear tumbled over her lashes.

"What's wrong? Is it Wardell?"

She swallowed twice before she could speak. Years of pretending to be someone else kicked in and she was able to say the words. "Your wife is waiting for you in the lobby."

The shock on his face told the entire story. She nodded. "So, it's true. You're married." Not a question. She knew by his expression it was true. "The boy I knew would never have done this to me. I guess the man isn't nearly as honorable as the boy." Her teeth clamped down on her trembling lip, and she shook her head. "I thought better of you, Hank." She hefted her bag onto her shoulder. "Tell your wife I said hello."

She spun on her heels before she broke down and made for the door.

The scrape of shower curtain hooks on the rod sounded from the bathroom. "Charlie."

There was no stopping her. She was out the door and down the hall in a second. The trip to her floor was a blur of gut-wrenching pain and confusion. Inside her room she stripped off her clothes and threw them into the trash, then crawled into the shower.

The hot water washed Hank from her skin, and the tears washed him from her heart.

Chapter Four

FIRST TRIMESTER

Until the ink dries.

An innocent enough phrase, unless someone's using it to refer to your impending marriage. Charlie tried and failed to ignore the roiling river of uncertainty swishing around her belly. Of course, that could just be the little alien taking up residence for the next seven or so months. Either way, she wished she was anywhere but in the Zachsville, Texas Justice of the Peace's office about to get married.

"Charlie, are you listening to me?" her publicist Marci asked.

"Huh? Oh, sorry. Yes, I'm listening. You just made a joke. Instead of until death do us part, it's until the ink dries on the new Carousel contract. Then Ron and I can divorce. Is that right?" She glanced at her manager, Ron—or should she say, her fiancé—who gave her a don't-give-me-any-crap look.

Marci cleared her throat. "Yes, that is what I said, but it doesn't have to be horrible. You love Ron and Ron loves you. You two have known each other for the past eight years. So who knows what might happen?"

Yeah, since I was almost sixteen. That's not creepy at all.

"Who knows, Charlie, you might decide you can't live without me.

Christ, you look like you're about to be sick again." Ron opened a canister of mints and offered her one. "Here, eat one of these before you puke all over my new suit."

She obediently plucked a tiny white sphere and popped it into her mouth. "I already can't live without you, Ron. If you left, who would run my life or bully me into doing things that are good for me? But I don't want to be married to you or anyone else." The refreshing peppermint soothed her traitorous stomach. She hated that he'd known it would.

He hissed out an exasperated breath. "Charlie, we've been over this a thousand times. If the Carousel Network finds out their biggest child star is pregnant out of wedlock, then they won't sign you to this new, highly lucrative contract."

She crossed her arms over her sensitive breasts. "Out of wedlock? Really, Ron? You sound like you just stepped out of a Victorian novel. And I'm not a child. I'm twenty-four years old."

"Not to Carousel you're not. It's how the network will see it. They're still not going to be happy even if we get married, because of the accommodations they'll have to make while shooting to hide the pregnancy. But they want you, and if we're married, they will overlook it. Trust me."

Trust him. Famous last words. She'd trusted her mother, who'd robbed her blind. She'd trusted Hank, and look how that had turned out. Her hand went unconsciously to her belly. Tiny tendrils of affection connected this pea pod to her heart.

No matter how deep Hank's betrayal cut, she'd never considered anything but continuing this pregnancy. She and Hank had loved each other once. And against good judgment and everything that had happened, that foolish young girl still loved him.

But not the grown woman.

Not anymore.

Ron snapped his fingers in front of her face. "Did we lose you again, Charlie?"

She shook her head and chewed her nail. "No, I'm still with you. Just trying to figure out if there is an alternative to marriage."

He laughed. "No wonder it looks like steam is coming out of your ears. Don't try to do the heavy lifting, Charlie. That's what you have Marci and me for. You just do what you do best—look pretty, be talented, and make us all lots of money." He chucked her under the chin. "This is the only option. We're going to take care of you."

Would there ever be a time where she didn't let these people run her life? She couldn't deny that they were terrific at what they did. It was just that what they did was exhausting for her.

The sad truth was that she'd never wanted this life and didn't know if she wanted to continue living it. Her current situation had forced her to take an honest look at things. But if she didn't take the deal, then how would she get the IRS off her back and support herself? Too much contemplation and too many hormones meant she hadn't had a clear thought in two months. So she'd fallen into the rhythm of her life where she let Ron and Marci make decisions for her. Really, it was all she knew. "You're right."

He squeezed her shoulder. "That's my girl. Now, Marci, is the media assembled outside the courthouse?"

Marci checked her phone. "Yes, they should be gathering just about now. When we're done here, then you'll exit out the front of the court-house and pose for pictures. I'll make a statement, reminding them that Charlie's been here in Podunksville caring for her ailing grandfa-ther for the last three months, then you and Charlie will take a few questions. They may ask why the wedding took place here instead of LA. Do you remember what you should say, Charlie?"

As if on autopilot she repeated the words that had been scripted for her. "I couldn't leave my grandfather, but I couldn't wait to marry Ron either." Even to her own ears, every syllable sounded flat as the pancakes she'd made her Pops for breakfast that morning.

Her publicist pursed her lips. "Right. Hopefully you'll be able to deliver it with more enthusiasm than that when the time comes."

"She'll do fine." Ron brushed lint from his lapel. "Do you think they know what this is all about?"

Marci shook her head. "If they do, no one's contacted me. It's helped that Charlie's been in the middle of nowhere for the last two months."

Ron rubbed his silver-flecked beard. Charlie was surprised he kept it. It made him look every bit his forty-one years, and the man had more vanity than the cast of all the Real Housewives shows combined. "Good. I'd like to surprise them with this news." He threw an arm around Charlie. "It'll play even better later when we announce that we're going to be parents."

What little food she'd choked down earlier threatened to make a reappearance all over Ron's expensive suit. *They* were going to be parents? She wouldn't let Ron parent a goldfish, let alone Hank's chi— She cut the thought off before she completed it. Hank wasn't a part of any of this.

Hank had a wife, and they were a family. There was no room for her and her pea pod in that mix. There was a nearly audible rip in the fabric of her soul at that thought. No, not of her soul, but of that idiot kid's she used to be.

"Oh, I like that, Ron," Marci said. "You and Charlie will move in with her grandfather to continue to care for him. Her fans will eat it up. We'll announce the pregnancy in the next couple of months. But first, we'll sign the Carousel contract tomorrow, then payday!"

The fist bump they exchanged seemed uncalled for considering they were discussing her freakin' life. She should be used to this. They always talked about her like she wasn't in the room and didn't have a say about anything, but now they were talking about The Pod like a commodity, and that was wrong.

Who was she kidding? This was all wrong.

Before she could tell them so, the door to the Justice of the Peace's office opened and in walked the JP himself, Larry Norris. Not two seconds later Sheriff Hank Odom strolled into the room too.

Her Hank.

No, not her Hank.

Her Hank was Mrs. Hank Odom's man. Whoever *she* was. She'd avoided any conversations about Hank for the last two months, avoided leaving the house unless absolutely necessary, and most definitely avoided Hank's many attempts to get in touch with her. Basically, she'd gone on a Hank Odom fast and had no intention of breaking it.

This morning's oatmeal churned at an uncomfortable rate in her stomach. The temperature in the room rose about a million degrees, and sweat pooled beneath what were rapidly becoming her pregnant, monster boobs. What were the freaking odds? Considering the lousy roulette game her life had become, about a million to one. Hell, even she'd bet against her own damn self at this point.

He was tall, golden and eat-him-up-with-a-spoon good-looking. Damn it, she'd hoped her overactive imagination had made that part up. Sadly, no. If anything he was more good-looking than she remembered, and she hated him for it. She hated his perfect hair, his perfect jaw, and his perfect teeth. His perfect everything.

Images of their one night together blasted through her. Lips, arms, and legs tangled in ecstasy. Her heart wrapped in the promise of finally being with the man she'd always loved. She placed her hand on the wall to steady herself. The best and worst night and morning after of her short twenty-four years. Her other hand went to her mouth. Damn him for making her fingers tremble. Even after two months, she could still taste him there. She hated him for that too.

"Oh, hell. I'm sorry, folks. Looks like I'm late," JP Norris said.

"Nothing to worry about." Marci extended her hand. "I'm Marci Malone, Ms. Kay's publicist."

"Larry Norris. Nice to meet you. If you give me five minutes we'll get this thing taken care of," Larry said.

Ron smiled and also offered his hand. "Ron Gaylord. I'm Charlie's fiancé and manager."

The other three occupants of the room continued with introductions and niceties, but she and Hank stood like statues, neither taking their eyes off the other.

She wanted to run and jump into his arms, beg him to get her out of this circus. Deep down, on a cellular level, she longed for him. Wanted him, not just sexually, even though that was definitely there. Her flesh and blood called out to him.

Dramatic much? Hello, idiot. He's married. And he lied to you.

They stood like that for what seemed like forever before she watched his armor fall into place. "What?" she whisper-yelled.

"Nothin'." The sadness on his face when he shook his head and gave a one-shoulder shrug tried to break through the angry shield she held between them.

She forced herself to remember the devastation of seeing the texts from his wife. That did it. She and The Pod turned their back on him. He didn't deserve one ounce of her attention, nothing but her contempt. And she'd do well to remember that.

"Larry, I need to be going. Fishing on Saturday?" Hank asked.

"You know it, Hank."

She glanced over her shoulder at the man who'd ripped her heart to pieces. He left the room without a backward glance in her direction, and her barely functioning heart took another crushing hit.

It was a one-night hookup, nothing more. Stop trying to make it something it wasn't. Plus, HE LIED!

A one-night stand that produced The Pod. She'd forgotten that the antibiotic she'd taken the week before their ill-fated night could render her birth control useless. Gah! How had she let this happen? She wasn't ready for a baby, could hardly take care of herself.

Ron and Marci will take care of it. It'll all be okay once this wedding is over. Her secret would be safe, and she could go on with her life with Sheriff Odom none the wiser.

Guilt pounded down on her like hail from a Texas thunderstorm. Could she really do this? Pass this baby off as someone else's, and never tell Hank about his child? Memories of wondering about her father scraped against her. She quickly brushed them aside. This was different. She glanced at Ron yucking it up with Marci and the Justice of the Peace and knew he'd never be The Pod's father.

The first clear thought she'd had in nearly two months slapped her in the head.

What was she doing?

"Charlie." Her grandfather limped into the room with his girlfriend Honey Jenkins on his arm.

"Pops?" She moved to him and helped him sit. "What are you doing here? I told you that you didn't have to come."

"You know him, Charlie. You can't tell the dern fool a thing." Honey's tone was stern, but Charlie could see the worry in her eyes.

Charlie knew how she felt. The sheen of sweat on her grandfather's forehead was concerning. He was improving, but he still didn't need to overdo it. "Has he had his meds today?"

Honey sat next to him. "No, he wouldn't—"

"Would you two quit picking over me like a couple of chickens? And stop talking about me like I'm not here. I didn't take my medicine because I don't need it. I know my own mind. You two need to remember that."

Honey's arm snaked around her grandfather's neck, and she kissed his cheek. "You're right, Wardell. We're just worried about you. You're doing so well we don't want you to lose ground."

He patted her knee. "I know, Honey Bee. But I'm perfectly fine to attend my only granddaughter's wedding."

Big, goofy love bloomed in Charlie's chest. It was good to know she had one person who loved her for just her. She sat on the other side of him. "Thank you, Pops."

Wardell glanced at Marci and Ron, who were now standing alone, both concentrating on their phones. He didn't try to hide the distaste on his face. "You sure you want to do this, Charlie?"

She lowered her head and voice so only her grandfather and Honey could hear her. "No, I'm not."

"What?" Wardell asked at full volume.

"Shhhhh. I said, no."

"You're gonna have to speak up, Charlie, if you want me to hear you."

"I swear, Wardell," Honey said. "Turn on your hearing aids."

He pulled them both from his ears and turned them on, then stuck them back in place. "Now what in the Sam Hill are you whispering about?"

Charlie poked her head up from their little powwow to see if Marci or Ron were watching. They weren't. "I said that I don't want to marry Ron." Just saying it out loud infused her with courage.

Her grandfather's slightly yellowed teeth winked at her when he grinned. "About damn time. That man's as useless as tits on a boar hog."

Honey laughed. "Wardell, you're so bad."

His warm, arthritic hand came to rest on Charlie's cheek. "I told you she was too smart to go through with this insanity." Even though he spoke to Honey, he never took his eyes from Charlie.

"You did," Honey agreed.

Charlie placed her hand over his and squeezed. In the two months that she'd been in Zachsville, she'd become addicted to this man's no-strings-attached affection. It was life-giving water to her splintered, dry soul. "Wait, you knew I wouldn't marry Ron?" He didn't know about the pregnancy. He might feel differently if he did.

Ron started yelling at someone on his phone.

Her grandfather made a disgusted noise. "Idiot."

Then again, maybe not.

Honey took her hand. "What can we do to help, darlin'?"

"Charlie, are you ready?" Marci asked. "JP Norris said he'd be back in a minute." She began typing something on her phone. "We're on a tight schedule."

Short, quick breaths jumped in and out of Charlie's lungs. Honey and Wardell blurred in her vision. "I don't know. I don't think they'll just take no for an answer."

Wardell and Honey shared a conspiratorial look.

"What?" She'd learned pretty fast that a look like that meant trouble.

"You need a diversion." Honey winked. "Leave it to us."

Wardell kissed Charlie's hand. "Follow our lead."

Follow their lead? What the hell? She stood when they did. No idea why—she just *followed their lead*.

Wardell yelled and clutched his chest, then crumbled to the ground.

"Pops!"

And receiving the award for best actor in a bogus drama...Wardell Pritchett. The big faker quickly winked at her, then proceeded to writhe in pain and gasp for air, all the while clutching his chest.

"Oh, my Lord!" Honey screamed and dropped to her knees next to him. "He's having a heart attack!"

Ron and Marci exchanged shocked looks.

"Don't just stand there, Charlie! Go get help!" Honey cried real tears and wailed, "Please don't take him, Lord. He's not done yet. He's not done." She threw her body over Wardell. Her ample breast smashed against his chest.

Charlie almost had her own heart attack when her grandfather, while still thrashing in agony, felt Honey up. Like full-on, handful of boob. "Ohhhh!" Honey let out a high-pitched squeal but quickly recovered. "Oh, Lord, save him."

Astonishment had Charlie's feet plastered to the spot. Apparently Ron and Marci were suffering from the same condition, because they didn't make a move to help.

Honey briefly broke character and cut her eyes to Charlie. "We need help, Charlie. Get help!" Then she continued her bawling and pleading with the Almighty. Charlie remained frozen until Honey slapped her leg and yelled, "Go!"

She went.

The clip, clip, clip of heels on the tile rang through the hallway. Shouts came from behind her. She glanced over her shoulder to see paramedics running for the JP's office.

She swung into the bathroom that was luckily a one-seater and locked the door behind her. A plan, she needed a plan.

Whattodo, whattodo, whattodo?

Her reflection in the mirror looked like it always did, but she could see the panic behind her eyes. What was she doing? Unless she was planning to run to Mexico, they were going to find her. She crazily wondered if The Pod would like Mexican food.

Are you kidding me, Charlie? Get a hold of yourself.

The window high on the wall caught her eye. It was small and rectangular like she'd seen in other old buildings. Could she fit? She'd never know if she didn't try. She flipped over the trash can, hiked up her dress, and with one hand on the sink and the other on the wall, climbed on top.

Relief flooded through her when she saw that the window faced a small alley at the back of the building. She didn't have to worry about paparazzi, or anyone else seeing her getaway. She tried to push the window up, but it wouldn't budge. Once more, with all the strength she had, and the window slid open with a terrible screech.

"Crap, that's loud enough for Pops to hear without his hearing aids." Now that the window was open she could see that it was a decent drop to the ground. It was farther to the grass below than it would be if she dropped back to the floor of the bathroom.

Someone jiggled the bathroom door handle. "Anyone in there?"

Her head jerked toward the sound. The air pumping in and out of her lungs didn't seem to be doing its job because the room spun and she almost fell from her perch.

A weird clicking sound had her looking around until she realized it was her own teeth chattering out of...fear? Adrenaline? The possibility of freedom? It was probably a combination of all three. Whatever it was, it was time to move.

She hoisted herself up, maneuvered her body through the window and swiveled around until her feet were dangling with the window sill wedged under her armpits. A quick look down told her she was a good six feet off the ground. Piece of cake, unless you were carrying another person. What if the fall hurt The Pod?

Just let go.

I can't.

Let go!

I can't.

Do it!

I can't.

A cool breeze fanned across her backside. It appeared she may have a bigger problem than she'd initially thought. A quick peek confirmed that her white slip dress was caught between her body and the building. The same slip dress she had to wear a nude thong with. Which meant her bare-ass cheeks were exposed to the entire world. Because fleeing your own wedding, pregnant and penniless, doesn't seem like quite enough humiliation. Let's add mooning the fine folks of Zachsville to the mix for kicks and giggles. "Are you shittin' me right now?"

"Would you listen to that. The teenybopper queen has such a dirty mouth."

Her head jerked around of its own accord. She knew the voice. She knew it and hated it.

"Sheriff."

Chapter Five

H ank tried to ignore the finely rounded ass of the bride currently hanging from the window of the old courthouse. He'd come outside to get himself under control, and this is what he'd stumbled upon. God must really hate him.

All these weeks later and he still craved every inch of her. The luscious globes of her behind taunted him. He'd traced every contour of her backside with his hands, tongue, and lips. She was beautiful even dangling six feet off the ground, pissed-off, and sweaty. "Need some help?"

"Not from you."

"That's an interesting position for you to take, as is the position you're currently in. Didn't I see this on an episode of *Charlie Takes the Town* once, minus the bare ass, of course?"

She glanced over her shoulder. "Kiss my bare ass, Hank."

He checked to see if his clothes were on fire. The searing glare she gave him left little doubt that she hated him. He deserved it. She couldn't hate him any more than he hated himself.

But that didn't stop irrational anger from burning him alive. She'd refused to let him explain that he and Karen had been on the last steps of divorce. He'd made the decision to be with her with a clean conscience, genuinely believing his marriage was over. Should he have stopped things and told her? Yes. But it ripped him up that she'd automatically assumed the worst of him.

Now she'd have to listen. "Charlie, I've been trying to talk—"

"Shut up, Hank, and go away. I don't care what you have to say."

"Tough." He was saying his piece, damn it. He kept one eye on her hands to make sure she wasn't about to fall. Regardless of what she said, he'd catch her if she slipped. "You're going to listen."

She readjusted her hands and gave him another death glare. "Are you married?"

He shoved his hands in his pockets. "Yes. But—"

"Then we have nothing to discuss."

"Charlie, please listen." He touched her ankle.

She kicked out her foot and caught him on the side of his head. "Don't touch me."

He rubbed the spot. He deserved that too. "We'd been legally separated for a month."

"So you were on a break? Perfect."

"It was more than that. Divorce papers had been filed. You see—"

"La-la-la-la. I can't hear you."

"Real mature, Charlie."

Both feet went to the wall, she pushed, dropped, and landed in front of him. She turned with fire flaring in her blue irises. Her small hands went to his chest, and she shoved. He stumbled back a few steps from the shock of it.

"You know what's immature, Hank? A stupid, starry-eyed girl who thought the boy she used to love would've grown into a good and honest man who didn't cheat on his wife." She balled her fists at her sides. "That boy was the only honorable person I knew, and I'm furious that you took him from me."

He didn't think he could feel worse than he already did. He was wrong. "I'm trying to be an honorable man."

"Are you back with your wife?"

"Yes."

She shook her head, and the disgust rolling off of her made him sick. "You have nothing to say that I want to hear." She pointed her finger at his face. "Stay away, Hank. We don't need you."

What was left of his heart turned to ash when she stormed off down the alley. Just as well. It was wrong for Charlie to own so much of him when he was trying to make things work with Karen. Still, it took everything in him not to go after her. But she'd made herself perfectly clear, and he'd made a vow to someone else.

There was just one question.

Who was "we"?

Chapter Six

The hot water rained down on Charlie. She'd been in the shower for thirty minutes and could still smell the funk from Haskell Jordan's pick-up truck. She'd flagged down Haskell as she'd left the alley, and he'd given her a ride home. Unfortunately, the inside of the man's vehicle hadn't been cleaned since the first Obama administration. The smell of dog, motor oil, and stale mayonnaise clung to every surface of the interior like mold on a three-week-old slice of bread. In fact, she was pretty sure Haskell had some kind of science experiment growing in a discarded fast food bag she spotted on the floorboard. She'd nearly had a reunion with her breakfast when her rescuer put the cherry on top of the toxic sundae being served to her olfactory system, by passing gas. The man seriously needed to adjust his diet. It had taken all her self-control not to yell, "For the love of God, man, eat a salad every once in a while."

The Pod still wasn't speaking to her.

Admittedly, she could've been pickier about who she caught a ride with, but she'd just been so mad and upset after talking to Hank. Fire and lingering nausea simmered in her belly over what had happened between them.

Scenes of that night ran over her like the water from the shower.

She still dreamed about it. It'd been everything her stupid, young girl's heart had hoped for. But she wasn't a young girl, no matter how the people around her treated her. She was a grown woman, and that night had proven it in more ways than one.

Speaking of the people around her. The last thing she wanted to do was have the confrontation with Ron and Marci that was sure to come. But no matter what they said, she wasn't getting married. They could either stay with her and take their chances or leave. She braced her hand on the shower wall. What would she do without them? Even though she hadn't been happy with her life in a long time, they'd always been the constant. Their presence was more stable than her mother had ever been.

A final rinse and she flipped off the water. She grabbed a towel, one of the few things that she'd bought for herself and her grandfather since she'd come to help him. The threadbare excuses for towels that her grandmother got from a laundry soap box back in the sixties just wouldn't work. Naturally, her grandfather had given her trouble about the expense, but she noticed he hadn't complained after he'd tried them.

She wrapped her hair, then slipped on a pair of yoga pants and an oversized t-shirt. If she was going to battle, then she was going in comfort. She lifted her shirt and turned to the side. Her hand went to her still flat stomach. Emotions she couldn't identify, but somehow knew would be with her forever, bloomed in her chest. "I've gotten us into a bit of a mess, Pod. But I promise I'll get us out of it, just give me time."

The clean, fragrant smell of her lotion helped settle her nerves. A sense of satisfaction at having made the body butter caused her to smile in spite of the day she'd had. It was her legacy from the grandmother she'd adored. The woman had been a modern-day alchemist. She could take any ingredient and make it into something lovely and good for your skin.

She pushed down the waistband of her pants and smoothed lotion on her belly. "Maybe one day I'll teach you to make soaps and creams like my grandma taught me, little Pod. I'm pretty good at it. My makeup artist on the set in Hollywood used to say I should bottle and sell it." She pulled her clothes back into place, capped the bottle, and an idea flashed through her mind.

I could sell this stuff.

It had been the dream that she and her grandmother had talked about all those years ago, but she quickly dismissed it. Yes, she'd taken some online business and accounting classes for that reason, but honestly, what did she know about running a business? What did she know about anything? There'd always been someone around to take care of every aspect of her life.

Not always.

Warm, happy thoughts of when she'd been a regular person came to a screeching halt when she realized all those memories involved Hank and a silly, love-struck girl. The misery she'd been battling snuck up on her again. Sometimes it hit her like an eighteen-wheeler, but usually it army-crawled its way through her chest like love-hating soldiers, silent and covert, lying in wait for an ambush. Most days she could handle it, but on days like today, her battered heart had a hard time holding off the assault.

She braced her hands on the counter and gave in to the misery, but only for a few minutes. That was all she could afford to give to the memory of her and Hank. She had a crumbling career, a life in shambles, and a Pod to raise. No time to nurse a broken heart. Several deep breaths and a few more sniffles later, and she was ready to face the music.

When she opened the door to the bathroom, she heard her grandfather raising hell downstairs. She made her way to the staircase, careful to stay out of sight. "No, you can't talk to her. I think she made herself pretty dern clear when she ran out on you."

"Listen, old man, we're not leaving here until we talk to Charlie." A note of barely restrained violence laced Ron's tone.

"Ron, calm down. I'm sure Wardell understands how important it is for us to speak to Charlie." Marci's ever-reasonable words tried to break through the tension filling the house.

Charlie patted her belly. "Hang on, Pod. Things are about to get bumpy." She made her way down the stairs and waded into the fray. "Ron, stop bullying my grandfather."

"Charlie, thank god." Her manager came to her and gently took by her shoulders. "We were so worried."

His reaction was so unexpected that she momentarily lost her ability to speak.

"Don't coddle her, Ron." Marci's words sliced the air like the blade of a sword. Gone was the voice of reason. "What she did was unbelievably irresponsible. How could you take a risk like that, Charlie? What if the paparazzi had seen you?"

Charlie glanced around the room to check for hidden cameras. This had to be a joke. Their role reversal had her head spinning. "I...um..."

"Stop it, Marci. Can't you see she's having a hard time?" Ron slid his arm over her back.

The anger in Marci's face had Charlie taking a step toward the protection Ron offered. "I don't care if she's having a hard time. I'm tired of her antics. We can't do our jobs if she won't do hers."

"Lady, you better watch what you're saying about my granddaughter." Wardell tried to insert himself between her and Marci, but Ron stepped in. "Marci, I think you should wait outside. You aren't helping."

"Fine." Her publicist agreed just a little too quickly.

Something about this whole scene had Charlie's spidey senses going haywire.

"Wardell, would you mind if I spoke to Charlie in private?" Ron asked.

Okay, now she knew something was going on. Ron hated her grandfather.

"Come on, Wardell." Honey took him by the hand. "Let's give them some privacy."

The fierce look he and Honey gave Ron settled Charlie's nerves. She hadn't had anyone in her corner like these two geriatric superheroes since she left Zachsville. This is what she wanted for The Pod. A life where he or she was treasured and protected. "We'll be in the kitchen, Charlie. You yell if you need anything," Wardell said.

"Anything," Honey agreed. She turned her attention to Ron. "Mister, if you try any funny business, I won't stop Wardell from cuttin' your tallywacker clean off." To reiterate her point, she made scissors with her fingers and mimed cutting.

Charlie bit her lip to keep from laughing when Ron shivered next to her. She didn't blame him. It was clear that Honey was dead-dog serious.

Ron waited until they were out of the room before he led her to the sofa. Then he sat on the coffee table in front of her and clasped his hands in his lap. "Charlie, can you tell me what happened?"

His empathetic gaze caressed her face like he was auditioning to be the next Oprah. Good grief. How stupid did he and Marci think she was? He'd never asked her opinion on anything. Ron was terrific at his job because of his single-minded approach and focus. Not because he polled the room to see what everyone else wanted to do. "I'm not marrying you, Ron."

He leaned forward, rested his elbows on his knees and placed his hands over her clutched fists. "But why? Is it because you think I don't care for you? I assure you that's not true."

She extracted her hands from his and crossed her arms. "No, that's not it. I know you care for me."

"Good—"

"Like any manager cares for his client and the money they can make him."

He reeled back like she'd punched him. Honestly, he should be the one with the acting career. "What?"

She stood and moved out of his reach. "Just stop it, Ron. I'm not buying this crap you're peddling. I don't know what this good cop, bad cop thing you and Marci have going on is, but it's not working. I'm not marrying you."

Some of his affability slipped, but he caught it before it fell away completely. He stood and tried to move to her, but she put her grand-father's recliner between them.

"Charlie, listen to reason."

"Call Marci back in here."

"What? Why?"

"Forget it. I'll do it." She marched to the screen door, swung it open, and almost hit her publicist in the nose. "Marci, I need you to come inside."

"Okay." The trepidation in Marci's voice was palpable. She gave Ron a questioning look, but her manager just shrugged, clearly tiring of this game.

"Sit, please." Charlie indicated the sofa. They both remained standing. Fine. She could do this standing up. "I appreciate everything you both have done for me, and how you tried to take care of me when my mom wasn't around."

"That's our job, Charlie." Marci sincerely broke off a tiny piece of her scarred heart.

It was only their job. She was their job, and she was bone sick of it all. "I appreciate that, Marci." The words were like jagged rocks rolling up her throat. "But I'm not going to marry Ron, or anyone else. If Carousel won't take me as I am, then they can keep their job. I don't want them anyway."

"They won't accept it. I can promise you that." The smug, condescending expression on Ron's face severed one more tie between them. They really did think she was the stupidest person in the world.

She shrugged. "Then we'll do something else. Surely there's someone else that will hire me. Or I can go to auditions. I'm not too good for that."

The color of Ron's face was an alarming shade of red. She'd never seen him this mad. "And what roles are you going to audition for, Charlie? Knocked-up best friend? Pregnant girl number one? No one will hire you while you're pregnant."

"Then I'll wait until I'm not pregnant to begin to look for another role." That could work, couldn't it?

"Charlie, in seven months you'll be irrelevant. A has-been." Marci did seem truly sad about that.

"Here's the deal, Charlie." Ron's hair stood out in every direction from plowing his fingers through it. "Either you marry me, and we pursue the Carousel deal, or Marci and I walk."

Her gaze shot from one to the other. "You would really do that? I mean so little to you two that you would dump me just like that?"

Neither said a word, but the guilty expression painted on Marci's face said it all. They did mean it. "Oh." They would leave her. What would she do without them? The answer was perfectly, wonderfully clear. Any damn thing she wanted. She'd be free. "I understand."

"Good. I think if we rub a little money in JP Norris's palm, then we can get him to do the ceremony now." Ron had that crazed look in his eye that he got when he was about to close the deal.

Charlie gave them both a sad smile and moved to the door. She opened the screen and stood with her back to it, one foot in the house and the other on the porch. "I accept your resignation as my representation. You'll understand if we don't invite you to stay for dinner."

They both just stared at her like they didn't speak the language.

"I said, goodbye."

Marci rushed to her and tried to take her hand. She calmly pulled it away. "Charlie, don't be like this."

"You two have made yourselves perfectly clear, and now I'm making myself equally clear. Get out. Get off my property. Get out of my life."

They both made their way out of the house without a word. Just before they got into the car, Ron lobbed his parting shot. "You were a nobody when I found you, Charlie. I made you who you are today. Without me, you'll go back to being a nobody. Is that what you want?"

"Nothing sounds better, Ron. Absolutely nothing. Drive safe." She closed the door on her old life and threw away the key.

Chapter Seven

"Mom!" Hank didn't know why he bothered to yell. Between the barking dogs and the screech of the screen door, people in Austin forty miles away knew he was at his mother's house.

"I'm in here, honey."

He followed the sound of her voice to the bathroom. His mom was leaning over the bathtub, up to her elbows in bubbles, while two squealing kids splashed and played in the water.

"Uncle Hank!" his four-year-old twin nephews yelled at the same time.

He leaned his shoulder against the door frame. "Hunter and Eli, are you giving your Grandma a hard time?"

"Hello, son." His mom grinned at him over her shoulder. She looked tired, but who wouldn't be after keeping these hoodlums all day, five days a week? "They found the one mud puddle in the yard and had a big time. I thought I'd bath them before Roxanne gets here, one less thing for her to do."

He rolled up his sleeves and knelt beside his mother. "Here, let me wash their hair." He grabbed the kiddy shampoo and squirted a dollop in his hand. "Come here, Hunter. You little maniac." He'd lay money on the fact that the mud fight started with Hunter. He was definitely the instigator of most of the trouble the twins got into.

His mom pushed herself up and sat on the toilet lid. "Thank you, son. I'm not as young as I used to be."

No, she wasn't. Patrice Odom had raised her kids. First Hank, then his twin brothers Derek and Jett had come along thirteen months later. Three kids in less than a year and a half couldn't have been easy, but she'd done it and done most of it by herself after his father up and left her high and dry.

His mom should be having lunch with her friends or participating in activities at the Senior Center. Instead, she was babysitting his irresponsible brother's kids. His brother Jett had taken off five months after Hunter and Eli were born, leaving his wife with two little boys to raise on her own.

"Uncle Hank, too hard," Hunter whined.

"Oh, sorry, bud." It was hard to control his emotions when it came to both his unreliable brothers. "Lean your head back." He poured a couple of cups of water over the boy's blond head, careful to keep it out of his eyes. "Alright, out you go." He slid his hand under Hunter's armpits, then handed the boy to his mother, who wrapped him in a towel.

"J-E-T-T sent Roxanne a thousand dollars yesterday." His mother always spelled his brother's name in front of the twins. Probably just as well—the news was rarely good.

He repeated the hair-washing treatment with Eli, who grinned at him the whole time. Where Hunter was a hellion, this kid was a charmer, and could usually cute himself out of most trouble. "Don't grin at me, kid. You're in as much trouble as him." He jutted his chin toward Hunter. Eli only laughed. God, he loved these kids. "J-E-T-T didn't happen to say where he was, did he?"

Patrice vigorously rubbed the towel over Hunter's head. "There was no return address and no note. Just a padded envelope with cash in it like before."

What kind of dumbass sent cash through the mail? But that was what Jett had been doing for the last three and a half years. According to the postage stamps, they'd come from Oklahoma, Louisiana,

Montana, and now Alaska. Hank was pretty sure his brother was working as a roughneck in the oil fields, but there was no real way to know. The only thing he did know was that the shithead broke his vows and ran out on his wife and babies, an unforgivable offense in Hank's eyes. "Okay, buddy. You're done."

The second twin was toweled off, then the two took off, naked as jaybirds. "Hey, come back here." The only answer he got was howling laughter as they ran from the room. He chuckled and pulled the plug in the tub to drain the water, then rose to his feet. He took his mom by the hand and helped her to stand. "Come on woman, I'll make you a cup of coffee."

"Make it a glass of wine, and you've got a deal." She winked.

"Like you'd drink with those two here. Not that I'd blame you."

She laughed and glanced at her watch. "I'm only half joking. Roxanne should be here any minute to get the kids, then I can have that glass of wine."

He held his arm out to her. "Then I'm at your service, and I think I'll join you."

"Where's Karen tonight?"

The vise that seemed to live around his neck tightened at the mention of his wife. "Teaching an extension class at the community college in Austin." He narrowly avoided a collision with a naked preschooler when he entered the kitchen. "Boy, get some clothes on!"

"Oh, she's doing that again? That seems like a lot with her full-time teaching job at the high school." His mother grabbed Eli and wrestled some underwear and a t-shirt on him before he wiggled out of her grip and took off after Hunter.

He pulled a bottle of his mother's sweet white wine from the fridge, then rummaged around in her junk drawer for the corkscrew. "It is, but she enjoys it. She teaches there on Tuesday and Thursday nights. This is her third week. She—"

"My eyes! My eyes!" The shrill girly scream came from the front room.

He glanced at his mom. "Lottie?"

A warm, loving smile spread across his mom's face. "Yes. She's staying with Roxanne tonight."

His seven-year-old niece ran into the room with a naked four-year-old hot on her heels. "Save me, Grandma!" She flung herself at Patrice laughing like an idiot.

His sister-in-law Roxanne grabbed the naked four-year-old and hauled a pair of underwear up his legs. "Stop tormenting your cousin, Hunter."

Hunter gave Lottie a loving smile. "But I wuv her."

A shirt and pants covered Hunter's body in two seconds flat. Eli got a pair of shorts and a kiss on the head. "Go play for five minutes, then we're leaving."

"'Lottie come wif us?" Eli asked.

"Sure, I'll come too." She took the boy's hand and started out of the room.

Hank cleared his throat. "Have you forgotten something, Lottie girl?"

"Oh." She ran to him, and he picked her up. Her skinny arms went around his neck, and she gave him a toothy smile. "Hello, Uncle Hank. I love you."

His heart, the one that had disintegrated in the alley when Charlie walked away from him, regenerated with Lottie in his arms. "I love you too." He put her down, and the three kids ran from the room.

"Hey, Hank." Roxanne wrapped him in a hug.

He kissed her head. "Hey, gal."

"Where's Karen?"

"She's teaching an extension course at the community college in Austin tonight." He poured his mom a glass of wine, then lifted the bottle to Roxanne. "Want one?"

The frazzled mother of two shook her head. "No, I need my wits about me for the evening."

He grabbed a beer from the fridge. "You have Lottie tonight?"

"Yeah, Hailey got called into the bar." She shook her head. "She's obsessed with keeping that place open, and her dad is no help." She took a cookie from the jar on the counter. "I don't mind keeping her. She's a big help with the boys. Besides, we Odom cast-offs have to stick together."

His mom coughed. They both turned to see her stricken face.

Roxanne went to her immediately and knelt next to her chair. "Patrice, I'm so sorry. I didn't mean..."

Anger boiled through him again at his shit-for-brains brothers. First, Jett left Roxanne without so much as a kiss my ass. Then his brother Derek left his wife Hailey for their next-door neighbor, flaunting the affair right in front of her face. He couldn't understand them at all. You make a vow, and you keep it.

His mom ran her hand over Roxanne's dark head. "Oh, darlin', I'm not upset with you. I love you. It's those lousy sons of mine whose necks I'd like to wring for hurting y'all." She wiped her eyes with the back of her hand. "I still don't understand. They weren't raised that way. Thank God for Hank. He seems to be the only one who understands commitment."

It was true. Regardless, or maybe because, of how his dad had taken off on his family, that was what they'd all been taught by their ever-faithful mother. It was also true that Hank seemed to be the only one who took it to heart.

"I'd feel like a total failure if it weren't for him." The look his mother gave him made the beer ferment in his gut.

Roxanne swiped a tear from her cheek and gave him a sad smile. "Yeah, Hank gives us all hope in men."

He gave her a tight-lipped smile. Oh, for fuck's sake. Someone stab him now. They knew about his and Karen's separation. Hell, the whole town knew because she'd filed for a legal separation and then divorce. Once the papers were filed, the gossip began spreading before the ink was dry. Zachsville was his town, his responsibility, but sometimes he hated living in such a small place.

That was why he'd been in Austin the night he ran into Charlie. He'd just needed to get the hell out of town and away from all the scrutiny and speculation. That night had been the happiest he'd been in years. It was shit timing that Karen chose that moment to try to patch things up.

He'd been trying to get her to go to counseling for months, and she'd refused. But once she agreed to get help, he couldn't tell her no. No matter what had just happened between him and Charlie or how horrible he felt about it.

He loved Charlie, always had, and after that night, he knew he always would, but that wasn't enough of a reason to break the vows he'd made to Karen. Sticking with his marriage was the right thing to do, and he always did the right thing.

Even if it killed him.

Chapter Eight

The sight in the hall mirror stopped Charlie in her tracks. A hot mess didn't even begin to describe her reflection. No sleep and nausea would do that to a girl. Her morning sickness was all-day and middle-of-the-night sickness—basically, debilitating nausea twenty-four seven. Yay. She didn't recommend trying to come up with a life plan while puking your guts up.

Thank God the paparazzi couldn't see her now. She pushed back her blonde waves and squinted at the woman that stared back at her. Even though she looked like hell, there was peace behind her eyes that hadn't been there in a very long time. Which was crazy, because her only hope of making any real money, and a life for herself and her tagalong, had driven away in a rented Audi yesterday.

Didn't matter. She was free.

The sound of gospel music and perfectly pitched humming floated down the hall to her. She should know—she had perfect pitch too. That and her natural comedic timing was why she was a household name. Why the Carousel Network had created a whole show around her and ended each episode with her performing a song, whether it made sense to have her sing that song or not.

Her hand went to her belly. She'd be a household name again for sure once word of this pregnancy was public knowledge. The good news, as Ron said, was that she'd be a nobody, and they wouldn't care for very long.

She followed the sound of the melody to the kitchen. Honey stood at the stove stirring a skillet. The older woman wore a Zachsville Raiders t-shirt that had 'Raider Pride' spelled out in rhinestones. Loose-fitting jeans tucked into fuzzy boots made to keep your feet warm rounded out the outfit.

"Good morning, Honey. Did you stay the night?"

Honey threw her head back and laughed. "Lord, no. This town would be beside themselves if I stayed the night with Wardell. Have you been away so long that you've forgotten this town has eyes everywhere and tongues ready to wag?"

"No. I remember that." She tipped her head at Honey's shirt. "Nice shirt." Coffee. She needed coffee. The sweet sound of the hot liquid being poured into a cup gave her hope for the day.

"It's game day, baby! Zachsville Raiders football is the hottest ticket in town. It wouldn't be fall in Texas without Friday night football." Honey pumped her fist in the air. "Go Raiders!"

Charlie raised her mug in a toast. "Go Raiders." Then she glanced around the kitchen. "Where is Pops?"

"Boys' morning out."

"What?"

"'Scuse me." Honey stepped past her to grab the salt and pepper shakers from the cabinet. "You know what boys' night out is, right?"

Charlie sipped her coffee and nodded.

"Well, the men at the Senior Center are all in bed by nine p.m., but every one of 'em is up at four a.m., cause they're old, so they get together early and play dominos and drink coffee once a week. This is his first day back since the accident."

A horrible thought hit Charlie. "He didn't drive himself, did he?"

"Oh, no. Regardless of what that man says, he's not ready to drive. I took him." She checked the clock on the wall. "I'm supposed to pick him up in an hour."

"I don't think I've ever asked...how long have you been seeing each other?"

Honey's skin took on a pinkish tone. "Truth be told, Wardell's been chasing me for a while." She struck a pose with one hand on her hip and the wooden spoon in the air like a wand. "You can see why, right?"

They both laughed. "Absolutely." Charlie loved this woman who was so good for her grandfather.

"And why wouldn't he? I'm the best thing to ever happen to him. No offense to your grandmother. Lila was a lovely woman."

Charlie leaned a hip against the counter and cupped her mug in her hands. "None taken. She was lovely, and I miss her every day, but she's been gone a long time now." Bitterness mixed with the coffee she'd drunk, making a nauseating concoction. Of all the things her mother had done, she'd never forgive her for not letting Charlie come back for her grandmother's funeral. Because of a stupid television show, she'd missed the opportunity to comfort her grandfather and say goodbye to her beloved Grams.

Honey patted her on the arm. "I know you do and so does Wardell, just like I miss my Joe, but life goes on. I think in the beginning Wardell just chased me to have something to do, and I told him so. I told him I wasn't interested in being anyone's second choice. But he kept pursuing, and I kept resisting. Then he was in the accident, and I almost lost him." Her bottom lip wobbled, and Charlie had to force down her own emotional lump. Honey waved her hand in front of her face. "Anyway, I knew it was time to fish or cut bait. And as you can see, the fishing is fine." Honey's happy laughter filled the kitchen.

Charlie wrapped her arm around the older woman's shoulder. "I'm so glad."

Honey leaned her head against Charlie's. "I'm glad I could be here to help, especially with you in your condition."

"What?" Charlie jerked her head back and chuckled. It sounded more like an admission than a nonchalant giggle. Suddenly she was very interested in the contents of the pot on the stove.

"Darlin', I may never have been pregnant, but I know the signs." One of Honey's drawn-on eyebrows slipped up her forehead.

Grits? Oatmeal? What was Honey cooking?

Don't make eye contact or she'll know.

Charlie turned and rested her butt against the counter. In a way, it was a relief that Honey knew, or suspected. But could she trust one of the town's biggest gossips with her secret? Doubtful. Then she remembered that Honey's niece, Scarlett, was married to Gavin Bain, superstar rocker. They had to have things they didn't want made public knowledge, and there hadn't been one bit of gossip from that camp, so maybe Honey could be trusted.

She glanced at the woman patiently stirring her concoction and took a chance. Frankly, it wouldn't be long before everyone knew. "Yes, I'm pregnant."

Honey threw her arms into the air and squealed. Then Charlie was wrapped in a fierce hug. "Oh, how wonderful!"

The scent of gardenias had nothing to do with the tears stinging her eyes. Someone besides herself was happy about the Pea Pod. She'd never be able to tell Honey how much that meant to her. She clung to her grandfather's girlfriend and let a few of those tears loose. "Thank you, Honey."

Warm, soft hands cupped her cheeks. "What's this?"

"It's just..." She choked on a sob. "That..."

"You're afraid?"

Charlie nodded as much as she could with Honey holding her head. "Yes. I'm by myself."

"Awww, darlin'." Honey pulled her back in for another soul-fortifying embrace. "You aren't alone. You've got Wardell and me, and that's all you need right now."

Charlie melted into the woman and stole as much strength as she could. Then she pulled away and gave a half laugh. "I'm sorry. I guess I needed to tell someone."

Honey handed her a tissue. "Wipe your face and sit down. We're gonna have a talk."

"Okay." She sat at the worn table and tried to get herself under control. Eventually, her shaking breaths evened out. A plate of food was placed before her. Eggs, two biscuits, and oatmeal. "Honey, I can't eat all of this."

"Nonsense. I see that bird food you've been eating, and now I'm gonna fatten you up. You're eating for two now."

"I only need an extra three hundred calories a day, according to what I've read online."

"Oh." Honey reached over and took one of the biscuits from Charlie's plate. "I'll eat this one then. I'm a giver like that." She winked one blue-shadowed eye.

Charlie snorted coffee out her nose.

Honey handed her a napkin. "Lord, girl, you're a mess."

That sobered her. "I've certainly made a mess of my life."

"No, you haven't. No more negative talk. This baby is precious, and we're going to celebrate it. Can you tell me who the father is?"

The delicious food suddenly lost its appeal. "I don't...it's complicated."

"Ha! If I had a dime for every time I'd said that about a situation that wasn't really that complicated, only took some courage to address, then I'd be as rich as one of them housewives on TV. Can you imagine? The Real Housewives of Zachsville, now that'd be a show. Instead of fightin' over men and where to go to lunch, we'd be fightin' over who got the biggest cucumber at the farmer's market, or who had the right to sit in the front pew at the Baptist church." She rested her forearm on the table. "What I'm saying is that most things aren't complicated, they're just hard, and it's easier to ignore them than tackle them head on."

She pushed her plate away and studied Honey. Oh well, in for a dollar, in for a married sheriff. "Hank Odom."

Apparently, that wasn't the answer Honey was expecting. She blinked several times like the words wouldn't compute in her brain. "Hank? Sheriff Hank Odom?"

Charlie bit her lip. "Yep."

"But when? How?"

"The how was the traditional way."

Honey gave her a look. "You know what I mean."

"The first weekend after Pops' accident. I ran into him at the hotel where I was staying." She shrugged. "Things...happened."

Honey reached for the remaining biscuit on Charlie's discarded plate and took a big bite. "This is... So, you and Hank? Did you know who he was?"

Charlie took mercy on the woman and told her the story. The whole story, including always being in love with him and the little matter of his wife.

"Oh, darlin'." Honey's liver-spotted hands covered hers. "He and Karen were legally separated. And I did hear she'd filed for divorce too. There'd been infidelity." Honey whispered the last word as any good Texas woman would.

"By Hank?" Had she just been one of many?

"No, by Karen. She and Matt Allen were having an affair. We were all shocked when she and Hank got back together."

A humorless laughed escaped Charlie's mouth. "Yeah, me too. Wait. Karen? Karen Williams?"

"Yes. That was her maiden name. Did you know her?"

Charlie rubbed her tired eyes. Did she know her? "Yeah, I knew her." Karen had been Hank's age and Miss Everything. Had had everything, except Hank. And she'd made no bones about the fact that she'd wanted him. Old jealousy slithered around Charlie's body. The competition between her and the other woman had been vicious.

Looks like you won after all, Karen.

Honey wrapped her in another hug. "I'm so sorry. Are you going to tell him?"

She disentangled herself from the embrace. "No."

"But why? Don't you think he'll figure it out?"

She shrugged. "I'll deal with that at the time. The boy I knew always did the right thing, no matter how hard or unpleasant it was. I can only assume he's the same as a man." She looked to Honey for confirmation.

"Yes, that's Hank."

"If he knew, then he'd try to do the right thing, and I don't want to be the reason for trouble in his marriage. I also don't want anyone in The Pod's life just because it's something they think they have to do."

"The Pod?"

"That's what I've been calling it." Her cheeks pricked with heat. Honey would probably think she was already the worst mother around.

"Isn't that adorable."

She couldn't stop the smile that spread across her face. "Yeah?"

Honey's warm hand cupped her face. "Yeah."

"Thank you for understanding."

"Oh, darlin', I don't understand. And for the record, I think you're wrong, but I'll support you no matter what."

Lovely streams of warmth spread through her chest. "Thank you, Honey. I...um...also need to ask you not to tell Pops until I'm ready."

Honey rose and took their dishes to the sink. "Well now, that will be tricky."

"I know. I hate to ask you to lie."

"It's not that, though I'd never outright lie to him. As much as I hate to admit it, the man is perceptive. He knows something's up." A quick rinse and the plates were loaded into the dishwasher. "That's why he insisted on going to that joke of a wedding yesterday. We had the heart attack scene planned and would've used it to keep you from getting married. As it turned out, you came to your senses on your own."

Charlie laughed. "You two are a dangerous pair. And thank you."

Honey chuckled. "You're welcome."

"What do you think he'll do when he finds out?" She asked the question that had been plaguing her since she took the pregnancy test.

Honey took the chair next to her again. "Baby, he'll honor your wishes. I'll make sure of it, if you know what I mean."

Coffee shot from Charlie's lips back into her cup. "I don't think I want to know what's involved in that."

A smear of red lipstick on Honey's front tooth flashed at Charlie when the woman let out a belly laugh. "I'm sure you don't either."

Chapter Nine

Hey, babe. Sorry, but I got tied up at work. I can't make it to dinner. I'll meet you at home later.

Hank listened to the message from his wife for the second time. He'd give anything to feel even one ounce of disappointment, but he couldn't ignore the river of relief that rushed through him.

This was bad.

He was committed to his marriage, so he better find a way to make this work. He fired back a text.

No worries. I'm going to grab a bite, then I'll be home.

He was about to exit his cruiser, when he noticed a commotion across the street. A group of reporters crowded around a car, yelling and snapping photos. In an instant, he knew it was Wardell's car. From there it didn't take long to understand that Zachsville's newest celebrity in residence must be in the car too.

Now this was a situation he could take care of. He started his car and made the block. The squawk of the siren got the paparazzi's attention as he pulled in behind the other automobile. He could see that Honey was in the driver's seat, and she was yelling at the press.

He unfolded from his vehicle and waded into the fray. "Alright, what's going on here?" The edge of anger in his voice wasn't manufactured after he got a look at Charlie in the backseat. Christ, she'd put up with these vultures for the last couple of months, and it was time for them to go.

"Charlie! Look here."

"Heard you were going to marry Ron Gaylord, why'd you call it off?"

"Are you pregnant, Charlie?"

These guys had to have the worse job in the world. Ninety-nine percent of what they reported was fabricated bullshit. He had no idea why she'd decided to marry her manager, but he was reasonably sure it wasn't because that old guy got her pregnant. No way were they sleeping together. He didn't know how he knew, just that he did.

Yeah, you don't know shit, Odom.

He wedged himself between the paparazzi and the car. "That's enough. Back off."

"We have a right to be here, sheriff," some big guy whose shirt didn't entirely cover his belly said.

"You don't have the right to harass the good citizens of Zachsville, son." He didn't feel one bit bad about the satisfaction he got from adding the 'son' to that sentence.

A skinny, pasty guy who looked like he was on vacation from his mother's basement shouted, "Come on, sheriff. We're just trying to do our job. Give us a break."

Hank took off his cowboy hat and smoothed his hair back with the opposite hand. "I get that, but you can do your job from the other side of the street. Now."

There was cursing and whining, but they did finally move like an amoeba to the opposite corner, where they restarted their barrage of questions and snapping cameras.

Once he was sure the coast was clear, he opened Honey's door. "Y'all alright?"

Honey exited the car and fanned herself. "At first it was excitin', but then they tried to open the car doors." She straightened her frilly top and pushed her red hair from her face. "I'll tell you right now." A red-tipped finger waggled in his face. "I know how to handle those jackals,

Hank Odom. You remember when they tried to come on our property when Scarlett and Gavin got married. I showed them."

He bit the inside of his lip to keep a straight face. "Killer, I believe we've had more than one discussion about the concealed handgun license you have."

The troublemaker's hands went into the air to indicate her innocence. "I know, and I'm not carrying today. But that don't mean I couldn't introduce them to the redneck side of the Jenkins family." She nudged him with her elbow. "Even though I don't have my fightin' shoes on, I'm pretty sure I could take that little pasty one."

He lost the battle with the laughter building inside him. "I'm pretty sure you could too."

"You okay, Wardell?" he asked the old man as he limped around the front of the car, leaning heavily on a cane.

"Just dandy. Thanks for the save. Unlike this lovely lady, I'm not in fightin' shape." He snuggled Honey to his side.

"No problem." Hank glanced toward the reporters to make sure they were still across the street. Once he was sure she was safe, he opened Charlie's door and extended his hand. "You alright, darlin'?"

She ignored his hand, and exited the vehicle. And elbowed him hard in the gut. "All you've done is made it worse. Now they think I've got something to hide. The best way to deal with them is to give them their pound of flesh." She yanked the ball cap she wore farther down on her head and turned to Honey and Wardell. She took them both by the arm and walked to the City Cafe. "I'm sorry they scared you. They're mostly harmless, but I know it can be overwhelming."

Honey patted her hand. "We're just fine. I'd say it's the most excitement we've had all week," she winked at Wardell, "but I can't."

Charlie choked. "Okay, you two, we're going to have to come up with a list of things you can talk about in front of me. And I can assure you that's not on it." She stopped abruptly and snapped her head around to Hank. "What are you doing?"

"Going to the City Cafe." Hank tried and failed to sound innocent. For whatever reason, he enjoyed the fact that his presence annoyed her.

"You can't. We're going to the City Cafe."

He opened the door to the restaurant and ushered the family inside. "You see, there's this thing called a public place. Do they have those in California?" He shouldn't mess with her. He didn't know why he was, but it was like when they first met. He couldn't help himself. She was snooty then, like she didn't have the time of day for him. It took months of picking at her to break her down.

The tight-lipped smile she shot him looked out of place on her face. It was so reminiscent of the girl she'd been that it hurled him back in time. Devastated and broken, he'd been nearly ruined when she left. It'd taken him years to get over her. It hadn't helped that she was on TV seven days a week, tormenting him.

"Yes, we have public spaces in California. I mean, we're having dinner as a family. Shouldn't you be having dinner with your family too? Where is your wife, by the way?"

Bullseye.

"Working." She knew exactly how to hit the mark and make it count. That was the danger in fighting with someone who knew you well.

Hell, at least she'd fight with him. When he and Karen had a disagreement, she wouldn't fight, she'd just leave. That was the reason for their legal separation. They'd had a disagreement about having kids. She didn't want to try. He did. But instead of talking it out or fighting it out, she left and said she didn't want to be married anymore. Now he knew it had nothing to do with having kids and everything to do with her affair with Matt Allen.

Let it go, man. That shit's in the past.

"Shame. Well, enjoy your meal, Sheriff." She led Honey and Wardell to a table in the corner, but Wardell dug in his heels.

"Let me buy you dinner, Hank. You shouldn't eat by yourself."

The mutinous look on Charlie's face had him accepting when he knew damn good and well he shouldn't. "I'd love to."

Honey and Charlie did that silent communication thing women do. He didn't understand what it was about. Maybe Charlie had told the older woman about what happened in Austin.

They took their seats, and Honey stopped him when he started to slide in next to the Hollywood celebrity. "I'd like to sit across from Wardell, Hank." She motioned toward the other side of the booth.

Yep, she knew alright. Shit. "Sure, Honey."

He scooted into the booth, followed by Honey, while Charlie and Wardell sat opposite them.

Honey clasped her hands on the table. "Well, isn't this cozy?"

Wardell took her hands in his and the look her gave her scorched the paint off the walls. Damn, these two needed to get a room. Which gave him the willies and apparently destroyed his mental filter, because he blurted the first thing that came to his mind. "So, Charlie, you're not as skinny as you were two months ago."

What. The. Hell.

Was he insane? Of all the things he could've said, why did that come out of his mouth?

There was a flash of panic in Charlie's gaze that was quickly replaced by annoyance. "Why, Hank, you say the nicest things." Sarcasm marched the words across the space between them and punched him in the face.

"What I—"

"It's good livin' and my cookin'," Honey said.

Charlie grabbed a menu from behind the napkin dispenser and studied it. "That's right. Good country living and Honey's delicious food."

He must've really pissed her off, because she wouldn't look him in the eye.

Wardell shook his head. "I don't see how she's gained any weight with as sick as she's been."

What? "You've been sick?" The desire to make sure she was okay was intense and so inappropriate.

She waved him off. "A virus. I'm all better now."

"It's lasted longer than it should," Wardell supplied. He held his thumb and forefinger close together. "I'm this close to sending her to Doc Sanders."

"Oh, Lord, don't send her to that quack. That man doesn't know a stethoscope from a hole in the ground." Honey stood and held out her hand. "Wardell, come with me. Sally Pruitt's over there, and she's been wanting to say hello and see how you are. I wouldn't let her come to the house, or we'd never get rid of her, but we should go say hi, that way we can leave when we want. Charlie, we both want the chicken-fried steak with all the fixins." She glanced at Hank. "'Scuse us."

"Sure."

Once they left, he and Charlie sat for several seconds in silence. They each took turns staring at the same spot on the linoleum table-top. The awkward vibe strumming between them played an off-key chord. He closed his eyes and sucked her wildflowers-after-a-spring-rain scent deep into his lungs. When he raised his lids, she had him in a dead-eyed stare.

He should leave.

Go home to his wife and enjoy the evening with her. But he still owed Charlie an explanation. He'd stay to give her one if she'd let him.

Also, he was a masochist.

* * *

Charlie's brain was whirring like the buzzing fan on the counter of the restaurant. What in the ever-lovin' hell just happened? She owed Honey for getting her grandfather out of there for a minute.

"So, you've been sick?"

Are you kidding me? She needed to nip this in the bud right now. "Yes, Hank. Do you really want to sit through the retelling of my adventures in regurgitation?"

He chuckled and rested his arms on the table. "You've still got a sassy mouth."

She gave him a flat stare and tried to ignore the fiesta going on in her girly parts at the sound of him talking about her mouth. Her brain, playing the role of the crabby neighbor to her party-loving anatomy, tried to put a stop to all the yummy vibes assaulting her. "Remind me again, you're married, right?"

He dropped his head and took a long breath. The pain in his eyes when he glanced up at her made her want to crawl across the table and curl into his lap. It physically hurt her to see him so...tortured was the only word. "Charlie, I'm so sorry. I would never intentionally do anything to hurt you. Please believe that."

Truth rang clear as a bell in the words. "I believe you." It was out of her mouth before she knew she was going to say it. But the sincerity of what he'd said drew them out of her like a snake charmer.

"You do?"

"Yes."

"I wish there was a way to make it up to you. I—you mean so much to me." His expression pleaded for her to understand.

She didn't, but she could accept his earnest apology. Maybe Honey was right, maybe she should tell him about The Pod. He cared for her. They could work something out. "Hank—"

"But I do need you to know that even though I'm sorrier than you can imagine, I'm committed to making my marriage work. I made a vow, and it's the right thing to do."

"And you always do the right thing."

He shrugged. "I try."

And there it was. This was who this man was, and she wouldn't get in the way of him doing what he thought was right. Her secret would stay her secret until he and his wife could get on firmer footing. She would tell him eventually, but not right now. "So, I guess the boy did turn into an honorable man." She hoped the sadness behind her smile didn't show, but when she saw the same emotion in his eyes, she knew it did.

He bit his lip and glanced away. "You know, I think I'm going to get my food to go. Tell Wardell and Honey thank you and that I'll take a raincheck." He stood to leave.

"I will. Bye, Hank." She had to maneuver the words around the mass of emotion in her throat. The smell of stale fries and her own disappointment chased away her appetite.

He lingered next to the table with one hand in his pocket, tapping the surface with the fingers of his other hand like he was trying to make a decision. After several long moments, he blew out a gust of air. "Goodbye, Charlie."

* * *

With every mile he drove from the diner, Hank put Charlie farther and farther behind him. He wouldn't lie to himself and say it didn't hurt, but nobody could mind over matter shit better than him. Now that he'd been able to apologize, he could put her out of his thoughts and concentrate on his marriage.

Speaking of mind over matter. The lights of his house were on when he pulled into his driveway, and he could see Karen talking on the phone and pacing in the front room. She gestured wildly then dropped into a chair.

Suspicion snuck past his resolve to make this marriage whole again. He shoved it aside. She wasn't doing anything wrong, and he wouldn't let insecurity beat him.

His phone vibrated in his pocket, and he pulled it out. "Hank Odom."

"Sheriff Odom, this is Agent John Sheridan. I'm with the DEA."

The Drug Enforcement Administration? He transferred the phone to his other hand and unbuckled his seatbelt. "What can I do for you, Agent Sheridan?"

"I'd like to set up a meeting with you tomorrow."

He exited the car and leaned his butt against the closed door. "Alright. What's this about?"

"I'd rather not say over the phone. Does 10 a.m. at your office work for you?"

"That'll work."

"Great, see you tomorrow."

"See ya then."

What the hell? There was obviously trouble here in Blister County. A charge of excitement shot through him. He passed his phone from hand to hand. It was doubtful the DEA wanted his help—it was probably a courtesy call to let him know they were investigating something and he should stay out of their way.

He pocketed his keys and made his way inside. "Hey."

Karen was curled into the corner of the sofa with a glass of wine in one hand and her phone in the other. She dropped the phone into her lap when she saw him. "Hey." The edges of her smile looked like one of those old faded photos in his mom's attic.

He slid the to-go box onto the table. "Let me grab a fork and beer and I'll join you."

She rose from the sofa. "Actually, I was about to head to bed. It's been a long day, and I've got a headache." She placed her hand on his arm and kissed his cheek. "Night, babe."

"Night."

He hated to admit that he was relieved when the bedroom door closed. While he was committed to working this thing out, he couldn't deny that he was still nursing a grudge. He'd get over it. He wasn't weak minded. He'd overcome these feelings. He would.

Once he finished eating, he sat back on the sofa with his beer, a ballgame, and his wife asleep down the hall. Was he happy? Not really. But this could be enough for now. And besides, happy was overrated. What defined a man was his word and if he could keep it or not.

Chapter Ten

Charlie sang along with the song on her phone and whipped her latest batch of body butter with her hand mixer. The smell of tangerine and honeysuckle filled the kitchen. This recipe she'd created to prevent stretch marks.

She'd gotten the idea while reading her pregnancy book the night before, then she'd combed through her grandmother's recipes and pieced together what she hoped would be something amazing. If it didn't help with stretch marks maybe the smell would make women feel so good they wouldn't care if they had stretch marks.

The little happy sphere she lived in while she was creating helped shave off the sharp edges of her broken heart and her panic, the evil twins that were her constant companions. In a lot of ways, real life sucked.

The truth was, life in the never-never land of Hollywood had shielded her from reality. There'd been moments in the last couple of months that she'd longed to retreat back into that cocoon. She could call Ron, beg for forgiveness. Then he and Marci would take care of her. They'd make the hard decisions and she wouldn't have to worry about a thing. But every day that she wasn't in La-La Land, she found that she had less and less desire to go back. No matter how hard her current life situation was.

Being a star had never really been her dream. Sure, she'd been excited in the beginning. It was thrilling to be the center of so much attention, but pretty soon after the production of the show began, she felt the undeniable pressure of being responsible for the jobs and livelihoods of the cast and crew. People with children and mortgages relied on her to deliver every single day, and that was overwhelming for a sixteen-year-old kid.

She thought of her grandfather and The Pod. They were her responsibility now, and somehow she'd figure out a way to make this all work.

Anger scorched her from the inside out, when she thought of the thousands of dollars in residuals from *Charlie Takes the Town* that could make this whole mess go away, but were instead going to pay off her astronomical IRS debt.

Several cleansing breaths to calm her resentment toward her mother, and she was on firmer emotional footing. For the millionth time, she wracked her brain as to why her mother would've done such a thing to her, and for the millionth time there were no answers. The only thing she knew for sure was that she'd have to get a job sooner rather than later.

"Oh, that smells wonderful." Honey stood in the doorway of the kitchen with her head tilted up and her eyes closed.

"Thanks. It's something new I'm trying." She lined up empty lotion jars she'd ordered off the internet.

Honey picked up her recipe. "These ingredients are lovely. Your grandmother was a genius."

Pride pounded through Charlie's chest. "Actually, this is mine. I took a little from several of Gram's recipes. But I was reading about skin care while you're pregnant." She whispered the last word. "This is for stretch marks."

"Really? Darlin', you have a talent. I gave Scarlett one of the bottles you gave me and she hasn't stopped talking about it. She loves it." Honey went to the fridge and grabbed them both a bottle of water. "She said you should sell the stuff."

Charlie laughed. "That's what my makeup artist and hair stylist used to say."

"Why don't you?"

She removed the pot from the burner. "Why don't I what?"

Honey set the water next to her on the counter. "Sell it. You said you needed a job."

"Honey, that's not a job, that's a business. I don't know anything about running a skin care business."

"Yet."

"What?"

"You don't know anything about running a skincare business, yet." She patted Charlie's cheek.

The woman had lost it. She was Charlie Kay, child star, not an entrepreneur. Her education once she moved to Hollywood had been spotty at best and neglected at worst. "I didn't go to college. I mean, I've taken a few business classes online, but that's not the same as attending college."

Honey shrugged. "I don't think you have to have a degree to run a business, but if you feel like you need some more classes, then take them."

"It's not that simple. I wouldn't even know where to begin to set up a business, or how distribution works, or anything."

"Isn't that what the Google is for? We had a speaker at the senior center that said she taught herself to make colored paper from that thing where you can watch all the videos?"

"YouTube?"

Honey nodded. "Yeah, that's it."

The lotion was poured into the bottles. "Hand me that towel, please."

Honey retrieved the towel from the kitchen table and handed it to her. "Plus, your grandfather ran the Zachsville Feed Store for forty years. He might not have owned the place, but he sure as shootin' ran the day-to-day operation." She rubbed her hands together. "I'm likin' this idea."

Charlie used the towel to clean the bottles. "Well, I'm not. Can we talk about something else?"

"Okay, let's talk about what you and Hank were in such a deep conversation about last night when Wardell and I left the table."

"Yeah, thanks for that, by the way."

The meddler pulled out a chair, sat, and crossed her arms over her chest, waiting for a full report. "Spill."

Charlie tossed the towel over the back of a kitchen chair. She leaned against the counter and crossed her arms, mimicking Honey. "Nothing to tell. He apologized. And I accepted. Then he left to go home to his wife." She shrugged. "Pretty uneventful."

What a crock. It was the turning point in her life. He was officially out of reach. Sadly, there'd still been a tiny part of her that'd wished it would all work out. That she could finally have the picket-fence lifestyle she'd always wanted with Hank and The Pod, but she knew now that it would never happen. Not with him, anyway.

You can still have that. You can make it happen for The Pod and you.

She didn't really believe that yet, but she had a minuscule hope that it was true. She didn't know how. But she'd get through this. She'd get a job and make a life for herself.

"Oh, my Lord." Honey looked up from her phone.

"What? Is it Pops?"

"No." She slapped her hand on the table. "I should've let Wardell at that manager of yours when he was here."

"You've lost me, Honey."

Honey held her phone out to her. "I get updates from *People* magazine."

Charlie yanked the phone from her hand and read.

Is Charlie Kay okay?

Ron Gaylord, the former manager of Charlie Kay, who starred in the Carousel Network's Charlie Takes the Town, said in an interview yesterday that Charlie recently fired her whole team, and implied that she may be mentally unstable.

"I fear that Charlie may be losing her grip on reality. We're all concerned for her, but I'm afraid that she may have turned a bend that we can't get her back from. We're all praying for her."

It should also be stated that while Mr. Gaylord may be praying for Charlie

Kay, he also said he hadn't ruled out filing a breach of contract suit against his former client.

She dropped into the chair next to Honey. She kept rereading the article like maybe if she looked at it enough times the words would rearrange themselves into something not so soul crushing. Then she dropped her head on her folded arms. "Ron, you vicious bastard."

"I could just spit fire. I'm so mad." Honey sucked in a sharp breath. "I just had a horrible thought. What if he leaks to the press that you're pregnant?"

Charlie never looked up. She continued to hide behind her crossed arms. "He won't."

"Why wouldn't he? He obviously wants to make you look as bad as possible."

She turned her head so she could see Honey. "It makes him look bad if his star client went rogue and got herself pregnant. A manager is supposed to be able to manage any and every circumstance. He didn't." Her elbows stayed on the table, but her hands came up to cradle her forehead. "Oh, this is bad."

Honey reached over and stroked her head. "We'll figure something out. I promise. You and this baby will be taken care of. It'll be alright, darlin'."

"No, it won't. Nobody is going to hire me, inside of Hollywood or out, if they think I'm unhinged. And how am I going to fight a law suit? It'll take what little money I have to defend myself against that." Her chair screeched as she shoved away from the table. "I need to call my attorney after I clean up this mess." She rose and started to clean up her supplies.

"I'll get this, Charlie. Why don't you go take a nap? Things will look better after you rest."

Tears stung her eyes at Honey's generosity. "Thank you."

She climbed the back stairs to her room. She appreciated the save, but Honey was wrong. In an hour, things would be so much worse. By then every entertainment news agency would have the story and there wouldn't be one person who didn't think she was having a nervous breakdown.

Which, ironically, wasn't far from the truth.

Chapter Eleven

Hank answered his phone on the first ring. "How's my favorite sister-in-law?" Hank hung his hat on the coat rack in his office, nearly dropping his phone in the process.

"I'm not your sister-in-law anymore, Hank," Hailey reminded him.

He opened the office blinds and took a seat at his desk. Anger at Derek, his witless brother, made his chest burn. "You're still my favorite."

She laughed. "You know Roxanne and I talk. We keep score on which of us is your favorite."

He chuckled. "You're both my favorite. I love y'all, and you know you can count on me for anything."

"I'm really glad you said that. Is there any way you can grab Lottie after school and bring her to the bar? I have to interview some people today. My dad and Irene are meeting with their wedding planner, and Derek is...well..."

He clicked a pen and wondered how someone as great as Hailey had ended up with his good-for-nothing brother. "Sure. Remind me what time she gets done?"

"Three thirty."

"Alright. I'll put it in my phone. The only thing that would keep me from doing it would be an emergency around here. If that happens, I'll get Barb to do it."

"Hank, you don't have to ask your secretary to pick up my kid. I'll work something out if that happens. I guess I can call Ariel, even though asking Derek's girlfriend to do anything makes me want to drive a nail through my eye."

He laughed. "Barb won't mind. She's always looking for an excuse to get out of here. Not sure what that says about me."

"You're perfect, Hank. Thank you for being the one stable man in Lottie's life."

"You don't have to thank me for that."

"How are things with Karen?"

He took a deep breath and blew it out. "Slow going, but we're getting there."

"I admire you for trying to make it work. As someone who's been cheated on, I don't know how you can try again. It killed me, and any trust I had in Derek."

He tossed the pen on the desk then rubbed the tension headache forming between his eyes. "I made mistakes too, Hailey. I left her alone a lot, and I wasn't emotionally available. Damn, I sound like a PSA for marriage counseling."

"I picked the wrong brother. Just one more reason to hate Charlie Klein. She already had you wrapped up by the time I met you and Derek."

"Haven't you seen her since she's been back?"

She snorted. "No. I've got nothing to say to her. She dumped us— all of us—and I can't forgive her for that. I just wished I'd realized it before I named Lottie after her. But I was young and stupid about a lot of things. There's a reason sixteen-year-olds shouldn't get pregnant and married."

"You're the best mother Lottie could ever have. And don't say that about Charlie. I think she could probably use a friend right now."

"Oh, yeah. I heard she's not mentally stable. Like she ever was."

"That's a lie, Hailey. You know it is. I just saw her, Wardell and Honey last night at the City Cafe and she's perfectly fine. That's just Hollywood shit."

"Okay, fine, she's not crazy, but I still don't want to have anything to do with her. Besides, she hasn't reached out to me either."

"Yeah, I think she's been pretty busy with Wardell's care."

"How is he?"

He relaxed back in his desk chair. "Good, I think. Still has a limp, but he seems to be back to his normal self."

"Glad to hear it. Well, I better go. We just got a delivery, and I need to inventory it. Thanks again, Hank."

"No problem."

He disconnected the call. And choked off Charlie's memory. Then he checked his watch. He had ten minutes until Agent Sheridan arrived. He slid his thumb across the screen and typed out a quick text to Karen.

I wanted you to know I was thinking about you. I hope you have a great day.

He'd get their marriage back on track if it killed him. He wasn't a quitter. Maybe if his brothers saw him fighting for his marriage it would teach them the lesson they needed to learn.

His office phone rang and he grabbed it on the first ring. "Morning, Barb."

"Morning, Sheriff. There are two DEA agents here to see you. Agent Sheridan and Agent Murphy." She sounded like she smelled something bad.

"Send 'em in, Barb."

He stood and greeted the DEA agents. "Hank Odom."

"John Sheridan, and this is Julie Murphy."

He extended his hand to the woman, who could be a model if not for her cop eyes. "How are you?"

"Just fine, Sheriff. Thanks for meeting with us."

"Y'all take a seat." He moved behind his desk and prepared to be put in his place. This was the shitty part of the law enforcement hierarchy. State and local government always played second fiddle to the feds. "What can I do for you folks?"

The two agents glanced at each other. "Go ahead, John," Agent Murphy said.

"Sheriff, we think you have a drug smuggling ring forming in Blister County, and we could sure use your help."

Hank didn't know what was more surprising—the fact that they'd asked for his help or the fact that they thought there was a drug smuggling ring in Blister County. "Can you give me more details?"

"Sure." Agent Murphy pulled a folder from her bag and slid it across the desk to him.

He surveyed the photo of an aerial view of someone's property. He glanced between the two agents. "What am I looking at?"

"Golden Leaf Garden and Holistic Farm," Agent Murphy said.

He rested his arms on top of the photo. "And..."

The agents exchanged another look. "We believe that cocaine is being smuggled through Golden Leaf Garden and Holistic Farm," Agent Sheridan said.

Hank couldn't control the snort of laughter that escaped him. "I'm sorry. But Ji and Lin Chang are not in the smuggling business. They're scared of their own shadows, honest to a fault, and they give back to the community. Where did you get your information?"

"We don't believe they are either. But we're fairly certain their son Thomas is, along with a man named Raul Perez."

"How? I mean, how are they transporting the drugs?"

"We've noticed an increase in cocaine in small towns from the Mexican border north, and Perez seems to be the only thing these towns have in common. On the surface, he's a new-age guy that distributes essential oils and plants to organic nurseries. He delivers his legit products in recyclable crates that we believe have a false bottom, and that's where he stores the drugs. Our working assumption is that he drops them off, the shop owners unload their product, then the drug dealers, dressed like Perez's employees, come back the next day and pick up his crates, where they retrieve the drugs."

"If you've had him on your radar, why haven't you arrested him yet?" Hank thought he knew the answer, but he wasn't doing anything with the DEA based on assumption.

"It's unknown if Perez is working alone or involved in a cartel, so for now we're watching and waiting while we build our case. We want to cut off the snake's head, not just kill it."

"Is he coming up from Mexico? Is Border Patrol involved?" Hank made a few notes on the pad in front of him.

"No. He's not crossing the border with the drugs. We believe he has a place here in the states that he either manufactures the drugs or gets them from someone in the states," Murphy said.

"And you think Thomas Chang is involved?"

The agent shrugged. "We're not entirely sure of anything right now as it pertains to Blister County, except the two men are doing business together. Perez has been making his way north from Mexico over the last year."

Hank shook his head to clear it. If this was true it would hurt two really good people. "Alright, what would you like me to do?"

"We want you to keep an eye on Thomas. If you're out and about and see him, note who he meets and where. We just need eyes on him while we build the case. We don't want him taking off on us."

Hank's fingernails dug into his palms. "I need a promise from you."

"Okay," Agent Murphy said.

"I need your word that you'll give the Changs the fairest shake possible. They're about to lose their son, I don't want them to lose their business too." He knew it was a ridiculous request. They didn't make those kinds of decisions. But he wanted them to know his stance on the matter.

They stood to leave. "We'll do our best, Hank. Can we count on your cooperation?" Agent Sheridan asked.

Hank came around his desk and opened the door for them. He extended his hand. "Anything I can do to help."

"We appreciate it, Sheriff Odom." Agent Murphy hiked her bag higher on her shoulder.

He closed the door behind them and leaned his head on the hard surface. "Shit." All he wanted to do was run to the Changs and tell them to get out now, but he couldn't. His job was to uphold the law, and sometimes he had to do the hard stuff in order to do the right thing.

Chapter Twelve

"I hate it when I'm right." Charlie sped out of Zachsville on her way to Austin. Great, now she was talking to herself. Maybe Ron was right—maybe she was losing it.

She'd woken up this morning with a renewed sense of...something. Ron would not beat her. Life would not beat her. She'd packed up every bottle of lotion and moisturizer she had in a wicker basket, dressed in her cutest, flirtiest dress, and headed to town to see if she could get some of the local shops to stock them for her.

The beauty salon was her first stop. What a crazy house. Those women all wanted a selfie with her, but none of them could see the screen without their glasses, but they didn't want their photo taken with their glasses on because it made 'em look old.

She didn't care. The more selfies she took, the more bottles of lotion she sold.

Excitement over having money in her purse because people had bought something she made was a shot of adrenaline to her resolve to be self-sufficient.

It was a foreign concept. She'd never taken care of herself. First her mother had run her life, but she was nothing compared to Ron. Once they hired him, he took over the duties of dictating Charlie's every move.

The irony that she'd been making all the money and should've had the power was one of the great paradigms of children in show business. The inequality of it all was what usually drove child stars to rebel.

Not her. She'd always been a good little compliant girl, and look what it had gotten her. Her name slandered by the one person who knew her best and who'd profited the most from her. And now everyone in Zachsville thought she was batshit crazy.

As she went in and out of one business after the other, she'd inquired about whether they were hiring or not. Even if they had a sign in the window they told her no. Then they looked nervous, like she might have a running, screaming fit.

She was upset alright, and seriously wanted to run screaming through the streets with Ron's head on a pike. But her murderous rage only extended to him...for now.

The bottom line was, no one in Zachsville would hire her. Hence this trip to Austin to hopefully find something there.

She hated to do it. Austin was an hour away from Zachsville, and that was farther away from her grandfather than she wanted to be. Besides, the thought of gas eating up the money she needed made her sick to her stomach.

Her cell rang and she hit the Bluetooth button on the steering wheel. "Hello."

"Charlie, it's Howard Leibowitz."

Oh, thank God, it was her attorney. It'd been hell waiting on him to return her call from the day before. "Howard, thanks for returning my call. I think I need your help." She wasn't really sure how to handle this. He and Ron had always taken care of any legal issues she might have.

Silence.

"Howard, are you still there?" She kept one eye on a blue truck barreling down on her.

"I'm here, Charlie. You should call Ron." The nerves in the man's voice made him sound like a warped record.

"What? Why would I call the man who's told lies about me to the media and who's threatening to sue me?" She eased off the accelerator and let the truck pass. The teenage boy in the passenger seat mooned her as they drove past. Nice.

"I'm sorry, but I can't help you, Charlie. Call Ron."

"Howard, if you tell me to talk to Ron one more time, I'm going to —wait. Why do you want me to call Ron?"

"Um...I think it would be best if you spoke to Ron yourself."

"You little weasel, you're in on this too, aren't you?"

"I have no idea what you're talking about."

She smacked her forehead with the palm of her hand. "Of course you are. Is Marci? Have you all three been conspiring against me? For how long, Howard? How long have you three been plotting against me?"

"Charlie, stop being so dramatic. For the love of God, haven't Ron, Marci, and I always taken care of you? This will all work out. If you just call Ron, I'm sure you'll see that." The click, click, click of a pen on Howard's end of the line was a sure sign he was nervous.

"Oh, you think I'm being dramatic now?"

"Call Ron."

The line went dead. It was just as well he hung up on her. She was about to make a bunch of threats that she had no way of enforcing. She set her elbow on the door and rested her head in her hand, while she steered the car with a death grip on the steering wheel. Tears burned her throat and pinched her eyes. This was about as bad as it could get.

No one in her life had prepared her to handle something like this. She didn't know why she'd thought she could get a straight answer from Howard. He'd always been Ron's lackey. He and Marci both did exactly what her ex-manager told them to do. She'd gone to Howard for help, and all he could say was, call Ron, call Ron, call Ron.

Hell would be an ice rink with skating pink flamingos before she called Ron for any reason ever again.

The glare from Boon's Saloon's giant sign nearly blinded her and made it hard to see the road for a second. The local dance hall that everyone just called Boon's, situated just outside of Zachsville, was the oldest dance hall in Texas. They had a plaque to prove it. Her best friend Hailey's mother had owned it when she used to live here. Her heart sank when she thought of Hailey. She'd left without a word to Hailey and Hank. She hadn't been able to see them and still leave. She and Hailey had been like sisters. They'd even snuck around with brothers.

She hadn't reached out to Hailey when she'd gotten back to town. She knew the woman probably hated her, and she hadn't had the emotional energy to cope with the problem. Also, dealing with a disabled grandfather, losing all her money, and an unplanned pregnancy meant she wasn't at her best. Lord, her life was an after-school special.

A help wanted sign caught her eye and she yanked the car into the parking lot. The front of the building rose up in front of her. Did she want to work in a dance hall? Not really, but she also didn't want to work in Austin. She maneuvered the car into a spot by the front door. She probably wouldn't get the job anyway. She had zero experience, including serving drinks.

Oh, well, plucky Charlie Kay from her television show would just waltz right in there and fake her way through any kind of interview. Of course, Charlie Kay would've already solved her money problems by having a lemonade sale and getting a local businessman to buy her beverage recipe for a million dollars, then sing a song about it. End of episode, end of problem.

Too bad life didn't work like that.

She thought of The Pod and how expensive she'd heard those little things were, besides the fact that she didn't have insurance anymore. That thought drove her from the car and right through the front door of Boon's Saloon. Even though it was the middle of the afternoon, the interior of the windowless building was dark. A minute or two to let her eyes adjust to the gloominess gave her time to assess the place. There were tables on three sides of a large dance floor that took up most of the huge room, and a bar ran almost the whole width of the building at the end.

This was a mistake. She should leave.

"Please say you're here because you want a job." A woman stood behind the bar with her back to Charlie. Her dark hair bundled on her head was thick and curly.

"Yes." Her vocal chords scraped against each other to create a croak.

"Come on over and have a seat. I'll be with you in a moment." The woman never turned around but waved her hand toward the end of the bar.

"Okay, thank you."

The woman walked through the swinging doors behind the bar as Charlie sat down. "So what experience do you have?" her potential boss called out from behind the doors.

This was it—when they told her thanks, but no thanks. "I don't actually have any experience, but I'm a quick learner."

The woman's bun bobbed around just beyond the door. "Girl, I don't even care. I'll train you myself. We're desperate for help."

What? This was fantastic. "That's great."

"When can you start?" The brunette came through the door and skidded to a stop.

Oh, shit. "Surprise." Charlie fanned her hands out by her face. "Good to see you, Hailey."

"You're fired."

"You haven't officially hired me yet."

Hailey reached up and adjusted her bun. "Good. Now leave."

"You said I could have the job. You said you were desperate."

Brown eyes speared Charlie to the spot. "Not desperate enough to hire you."

"But—"

"Get out of my bar."

Charlie cocked her head to the side. "You own the bar now?"

Hailey crossed her arms. "What do you care?"

"I care. I've always cared."

"Don't give me that load—"

"Mama!" A little brown-haired beauty came running around the bar and threw herself at Hailey. "I got to ride in Uncle Hank's squad car."

Uncle Hank? Oh, hell no.

"You did? Well, isn't that fun."

"Lottie, are you gonna make me carry this backpack all the way to your house?" Hank came ambling in looking better than he had any right to look.

"Lottie? You named her Lottie?" Hope that Hailey didn't hate every part of their past together wiggled and came to life.

The little girl turned to Charlie. "My name is Charlotte Claire Odom, but everyone calls me Lottie. And you're Charlie Kay." Her big eyes looked from her mother to Hank, then back to Charlie.

"Yes, I am." This little thing was adorable and Charlie loved her instantly.

"What are you doing here?" The reverence in Lottie's voice made it sound like she was speaking inside a church rather than an old honky-tonk.

"I'm trying to get a job from your mom."

"Are you going to work here?"

She only felt a little bad for what she was about to do. "That depends on your mom." She lifted her eyes to Hailey and grinned.

Lottie spun to Hailey. "Is she, Mom? Is she going to work here? I can tell all my friends that Charlie Kay works at my mom's bar. Please say yes." She folded her hands under her chin. "Please, please, please."

The go-to-hell glare Hailey shot Charlie was almost enough to make her run from the room. But she had a Pod now too, and she'd stand up to anyone for that little hitchhiker. She raised her brow the way she used to during a particularly dramatic part on her show.

Hailey smoothed her hand over Lottie's head and smiled down at her daughter. "Sure, honey."

Lottie jumped around and squealed her delight, while Hailey mouthed *I hate you* over her head at Charlie.

She didn't care. If it hadn't been inappropriate, she would've jumped and squealed with Lottie.

"Come on, hon, I'll take you back to my office. I've got a snack for you there." Hailey turned the still-hopping Lottie toward the swinging doors.

"When do I start?"

"Tomorrow. Be here at six," Hailey barked.

"I'll be here, boss lady."

Hailey shot her the finger over her shoulder, out of view of Lottie.

Hank chuckled, then a frown creased his forehead. "Why are you trying to get a job at the bar? Are you researching a role or something?"

Why not? She wasn't going to lie, but she was willing to let him think what he wanted. So she gave him a noncommittal, "Mmmmm."

"You might want to get some of that high-priced security from Hollywood down here, because Hailey's going to murder you."

She slid off the barstool and looped her purse across her body. "I'll take my chances."

As she passed him, he wrapped his warm hand around her upper arm. The electric heat from his thumb sliding across her skin momentarily short-circuited her brain. This had to stop. She glanced at his fingers gripping her arm and then back to him.

"Sorry." His hand released her but not his gaze. "How are you?"

Exposed. He peeled back all of her defenses and left her bare. Damn him. "I'm not your problem, Hank. Now if you'll excuse me, I have a job to celebrate." She strode out of the bar and turned her face to the sun. She'd done it. She'd gotten a job...as a drink server...in a bar.

She'd never been prouder.

Chapter Thirteen

"Charlie, this isn't going—"

"She's gone." Hank grabbed a peanut from a bowl on the bar, cracked the shell, then threw the two nuts in his mouth.

Hailey glanced around. "Gone? Where'd she go?"

"To celebrate her new job." He held the peanut shell up to Hailey in question.

She waved a hand. "Just throw them on the damn floor, everyone else does. I hate those effin' things. It was Dad's big idea to have them here, but who's responsible to make sure that shit gets cleaned up? Me." The evil sneer she wore made him uncomfortable. "Maybe I'll put my new employee in charge of peanut shells. That should run her off pretty fast." She readjusted her bun. "Why is she even applying for a job? I'll tell you why. Just to annoy me."

He laughed. "Settle down there, killer. She's researching a role."

She grabbed her own peanut, but she put the shell in the garbage. "Is that what she said?"

"Yeah... You know, she never actually said that. I asked if she was and she didn't say she wasn't. That's weird, isn't it?"

"She didn't seem very glad to see you." She began slipping glasses in the slots above the bar. "What's that about?"

What, indeed. Could he tell her? She was his best friend, had been since they were teenagers. "Is there anyone here but us?"

Her hand stopped in mid-motion. "No. Why?"

He dropped his hands to his lap and bowed over the bar. The boa constrictor around his chest tightened its grip. Pain burned his throat. When he raised his head his neck and face burned. "Swear you won't say anything."

"Oh, my Lord, what's wrong?"

"Swear."

She came around the bar and sat next to him. Her cool hand went to his arm. "I swear. Tell me."

"Two months ago, right after Wardell's accident, I'd gone to Austin to stay in a hotel. I just had to get out of this town, you know? All the starin' and talkin', I needed a break." He rested his elbow on the bar and slid the peanut bowl from one hand to the other.

"And?"

"And I ran into Charlie in the hotel. It was..." The memory of that night slammed into him. Longing gripped him and pain sloshed through him like raw sewage. He swallowed past the regret lodged in his throat and turned to Hailey. "We slept together."

Her hand went to her mouth. "Oh, no. That's the weekend you and Karen got back together. I remember because Lottie and I picked flowers for Wardell and she wanted to bring some to you too. When we got to your house, Karen had moved back in." Her hand moved from her mouth to her chest. "What happened, Hank?"

He dropped his head to his arms on the bar and groaned. "The next morning, I was in the fucking shower. Happier than I'd been in my whole miserable life. Then Charlie came in and said my wife had texted me."

Hailey gasped.

"Turned out Karen was in the lobby."

"Shit."

He turned to look at her without lifting his head. "It was ugly. Charlie was crushed, Hay. I crushed her. And I feel like a complete ass."

She rubbed circles on his back. "Karen had filed for divorce and was with someone else. You had no way of knowing she'd come back."

"I know."

"Why did you take her back, Hank?"

"She's my wife. I made a vow, and even though most of the Odom men don't seem to give two shits about that, I do. Besides, I made mistakes too."

She slapped the bar. "That's total bullshit and you know it. You've been a great husband to her, way better than she deserves."

"I'm prideful, Hailey. I didn't give her what she needed because of my damn pride. Look how the Odom pride has ruined your life."

Her back went ramrod straight. "My life's not ruined. I have Lottie and a business and friends. What I don't have anymore is a man who didn't appreciate what an amazing family he had, and I say good riddance." She made her way back behind the bar. "How dare you pass judgment on my life."

"That's not what I meant and you know it. But you can't deny that my brother's inability to keep his promises has caused you and Lottie pain."

"It has, but we're not your problem, Hank. You don't have to save us. I'm doing a pretty good job of saving us myself. Maybe you should worry about your own life. I'm mad as hell at Charlie, but she didn't deserve what you did to her. You two could've probably had something great. But instead, you're settling for Karen. I never understood why you married her in the first place."

"I'm not settling for Karen. I loved her." He shook his head. "Love her. And that's why I married her. It was time to move on with my life. I couldn't continue to let a high school relationship get in the way of... everything. Karen made me forget the past and for the first time, visualize a future that didn't include Charlie. She was sweet, funny, and beautiful—every man's dream."

Hailey arched a brown brow.

"That's a low blow."

She held up her hands. "I didn't say a word."

"You didn't have to. I know what you're thinking. That she was so much every man's dream that she had an affair."

The shrug Hailey gave him pissed him off. He tunneled his fingers through his hair. "Listen, I'm just trying to do the right thing for everybody here."

"Yeah? Well, maybe you should do what's right for you."

Before he could respond she disappeared through the swinging doors to the back room. He grabbed his hat and headed for the exit. Great. One more woman he'd let down.

* * *

Hank drove around for an hour and found himself by Golden Leaf Garden. As he approached he saw Mr. Chang at the mailbox by the road. The Changs' house and farm were all on one piece of property. He slowed the cruiser and rolled down the window. "Evening, Mr. Chang."

The older man flipped through his mail and stuck a magazine under his arm. "Sheriff. How are you?"

"I'm good. How are you and Mrs. Chang?"

"We're fine. Very nice." He smiled, revealing a gold eye tooth.

Hank rubbed his hand over the steering wheel. "How's business?" Real subtle, idiot.

Mr. Chang laughed. "It's very good. Thomas runs the business now. We retired."

That was news. "Really, when?"

"Last month. We're moving to Taiwan with Li's sister next week." He laughed again. "Your face is funny."

Hank chuckled. "Sorry, I'm just surprised. This seems kind of sudden."

The man nodded. "Yes, Li's sister is very ill. We go to take care of her. Thomas does a good job running the farm. He bought us out, so no more farming for me." He laughed.

"Well, I'll be. Isn't that somethin'." He extended his hand. "Congratulations, Mr. Chang. Tell Mrs. Chang I said best of luck."

"I will. Good knowing you, Sheriff. You're a good man."

Yeah, tell that to the women in his life.

Hank turned into Mr. Chang's driveway and did a three-point turn and began driving back into town. The sun was just about to set and the sky was a kaleidoscope of fire and ice. The wheat plants swayed in the early evening breeze and Hank rode with his window down. He did love these country roads. Then a black SUV parked down one of the overgrown side roads caught his eye as he drove past. Was that Karen's car? He whipped his vehicle around and headed back. What would she be doing out here? The thump, thump, thump of his heart shoved adrenaline through his veins. He stopped at the entrance of the tree-lined lane but there was no one around, just a deer standing in the middle of the gravel road.

He glanced at his watch. No way it could be Karen. She was still at work.

Damn, Odom. You need to rein in the paranoia. That's no way to fix your marriage.

He turned the car around and then, because he couldn't help himself, he drove past Wardell Pritchett's house.

Chapter Fourteen

Charlie bolted out of bed and barely made it to the bathroom before she started dry heaving. She wasn't going to lie. She was pretty sick of this mess. The pregnancy books said the morning sickness should get better around twelve weeks. Ugh, four more weeks of this might do her in.

She leaned back against the tub and rested her hand on her belly. "When we hit twelve weeks, dude, I'm going to expect you to get with the program and move on. You can't live in the past."

Boy, didn't she know that.

Been there, done that, and had the extra person to prove it.

With an effort that would embarrass her disabled grandfather, she climbed to her feet and swished her mouth out. That wasn't enough. She grabbed her toothbrush and took the first step to feeling human.

She dried her mouth and addressed the stowaway in her body. "Listen, up, Pod. I'm gonna need you to get with the plan. I'm doing all I can to keep us going, and I expect you to do the same. And don't give me that *I'm the size of a cherry* crap. You're better than that." She chuckled and looked down at her stomach. "I'm just joking, you grow big and strong, and I'll do the heavy lifting."

Little pinpricks of anxiety tried to bust in on her conversation with Pod. She shut them down before they could get a foothold.

The house was quiet as she moved from the bathroom back to her bedroom. The raw ache in her stomach had her pulling out her laptop to research whether someone could die from dry heaving. Her email icon said she had a message. She opened it, and the final nail in the coffin of her life in Hollywood slammed home. It was an email from her agent, Rhonda.

Charlie,

I regret to inform you that I am exercising my option to end our association, effective immediately.

Sincerely,

Rhonda Cooper

Talent Agent

The raw ache turned into a full-on crampy, seizing churn fest in her abdomen. Sweat beaded her brow and upper lip, and she thought she'd have to dash back to the bathroom.

It was really over. She'd wanted out, had been plotting how to get out before her grandfather's accident, but acting was her ace in the hole—she'd known she could fall back on it if she really got desperate for work. But not anymore. With all the lies Ron was spreading she'd never get another agent worth having to represent her.

These people were supposed to be on her side, in her corner. She'd eaten with them, shared holidays with them, made them all tons of money, and when push came to shove it didn't matter one little bit. Everything, including love and loyalty, was expendable.

She was expendable.

Put it away, Charlie. What'd you tell Pod? Move on, dude. You can't live in the past.

Her phone buzzed with a text. A screen swipe showed she had three texts and a voicemail. She selected voicemail and listened.

"Charlie, this is Maureen down at the Dip N Do. Listen, hon, we need some more of that lotion you brought by yesterday. That stuff's more popular than a cupcake at a diet club meeting. I need ten more bottles and ten more bars of soap. Though why anyone would pay what you're charging for a bar of soap, when you could go to the Shop and Save and buy six bars of Dial soap, is beyond me. Anyway, I need 'em as soon as you can get 'em to me."

She listened to it again, then stared at the phone. Then checked her texts. They were from the other stores where she'd left her products, all wanting more. Her surprised laugh filled the room. "Can you believe this, Pod?" Even though the troublemaker remained silent on the subject, Charlie took the easing of her nausea as Pod's approval.

The swelling in her chest wasn't because of gas, though that was a new development in the last week. Pregnancy was a messy business. The fullness behind her ribs came from solving a problem and taking care of herself and her Pea Pod.

The clock on her phone said eight a.m. She needed to get going and fill these orders if she was going to make it to work at Boon's by six. She threw on a t-shirt and yoga pants, her new uniform, and headed for the kitchen.

The sun streaming through the window over the sink shone off her grandfather's nearly bald head as he sat at the table drinking a cup of coffee and reading the *Zachsville Herald*. "Morning, Pops." She poured herself her own coffee and began pulling out the pots she used for her lotions.

"Morning." His greeting was so flat that it was almost non-existent.

She glanced his direction to see if he was okay. "You alright, Pops?"

"Mmhm. How are you?"

She couldn't control the smile that spread across her face. "I'm great."

He finally gave her his attention. "Really? After all that gagging and retching that went on, I'd think you'd be exhausted."

She waved him off and turned back to the stove. Fingers crossed he hadn't read anything in her expression. "I must've eaten something bad. I feel fine now. Thanks for asking."

The crinkle of the newspaper being folded and her pots clinking together were the only sounds in the kitchen. "So your stomach's not still upset?"

Of course it was. She lived in a constant state of nausea. Every day she played a different game of Russian Roulette with the contents of her stomach. Instead of saying that, she smiled her *you can totally trust me* smile. "Nope. I feel fine."

"That's good." He smoothed his hand down the crease in the newspaper. "That's good." The second time he said it was almost to himself.

"Yep. Fit as a fiddle." Fit as a fiddle? When had she ever said that? And why was she talking so loud?

He got up and poured himself another cup of coffee, then returned to his seat.

The air and the vibe in the room rippled with some kind of unspoken weirdness. She ignored it and measured glycerin and mixed it with the water.

"Let me tell you what I found this morning."

He'd been quiet for so long she thought he might have done that thing he did where he fell asleep sitting straight up and down. It was weird, and the first time she saw him do it she thought he'd died. But this subject was preferable to any discussion of her being sick. "What'd you find, Pops?"

"A dead squirrel behind the shed."

Gross. Weird that he'd feel the need to share that with her. "Really? That's sad." What was she supposed to say? She didn't know the squirrel.

"Yeah, it'd been there a while. It was kind of in pieces."

Oh, shit, shit, shit. The cauldron that was her stomach began roiling and swirling. She made the most *I am not about to puke* sound possible.

"And the smell, Lord it was rancid. The stench hung thick and heavy in the air. I'm not ashamed to say I almost lost my breakfast."

Her belly spasmed, sweat broke out on her upper lip, and she fought to swallow the bile barreling up her throat. "Pops—"

"When I saw what was crawling—"

"Stop!" She turned and retched in the sink, but it was more of the dry heaving. Pain from the strain on her neck and chest muscles made her moan.

A bottle of water and a dish towel appeared in front of her face. She took the water, swished her mouth out, and placed the cold bottle against her clammy forehead. "Thanks."

"Your grandmother used to be sick like this when she was pregnant with your mama." His watery blue eyes dared her to deny it.

"How long have you known?" She wet the dish towel and placed it on her neck.

"I've suspected it for about a month, but I've been pretty sure for the last week."

Another swig of water and she was starting to feel human again. "Why didn't you say anything?"

He crossed his arms over his chest. "Why didn't you tell me?"

She closed her eyes and let her head fall back. "I just...I figured you had enough to deal with."

"Like you don't have enough to deal with too? You've been taking care of me, dealing with your money woes, fighting off that manager of yours, and all the while you were pregnant and sick as a dog." He wrapped his arms around her and she went willingly into his embrace. "Sweet girl, you don't have to carry all this by yourself."

That was all it took for her to fall silently apart. All the fear, loneliness, and sadness from these last eight weeks—hell, the last eight years —came pouring out of her onto her grandfather's shoulder. Once she started she couldn't seem to stop.

He gently patted her back and rocked her back and forth. "You're home, now. I've got you."

Once her tears stopped he led her to the table and handed her the water again and a tissue. "Thanks, Pops."

"No problem." He took his seat next to her. "Better?"

She nodded and sucked in a chestful of air.

"Okay, now tell me who the father is." He pinned her with a look that told her he meant business.

Well, she meant business too, and she wasn't telling him yet. He'd go straight to Hank and demand that he do the right thing, and Hank, being the *do the right thing* junkie that he was, would jump into action.

That wasn't what she wanted for herself, and certainly not for Pod. The only people that got to be in their lives from now on were people she could count on. "Pops, I know you're not going to like this, but I'm not going to tell you yet."

"Why the hell not?"

She twisted the tissues he gave her. "Because I don't want him to know yet, and if I know you, you'll storm out to find him even though you can't even drive yourself anywhere. I'm not going to swear I know what I'm doing, but this feels right for now. I'm asking you to trust me."

The side of his fist came down on the table. "Now why'd you have to go and say that?"

"Say what?"

"To trust you." He took both her hands in his. "Of course I trust you. And that means I can't go kick this SOB's butt for leaving you to deal with this alone, and for potentially hurting our precious baby."

The water works began to leak again. Never mind the fact that the man could barely make it from the front door to the back door. He was willing to defend her honor and protect Pod. She loved this man.

Chapter Fifteen

H ank slipped the tan shirt of his uniform on and tucked it into his pants. "So how's the teaching extension job?"

"Fine." Karen cinched her blue robe tighter and continued to put on her makeup.

He leaned his shoulder against the bathroom door frame and crossed his arms. "Any favorite students?"

She shrugged. "Not really."

He moved in behind her, slid his arms around her waist, and rested his chin on her shoulder. "Not even one good story to tell?"

She stiffened slightly, then relaxed. He didn't hold it against her. They were both finding their way back to each other. It would happen. He was willing to take the lead to get them back to where they were when they got married.

She gave a small chuckle. "Well, there is this one kid who told me his dog ate his homework. When I called him on it, he showed me the half-eaten paper. He even had the bill from the pet ER, where he had to take the pooch."

Hank laughed. "That kid's a planner."

She pulled out of his embrace and picked up the clothes she was going to wear. "I need to get dressed."

He grabbed his electric razor and flipped it on. "Go ahead. You won't bother me." He tried to give her a flirty smile, but he must've missed the mark because she grimaced. "Hey. I want you to know that I'm all in, one hundred percent committed to making this work."

The weak smile she gave him did not instill confidence. "Me too." She hitched her finger over her shoulder toward the closet. "I'm just going to..."

He tried very hard not to grind his teeth when she disappeared behind the door. Suspicion danced around his head like a cobra, but he beat it back into its box. This was hard for both of them. If she needed time, then he'd give her all the time she needed.

His heart bucked. It wanted out of the prison his iron-clad will had put it in. But that wasn't happening. That organ would only be allowed to run free once Hank could trust it to love the right person. And so far, it wasn't cooperating at all.

Chapter Sixteen

✦❦✦

Charlie's thumbnail might not survive her new life. She'd gnawed it to the quick and was about to start on the other one when Boon's Saloon came into sight. The tingling in her hands and fingers didn't seem like a good sign. And when had her left eye started twitching? She worried that she might be about to have a stroke.

Pull yourself together, Charlie. You've done harder things.

She'd had to kiss her co-star, Lance Peters, for two seasons, and his breath smelled like what they'd served at craft service the day before. If she could fake her way through that, then she could do this. And she'd acted the hell out of that too. She and Lance had been voted TV's most swoon-worthy couple both years. Who said she couldn't act? Screw them, whoever they were.

Before she could talk herself into turning around and going home, she exited the car and locked it. The sweat on her hands made a wet streak on her jeans. She hoped she'd dressed appropriately. Hailey hadn't told her what to wear, so she'd dressed like she was going to a country and western club. Boots, jeans, and a loose-fitting top.

The music was playing, and the club was darker than it had been the day before. The smell of stale beer and peanuts had her breathing through her mouth, which wasn't doing anything for her nerve-induced dry mouth.

Why did it have to be peanuts? She puked every time Wardell pulled out the peanut butter at home, and he ate the stuff on everything.

Keep it together, Pod. I'm not joking. Hold your nose and think about rainbows and unicorns.

She quickly ducked into the bathroom that was blessedly empty. Once she was safely ensconced in the stall, she began bargaining with the one that seemed to be in charge of her bodily functions lately. "I'll make you a deal, Pod. You stay quiet and don't cause a ruckus, and I'll eat an extra dessert tomorrow just for you. Deal?" She leaned her forehead against the metal door, then quickly yanked it back. Now she had to disinfect her whole face. The courage she sucked into her lungs came with a small dose of fetid air, and she waited to see if Pod would throw a fit. She took the nonreaction as a good sign.

"Alright, Pod, let's go to work."

She flushed the toilet for good measure and exited the stall, and nearly had a heart attack when she saw Hailey standing by the sink with her arms behind her back. "Oh! You scared me."

"Who were you talking to?"

"Myself." Crap, crap, crap. This was not good. She couldn't tell the truth, but she also didn't want Hailey believing the rumors about her mental instability. Charlie eyed the door. She needed to get out of this bathroom before The Pod revolted.

"Who's Pod?"

"Huh?"

"Who is Pod?" Hailey said the phrase like Charlie wasn't an English speaker.

"Um..." Who indeed? "It's my pet name for myself." She chuckled and flicked her hand like it was no big deal that she'd just been caught talking to her alien tagalong. "It's a Hollywood thing. Everyone has one. Jen Lawrence is Candy because she eats a lot of candy, Zac Efron is The Stud."

Hailey gave her an unimpressed scowl. "Of course he is."

"Right? I know. But he's not really stuck up at all. He's actually very cool—a real sweetheart. And Chris Pratt is Mongoose, no idea why he chose that name. We don't really speak anymore." She flicked her hand and rolled her eyes. "Don't ask. Anyway, it's an acting trick to help combat performance anxiety." A self-effacing shrug to show she was sincere. "I'm a little nervous about tonight."

Hailey's eyes squinted like she was trying to decipher some kind of code. "Mmhmm."

"Well, let's get to it, shall we?" Charlie stepped around her old best friend and grabbed the door handle.

"Ah, Pod? You forgot something."

"What?"

Hailey pulled something from behind her back. "Your uniform."

"My..."

"Uniform." The glint of vengefulness in Hailey's eyes let Charlie know that her boss was going to enjoy making her wear the Daisy Duke shorts and low-cut baby-doll top.

"Can't I just wear my own clothes? I mean, I'm dressed to go to a country bar." She held out her hands in case Hailey couldn't see she looked like a damn rodeo queen.

"Sorry, that won't do. We have a strict uniform code here at Boon's Saloon." She extended said uniform toward Charlie and shook it.

This was ridiculous. "What if it doesn't fit?"

Hailey shrugged. "If it's too big, I have some safety pins in the office, and if it's too small...well, more tips for you. Meet me at the bar in ten minutes."

When the door closed behind her, Charlie held the scraps of material up. The shorts looked more like a collar than something you'd wear to cover your butt. At least the top wasn't a halter and wouldn't be tight-fitting around the middle.

She took the clothes back into the stall. She eyed the waistband of the shorts and knew immediately there was going to be a problem. Her shirt came off first—no way was she standing in the bathroom of Boon's Saloon in only her underwear. The necKlein of the top was so low and tight that her boobs looked like two water balloons one drop of liquid away from exploding. If Hailey was right about tighter clothes meaning more tips, then her money woes were over.

Now for the pants. She got rid of her jeans, then shimmied the shorts up her legs and over her hips, but there was no way in hell those bad boys were buttoning. She pulled a hair tie from her wrist and hooked one end to the button of the shorts, looped the band through the hole, then looped it back over the button to give her another inch or so. Even then they were riding up her butt.

She surveyed herself in the mirror after exiting the stall. "Oh, my Lord. Pod, cover your eyes." She looked like the topper for Hugh Hefner's birthday cake. There was nothing whatsoever left to the imagination in this outfit. The only good news was that you couldn't see her slightly rounded belly.

Oh well, nothing to do but gut it out. The good news was that it was dark in the bar and her hair was long enough to cover her heaving breasts. The porcelain of the sink was cool on her sweaty hands as she gripped the side. Her blue eyes were a little wild, and her skin was a bit pale, but it didn't matter. She'd be grateful for this job and this hoochie-mama outfit if it helped her and The Pod survive. One last breath in, then out. "Okay. Let's do this thing."

Music rang through the speakers, and the neon lights above the bar gave the room an otherworldly glow, like aliens had perpetrated a redneck abduction. Hailey was at the bar with two other women dressed exactly like Charlie, except their uniforms fit.

"Tracy and Maria, this is Charlie—"

"OMG! You're Charlie Kay?"

A real smile spread across her face at Maria's sincere enthusiasm. "That's me."

"It's so great to meet you," Maria gushed.

"Thank you. It's nice to meet you."

"Wait. Why are you working here?"

The confusion on the girl's face would've been funny if Charlie weren't currently trying to figure out something to say without lying. "I—"

"She's researching a role, okay?" Hailey said. "Can we get down to business?"

"Ooooh, really? That's so cool." The admiration in Maria's eyes escalated to just above fan and just below stalker.

She wasn't going to outright lie, but she was willing to let them think what they wanted.

"'Sup," Tracy said, and gave Charlie a nod.

"Hello." These two seemed friendly enough.

Her cranky boss glared at the three of them. "Are we done becoming BFFs?"

"I'm ready to get to work, Hailey." Kill 'em with kindness, as her grandmother always used to say.

Hailey gave her the same look she did when she'd handed her the uniform. "I'm so glad to hear you say that, Charlie." She grabbed a broom that was leaning against the bar. "How do you feel about peanuts?"

She glanced around at all the shells on the ground. Suddenly, peanuts were all she could smell. Pod threw the mother of all fits.

She turned and sprinted for the bathroom.

That kid was so grounded.

Chapter Seventeen

Hank kept Thomas Chang's taillights in sight. He'd stayed three car lengths behind him, but in Zachsville that didn't mean much, since there were hardly three cars on the road right now.

Following Thomas had been a spur-of-the-moment decision. He'd been pulling out of the gas station after filling up his truck and seen the young man drive by.

Unfortunately, or fortunately, since he was in civilian clothes and not currently on duty, he hadn't seen the guy do anything out of the ordinary. He followed as Thomas turned into Boon's parking lot and disappeared into the honky-tonk. If Thomas was going in, then so was he.

The dimly lit, familiar room engulfed him as he entered behind his suspect. There was a pretty good crowd for a Thursday night. Couples danced, a group of men and woman played darts in the corner. It was all pretty normal except for Thomas Chang and the Hollywood star sweeping peanut shells.

And...holy shit. Against his will, he followed the motion of her hips as she moved the broom back and forth. Her barely-there shorts and cowboy boots made her legs look like the runway to paradise that he knew they were. The image of those legs wrapped around his hips made him grip the wall to steady himself.

While the sight of her backside conjured all kinds of amazing memories, nothing could've prepared him for the sight of her when she turned around. It was all he could do not to rip off his own shirt and throw it over her. Her breasts were practically coming out of the top. Being at home had done her some good and put a little meat on her bones. Unfortunately for him, the extra weight seemed to be in her chest. She looked like every cowboy's wet dream, and it pissed him off.

His prey forgotten, now his quarry had changed. He made a beeline toward the scantily clad Hollywood starlet. This had nothing to do with the fact that they'd slept together, or the feelings he'd shoved from his life—this was about her protection. At least that was what he told himself, but even he didn't believe it.

White-hot anger fueled his approach, and he yanked the broom out of her hands. "What the hell are you wearing?"

Her big, startled eyes briefly gave him a pang of regret for coming at her that way, but then she flipped her hair out of her face, and her brows slammed down over her furious icicle-blue eyes. "What the hell are you doing?"

He took her by the elbow and maneuvered her down a small hall behind the bar. She jerked away from him when he stopped moving. His arms went across his chest, and he blocked her way out of the hallway. "You can scowl at me all you want, Charlie, but you aren't going back out there in that outfit." He knew he should stop. Why had he done this? It was wildly inappropriate, but for the life of him, he couldn't stop. It was like this pissed-off blonde beauty had cut the breaks on his self-control.

"And who's going to stop me from going back out there, Hank?" She advanced on him, and he got lost in the way her breasts bounced above the neck of her top, which only made him angrier. A long, slender finger jabbed at his face. "You have zero say in my life."

"Someone needs to have some say if you're going to go around dressed like that." He kept one arm across his body and gestured toward her uniform with the other.

"You are unbelievable. You know that? I'm a grown woman, and nobody gets to tell me what I'm going to wear. Are you insane? You're not my daddy, my boyfriend, or my husband." Her fists slammed to her hips. "In fact, you're someone else's husband. What's your wife wearing tonight, Sheriff? Huh?"

That should've been enough to make him walk away from her, but they were nose to nose, and he just wanted one more minute to pull her scent deep into his lungs.

Wrong, wrong, wrong, his brain screamed at him.

He shouldn't be alone with her in a dark hallway. He shouldn't care what she wore, and he sure as hell shouldn't be sporting wood just because the heat of her body wound around him like silken shackles. His inability to step away from her kept him rooted to the spot.

The closeness had them exchanging breaths.

Breathe her in. Breathe her out.

Against his will, he looped a stray hair behind her ear. His finger skimmed the warm skin just behind the lobe. Her lids slid shut, and she leaned her head toward his hand. He wouldn't identify what that slight tilt of her head did to his heart, but he would suck it in, soak it up, and savor it for a bit longer. The moment hung between them like paper flowers in the rain. Beautiful, remarkable, and fragile as glass.

Breathe her in. Breathe her out.

The neon lights screwed with his vision. Alabama's *Feels So Right* blared through the speakers. The combined scents of cologne, stale beer, and peanuts assaulted them. She hated him. He was furious with her. It was too dark, too loud, too oppressively hot.

Didn't matter. It was the most perfect moment he'd ever lived. It floated between them like the final notes of the saddest song he'd ever heard.

Breathe her in. Breathe her out.

The song changed to a fast two-stepping tune. A cheer rose up from the dart game. One of the neon lights flicked off then flicked back on, and the spell shattered, blown apart by reality and fucking horrible timing.

Her eyes opened with a dreamy haze. It cleared faster than fog in a strong wind, and she pulled away from him. No, that wasn't quite right, she removed herself from him with a clear, definitive step away from his body. "I have to get back to work."

A nod was all he could manage. That moment had been more intimate than anything he and Karen had ever shared, and it rattled him to the core.

She stepped around him, walked to the end of the hall, and paused. She didn't face him. "Don't ever do that again, Hank. We're not friends, you're not my boyfriend, you're just someone I used to know, who I made a huge mistake with. Now leave me alone."

The command pierced through him. She was right, of course. He needed to leave her alone. She wasn't his business anymore. Nothing but memories tethered them to one another now.

Chapter Eighteen

Charlie couldn't wait to get home and drown her sorrows with multiple containers of Greek yogurt. Her first shift at Boon's had not been a rousing success. The events of the night looped through her brain like one of those crash test dummy commercials—a series of horrible disasters in slow motion, the most dramatic of which was her running to puke three times.

Pod was in time-out, and she had a date with some non-fat, gluten-free, low-sugar dairy products. Lord, she was pitiful. She didn't even know how to throw a proper pity party. Just one more thing she didn't know how to do. Like sweep peanut shells, apparently.

Sweeping those freaking husks had been the worst thing Hailey could've made her do. The smell of peanut was permanently embedded in her nostrils. Just the thought of it caused her to blow little puffs of air from her mouth.

Then there'd been that stupid uniform. The shorts rode up her ass all night long. She'd pulled them out of her crack so many times that she had blisters forming on her thumb and forefinger. No idea why she bothered, because every time she yanked them free, her butt cheeks would gobble them back up. Humiliating, not to mention uncomfortable.

The top hadn't been any better. She'd spent the entire shift trying to harness her pregnant boobs in the barely there neck. No small feat, considering they'd begun to take on a life of their own. Every time she moved, they looked like ocean buoys in rough seas. How had they gotten so big in such a short time?

She turned into her grandfather's drive and rolled to a stop. The real reason for her crappy mood, though, was the encounter with Hank. He was a jumble of mixed messages that her inexperienced heart had no way of deciphering. What had he been thinking? They weren't lovers. Hell, they weren't even friends. That thought caused an ache beneath her ribs.

She switched off the car and was just about to open the door when a flash of light from the backyard caught her attention. What the hell? She blinked a couple of times. She must've imagined it. No. There it was again. The beam moved back and forth like a pendulum. Who could be in their backyard with a flashlight at one in the morning?

An intruder.

The two pieces of her broken heart began to beat double-time, each trying to out do the other.

Was Pops safe? She had to protect him. He was old and still recovering from his accident. This would scare him to death. She reached for her phone to dial 9-1-1, but the damn thing was dead.

Shit.

How far was it to the front door? Could she make it inside before whoever was in the backyard saw her? There wasn't a back fence, so they'd have no trouble getting to her if they wanted to.

Even though it was a chilly fall night, sweat broke out around her hairline and on her neck. The baby hairs around her face stuck to her damp forehead. Each inhalation did less and less to fill her needy lungs until she was dizzy and lightheaded.

She needed a plan. The neighbor? No. They were a half a mile up the road. She couldn't leave Pops alone with some bad guy toting a flashlight, and God knew what else.

From her vantage point, she could see around one side of the house and a small part of the backyard, where the light still swung back and forth.

Get inside and call the authorities. That was her only option. One attempt, then two to unbuckle her seatbelt, and finally, on the third try, her trembling fingers were able to manipulate the release. She flipped the switch so the interior lights wouldn't blow her cover when she exited the vehicle. As quietly as she could, she opened the car door, thanking God for the lack of streetlights and that there wasn't a full moon.

Her sweaty fingers slid under the door handle once she was out of the car and she gently closed it. She took just a second to make sure her nerve-rattled legs would hold her before she made a run for it, hoping like hell she could make it.

She never got a chance to find out. A scream ripped up her throat and died against the hand over her mouth.

"Don't say a word."

She tried to fight, but he was too big.

"Charlie, it's me, Hank. Stop fightin'." He barely breathed the words into her ear.

As soon as the meaning of his whispered command reached her brain, she immediately relaxed. They were saved. Hank was here, and he'd protect them.

"Are you going to scream?" It was wrong that his soft words would cause goosebumps to break out on her skin. She blamed the pregnancy hormones. She shook her head as much as she could with his big paw over her mouth.

"Okay, I'm going to take my hand off your mouth."

As soon as he did, she spun to face him, and spotted the glint of his service revolver in his hand, pointed at the ground. "Hank, what are you doing here?" She kept her voice as low as he had.

"I followed you home to make sure you made it without any trouble." He never took his eyes from where the beam of light still roamed the backyard. She didn't know if that was because he was a good cop, or because he was embarrassed about having admitted he followed her home.

She slid her arms around his middle and squeezed as hard as she could. "Thank you." The hand not holding his gun went to the back of her head. She took a tiny second to burrow into the safety his big body provided. Not too long, and she tried not to enjoy it too much. Her high susceptibility to the addictive powers of his scent forced her to use restraint.

His mouth came to her ear again. "I need you to get to the house and make sure Wardell is alright."

Her fingers curled into the folds of his shirt and she held on tight. "I'm not leaving you out here alone."

He did look at her then, and she glimpsed a flash of white teeth. "Sheriff. Remember?"

A puff of nervous laughter popped from her mouth. "Oh, yeah, right." Even clinging to him, her whole body trembled and shook.

There was a gunshot and a curse from the backyard. "Hold still, you son of a bitch. I've got you now."

She glanced at Hank, who was staring at where the suspect was located. "Is that..."

"Wardell?"

Was her grandfather fighting with the robber?

Hank took off at a dead run for the backyard. She took off for the house.

As soon as she was inside, she ran to the back porch, flipped on the floodlights, grabbed the landline, and stretched the cord across the kitchen to look out the back window. Thank heaven she did.

Hank was in his cop stance, with his gun drawn on Wardell, who stood in nothing but his thin cotton boxers and cowboy boots. In his hands was a shotgun pointed at the ground. Her grandfather squinted against the floodlights, and his wispy white hair blew in the breeze. He looked like a blinded dandelion.

Ho-lee crap.

Chapter Nineteen

E ven with all his training, nothing had quite prepared Hank for the sight of Wardell Pritchett in his underwear toting a shotgun. His spindly bird legs, rising out of old, worn cowboy boots, looked like a couple of white, fuzzy pipe cleaners. "Wardell, what in the hell are you doing? Put down that gun, right now." He still had his gun trained on the old man, but his finger wasn't on the trigger.

Wardell let go of the shotgun with one hand to shade his eyes. "Hank?"

"Yes. Put down the gun."

The screen door screeched, and Charlie walked onto the porch. "Pops?"

Wardell dropped his weapon. "Oh, for the love of... What are you two doing here? Hank, put that fool thing away." The man sounded downright testy.

Charlie stepped off the porch and went to Wardell. "I came home from work and saw the flashlight in the backyard. I thought someone was breaking in." She placed her hand on the old man's arm. "Why were you out here with a shotgun, Pops?"

Hank could tell by her tone that she thought the old guy was having some kind of episode. He knew better. "Racoons?" His weapon went into the holster under his arm.

"Hell, yeah." Wardell shook off Charlie's touch, and his hands went to his hips. "They get in my dadgum garbage, eat my garden, and shit everywhere. I've had it with 'em."

"So you were going to shoot them?" Charlie rolled the whole question around in disbelief, before serving it to Wardell.

"I sure as hell was. I'd have had him too if the little bastard hadn't come at me." He waved to the side of the porch where there were buckshot holes.

"Pops! You shot at the house. Did it ever occur to you to just set a trap?" Now her hands were on her hips, and Hank let out a bark of laughter. She pointed her finger at him. "You, be quiet."

He bit his lip and held his hands up in surrender. "Yes, ma'am."

Wardell shuffled his feet and wouldn't look either of them in the face. "I...um...I guess I could get a couple of traps and set them out. I hadn't actually thought of that."

Charlie wrapped him in a hug. "We'll get some tomorrow. You need to get inside before you catch your death of cold. It's damp and chilly out here." She began to lead him toward the back door.

The old man stopped and pointed at Hank. "Good to see you, Hank."

"Good to see you, Wardell."

"And stay off my roof," the old man said.

Hank chuckled and watched them make their way across the porch, wanting more than anything to follow them inside and make himself at home.

He should go.

She glanced back at him and mouthed, *stay*.

That one word kept him rooted to the spot. It was a mistake, but he wanted to try to make things right after he'd behaved like an idiot at the club. He grabbed Wardell's shotgun from the ground, checked the chamber to make sure it wasn't loaded, then propped it against the wall of the house, next to the back door.

A light fall breeze cooled the stress sweat that had his shirt plastered to his back. The crisp air carried the earthy smell of damp leaves and dirt along with the slightest hint of wood smoke. With his shoulder against the porch rail, his hands in his pockets, he examined the old oak tree he used to climb to get to Charlie's window. A warm glow of happiness tucked in around his chest. They'd had the best times together...until they hadn't. He dropped his chin to his chest. The back of his boot heel tapped against the front of the top step. She'd gone and never come back.

The sound of the refrigerator opening made him glance over his shoulder. Through the open back door, he could see her. She was standing with her hair piled on top of her head, the light of the appliance illuminating her lovely face. Pressure built in his chest until air could barely squeeze through his lungs. He didn't want to want her. Hated the war of emotion her presence inflicted on his resolve to do the right thing. But there was something so basic about their connection that he didn't know if he'd ever be able to fully extricate it from his life.

"Wanna come in?" She stood with the screen door open, two bottles of water dangling from her fingers.

He shook his head then cleared his throat. "Better not."

She nodded like she'd known what his answer would be. She handed him the drink and took a seat at the patio table.

"Thanks." He took the chair opposite her.

They drank their water in silence until he shook his head and chuckled. When she snorted water out of her nose, they both cracked up laughing.

They laughed until his sides hurt. Every time he thought he'd gotten a hold of himself, they'd make eye contact, and he'd lose it all over again. "What the hell just happened?"

She wiped her moist eyes with the sleeve of her shirt. "I have no idea."

"His boxers were so thin, I saw his junk." He scrubbed his hand over his face. "I'll have nightmares about that forever."

She frantically waved her hands in front of her face. "TMI! TMI! TMI!" She dissolved into a fit of giggles again.

The air backed up in his lungs at the sight of her flushed face and dancing eyes. He wanted it to be like this between them all the time. Not like the ugly scene at the bar. "I'm sorry, Charlie."

Her laughter dried up like the dead leaves in the yard, and her back went straight as a board. "For?"

"Tonight. Hell, for everything." He crossed his arms on the table top. "But most recently for tonight. I was a jackass. We have no tie to each other, what you do is your business. Will you accept my apology?"

The strangest look passed over her face, then she nodded.

"Thank you." He tapped his fingers on the tabletop. "I'd like us to be friends if we can."

She cocked her head. "Friends?"

"Yes."

"And how would we go about doing that, Hank?"

He shrugged. "I don't know. We talk to each other. I won't act like an ass, and you won't get mad at me." He took her smirk as acceptance of his terms. "Why don't you tell me a little about Hollywood?" There was so much about her that he wanted to know. He reached for his water, then leaned back in his chair. "When do you have to go back?"

She glanced away, and there was a real danger she'd chew off her gorgeous bottom lip. "I'm...um..." She blew out a breath and sat up straighter. "I'm not going back. I'm staying in Zachsville."

The bottle halted halfway to his mouth. "I don't understand."

"I've retired. Surely you heard about me firing my management team? I'm done."

"Yeah, but I thought that was... Won't you miss it? I mean, all that fame and fortune would be hard to walk away from." Some bizarre combination of panic and joy gripped him. This was the best and worst news he'd ever heard.

"Will I miss it?" She shrugged and picked at the label on her water bottle. "Some of it, maybe, but if I'm honest, it's a huge relief. Stardom isn't what it's cut out to be. Or it wasn't for me anyway."

That wasn't what he'd expected her to say at all. He'd always assumed that she'd never gotten in touch with him because she loved her life in LA. That she'd had no place for a country bumpkin like him. "Really? I thought you were happy there." He propped the statement up with as much nonchalance as he could pull together.

"No." Her face reflected all the regret he'd lived with since she left. "I missed home. I missed my family. I missed...you."

He was about to lose his freakin' mind. He'd given up on her when she turned eighteen and hadn't come back to him. When she was old enough to make her own choices, and didn't choose him. "But you never came back or reached out to me. I thought you didn't want..." He had to get more moisture to his throat. Another swig of water, then another. "I thought you were happy."

Both lips disappeared between her teeth, and she shook her head. "My mom wouldn't let me have contact with anyone here in Zachsville, even Pops and Grams." The pain etched in her expression gutted him. "She didn't even let me come back for Grams' funeral." One shoulder rose then fell. "After so much time had passed, I figured you'd moved on without me."

Shit. Shit. SHIT.

"Charlie, I called all the time, then your number changed, and I couldn't get in touch with you. I waited for you to come back when you turned eighteen, but you never did."

"And you moved on."

"Yeah." He could hardly believe his own answer. "Karen and I started dating about nine months after your eighteenth birthday. We got married a couple of years later." What a massively screwed up situation.

A sad smile pushed at the corners of her mouth. "I understand, Hank. It wasn't your fault. I made an assumption about you, about us, and it was wrong. I shouldn't have done that. I should've called or come to see you when I was no longer under her control. That's on me."

His whole relationship with Karen was based on his belief that Charlie hadn't wanted him. The house of cards that was his marriage began to wobble under the weight of this revelation. He strained to keep it upright.

"Wait. If you've retired, then why are you working at Boon's? You said you were studying for a role."

Two pink spots appeared on her cheeks. "I never said that."

"Yes, you did. I asked if you were studying for a role, and you said you were."

"No." A little mischief crept back into her voice. "You just thought that's what I was doing, and I didn't correct you."

"Then why?"

She eyed the door, then chewed on her thumbnail.

What was going on? "Charlie?"

When she looked at him, her eyes were blue ice. "I'm broke."

"Broke? How?"

Her slender fingers massaged her temples. "My mother."

"What did that bitch do?" Shelly Klein was the worst, most vindictive, self-serving person he'd ever met. And considering he was in law enforcement, that was saying something.

A humorless huff shot from her mouth. "Now that *is* a long story. I'm tired, and not in the mood to tell it." She stood and took both their empty bottles.

His head spun with all of the information that had just come his way. "What will you do?"

She smiled like a woman who'd just broken out of prison. "Whatever the hell I want to do." Her eyes dropped away from him briefly. "I'm going to bed. You'll understand if I don't walk you to your car."

"Sure." It was about the only thing he'd understood in the last fifteen minutes. She was done with Hollywood. She hadn't rejected him. And she was in Zachsville for good. How was he supposed to move on now?

He thought of his wife. His vow. And solidified his resolve.

He would.

Somehow, he would.

Chapter Twenty

Pain jolted Charlie awake. A cramp in her calf had her writhing in pain. She tried to flex her foot to stretch out the abused muscle, but the jolts of agony made it difficult. Finally, she was able to work it out, and the torture subsided. She wasn't surprised her body was rebelling—she'd been on her feet and doing physical labor all night at the bar. One thing she could say about Hailey, she sure could hold a grudge.

Besides the physical pain, she had an emotional hangover as well. It'd taken her forever to fall asleep after Hank left. He'd all but told her that he only started dating Karen because he believed she didn't care. She'd done all of this to herself because she'd taken the easy way out. Fear of rejection had kept her from reaching out to him, and now she'd lost him.

"I'm such an idiot." She yanked the covers over her head, then quickly flipped them back when her phone buzzed with an incoming text from Maureen at the Dip N Do.

Girl, are you putting crack cocaine in that lotion? Cause we're completely out, and I need some more as soon as possible. These dry-skinned natives are getting restless.

Her supplies were low, which would mean a trip to Golden Leaf

Garden. Her phone said 10 a.m. She had time to grab supplies and get a couple of batches made before she had to be back at the bar tonight. The muscle in her leg tightened up again.

She glanced back at the text. Could she start her own business? Be a part of the community?

The memory of her and her grandmother dreaming of owning a little shop where they'd sell pretty things that smelled nice and made women feel good about themselves was as real as the spasm in her leg, and just as visceral.

From the moment she'd rolled back into Zachsville she'd had an overwhelming sense of nostalgia. A desire to belong in this quirky little Texas town again. And now, with Pod on the way, that desire had grown into a full-blown, soul-deep ache to put down roots someplace that mattered. A place with tradition and pride. But more than anything, she wanted Pod to be raised the way she should have been, with unconditional love and acceptance. Her hand covered her belly. Moisture gathered in her eyes, and a lone tear escaped and rolled into her hair. "You'll have that no matter where we live, little Pod. I promise."

Ugh, pregnancy hormones. She needed coffee.

She threw back the covers, gently placed the foot of her abused leg on the ground, and stood. Nothing buckled and there wasn't any pain, thank God. A quick shower to wake up, then she ran downstairs. Her grandfather was at the table reading the paper. "Hey, Pops." She kissed his balding head.

"You're in a good mood today."

"I got more orders for lotion. I need to check my supplies and then head to Golden Leaf Garden to replenish." She pulled her box of ingredients from under the cabinet. After jotting down a few things, she returned the box to its place.

"Do you, now?" He grinned at her from behind his coffee cup. "Well, that's just dandy. You have them bill that to me."

"I know. I can't believe people like it so much. I mean, it's Gram's recipe, so I know it's awesome, but I'm still surprised. And thank you, Pops, but I can pay for my own supplies." For a while, anyway—she still had a small reserve of money to work with.

"Yoohoo!" Honey said as she walked into the kitchen. At her side was a redheaded beauty with the most adorable little boy on her hip.

"Good morning, Honey," Charlie said as the woman wrapped her in one of her all-encompassing hugs.

Honey released her and took the redhead by the hand. "Charlie, I want you to meet my niece, Scarlett. And this little towhead is Aiden."

"Hello." Charlie extended her hand.

Scarlett ignored it and threw one arm around Charlie for a hug. "It's so nice to finally meet you, Charlie."

Aiden, who'd gotten caught in the hug fest, started to squirm. "Down."

Scarlett laughed. "Okay, bud. Don't get into anything." When she set the little boy down, he grabbed her dress and pulled, revealing a definite baby bump.

"You're pregnant." Prickly warmth stung Charlie's cheeks. "I'm sorry. I just blurted that out."

The smile that spread across Scarlett's face was enough to blind the whole town. "Yes, and don't be sorry."

"When are you due?"

Scarlett's hand moved lovingly over her belly. "In a few months. She's a girl." Her blinding smile became more brilliant.

Honey leaned down and kissed Wardell on the cheek. "How are you, lover?"

Wardell patted her face. "Better now that you're here."

Tears pricked at Charlie's eyes. She was so happy that her Pops had Honey.

As if her thoughts drew the woman's attention, Honey glanced at Charlie and winked. "We've got some serious business to discuss, Charlie."

"Oh, okay. I was just leaving." She grabbed her purse from the counter. "I'll get out of your way."

"No, darlin'. I mean, you, Scarlett, your Pops, and I have business to discuss."

She looked at Scarlett and her grandfather both grinning like they were in on whatever this was. She dragged in a breath and sat in one of the kitchen chairs. "Alright, what is it?"

Honey took the seat next to Wardell. "Darlin', you need to go to the doctor." Honey bit her lip and looked slightly uncomfortable. "I hope you don't mind, but I told Scarlett about your little blessing, hoping she could help us. Turns out she can."

"I know I should've already gone, but I've been worried about..."

"The wrong people finding out?" Scarlett supplied.

Charlie played with the ring she'd bought herself after she won her first Teen Choice Award. "Yes. I'm not ready for the press to know."

Scarlett took the chair next to her. "I completely understand. Gavin and I had the same concern."

Honey got up and poured herself a cup of coffee. "We're real lucky that the media found out about the sex scandal on that reality TV show. Once that story broke the paparazzi hightailed it out of here like their clothes were on fire. So at least we don't have to worry about them following you to the doctor."

Scarlett placed her hand on Charlie's. "My OB, Dr. Shelton, is fantastic, and she and her staff can be trusted to keep things confidential. I know the law requires it, but you and I both know people can be bribed and coerced into telling things they shouldn't. I totally trust Dr. Shelton and her people."

Charlie eyed her grandfather. "You knew about this?"

Wardell smiled. "I did. It was my idea for Honey to ask Scarlett about her doctor." He reached over and took her hand. "You're my granddaughter, and..." He turned to Honey. "What'd you say she's calling it?"

"The Pod," Honey said.

"That's right." His attention went back to Charlie. "And The Pod is my grandchild. I'm for damn certain gonna make sure the two of you are safe."

"Damn certain!" Aiden yelled.

Scarlett pulled the boy onto her lap. "Aiden, what have Daddy and I said about bad words?"

"That they're bad." He gave her a toothy grin.

"And?"

"And I shouldn't say them even though my daddy does." The mutinous look on his face was hilarious.

"Yes, well..." Scarlett said, while Honey choked on a laugh.

"I guess I'm gonna have to watch my language from now on," Wardell said. "Sorry about that."

Scarlett waved him off. "Clearly, he's heard it before. We're just trying to nip it in the bud before he goes to school next year. I don't want him known as Potty Mouth Bain."

Aiden dissolved in a cascade of giggles. He took Scarlett by the face and looked her in the eye. "I not a potty mouth, mama. Daddy's a potty mouth." Then he fell into laughter again along with everyone else.

As Charlie watched Scarlett and Aiden together, a heady cocktail of fear and joy rushed through her. What would it be like after Pod was born? She could hardly imagine it.

"Oh, Charlie. I almost forgot," Scarlett said. "I was hoping to buy some lotion from you. I picked up a tube in town, but Honey said you were working on one for stretch marks. I'd like several containers of that one."

"I'm still tweaking that recipe. It should be ready next week. Would that work?"

Scarlett scooted a plate out of Aiden's reach. "That would be perfect. Just tell me how much I owe you."

She waved the other woman off. "Don't worry about it. You can just have it."

"Nonsense. I'll pay for it like any other customer. Speaking of paying for it, you need to raise your prices. I'm sure you know that you can get twice what you're selling it for in a boutique somewhere."

"Yes, but this is Zachsville. I didn't think I should price it so high. I want people who would benefit from it to be able to get it." That was another of her grandmother's traits rubbing off on her. She had been all about helping people.

"I see what you mean, but it's a shame because the stuff is golden. My elbows and feet have never been so smooth," Scarlett said.

"Wardell says my skin is soft as a baby's bottom." Honey cupped Wardell's face in her hand and kissed him on the lips. "Isn't that right?"

"That's right, my Honey Bee."

Scarlett and Charlie shared a look indicating that both wished they were in another room...or state.

"I guess I could buy some less expensive ingredients and make two different lines. One would be more affordable, and the other would be priced as a high-end item."

Honey tapped the table. "And you said you didn't know anything about business. But look at you coming up with that fantastic idea."

"That wasn't business, Honey. That was just common sense." But a little thrill of excitement jetted through her at the thought of making this into a business.

"That's ninety percent of what business is, common sense. And Honey's right," Wardell said.

He should know. He'd run the local feed store for forty years. "You always think Honey's right." She stood and gathered up her purse.

"I agree with Honey too," Scarlett said. "And I rarely think she's right."

Honey grinned, wadded up a napkin, and threw it at her niece. "You're a liar."

"Liar, liar, pants on fire," Aiden sang.

While the kitchen broke out into laughter and song, the wheels in Charlie's brain were churning.

If she was doing this, then she needed a plan, and a damn good one too.

Chapter Twenty-One

"I don't know where she could be." Hank checked his cell for the fifteenth time. "She knows about the appointment. I confirmed it with her a couple of hours ago."

Stan Middleton, their marriage counselor, checked his own phone. "We've still got a couple of minutes."

Hank paced to the window and glanced out. "She's usually very prompt." And wasn't it a shame that at the moment he couldn't come up with any of her other good traits?

"Yes, she's been uncommonly prompt for your last few appointments." Stan said it like he could read Hank's mind, and also thought it was pathetic that Hank was having a hard time coming up with any of Karen's attributes.

Hanks phone rang. "It's her." He swiped the screen. "Hey, babe."

"Hank, I'm sorry, but I can't make it this afternoon. One of the other teachers got sick, and I need to cover her extension class tonight." Karen's distracted tone told him she was driving.

He ran his hand down his face. "I wish you'd have told me sooner. Stan and I have been waiting."

"I know, and I'm sorry. Please tell Stan that I'm sorry too. I need to go."

"Alright. I'll see you—" The line went dead. "At home." He pocketed the phone. "She's not coming. She got called in to teach a class tonight at the junior college."

"Does that sort of thing happen often?" Stan asked.

He rubbed the back of his neck. "Not really...sometimes...more lately than when she first started. They're having trouble finding instructors to teach the evening classes."

"Uh-huh."

Hank slapped his thighs with his hands in the universal gesture of *this is awkward, so I'm leaving.* "Well, I won't take any more of your time. Maybe you can knock off early." He couldn't get out of this room fast enough. Stan's all-knowing gaze was hard enough to take when there were two of them to share it, but alone it was nearly impossible to stand.

"Why don't we continue without her?" The counselor turned and made a note in his calendar.

"Ah... I don't know if that's necessary." He hitched his thumb over his shoulder. "I think it's best if I wait for Karen."

Stan took his glasses off and cleaned them with his tie. "I often see either the husband or wife alone, it wouldn't be out of the ordinary at all."

Well, shit. There was no way out. "Alright. Let's do this then." Actually, he was warming up to the idea. Maybe Stan could help him with a strategy to put his marriage back together.

Stan picked up his legal notepad and pen. "Great. Why don't you tell me how things have been going?"

Hank sat on the sofa, leaned back, and put the ankle of one leg on the knee of the other. "Great. Things are really going great."

"Good." Stan scribbled something on the pad. "So no arguing?"

"None." He couldn't help the smug tone in his voice.

"Really?"

"Our schedules are kind of crazy right now. We're hardly ever home at the same time."

More scribbling. He hated when Stan wrote something without saying anything.

"You know she's really busy with this second job, and my job is always insane. But we're making it work."

"How?"

"Beg pardon?"

Stan glanced at him over his readers. "How are you making it work if you hardly ever see each other?" His pen was at the ready for the next words that came out of Hank's mouth.

"Well..." He rubbed the back of his neck, and it came away damp. Was it hot in here? "I'm trying to be more kind and interested in her job when I see her. I try to not only talk about my job or family."

"Mh-hm." Scribble.

"I'm also helping around the house more. I cook for us a couple of nights a week, though she's usually so tired when she gets home she goes straight to the bathroom to shower, then falls into bed." That fucking nagging doubt pounded against the lid of the box he'd put it in. He stomped it closed.

"Interesting." Scribble, scribble.

"Why is that interesting? The woman's working two jobs and she's tired. I'm doing all I can to show her I've changed and that I can be the kind of husband she needs."

"What about your sex life?"

Hank sat up taller on the sofa, trying to gain some advantage in this discussion. "How do you mean?"

"How's it going? Have you been able to reconnect? With what regularity are you having sex?"

This time he caught a bead of sweat from running down his forehead with his fingers. "We've...ah...we haven't, actually."

Stan cocked his head. "Actually what?"

The bastard was going to make him say it. "Um...had sex since we got back together. It's hard for her. And for me." He quickly added. "We're working our way up to it."

We're working our way up to it.

What kind of lame-ass answer was that? Like it was a chore, and they had to make sure they could stomach one thing before they moved to the next. Heat burned under his skin from his neck to the tip of his head. When he said the excuse he'd been telling himself for two months out loud, it sounded fucking pathetic.

"Hmmh." Scribble, scribble, scribble.

The silence, except for that fucking pen moving over the page, made him want to run from the room screaming. He couldn't take it anymore. He uncrossed his legs and leaned forward with his elbows on his knees, and his hands clasped. "Listen, Stan. It's not an ideal situation. I know that. We're both dealing with a lot of stuff. But I can promise you one thing. Nobody will work harder to make this marriage work than me. I can mind over matter shit like nobody's business."

Stan set his pen and pad on the table next to him. "I don't doubt that, Hank. It's the thing people admire the most about you."

Pride rose up in him like the sun on the Serengeti. "Well, thank—"

"It's also useless in this situation."

The slap of truth infuriated him. "I beg to differ. I can make my marriage work. I made a commitment, and I plan to keep it. Other men would've walked away from this situation when she had the affair, but I'm not most men. I can beat this."

Stan crossed one leg over the other. "Beat what?"

"This, this, this..." He waved his hand like the answer was printed in the air between them. "This affair, and the marriage falling apart. I. Can. Beat. It."

"Hank, you can't will another person to get on board with your plans. This isn't just about you."

"I know that. But Karen wants this too."

"Really? Then where is she? And why is it that when we have these sessions, it's like pulling teeth to get her to engage?" He held his hand up in surrender. "I'm not making accusations, I'm simply pointing out that this can't be one-sided to work."

Hank shot to his feet. He had to get out of this office with its soothing paintings, mellow music, and lavender oil in the humidifier thing. He'd show Stan. He'd show everyone that he didn't fail. "Thanks for your time, Stan, but I'm afraid I need to go."

Out on the street, nausea cramped his stomach. It had to be something he ate and not the double portion of truth sandwich that'd just been shoved down his throat.

An hour and a half later he was pulling into the parking lot of Austin Junior College with Karen's favorite sandwich and fizzy water. She'd most likely not been able to eat dinner since she'd had to come straight here from her other job. The school was quiet in the evenings, but he found the administration office easy enough.

A pretty middle-aged woman sat behind the front desk. "May I help you, Sheriff?" She looked and sounded nervous.

He forgot he was still wearing his uniform. "No, I'm not here in any official capacity. I'm just here to bring dinner to my wife." He held up the sandwich and water for her to see.

"Well isn't that nice. Is your wife a student?"

"No, she's one of your teachers, Karen Odom."

"Karen?"

He grinned because she was back to looking nervous. "That's right."

She fiddled with the flower necklace she wore. "Um...Karen hasn't taught here since the spring, Sheriff."

Doubt broke its chains and began running around like a wild man on a killing spree, murdering every ounce of goodwill and hope he'd manufactured about his marriage. "Since last spring, you say?"

The pity in her eyes made him want to hit something.

"Well, thank you for your time." He turned on his heels and calmly left the building. There had to be a mistake. Karen must've given him the wrong name of the school. Maybe the lady at the front desk had her confused with someone else. Homicidal doubt would have none of his excuses, and shot them down one by one, until they lay in a dead heap on the ground.

Just like his marriage.

Chapter Twenty-Two

There were more people in the bar than there had been the night before, Pod was behaving, and Charlie was about to murder her boss with a broom and dustpan.

"Charlie, how hard is it to sweep a floor?" Hailey yelled above the music.

There'd be a hole in her tongue by the end of the night from biting it. She didn't want to get into it with Hailey. There was still the hope that they could patch up their relationship. "I'll make another pass through."

"Before you do that, I need you to get the garbage from the bathrooms and take it to the dumpster out back." The glint of enjoyment in her boss's eyes wasn't encouraging. This must be another crappy job.

"I'm on it." Honestly, she was sort of glad to be able to leave the bar even for a few minutes. The singer on stage was maybe the worst she'd ever heard. It didn't help that he was clearly drunk.

The guy hit a particularly terrible note, and she fought the urge to cover her ears. The squeal from the monitor as he stumbled into it only added to the auditory assault.

"Damn it." Hailey threw her towel onto the bar. "That idiot is going to drive away all my customers."

"Why don't you get rid of him?" Charlie took a step back in case the question sparked violence in her boss.

"Chester's in here every night even when he's not singing, so that could get awkward, plus he's a friend of my dad's, and he won't let me fire him."

"That doesn't seem fair since you're the one that's always here." She'd never seen Hailey's father at the bar.

"I didn't ask your opinion about my bar or how my family and I run it. The only thing you need to worry about is doing your job, which includes the bathroom garbage."

She and Hailey would need to have that talk sooner rather than later. Charlie had been trying to give her former friend time to adjust to her being back in town. She was prepared to eat crow if it meant they could get their relationship back on track, even though the viciousness seemed a little over the top just for her leaving town without saying goodbye.

Too late, Charlie realized she needed a pair of gloves. But she'd rather scrub the skin from her hands than go back and ask Hailey for anything. She gathered the garbage from the women's bathroom, careful not to touch anything but the edge of the bag, and even that caused bile to lodge behind her tonsils.

Next was the men's restroom. She stared at the door for several seconds, not sure how to proceed. This was ridiculous. She just needed to knock and run in to do her job. "Anybody in here? I'm coming in to grab the garbage." When no one responded, she made her way through the door, and quickly realized she needed gloves *and* a mask for this assignment. A series of gags made the muscles in her chest and neck contract. Several attempts to swallow them down, then finally the retching stopped. Close call. Pod had almost had a meltdown. How horrible would it be to get sick in the men's restroom?

Ugh. The garbage hadn't been emptied in a while. It was a large metal can and was full to the brim. She gathered the edges of the bag and pulled. The awkward angle meant she couldn't get the correct leverage, and the greasy film on the floor didn't help at all. She tried not to think about the bacterial equivalent of Woodstock partying it up under her feet.

She did a shuffle, slide, step thing then maneuvered to the other side, yanked, and lost her footing.

She hit the ground. Hard.

Pod!

A quick roll to her side and her body instinctually curled around Pod. She gripped her stomach and waited.

And waited.

And waited.

No pain in her abdomen. No weird wetness between her legs. Just a sore backside. Her muscles went lax, and she said a grateful prayer.

Then the door swung open, and Hank walked in. Why did he keep showing up at the worst possible times?

The look on his face would've been hysterical if she hadn't been coiled in the fetal position, holding The Pod, on the men's bathroom floor.

"Are you alright?"

She gulped past the instinctive panic that was lodged in her throat. "Yes. I slipped and fell trying to get the garbage out of the can."

He squatted down next to her. "Are you hurt?"

"Just my pride." Thank God.

He reached for her hand. "Let me help you up."

"Better take my elbow. Hailey didn't give me any gloves to do this job. I don't think you want to touch my hands. As it is, I'm going to have to burn these clothes and sterilize my body." She held out her elbow and he helped her to her feet.

"What was Hailey thinking? I'm gonna tell—"

"No."

Confusion was all over his face. "No, what?"

She made sure her shirt covered the ever-growing bump. "You're not going to say anything to Hailey. This is my job and my business. I can handle it."

"You're right."

"I can take—wait, what?"

He lifted the bag of garbage from the can. "You're right. You can handle it. You're more than capable. You're a grown woman and perfectly able to handle your life." He tied a quick knot in the top of the bag and handed it to her.

A stray hair hung over her face. She blew it out of the way. "You're serious?"

He shrugged. "Yes. You're beautiful and appear delicate, which causes people to underestimate you. But I know you. I just forgot for a second how smart and capable you also are."

She searched his face to see if he was sincere. There wasn't a trace of sarcasm on his achingly familiar face. He meant it. The tears pricking her eyes weren't because of the smell in the bathroom, though that was god-awful, but because he'd just said the sweetest thing that anyone had ever said to her. The organ in her chest that she was only using to stay alive and care for Pod gave a huge double thump. "Thank you."

He grinned and held the door open for her. "You're welcome."

As soon as she came close to the bar, Hailey started in on her. "Where the hell have you been?"

Hank's words came back to her, and her spine got a little straighter. "Hey! Get off my back. I'm doing the best I can. And next time, you better have some gloves, or you can do this yourself."

The bar owner's eyes went round, and she stopped washing glasses. "Alright."

"Okay. Now get the door for me before I drop this all over the place."

"Careful. I'll let you get away with the first bit of sass because you're right. I should've given you gloves. But I can still fire you. Don't forget that."

"Please, you love having me here. Who would you pick on if I were gone?"

Hailey held the door open and stood aside for Charlie to step outside. "I'd find someone."

Charlie laughed. "I'm sure you would." She reared back and threw the first bag into the dumpster. Easy enough. Just as the second bag was about to clear the lip of the dumpster got caught on something and ripped, showering her with its contents. "Shit! Shit! Shit!"

Hailey laughed so hard Charlie thought she might hyperventilate. Then she disappeared inside the club. There was garbage everywhere, and it had touched her head and face. Disgusting!

A pair of gloves were shoved at her. "Here."

Charlie took them wearily.

More laughter bubbled out of her old friend's mouth. "You're right. I think I would miss you. Now clean this up."

Hailey disappeared into the building. A survey of the ground around her confirmed that it was as big a mess as Charlie thought it was. She could leave. She didn't have to take this shit from Hailey or anyone. She was Charlie Kay, for cryin' out loud. Then Hank's words came back to her. *I forgot how smart and capable you are.* Pride shoved her ego out of the way. She tugged on the gloves and went to work.

* * *

Charlie returned to work after scrubbing every inch of exposed skin three times. Tracy and Maria were huddled together at the bar. Tracy gestured wildly, but it was clear they were trying to keep their voices down. She glanced around to find Hailey was nowhere in sight.

"Hey, guys. What's going on?" She tried to act like she didn't know they were in the middle of a private powwow.

Maria peeked over her shoulder, then back to Charlie. "Hailey's ex is here with his girlfriend."

"The one he cheated on Hailey with." Tracy glared daggers Derek's way. "Bastard."

"Where?" She tried to look over Maria's shoulder, but both women shut her down.

"Don't look," Maria whispered.

"Okay. Why are you two huddled in the corner?"

Maria chewed on her lower lip. "We're arguing over who has to wait on them. I don't want to. I don't like uncomfortable situations."

"And I don't want to because I'm slammed and have a party of rowdy frat brothers." Tracy picked up her tray of drinks. "Speaking of which, I need to deliver these to their table. You're on your own, Maria."

The young waitress glanced over her shoulder again. "Fine, I'll go."

"Wait." Charlie stopped her with a hand to her arm. "Where's Hailey?"

"She's in the back. Derek brought Ariel up to the bar to order their drinks and say hello. He's a mean son of a bitch." She picked up her tray with the cocktails the couple had requested. "Well, I better go take them their order."

Fury burned up Charlie's insides. She and Hailey were on the outs, but that didn't mean she couldn't hate her ex for her. Derek always did have a cruel streak. She snatched the tray from Maria. "I'll go."

"But—"

"I'll go." She gave Maria the same look she gave handsy costars just after she threatened to ruin their careers.

Maria backed off. "Yeah, okay."

She took a minute to get into her sweet, wholesome, and a little airheaded Charlie Kay character. It was like slipping on an old comfy pair of slippers. She made sure her boobs were still contained in her super tight uniform, happy for once to have it. It would play nicely into her plan. With a bit of extra sway to her step, she sashayed up to the table. They were cuddled up together like two nasty bugs during mating season. "Hey, Derek, long time no see." She smiled so widely she was surprised she didn't sprain her cheek.

"Oh, hey, Charlie. I heard you were working here to study for a role."

She shrugged. "Who's your friend?"

"Um..."

The woman stuck out her red-nailed hand. "Name's Ariel, and you can back the fuck off my man."

In a perfect Charlie Kay way she laughed like that was the silliest thing she'd ever heard. "Oh, Ariel, you're funny. Derek and I are like brother and sister. Don't worry. I've got no designs on your man." The tray with the drinks teetered slightly, and she righted it. "Woo. I'm still getting the hang of this."

"Do you want me to help you with that?" Derek asked.

She moved between them. "No, I think I've got it." She brought the tray around with her tongue stuck between her teeth like she was removing a kidney, not serving drinks. Just as she maneuvered it over Ariel, the drinks slid and toppled onto the woman's head. "Oh, my gosh."

"What the fuck?" Ariel screamed.

"Ohmygosh, ohmygosh, ohmygosh." She tried patting Ariel down with the dirty bar rag tucked into her apron. While the spilled drinks had been planned, the yucky bar towel had been a happy, impromptu addition to this karma sandwich. Speaking of karma, Ariel should be glad Hailey used plastic cups, or she'd have a concussion as well. That part of the plan hadn't been very well thought out. Oops.

"Charlie, get out of the way," Derek yelled. "You're making it worse."

"I'm so sorry, Ariel. Please send me the dry cleaning bill."

"You can bet your ass I will. Let's get out of here, Derek." She yanked her purse off the back of the chair. Charlie stifled a giggle as liquor leaked from the designer bag, leaving a wet trail behind Ariel.

"Wait." Charlie jogged to catch up with the spitting mad cow.

"What?" Ariel cried.

Charlie reached up and tugged a cherry from the woman's hair. With a weak, apologetic smile, she held it up to her. "And a cherry on top."

Ariel let out a frustrated scream and shoved Charlie aside. "Get out of my way, you idiot." She was out the door before Charlie could respond.

The look on Derek's face was priceless. "You did that on purpose."

Charlie shrugged and dropped her Charlie Kay persona. "The two of you deserve far worse." She glanced toward the door. "She's a real winner, Derek. Enjoy your life."

"She hates you, you know?" The sneer he wore reminded her of the old Derek that used to tease and ridicule her and Hailey.

Her hand went to her hip. "Who, Ariel? You think I care?"

"No, Hailey." He leaned toward her and got in her face. "She hates your guts. So you just made an enemy for nothing."

She crossed her arms over her chest, and refused to give him the satisfaction of knowing how his words broke her heart. "Not for nothing. That's the most fun I've had since I got back to Zachsville."

Ariel poked her head back in the door. "Derek!" The screech had dogs in three counties barking.

"You have a good night, Derek." She turned to clean the table and caught Hailey staring at her from behind the bar. After a few seconds, a small smile ghosted across her old friend's face.

Not for nothing then.

Chapter Twenty-Three

Hank pounded the nail like it had personally offended him. His arm ached, and sweat ran down his face, but he welcomed the chance to work out his frustration. He'd been so happy when his mom called and asked him to help with her broken fence. Of course, then he'd had to field questions about his and Karen's relationship. Which he side-stepped like he was line dancing at Boon's.

He'd come home from the junior college the other night prepared to lay into her about her lie, but before she could get home, he'd been called into work for a bad car accident with fatalities. The paperwork had kept him out all night. He'd headed home hoping to catch her before she left on a scheduled trip to see her parents. But he'd been too late, which meant he still had a million questions and not one damn answer.

And yes, he had called her mother to confirm the visit was legit. With so much distrust, could this thing between him and Karen be fixed? Could they ever get back to where they'd been in the beginning? He had loved her in the beginning. True, it hadn't been the kind of love that makes you feel like you're hanging by your fingers on a giant Ferris wheel covered in lights with music ringing from the speakers.

But it was sound, sturdy, and steady. There wasn't a damn thing wrong with sound, sturdy, and steady, it was something they could build a life on... were building a life on, until one day they stopped. And the sad truth was, he didn't know who quit first. All he knew was that he'd only ever had that swooping, flying, scream-it-from-the-mountain-tops kind of love with Charlie.

And that was his problem.

But Charlie was his past, and Karen was his future. The one he'd committed to. The one he'd made promises to. Promises he wanted to keep.

Yes, she'd broken hers, but they were working that out. Or at least he'd thought they were.

"When you're done there, I've got a list a mile long that you can start on." Derek leaned against his truck.

Where had he come from? Some lawman Hank was. So lost in thought that he hadn't heard his brother's truck pull up the drive.

He loved his brother, and that was what made being angry with him so hard. "Hey, what're you doing here?"

Derek hitched his thumb over his shoulder toward the house. "Just came to drop off Lottie."

Hank slipped his work gloves off and stuck them in his back pocket. "Isn't this your weekend to have her?"

"Yeah, but Ariel wants to go to Houston for the weekend. Mom doesn't mind keeping her, and Lottie doesn't care."

"Are you kidding me right now?"

His brother looked offended. "No. Why do you care?"

"I care, Derek, because I love that little girl, and she misses you." He advanced on his sibling. "I can't believe you'd throw her over for a piece of ass."

Derek shoved him. "Watch your mouth. That's my woman you're talking about."

"Oh, please. You and I both know that she's just the flavor of the month. You can't spell commitment let alone keep one." They were nose to nose now, spitting and heaving like the wild bulls their mother used to accuse them of being. "I never thought I'd see the day that I was ashamed to be your brother, but that day has come."

An ugly sneer marred his brother's face. "Speaking of a piece of ass, have you seen Charlie lately? She's gotten fat, man."

Hank's fist came around and connected with his brother's mouth. No forethought, no planning, just a pure, unadulterated, furious reaction.

Derek wiped blood from his lip with his thumb, looked at it, then wiped again. "You want to talk about being ashamed. Let's talk about my pussy-whipped brother. Your old lady fucked some other guy, and you're still around, now that's embarrassing. One thing I can say about Hailey, at least she had the balls to leave my ass when I screwed around with Ariel." He snorted without humor. "She's more of a man than you."

Fire flashed up Hank's neck and face. "You don't know what the hell you're talking about."

"I know that I just insulted your wife, and you didn't do jack shit. But I said your old flame was a piece of ass, and you knocked the shit out of me." He shook his hair back. "I saw the way you were watching her last night at the bar. Looks like saint Hank's halo might've slipped a bit." He turned his head and spit blood on the ground. "Face it, you're no better than Jett or me."

Hank jabbed his finger toward Derek's truck. "Get the fuck out of here. I'm sick of listening to you."

Derek shrugged. "Gladly. I got places to go."

When his brother was out of sight, Hank leaned against the fence and tried to get his breathing under control. Derek was a jackass. Hailey and Lottie were better off without him.

But was he right? Was Hank no better than his brothers?

* * *

"Uncle Hank, can I get two scoops?" Lottie skipped along beside him as they walked to Zachsville's only ice cream shop, Scoopalicious.

"Can a little thing like you eat two scoops?"

She stopped abruptly and jutted her chin out. "I'm not little. I'm almost eight."

The stubble on his face scratched his hand as he rubbed his jaw.

"Are ya, now? Turn around, let me get a good look at ya." She obliged with shoulders squared and back ramrod straight. "I reckon you're big enough. Two scoops it is."

She pumped her fist in the air. "Yes!"

He laughed and wondered for the millionth time how Derek could be such a dumbass to walk away from this amazing kid.

"Where's Aunt Karen?"

"She's visiting her parents. I would imagine she and her mother are shopping right about now."

She scratched her leg while still skipping, making her do this one-leg hop thing. "Oh, I like shopping too."

He held the door to the ice cream shop open for her. "You do, huh?"

She gave him a giant you-know-you-want-to-buy-me-something grin.

He laughed. "Get in there, trouble."

"Okay." She ran to the display and pressed her nose to the glass.

"Hey, Sheriff Odom," Kelly Marks, the owner's daughter, said from behind the counter. "Oh, hi, Lottie. I didn't see you there. What can I get y'all?"

Hank held his hand out to Lottie. "Ladies first."

"I'll have a scoop of bubble gum and a scoop of peppermint in a cup, please."

"You got it." The teenager began dishing up the ice cream. "Tell Mrs. Odom I said hi, Sheriff."

"I'll do that." One thing he could say about his wife, she was one hell of a teacher, and since she'd gotten out of the classroom and started working with some of the kids with learning issues, she'd really found her calling.

Kelly plopped a ball of blue ice cream into a cup. "I'm really going to miss her."

Hank examined the girl. Karen's graduating students often said that, but Kelly was only a sophomore. Was she moving? He hadn't heard the Marks were leaving town.

"I think it's totally crappy what they're doing to her."

What in the hell was this kid talking about? "You do?"

"Yeah, she's the best teacher at Zachsville High, and it's stupid that they're shutting down the program she's working in. I don't know why they won't keep her and let her teach a regular class, or at least let her finish the year. If I were her, I wouldn't have come back. It was shi— um, crappy, that they didn't tell her until the first week of teacher in-service." She handed the ice cream to Lottie. "Does she know what school she's going to next?"

He shook his head. It was all he was capable of with the sirens screaming in his brain. Karen's job was going away? Wait. Did Kelly say that she found out right before school started? That was when she'd told him she wanted to get back together.

"Sheriff?"

"I'm sorry, what?"

Kelly laughed. "I asked what I could get for you."

"Oh. Nothing for me."

"I thought you were getting rocky road, Uncle Hank?" Lottie already had a ring of blue around her lips.

"I changed my mind, kiddo." He couldn't have eaten if someone shoved food down his throat. How had he not known this?

Derek was right. He was a fucking embarrassment.

Chapter Twenty-Four

Charlie, Scarlett, and Honey waited in an examination room in Dr. Shelton's office. They'd been kind enough to let them enter through the back door to avoid any accidental sightings. The scent of vanilla soothed her tattered nerves. Honey and Scarlett's steady stream of conversation helped to distract her from the inkling of fear that'd been her constant companion since she first saw those two blue lines on the pregnancy test. What if she was a terrible mother? She knew nothing about raising a baby and even less about growing one.

She was nearly at the end of her first trimester, and she was just now going to the doctor. She probably wouldn't get any mother of the year awards for that. But disbelief had kept her paralyzed for a month. Once Marci and Ron had found out, they'd insisted she not tell anyone or see a doctor. Then they left her. She'd always had people to handle things like this for her. That terrible voice reminded her that she didn't know how to take care of herself, so how did she think she'd be able to take care of another human being?

That thought got shoved into the nasty place with the rest of her insecurities. She had no time or energy for that crap. She had a Pod to grow and a life to build, and one way or the other, she would do this. Even if all her decisions weren't the best, she'd figure it out.

Probably.

Maybe.

Who the hell knew?

Honey laid her soft, liver-spotted hand over hers. "You alright, darlin'?"

She exhaled the bad and inhaled Honey's Jungle Gardenia fragrance. "I'm fine."

"I was so nervous my first appointment," Scarlett said. "Though I wasn't as bad as Gavin. He was a wreck."

Charlie crossed her legs and adjusted her position in the chair. "Really? He seems so tough, or at least that's his persona."

"Lord, that boy ain't nothing but a big ol' softie," Honey said.

Scarlett laughed. "It's true. They had to offer him a chair during the sonogram because all the color drained from his face. Then he started to hyperventilate. And I'll swear you're a dirty liar if you ever tell him I said that."

Charlie made a zipping motion in front of her mouth. "Your secret's safe with me."

The door to the room opened, and Dr. Shelton came in. "Hello, Scarlett." She shook Scarlett's hand. "How are you feeling?"

Scarlett gave her a blindingly happy smile. "Peachy."

"That's good to hear. And Miss Honey, are you still getting into trouble?"

"Yes, ma'am. I'm too old to change now."

They all laughed, and Charlie was grateful that Dr. Shelton had given her a few minutes to adjust to her presence. Coming face to face with a doctor made this all so very real.

Dr. Shelton extended her hand. "And you must be Charlotte?"

The physician's warm, competent demeanor instantly put her at ease. "You can call me Charlie."

"Alright, Charlie, it's lovely to meet you."

"Thank you. You too."

Scarlett stood. "Dr. Shelton, is there someplace Honey and I can wait?"

Dr. Shelton washed her hands in the small sink in the corner of the room. "Yes, there is a small waiting room next door."

Honey smoothed her hand down Charlie's head. "Darlin', we'll be next door if you need us."

"I'll be fine, Honey." As grateful as she was for Scarlett and Honey's help, she would do this alone. She'd gotten herself into this, and she'd take care of it by herself. She'd spent too many years letting other people handle things for her. She would handle this.

The two left, and Dr. Shelton sat in the chair next to her. "I like to sit and chat for a minute with my new OB patients. Do you have any questions?"

"Have I ruined things by waiting so long to come to the doctor?" The words shot from her mouth. She hadn't even known she was going to say them.

The doctor gave a deep, rich chuckle. "I seriously doubt you've ruined anything. How far along do you think you are?"

"Almost three months. I know exactly when it happened."

Her caregiver reached into her pocket and withdrew a round paper disc thing. "Tell me the date, and we'll see when you're due."

Charlie gave her the date and ignored the pain that always came when she remembered that night, or rather the morning after.

"It looks like your due date is June fifth. A June baby will be nice."

Baby. She held onto the arms of the chair. She'd never used that word. Her ever-present friend, nausea, threatened to crash this party.

"Okay. Why don't you step behind the curtain and undress from the waist down?" The doctor opened a drawer and pulled out a gown. "Put this on, and I'll get my nurse in here." Panic must've flashed across Charlie's face. "Don't worry. My staff is absolutely trustworthy and discreet."

"Thank you." Behind the curtain, she did as instructed. The whole situation was surreal, like it was happening to someone else. When she emerged from the curtain, there was an older woman with a streak of purple in her black hair.

"Charlie, this is Beth. She's my nurse." Dr. Shelton patted the table, indicating she should have a seat. "She'll be the one to call with the results of your blood work and any other test we may choose to do."

Charlie smoothed down the pink paper gown. "Nice to meet you."

"Same here." Beth held up her arm like she was asking Charlie to arm wrestle. "Give me your hand, and I'll help you lie back."

Once Charlie's feet were where they needed to be, Dr. Shelton rolled a machine with a screen over to the table. "Alright, let's get a look at this little bun." She took something that looked like a curling iron and rolled a condom over it.

"What is that? And is it going where I think it is?" Even Charlie could hear the distress in her voice.

The physician chuckled. "It's the ultrasound wand, and yes, at this stage of your pregnancy, it's the best way for us to see your little guy or girl. It doesn't hurt, it's just a little awkward."

With her feet in the stirrups and a paper gown the only thing between her hoohah and the world, how much more awkward could things get? "Okay."

"Alright, here we go." Dr. Shelton placed one of her hands on Charlie's abdomen, and then the other was between her legs. "Take a deep breath and blow it out." She inserted the wand in one smooth motion.

Beth squeezed her hand. "See, that wasn't bad at all."

Charlie nodded. Best to just pretend there wasn't a long, probing instrument inside her vagina. She kept her eyes locked on the screen. She had no idea what she was seeing, but she kept her gaze firmly on the window that looked like static on an old black and white television.

The doctor made a sound in the back of her throat. She removed her hand from Charlie's stomach and punched a few buttons on the machine. "Beth, can you dim the lights, please?"

"Sure."

The seconds ticked by, one after the other. Every tick of the clock notched Charlie's heart rate higher.

"How's the weather out there today?" Beth asked.

Unease crawled over Charlie's skin. Her eyes stayed glued to the monitor. "What?"

"The weather? Is it humid today? My hair feels like it's humid," Beth said, like the fate of Charlie's life wasn't unfolding in the display window of the sonogram machine.

"It's not too bad." But this was. Beth was trying to distract her.

Something was wrong. Dr. Shelton was too quiet, and Beth was too chatty. Agony like she'd never experienced before cracked and splintered the very fiber of who she was. "Is some—"

"There you are," Dr. Shelton said.

"What?" The word came out feeble and weak.

"There's your baby." The physician pointed to the screen. "See, there's the heartbeat. Oh, you've got a strong one."

The screen still looked like a lot of static, except for the hollow where her little stowaway floated. She raised her hand toward the screen. "Hey." The wonder and affection in her voice filled the room. "That's Pod's heartbeat?" The fluttering beat mesmerized her. With every tiny hummingbird flicker on the screen, she lost more of her own heart.

Look what we made, Hank.

"Pod?" Beth asked.

"Like a pea pod." Tears spilled from her eyes and a sob caught in her throat. Suddenly, she didn't want to do this by herself. This miracle should be celebrated. "Would you mind getting Honey and Scarlett?" She wiped a tear that was running into her ear. "I want them to see."

Dr. Shelton smiled like she knew exactly what Charlie was feeling. "Sure. Beth, would you mind?"

"I'll be right back."

In minutes the little room was full of people. Her people. Honey and Scarlett each took one of her hands, both ooing and aahing over Pod.

"Looks just like its mama," Honey said.

"Look what you're growing, Charlie, a strong, healthy baby," Scarlett encouraged.

The Pod was strong. Strong and fierce. And Charlie promised the image on the screen that she'd be just as strong and fierce for the two of them.

Chapter Twenty-Five

Charlie would live at the Golden Leaf Garden nursery if she could. She loved the herbs and flowers that covered the Changs' property, some imported and some homegrown. The quality of her lotions and soaps had gone up exponentially since she'd started buying her supplies from the Changs. She'd had a great place in California where she shopped, but even they didn't compare to the Golden Leaf.

"How are you today, Miss Charlie?"

She whirled around and saw Thomas Chang leaning against a support pole. "I'm great." And she was. Seeing Pod the day before had solidified a few things for her. She, Honey, and Scarlett had talked about her opening her own shop all the way home from the doctor's office. She was going to do it. "Are you all exporting things now?" She pointed to the back of the garden, where a few men were loading wooden crates onto a truck.

"Oh, no. Those are the crates our essential oils come in. We recycle them." He held up two fingers in a peace sign. "Save the world."

She laughed and returned the peace sign. "Save the world."

"How can I help you today?"

She handed him the list. His dark brows climbed up his forehead.

"This is a lot more than you've been buying."

The smile that spread across her face was uncontrollable. "Yes, it is. I'm going into business, Thomas." She'd done the math, and she was only buying what she could afford. The profits from what she'd already sold would pay for this larger order.

If possible the brows rose even higher. "Really?"

"Do you think I'm crazy?"

He shook his head. "No way. My mother loves the lotions you've given her. So are you going to make and sell them from your home, or are you going to have a store?"

A thrilling excitement made her spine straighter. "A store."

He held out his hand. "Let me be the first to shake the hand of Zachsville's newest successful business owner."

She took his hand and laughed. "I have a lot to learn, but thanks for the vote of confidence."

"Once everyone finds out Charlie Kay has a store, you'll sell out of everything."

"Klein."

"Pardon?"

"Charlie Klein." She couldn't help the steel in her voice. "Charlie Kay is dead and gone."

He chuckled. "My condolences."

He shouldn't be sorry. She wasn't. Not one little bit.

"Let's get this order filled." He led her to the back where they kept a lot of the herbs she used to make her own essential oils. "You know, Miss Charlie, if you're going to start buying more, then you're going to want to buy in bulk. I can introduce you to our wholesaler if you'd like."

"Oh. That would be great. Yes, thank you, Thomas."

"He'll be here tonight. Will you be at Boon's?"

She ran her fingers over the leaves of an African violet. "Yes, I'll be there."

"Maybe during your break, I can introduce you."

"Thank you, Thomas. What would I do without you and Golden Leaf Garden?"

"Let's hope you never have to find out."

Chapter Twenty-Six

Hank checked his email on his phone while he waited for Karen to join him at the City Cafe. He was beginning to doubt the wisdom of doing this over lunch. His gut was a knotted mess, no way he could eat anything. But they'd no doubt have an audience, and that was why he'd decided to do it in public. It would make it harder for her to storm off if things didn't go well. Nothing says you don't matter more than another person turning their back on you and walking away.

He was going to give her a chance to tell him the truth about the high school job and the timing of when she found out they were pulling the plug on the program. Now that he'd had a little time to cool off, he couldn't swear she'd only come back to him because she was about to be jobless. And in the grand scheme of things, the timing didn't really matter, the deception did. It only compounded the lie about the teaching job at the community college.

He hadn't known she wasn't being paid for that job, since she'd insisted they keep their bank accounts separate when they got back together. He hadn't argued. Like the rest of their relationship, he'd believed they could bridge the gap and once again merge their lives together. That nasty voice in his head called him the biggest fool in Blister County, and he was starting to believe it.

But if he was a fool, then so was she. Did she think he wouldn't hear about her losing her job at the high school? If they lived someplace else, he might not find out about her job going away, but not in this fishbowl of a small town. She had to know that. As hard as he tried, he couldn't figure out her thought process. Was she just planning to spring it on him at the last minute?

Hell, he didn't know. He didn't know much of anything, but that he'd loved Karen once and he'd made a commitment to their life together. If there was the slightest chance it could work out, then he'd exhaust every possibility to save it. But it all hinged on her telling him the truth. Right now. Today.

Email checked, he slipped his phone into his pocket and scrubbed his face. He knew people were calling him crazy for staying with Karen, but they didn't have the irresponsible Odom men label. And hadn't grown up the way he did, without a father, and wondering what he'd done wrong to make the man who was supposed to love and take care of him leave. Fuck 'em. They didn't have to understand, and he didn't much care if they did or not. He was trying to change the lineage of his family.

"Hey. You look deep in thought." Karen bent to kiss his cheek, then took a seat.

"You know me, solving the world's problems." He chuckled.

She flipped her straight mahogany hair over her shoulder. "Come up with any solutions?"

"Not yet. I'll let you know when I do." Banter like this used to come as natural as breathing, but now it was stilted and awkward with a million subtexts.

Hey, what are you thinking about?

I'm wondering if we have a chance.

What's your verdict?

Depends on if you can be honest with me or not.

Her smile was affectionate but reserved. More than anything he wanted to bridge this distance between them.

He placed his hand over hers and tried to ignore the slight flinch of her body when he did. "How long do you have before you have to get back to the school?"

"I have forty-five minutes."

Twenty seconds was as long as it took for her to disentangle their hands. A frigid breeze of defeat blew across the tiny flicker of hope he had for them. The knots in his stomach jerked tighter. "How are things at Zachsville High?" He attempted to make his tone casual. He had no idea if he succeeded, and with every excruciating second that passed he cared less and less.

"Oh, you know." She plucked a saltine packet from a bowl on the table, opened it, and ate the cracker. "Same old, same old."

"Yeah? Nothing new, good or bad, happening? Your program's still going strong?" Geez, he may as well hold up a sign saying, I know your job is going away. Please tell me the truth.

Her shoulders slumped, and her body language clearly communicated defeat. "Well, I was going to wait until this evening to tell you, but they've pulled the funding on my program. I'm done in just a few weeks."

Hallelujah. One hurdle down, now to see if she'd tell him everything. "That's horrible. Did they just spring that on you today?"

She played with the empty saltine packet. "No..."

"Hi, I'm Jenni-Lynn." Their waitress sauntered up to the table. She was new, which was weird. Most of the servers came over on the Mayflower then got a job at the City Cafe. "Jenni with an 'i'." She tapped her name tag with her pencil. "What can I get you today?"

Crap. Jenni with an "i" had shit timing. The thought of trying to shove food down his gullet seemed impossible, but he'd asked Karen to lunch, so he needed to order. "I'll have today's special and a sweet tea."

The server wrote down his order. "White gravy or brown?"

He found his first genuine smile of the day. "Do you even have to ask?"

She laughed. "I guess not. White it is." Her attention turned to Karen, and she cocked her head. "Hey, don't I know you?"

"No, I don't think so." His wife was friendly enough, but her words sounded like they were being sliced from her tongue by a switchblade.

"I'll have the chef's salad and unsweet tea." She folded her menu and placed it in the holder on the table.

Jenni-Lynn scribbled their order down. "That's so weird. I would swear I know you." She shoved her pencil behind her ear. "Do you have kids? Maybe I know you from school."

"Yes," Karen quickly answered, then chuckled. "I mean, no, but I am a teacher. That's probably where you've seen me."

Little frown lines slashed across Jenni-Lynn's forehead. "Do you teach at the elementary school? Because I thought I knew all those teachers. I volunteer a couple of days a week."

"No, I'm at the high school. But good for you for volunteering. Parental involvement is so important." Karen was back to pointy words and no eye contact.

"Oh, don't I know it. I just wish I could do it more." She placed her order pad in the pocket of her apron. "But I have a second job at the Sleep Away Inn in the next town over..." Her wide eyes went to Hank, then back to Karen, then back to him. A smile that looked like it was being held in place by a broken pulley wobbled on her face. "Um... well...I'll turn your order in. I'll be right back with your drinks."

Holy, fucking shit.

The Sleep Away Inn. That must've been one of the motels Karen and Matt Allen visited during their affair. Rage he thought he'd conquered reared its beastly head. Neither one of them said a thing. They both just stared at the white tabletop.

"Hank—"

"Don't."

The bell over the door dinged. He glanced up to see Scarlett Bain coming in carrying her little boy, followed by Luanne Price, and—because life hated him and enjoyed kicking him in the balls—Charlie Klein.

Scarlett spotted him and made a beeline to his table, her posse in tow. Which meant within a matter of seconds Charlie was standing directly in front of him and Karen. "Hank." Scarlett switched the kid to her other hip and put her hand on his shoulder. "Honey told me how you helped her, Wardell, and Charlie with the paparazzi a couple of weeks ago. I wanted to thank you for intervening before she went and did some fool thing." She pushed her red mane from her face. "You know how she is. Oh, sorry. Hi, Karen."

He glanced at his wife, who'd just slid her hand up his arm and around his shoulder. "How are you ladies today?" she said to the group at large, but her eyes stayed fixed on Charlie.

What was going on? She hadn't voluntarily touched him since they'd been back together. And given the recent revelation, compliments of Jenni-Lynn, it was entirely unwanted. The tremor that went through him when she ran her fingers through his hair wasn't a that-feels-fantastic kind of shiver, but more a get-these-fuckin'-spiders-off-of-me shudder.

What was Scarlett saying? Oh, yeah. "It was no problem, Scarlett. And yes, Honey is a pistol."

"I wuv Honey," the little guy said.

Scarlett patted his back. "I know you do, baby."

"She's bootiful," Honey's biggest fan proclaimed.

"She told you to say that, didn't she?" Scarlett asked.

The kid grinned like he understood the joke and nodded.

Everyone chuckled, but the tension between him, Karen, and Charlie was strung so tight you could practically see it.

"So, Charlie, how long are you in town for?" Karen's question was as harmless as could be, but the innocence was manufactured, and he knew it.

Charlie pulled her purse in front of her like a shield. He didn't blame her. The look in his wife's eyes was armed with daggers. "Indefinitely. Zachsville's my new home." She rocked her head side to side. "Well, old home."

"Mmhmm, I hope it works out for you. You'll probably find that most things are still the same." His wife wrapped her other hand around his forearm. "But some things are very different."

Charlie glanced to where Karen's other hand had covered his arm, and Charlie Klein slipped away as Charlie Kay took her place, complete with a phony smile and ridiculous eye roll. He hated it. "Oh, golly, don't I know it. Thanks for the heads up, though." She turned to Scarlett and Luanne, who looked at her like they didn't know her. "I need to go to the ladies' room. I'll catch up with you at the table. Good to see you, Karen. Hank." She never broke character as she bounced out of the room.

Any other time, he'd see this newfound affection as promise that his marriage was on the right track. But from the way Karen's gaze sliced through Charlie, he knew it was just trying to win a pissing contest.

Wrong.

There was something very wrong about what was happening.

"We better grab a table before they all fill up," Luanne said. "Good to see you both."

Karen straightened in her seat and removed her hands from him. "Oh, Luanne, congrats on your marriage."

"Thanks, Karen. See ya around, Hank."

"Bye." Scarlett waved, then she and Luanne made their way to a booth in the back.

"What was that?" It was out of his mouth before he could call it back.

Karen unrolled her silverware from the napkin. "What was what?"

He lowered his voice since they were the chief guppies in the fishbowl right now. "You know what? I'm surprised you didn't pull out a brand and put your mark on me."

She shrugged. "I don't know who she thinks she is, marching in here like she owns the place and making lovey-dovey eyes at you. I knew this would happen the minute I heard she was in Austin after Wardell was hurt." Her angry eyes followed Charlie as she made her way from the facilities to her table with Luanne and Scarlett.

"Wait, you knew Charlie was in Austin? How?"

She flicked the question away with a bend of her wrist. "Doesn't matter. The fact is, she's back, and she's not getting what's mine."

He angled his body, sliding his arm along the back of her chair and his other onto the table in front of her. "Whoa, slow down. Tell me how you knew she was in Austin and when you found out."

Her brown eyes the color of muddy water went wide. Whatever she saw in his gaze must've convinced her to spill her secret. "Carrie Rhodes told me. She works at the hotel where Lil' Miss Hollywood was staying and saw the two of you talking in the lobby. I mean how pathetic can you get, than to cry on the shoulder of your ex-boyfriend. Seriously, it's sad, really."

Hank wanted to cover his ears as the deafening sound of puzzle pieces collapsing into place crashed around him. "Is that why you came back?" His tone was all cop, not one hint of affection.

She tried to laugh it off, but the nervous hysteria behind it betrayed her. "No, of course not." Her gaze cut to the room then back to him. "Hank, people are watching," she said through her plastic, happy expression.

He didn't say a word, but waited for the truth.

She sucked in a deep breath and took the full brunt of his lawman's stare. "I'm not going to lie. When I found out she was back and that the two of you were talking, it made me realize what I was throwing away." Her hand went to his cheek. "I finally understood what I've known all along." Her smile was reminiscent of the one she'd bestowed upon him on their wedding day, and it sliced him to ribbons. "You're who I want."

Lie.

Lie.

Lie.

He stood and peeled off several bills and threw them on the table. "I'm not hungry anymore." Then he turned his back on her and walked away.

He hoped she got the message.

Chapter Twenty-Seven

C harlie popped a peppermint into her mouth to settle her sour stomach. Whatever she'd eaten at the café hadn't sat well with her. Yeah, that's what it was, not her interaction with Hank and Karen. The woman was still beautiful, still mean as a snake, and still hated her. There was no doubt that she'd make Hank's involvement in Pod's life miserable for everyone involved. Ugh, her unplanned pregnancy just got a whole lot more complicated.

"So what do you think?" Scarlett practically bounced up and down with excitement.

"I'm sorry." She needed to get her head out of the clouds. Her friends already thought she might be losing it, because of the Charlie Kay response to Karen from earlier. They'd quizzed her about it at lunch, but she'd blown it off as high-school rivalry. Thankfully, they'd let it go. "What did you say, Scarlett?"

"I said, what do you think?"

Sunlight streamed through the windows of the empty storefront they stood in. Situated on the town square, the building wasn't very large, but it was airy, with vaulted ceilings and tons of natural light. "It's beautiful. Whose is it?"

"Yours," Scarlett and Luanne said together.

She coughed to keep the mint out of her windpipe. "What?"

Scarlett took her by the arm. "Lou and I own it. Isn't it great?"

Aiden ran around with his arms outstretched making airplane noises. He ducked behind a counter in the back of the store that would be the perfect place for customers to pay for their products.

Luanne moved around the room, opening more window blinds. "It used to be the old Emporium, among other things, but we thought it would be the ideal place for your shop."

Charlie opened her mouth several times, but words failed to make it past her lips. Stunned stupid didn't even begin to cover it.

"Oh, don't cry—oof." Luanne tried to stay upright when Aiden barreled into her and wrapped his arms around her knees. She ran her hand over his head and smiled down at him. "Hey, bud."

"I wuv you, Lulu." Aiden's toothy grin melted Charlie's heart, and he wasn't even talking to her.

"I love you too, little man. Can I have my legs back?"

He giggled and sprinted off to play.

"Sorry." Scarlett winced. "Did he get you dirty?"

"No. He's fine," Luanne said, and spread her arms. "We want you to use this building for your new business."

Unless they were using air as currency, then there was no way she could afford it. "Y'all, I can't commit to renting this beautiful place." And wasn't that a shame. The space was perfect. Right on the square, not too big, with tons of natural lighting.

Scarlett pushed her red curls from her face. "You'd actually be doing us a favor if you used it."

Charlie's hand splayed across the spot where her hip bones used to be until Pod moved in. "Really, and how's that?"

Luanne went to one of the front windows. "We haven't been able to rent it. It's too small for a restaurant or most retail spots. We thought we'd make it a tearoom." She gestured to Scarlett. "But then fertile Myrtle over there went and got herself knocked up."

Prickly heat crawled up Charlie's neck. "Must be something in the water." They'd told Luanne about the pregnancy at lunch and sworn her to secrecy.

Luanne crossed two fingers over each other and held them up. "Then you two keep your water to yourselves."

"This is so kind, but—"

"It's just sitting empty. If it stays vacant for much longer, it'll start to deteriorate." Luanne glanced up at the painted tin ceilings. "And that'd be a shame."

"Honestly, Charlie, we'd just let you use it for a while until you can get your feet underneath you, but I know you won't do that, so we're prepared to make you an offer you can't refuse." She waggled her brows, and they all laughed.

"You guys, I don't even know how to apply for a loan at the bank. I've never done that. I always had people to do things for me." She nibbled on her thumbnail. "Do you really think I can do this?"

Scarlett wrapped her arm around Charlie's shoulders. Honeysuckle and citrus swam around her. "I believe you can do this, and you don't have to do everything by yourself. There are plenty of people who'd be willing to help." She waved her hand at Luanne. "And we'll sic Luanne on them to make sure they're trustworthy. She can smell a liar a mile off."

"Damn straight," the little pixie with the big personality said.

"Damn, damn, damn," the little blond-headed magpie mimicked as he darted past them.

"Lou, I've told you that you can't say those words in front of A-I-D-E-N."

"Lulu gots a potty mouth," Aiden sang as he continued to make laps around the room.

The front door opened. "Come here." Gavin Bain snagged his son and held him above his head. "Who's got a potty mouth, boy?" He'd come in with another man that Charlie didn't know.

"You gots a potty mouth too, Daddy." Aiden giggled.

Gavin settled Aiden on his hip. "That I do, son. Don't grow up to be like your old man." Long, graceful, predatory strides took him to Scarlett's side. His hand went to the back of her head, and he kissed her long and slow. The intimacy of it caused Charlie's cheeks to burn. When he pulled back and rested his forehead to his wife's, tears shoved against Charlie's lids. "Hey, fireball. I missed you."

Scarlett rolled her eyes. "I've only been gone for an hour, rock star. Surely you can occupy yourself for that amount of time."

"I can, but I'd rather have you there occupying me," he murmured against her lips.

Charlie didn't miss Scarlett's sigh. Truthfully, she might've sighed herself. The sex appeal rolling off the rocker was thick as honey, and it was all directed in one direction, straight at the mother of his children.

"Get a room," the tall, gorgeous man who'd accompanied Gavin said.

"Shut up, Jack," Scarlett and Gavin both said, and everyone laughed. Must be an inside joke.

Scarlett moved out of her husband's embrace. "Guys, this is Charlie Klein. Charlie, this bad man is my husband, Gavin Bain, and that ugly guy is Jack Avery, Luanne's new husband."

Honestly, the introduction to Gavin was unnecessary. Who didn't know who the superstar was? "Nice to meet you both."

"Good to meet you. We actually worked with the same producer once, Charlie," Gavin said.

"Really?" She'd recorded several albums with songs she'd performed on *Charlie Takes the Town*. Carousel wasn't stupid. They'd figured out how to make money off of her two ways, on the show and off album sales—a two for one. Not to mention memorabilia and appearances. She'd been everyone's cash cow. Relief flowed over her like a cool, unexpected rain on a sweltering summer day. She was free.

"Yeah, Rip Farmer. He said you had the most perfect pitch he'd ever heard and it was a shame your talent was wasted on the bubble gum sh—"

Scarlett cleared her throat.

Gavin grinned at his wife. "Crap Carousel made you sing."

"Oh, I love Rip. He always treated me like a professional. Not like a kid. The man is good at what he does." Weird how that life already seemed a million miles away.

"Charlie, it sounds like you could use our help." Jack handed her a card then threw his arm around Luanne. "Pretty soon, we'll both be practicing entertainment law, and I'd love nothing more than to nail that slimy manager of yours to the wall for defamation of character."

That took her back. "Can I do that?"

"Hell, yeah," Luanne said. "He went on record and called into question your character, your sanity, and cost you millions in lost wages. You could own him." She elbowed her husband in the ribs. "I didn't say anything earlier because I wanted to discuss it with Jack first, cause he's the expert when it comes to this kind of thing."

Charlie worried her bottom lip. "I could use some help. But he hasn't actually cost me millions in lost wages. No one's knocking down my door to hire me."

Jack shot her a cocky grin. "Exactly."

She chuckled and shook her finger at him. "I see what you did there." All she wanted was to be free of Ron, and if it'd just been her she'd have told Jack that she didn't want anything from her former manager, except money to pay for his services and for Ron to go away. But it wasn't just her. She thought of Pod and all the things she wouldn't be able to give him or her. "I don't want to own him. But I would like some compensation for...um...for my future."

"Piece of cake." Jack gave her a grin that made her almost feel sorry for Ron.

She stuck out her hand. "You're hired."

He took her outstretched hand. "Call the number on the card, and we'll make an appointment."

"Careful, Charlie," Gavin said. "Once he goes to bat for you, you'll never be able to get away from him. Believe me, I've tried."

Jack kissed the air in Gavin's direction. "You know it, sweetheart."

"Home!" Aiden yelled, and wiggled out of Gavin's arms.

"Are you guys done here? I can take him if you need more time." Gavin kissed Scarlett's temple, and his big hand went to her baby bump. It was so tender and loving that it stole the air from Charlie's body. This was what she wanted for herself and for Pod.

There was so much love in this small room that it was intoxicating. Between that, her run-in with Hank and Karen, and Scarlett and Luanne's generous offer, her pregnancy hormones couldn't take much more. Water covered her retinas. She needed to go home and cry in private like any self-respecting celebrity would do. But she wasn't a celebrity anymore, and these women were her friends and had just given her an unbelievable gift, so she let the tears fall.

Scarlett wrapped her arms around Charlie's shoulders. "Aw, honey, why're you crying?"

"It's just so... Thank you."

"So it's a yes?" Luanne asked.

She nodded. "It's a yes."

And just like that, she had a building for her little shop. Now she just had to figure out how she was going to pay for it. Time to talk to the bank.

Chapter Twenty-Eight

I t was a beautiful day in South Central Texas, and Charlie was sweatin' like forty hells up in the Zachsville National Bank. When, in fact, it was a pleasant sixty-eight degrees inside one of the town's oldest buildings. She was about to have a come-undone right there in the lobby. In spite of her nervous anxiety, she smiled. The longer she was in her hometown, the more and more she sounded like her grandmother.

Her hometown.

She was counting on her ties to the community and her excellent credit to convince the loan officer to take a chance on her. Honestly, it was probably a fool's errand—who gave a loan to someone with no money? But for better or worse, her nature was to give it a shot, and if she got shut down in the process, then she'd try something else. Maybe she was too stupid to know any better, or maybe she was so determined to take care of her little package that she'd try just about anything.

Thanks, Mom, for putting me in this position.

The flatline sensation she always got when she thought about her mother wrapped around her. Not fury. Not hurt. Just, nothing. You know things are done when someone betrays you so severely that it siphons away all feeling.

Her fingers danced over her lower abdomen. She'd made a promise to The Pod and to herself to be the kind of mother that inspired big love. The kind that stayed with you long after that person was gone. Did she have any idea how to do that? No, but if she accomplished nothing else in her life, she'd figure this one thing out, and wouldn't stop until she'd learned to do it the best she could. Pod deserved it, and so did she.

"Ms. Klein, Mr. Fitz will see you now," an older woman with a short brown bob and pink readers on her nose said.

Charlie ran her damp hands down the skirt of her dress and followed the woman.

Mr. Fitz's office was all hard, masculine lines with rounded feminine corners. Two big chocolate brown leather chairs sat in front of a polished walnut desk, which was decorated with two small stained glass lamps with tassels hanging from the globes.

On one wall were action shots of the Zachsville Raiders football team, along with a signed football with *District Champs* written on it in black Sharpie.

The other wall was covered in pictures of a black standard poodle. A plaque that read *Miss Shoog* hung above a photo of the lady herself on a plush red pillow that sat atop a throne. The bedazzled tiara the dog wore and the bouquet of roses at her feet clearly stated that Miss Shoog was the queen of Mr. Fitz's world. The rest of the photos were of the animal in various poses and outfits. One was of Miss Shoog with several blue ribbons hung around her neck. In one she wore a yellow polka dot bikini and a pair of red sunglasses.

"Charlie Kay!" Mr. Fitz rushed toward her with both hands extended. His big hands engulfed her smaller appendage in an adoring grasp. "It is such a pleasure to meet you."

It was Klein, but it appeared Mr. Fitz was a fan, and she wouldn't correct him—not if it could help her.

"It's very nice to meet you, Mr. Fitz."

"Martin, please." He stepped back and swept his long arm toward the chair in front of his desk. "Have a seat. May I get you a beverage?"

"No. Thank you."

He moved behind his desk and sat in his large chair. For several long seconds, he only stared at her with an adoring grin on his face. "I just can't believe I'm meeting *the* Charlie Kay. Truly it's like a dream come true. Miss Shoog and I still watch your show." He ducked his head as if embarrassed. "I know it's a kid's show, but the humor is wonderful, and your comedic timing is impeccable."

The humor on that show was the corniest possible, but to each his own. "Thank you, Mr.—um...Martin."

He rested his chin on his clasped hands. "So, tell me about your next acting project."

She gathered her hair at the nape of her neck. "I don't have anything in the works."

"Oh, really?" He said it like he'd just heard he missed the deadline for Miss Shoog's next contest.

"It's true. I've retired from show business."

"What?" The horror in his voice was a living thing. "Say it isn't so."

She laughed and shrugged. "Afraid so. I'm moving on with my life here in Zachsville."

"Oh, well, at least we'll have you all to ourselves."

His kind eyes warmed her soul, but she wasn't interested in being adored. She wanted her loan.

He seemed to get the telepathic message she was sending, because he clapped his hands together and rested them on the desk. "Now, what can we here at Zachsville National Bank help you with today?"

She pulled papers from her purse and slid them across the desk. "Martin, I'd like to apply for a small business loan. This is my business proposal." She'd googled how to write a business proposal and found a template that had allowed her to not look like a complete idiot when she walked into the banker's office.

Martin's eyebrows shot straight up his forehead when she slid the papers to him. "Really?"

"Yes. I'd like to open a lotion and soap emporium here in Zachsville. I've already secured the space next to Grant's Furniture." Her sweat glands went nuclear as he looked over her proposal.

"I have to tell you, Ms. Kay—"

"Charlie, please."

The smile he gave her made her wish she had the sunglasses Miss Shoog wore in her bikini photo.

"As I was saying, Charlie, this looks just like something Zachsville needs. With all the additional tourism due to our quarterly festivals, and how the Chamber of Commerce is playing up our famous residents Gavin Bain, Boston Blades star Jackson Carter, and, of course, Charlie Kay, Zachsville is quickly becoming a fun little getaway destination. Did you know Jackson Carter when you lived here?"

"I knew of him. He was older than me."

Fitz nodded. "Hell of a hockey player. And his mama, Lord, she's the sweetest woman you'd ever want to meet."

"So I've heard." She fought the urge to move her hand in a let's-get-on-with-this motion.

"Just between you and me, you're our biggest draw, though."

She bit the inside of her cheek when he gave her a conspiratorial wink. The thrill began in her toes and quickly worked its way up her body. This might actually happen. She'd be able to take care of Pod and herself. That was all she wanted in the world right now. "I'm so glad you think so, Martin."

"Did you fill out an application online?"

"Yes."

The click, click, click of the keys and the tiny frown line that crossed his forehead like a warning label leached all of the hope from her stupid heart. "Is there a problem?"

A horrible shade of scarlet slithered up his neck and consumed his face. "Ah... Charlie, your finances are..."

This was it. She took a big gulp of pride and swallowed. "Martin, the truth is my finances are not good."

He stared at the screen then glanced at her like maybe she didn't understand the meaning of *not good*. "That's one way to put it. Do you mind me asking what happened?"

She didn't want to go over this with him, but for Pod, she'd lay herself bare. "My mother stole all of my money, Martin. I know it looks bad, but you said yourself that Zachsville has become a tourist destination in part because it's my hometown. Surely that counts for something." She bit off another mouthful of pride, and it scraped its way down her throat. "I'm begging you to take a chance on me and give me this loan. I swear, I'll work harder than anyone else you know. And I'm not completely without resources—my grandfather, who has forty years of experience running a successful business, is going to help me. Also, I have excellent credit."

"This." He turned the computer screen toward her. "Is not excellent credit."

* * *

The drive from the bank to her grandfather's house was a complete blur for Charlie. Martin's words assaulted her mind the whole way home.

"I'm sorry, even if I wanted to, I couldn't loan money to anyone with a credit report as bad as this."

There was a time she'd been worth more money than she ever knew existed. How was it possible that she could have credit so bad that no one would give her a loan? The answer became blindingly clear when they'd delved into the report. Twenty credit cards had been opened in her name, and only one was actually hers.

One guess as to who'd opened the others. Dear old Mom was number one on the suspect list. Every time she thought she'd gotten to the bottom of her mother's deception, the hole would open up wider and deeper.

To compound her humiliation, Martin had to instruct her how to contact the credit card companies and credit agency to dispute the ownership of the accounts. Then he'd escorted her to the sheriff's office so she could file a report. She'd had to endure Hank's muted pity, which was more than she could stand. No one knew if it would do much good. Her mother was dead, and a few had been opened years ago. The strange thing was that some were still open and active. She'd closed them and requested statements. Hank assured her he'd look into it, but told her that most of the time these things are never solved.

Her grandfather's house came into view. The contents of her

stomach bubbled like rancid sewage. Would opening this store solve all her financial problems? No. In fact, it could make them worse. But at least she'd be doing something. Moving forward. Taking care of her own damn self.

She turned the car off and crossed her forearms on top of the steering wheel, her forehead resting on them. She'd sacrificed her life to her career, and there was nothing to show for it. The only other time she'd ever been this hopeless was boarding the plane to LA that took her away from this life. She was nothing but a washed-up, cautionary tale with another person on the way who was depending on her.

Her dress stretched tight across her breasts reminded her of her situation. Maybe she should tell Hank. At this point, she was going to need help with expenses. But then a horrible thought shook her. What if he tried to take Pod from her? Could that happen? Probably. What the hell did she know about raising a kid? Not to mention the fact that he had a steady job with benefits, and he was married. The sour taste of bile in the back of her throat made her gag. No, she wouldn't let that happen.

"Darlin', are you alright?" Honey asked. Her smile must've been as watery as it felt because Honey opened the car door and pulled her from the vehicle. "What's wrong? You look like something the cat dragged in and buried in the litter box."

All Charlie could do was shrug, which flipped some switch, and the water started flowing.

Honey put her chubby arm around Charlie's shoulder and led her toward the house. "Oh, darlin'. Things didn't go well at the bank?"

"No," slipped out between the tears rolling down her face.

"Come on inside. I'll fix you a nice glass of lemonade and we'll all talk." The screen door screeched when she pulled it open. It sounded how Charlie's insides felt.

"I don't want to talk. I just want to go to bed." And curl up and die, but she didn't say the last part.

"What in the world is wrong with her?" Her grandfather limped in from the kitchen.

Honey walked her to the sofa. "Things didn't go well at the bank."

"What? How is that possible?" Wardell dropped into his recliner. "Who'd you talk to at the bank?"

"Mr. Fitz." She grabbed a tissue from the box on the coffee table and mopped at her face. "It's not his fault. He was very nice."

"Like hell, it's not his fault. Who in their right mind wouldn't give you a loan?" He gripped the arms of his chair so hard his fingers turned white.

"Someone who was worried about getting his money back." The tissue muffled her words, but he and Honey must've heard her because they both wore the same confused expression. "My credit is awful. Someone, probably Mom or some of the men she paraded in and out of our house, opened a bunch of credit cards with gigantic limits in my name. Some are maxed out, and some lapsed into nonpayment." A hiccup caught in her throat. "They wouldn't loan me a piece of paper, let alone start-up money for a business."

The golden color from her grandfather's skin leached from his face. "Shelly did that?"

Anger shot to the top of the list of emotions she was experiencing at his bewildered tone. "Of course she did, Pops. Why would that be a surprise to you? She stole from me, and she stole from you. The only difference in the two of us is that you gave her permission to steal from you."

"Charlie, you stop that right now."

Honey's reprimand had zero effect on her indignation. "I won't, Honey. He needs to hear this." She turned to her grandfather. "She was a terrible person, Pops. She used me, sold me out, and she did the same thing to you. But you could've stopped her, and you didn't. You just gave her permission to clean out your account while you looked the other way."

For a brief second guilt at his disillusioned expression nearly stopped her, but she remembered Pod and let her anger take her further down the rabbit hole. "You let your love for her blind you to who and what she really was, and worst of all, you didn't see fit to warn me that she was that person." She rose from the sofa and headed for the stairs.

Wardell grabbed her hand as she passed. "I'm sorry."

The water pooling in his eyes made her sicker than she already was. "I know you are, but it doesn't change anything. I'm still broke and pregnant with no way to take care of us." She made her way upstairs and closed her bedroom door.

The pity party she had planned for herself would have to wait. She needed a nap, a shower, and to get to work. Especially because after the afternoon she'd just had, she needed her job at Boon's more than ever.

She stripped off her clothes and crawled into bed. Her arms went around her belly that was getting bigger every day, and curled around her baby. Who knew what would happen in June, but for now Pod was safe and sound with her.

* * *

Charlie clawed her way out of a nightmare. She'd never been one for naps, but since Pod came into her life, she'd become a world-class napper. The only downside was the daytime nightmares. Nothing worse than a bad dream in the middle of the day.

The foggy vision of her building a house for herself and Pod out of mud in the pouring rain slowly dissipated. Her rapid breaths sawed in and out until she got her bearings.

She stumbled to the bathroom and took a long, hot shower to loosen her knotted muscles. The scent of the new soap she'd made for peace and tranquility filled the steamy shower. Grapefruit, lavender, and peppermint swirled around her and helped as much as the hot water to soothe the aftershocks of the bad dream. A little ginger wouldn't hurt anything, and she made a mental note to add some to the next batch of Calm she made. Though she wouldn't need much, since she'd just be making small quantities for herself and the few stores that carried her products since the bank declined her loan application.

The low-level panic she'd lived with since the day she first peed on the stick cranked up a notch or two. What would she do? She had no real skills, and there were so many things she didn't know how to do, including being an adult.

Thank you, Hollywood.

La-La Land was a mythical place. Nothing was real in LA. Everything was an illusion, manufactured and manipulated for the public's enjoyment. The problem came when people started believing the illusion was real. She'd fallen victim to that way of thinking. Hard not to when that was the diet you're fed from the time you step into that wonderland.

She needed to hurry. The package on the dresser in her room made her smile in spite of the day she'd had. She'd ordered some maternity Daisy Duke shorts. Oh, the irony. Daisy Duke shorts were, by definition, sexy, but these bad boys were anything but. The stretchy material in the front was hideous, but at least she'd have blood flow to her lower extremities.

A dash of makeup, with a little contouring to help disguise the fact that her face was growing rounder by the day, and she was ready. She rummaged through her purse, procrastinating. The conversation with her grandfather that needed to happen before she left for work loomed in front of her like a regret-filled cloud. She shouldn't have yelled at him. That one thing propelled her from the room. She needed to apologize.

She found him in the kitchen making himself a sandwich. "Where's Honey?"

The tinkling sound of salty chips being poured on a plate made her mouth water. "She's singin' at a weddin' this weekend and had to go rehearse for it."

The chair she pulled out scraped against the worn linoleum. "Pops, I'm sorry about what I said earlier. I shouldn't have yelled at you. Will you forgive me?"

He set his sandwich aside and took her hands. "Of course I will, but you didn't do anything to warrant forgiveness. I always had a blind spot when it came to your mama. Everything you said was true, and I want to make that up to you." He reached into his back pocket and retrieved an envelope, which he slid across the table to her.

"What's this?"

He took a bite of his ham and cheese. "Open it."

The envelope wasn't sealed, so she flipped it open and withdrew the bundle of papers. She knew what it was as soon as she unfolded the pages. "No."

His watery blue eyes watched her over the rim of his iced tea glass. "Yes."

She shoved the envelope and its contents at him. "No, Pops. I won't let you do this."

He shrugged. "It's already done."

"Pops, I won't let you mortgage your house in order for me to get this loan. That's crazy." She couldn't control the tremble in her hands as she tried again to give him the envelope.

His warm, calloused, and wrinkled hand covered hers. "Charlie, I'm partially responsible for why you had to apply for this loan in the first place, and more than a little responsible for the person your mama turned out to be. I knew she couldn't be trusted and I gave her access to that account anyway." He fiddled with the edges of the envelope. "I raised her, and we never let her experience the consequences of her bad behavior. We just came behind her and cleaned up her messes. That's why she always felt she was entitled to what everyone else had, including her father and daughter, and it ruined her and cost her her life."

"You're not responsible for her actions, Pops."

"Maybe not, but I feel like I am. Let me do this for you. I believe in you. I know you can make this shop, or anything else you want to do, work."

She gripped his hand and held on. "Pops, this isn't some romance novel where everything works out in the end. There's a very good chance this will fail, and we'll lose the house. Do you know how much pressure that is to put on me?" Her heart pounded like a herd of stampeding elephants. Sure, Jack had said he'd get compensation from Ron, but that could take years...if it ever happened.

"Darlin' girl, it's no pressure at all. If that were to happen, we'll figure it out. Together. We're not destitute. But this is going to work. Besides, I can't think of a better way to honor your Grams than to make a real go of this store where you sell her potions." He winked.

The tears rolling down her cheeks were as much about the grandmother that she'd loved more than life as they were about his faith in her. "You know she'd get your goat if she heard you call them her potions."

He covertly swiped a tear from his own eye. "She would indeed."

She bent and kissed his fingers, then met his eyes. "Are you sure?"

His warm hand cupped her cheek. "More than sure."

Her arms went around his skinny shoulders. "Thank you, Pops. I swear I'll pay you back."

"I know you will. I have one hundred percent confidence in you."

She wished she had the same confidence in herself.

Chapter Twenty-Nine

"Do you want to puke before or after you sweep the peanut shells?" Hailey came around the bar and handed Charlie the broom and dustpan.

She took the instruments of her trade. "Haha. Sue me. I don't like the smell of peanuts." A lot of aspects of her job had gotten easier over the last two weeks—everything but the smell. Every time she walked into the bar Pod threatened to stage a mutiny. Ironically, the stale beer and cologne aroma seemed to help neutralize the effects of the peanut stink. Pregnancy was weird.

Hailey leaned her back against the bar and crossed her arms. "You know, Ariel is going to probably charge you a thousand dollars for her dry cleaning."

Charlie tied her apron around her waist. It was still early, and the bar was empty except for a group of guys playing darts in the beer garden. "Worth it."

A smile pushed against Hailey's lips. "Yeah?"

"Yeah. Nobody messes with my friend." Charlie couldn't help the hopeful tone in her voice.

The amused expression on Hailey's face slid away like ice melting on a warm winter's day. "We're not friends."

"We used to be. I'd like to be again. I know you're mad at me because I left without saying goodbye, but—"

Hailey pushed off the bar, and her fists went to her hips. "That's what you think I'm mad at you about? You don't have a clue, do you? I didn't blame you for leaving without saying goodbye. I understood. It was hard for all of us."

"Then why..." *Why do you hate me?* But she couldn't say the words. It gave them too much power.

"Because I needed you, and you turned me away."

"What are you talking about, Hailey? I never turned you away."

The tears swimming in her oldest friend's eyes sliced at her heart. "After Lottie was born, and I was lonely and depressed, I tried to get in touch with you. I called you, but you'd changed your number, so I called your mom. At least she was nice to me, unlike her superstar daughter who didn't have time for her small-town friends."

"Hailey, I never got any messages. I would've called you back."

Her boss swiped the tear that ran down her cheek like it personally offended her. "Don't lie, Charlie. Your mom told me that she gave you the messages. I wasn't important enough for your time."

Her mother was the worst person ever. Lord, she'd probably be in therapy for the rest of her life dealing with that shit. "I swear to you that she never gave me any messages from you. She kept my phone and monitored my calls. I wasn't allowed to call anyone back home. I tried more than once, and she finally changed my number. By the time I realized I didn't have to do everything she said, it'd been so long since we'd talked that I thought you'd have moved on without me." Her voice shredded as she thought of the years of anger at her mother and herself for not standing up to the people around her. For letting them make her decisions for her.

The person who'd meant the most to her stared at her, too many emotions to catalog washed across her face. Then she turned and walked away.

"Hailey."

"Sweep up the shells...please."

Please. She'd take it. At least Hailey hadn't kicked her out of the club. Baby steps. She grabbed the broom and swept up the shells around the bar, all the while breathing through her mouth. She'd found that little trick minimized the adverse effects of the dreaded legume.

"You still on peanut duty?"

She whirled around to see Hank in jeans, a blue pearl snap shirt, and his signature cowboy hat. Everything that was Hank, except his eyes didn't twinkle with mischief. "Hey. You alright?" She shouldn't care or ask, but he was Pod's father, and her... He was her nothing. But she still cared about him. Her little secret made it hard to look him in the eye. She needed to tell him. She would tell him, just not yet. There wasn't anything he could do right now, and it wouldn't help him in repairing his marriage.

He grinned, but it was stiff and mechanical. "Yeah, I'm good. How are you?"

"I'm great, but I better get back to work before Hailey takes my head off."

"Things not any better?"

She shrugged. "They're not any worse."

His presence tugged on her. She leaned toward him. He leaned toward her. It was like they had their own gravitational field that drew them to one another, always circling but never intersecting.

Hailey came out of the back with a case of beer. "Am I in danger of being raided, Sheriff?"

He turned from Charlie to address Hailey, and it physically hurt. "I don't know. Are you doing anything to be raided for?"

"Nope, unless you count the cockfighting and prostitution we run out of the back room."

Charlie laughed. One of the things she'd always loved about Hailey was her smart mouth and quick wit.

"Lucky for you I'm off duty." He climbed onto the stool and faced the bar. "I'll have a beer."

Hailey slid open the cooler door. "The usual?"

"Yep. And can I get a separate bowl for my shells?" He winked at Charlie.

Damnable tears pricked and poked at her eyeballs. Why did that little kindness grind a boot heel into her heart? She couldn't be around him when he was sweet like this. Fleeing was her only option, so she took her broom to the other end of the bar to tackle the ever-growing layer of peanut shells.

One more surreptitious glance over her shoulder for one more glimpse of him. A long, deep breath in and out on a sigh to help focus her mind on the task at hand. She couldn't think beyond this moment. If she did, then the panic became too much for her. One thing at a time.

Sweep the shells.

She could do that.

Then move on.

Easier said than done.

"Hey, Charlie." Thomas Chang sauntered up with a beautiful Hispanic man. That was the only word for him—beautiful. He could make a million dollars in Hollywood without ever saying a word. "Hello, Thomas."

"This is Raul Perez. Raul, this is Charlie Kay."

"When Thomas told me he knew *the* Charlie Kay, I thought for sure he was lying." Raul took her hand and kissed her fingers. "You are as lovely in person as you are on the screen."

Yeah, he could make as much money as he wanted in Hollywood if he spoke. His voice was like fine silk over naked skin. "Nice to meet you, Raul."

"I hear you're interested in possibly doing business with me."

Honestly, it was a little hard to concentrate on what he was saying because the cadence of his voice was so hypnotic. "Um...yeah, I'd love to talk. I'll get a break in about an hour. Can you hang out for a while?"

"For you, I'd wait forever, love." He winked.

Oddly, as lovely as he was, that wink did nothing for her. Not like when Hank winked at her earlier, which nearly turned her stomach into an origami swan. "Alright, talk later."

Not even the smell of the peanuts could break through her happiness. Things were falling into place. Piece by piece, brick by brick, she was building a life for herself and Pod. She rolled the garbage can she'd been dumping the shells into to the back hall.

"Who was that with Thomas?" Hank was standing right next to her.

She slapped his arm. "You scared me." She glanced around. "What are you doing back here?"

He didn't answer her question with the steely words that came out of his mouth. "Who was the man with Thomas?"

Irritation crawled all over her. This was where the infamous wardrobe discussion had taken place. She wanted out of this secluded hallway to where they had an audience. "That's Raul Perez. He's a wholesaler that supplies the Changs. I'm going to talk to him about…" It occurred to her that she hadn't told anyone except Honey and Scarlett what she was thinking of doing. Suddenly her annoyance fled, and she couldn't wait to tell Hank. She knew he'd be excited for her. "I'm going to open a shop and sell the soaps and lotions that my grandmother taught me to make."

"No."

"What?" The music had to have messed with her hearing. And why was he frowning at her?

His hands went to his hips. "I said, no. You're not doing business with him."

"Why? What's wrong with you?"

"Not a damn thing. I don't like the look of him."

Oh, my gosh. Was he jealous? Lord save her from stupid men. "Let's go over this again, Hank. You don't get to tell me to do anything. Nothing. And, yes, he's a handsome man, but this is strictly business. Not that it's any of your business."

"I need to tell you something—"

"Charlie, get back to work," Hailey yelled over the music. "Those shells aren't going to sweep themselves. And when you're done take the garbage out, and try not to make a mess this time."

"Stay away from me." She side-stepped past him as fast as she could. Yeah, taking out the garbage was preferable to being around him.

Chapter Thirty

Hank wanted to kick himself. Why couldn't he leave Charlie alone? Because she lived under his skin, that's why. What did it matter anyway? Even if his marriage was imploding, she wanted nothing to do with him. She'd made that perfectly clear. But now he had a new problem. Raul Perez was the big fish that the DEA wanted.

With an eye on Charlie, Thomas, and Perez, he sat at the bar nursing a beer.

"Who peed in your Post-Toasties?" Hailey wiped down the bar across from him.

He glanced at her, then back to where the trio sat talking. "Nobody."

"He's a handsome devil." She never looked up from her task, but kept cleaning the wooden surface.

"Who?" He knew who she was talking about, but he wasn't going to give her the satisfaction of confirming it.

"That guy with Thomas Chang. Though I wouldn't kick Thomas out of bed either." She did look at him then, and gave him a snake's smirk.

"Ugh, now I'll have that image to deal with for the rest of the night. Thanks for that." He took a swig from the bottle he held.

She laughed. "Happy to help. But seriously, you need to stop spying on her. It's not healthy, and if you're trying to patch things up with Karen, then that can't possibly be a good idea."

He tipped his hat back on his head. "I'm not spying on her. I just don't like the look of that guy. Call it a cop's instincts."

"Well, you can rest easy. She's done talking to them." She nodded in the direction of the threesome.

He shrugged. "Good for her." The stool swiveled, and he faced Hailey. "See, I'm not involved."

She smiled while she washed and dried glasses. "Lottie said you took her for ice cream. Thanks for doin' that. Fucking Derek, it's hard for me to remember even one redeeming thing about him." She seemed to realize what she'd said, and her brow furrowed with deep lines. "I'm sorry. I know he's your brother, and blood is thicker than water...."

He shook off her apology. "You and Lottie are my family, too. I don't understand him anymore. It's like he's on a mission to live as recklessly as he can."

She shrugged. "If I'm being rational, which I rarely am, I'd say that you can't blame him. We were so young when I got pregnant with Lottie. He never had a young adulthood."

"That's bullshit. You were sixteen when you got pregnant. You didn't have a young adulthood either, and you've never once wavered in your commitment to Lottie, or my idiot brother, until he made it impossible for you to stay with him."

A ticket for a drink order printed from the little machine in front of her. She began mixing a drink for a customer. "Lottie was probably always more mine than Derek's. I know he resented me for the pregnancy."

"That's bullshit too. He was the one with experience, not you. He didn't take care of you then, and he's not taking care of Lottie now." He wished he'd hit his brother harder the other day.

His father, Derek, Jett, hell, even his grandfather, none of them stuck. They all ran at the first sign of trouble, usually trouble they started. This was the cloth he was cut from, and it made him sick to his stomach.

"I don't need Derek to take care of me. I have Lottie and Roger, and that's all I need right now." She sat the drinks she'd mixed at the end of the bar for the waitresses to pick up.

"How's that going?" She'd started dating Roger Weston not long after the divorce. Nice enough guy, if a little boring.

"It's fine. He travels a lot."

"Is it serious?" The guy didn't seem Hailey's type at all, but he wasn't in any position to pass judgment.

One of her shoulders rose and fell. "Maybe. He checks a lot of boxes."

Thomas and Raul stood to leave. He'd wanted to chat with the men before they left, just as a subtle warning that he was here and he was watching them. "Excuse me. There's someone I need to speak with."

She rolled her eyes and waved him on. "Go ahead and make a fool of yourself. See if I care."

He chuckled and threw a five on the bar. "Keep the change."

The money disappeared into the register, and she gave him a finger wave.

Trying to look as benign as possible, he ambled up to where Thomas and Perez were standing. "How are you fellas tonight?"

Thomas never missed a beat but extended his hand to Hank. "Sheriff Odom, how are you?"

"Mighty fine." He took the man's hand. "Who's your friend?"

"Raul Perez, Sheriff." The Hispanic man offered his hand and Hank took it. Not a callus to be found. This man didn't do manual labor.

"Are you new to Zachsville, Raul?" It was Hank's business to know everyone in his town.

The man leaned his butt against the chair behind him, crossed his arms and legs, and gave Hank the most innocent smile he'd ever seen. "No, I'm only here for the day. I'm driving back to Austin as soon as we leave here."

"Raul's one of our suppliers at the farm." Thomas took the last pull of his beer and sat the bottle on the table.

"Really? You got a pretty big operation?" Hank was fishing. He just hoped it wasn't too obvious.

The humble shrug Raul gave him didn't fool Hank for a minute. This man was up to something. "Naw, just a little mom and pop organization, but we do have the best products in the state. It's something we take a lot of pride in."

"Mom and pop? So is it a family business like Golden Leaf Garden?"

"No, I'm the sole proprietor. Thomas here was one of my first customers in this area a little over a year ago." He straightened. "I better get going, Thomas. Thanks for the drink." He turned and once again extended his hand. "Nice to meet you, Sheriff."

"I'll walk you out." Thomas slapped Hank on the arm. "Good to see you, Sheriff."

He watched the two men leave. Then out of the corner of his eye saw Charlie head out the back door with her garbage bags in tow. He had a mess brewing in his little town, and he didn't like it one bit.

Chapter Thirty-One

Charlie wondered what it said about her that she'd grown to enjoy the nightly ritual of taking out the garbage. She knew Hailey had given her the job to humiliate her, and in the beginning, it had. But there was something basic and fulfilling about performing a necessary task that required very little thought.

Besides, it gave her a chance to get out of the loud club. And even though the Zachsville City Council had banned smoking in any establishment a couple of years ago, it seemed the ghosts of every smoker in Blister County lived within the four walls of Boon's Saloon. The cooler evening air chilled her neck and helped settle her stomach. She couldn't wait for the whole "you feel great in the second-trimester" thing.

The sound of moaning caught her attention as she leaned against the wall of the club. Was there a wounded animal somewhere? There it was again, but this time it was accompanied with a long moaning, "Yeees." Somebody was getting it on in the parking lot. Heat fired her cheeks, and the sense of being an interloper gave her the creeps. Her feet slipped on the gravel as she tried to get to the door and get inside.

There was another loud cry from the female half of the couple.

Something about it made her turn in the direction of the noise. A black SUV was parked just out of the ring of light, about five cars down from where she was standing. The vehicle rocked in time with the grunts and moans of the couple.

She should go inside, but she couldn't. The instinct to investigate was so strong that she couldn't fight the pull. What kind of pervert was she that she was compelled to see the faces of this couple? But she also needed to make sure it was consensual.

As quietly as she could, she moved along the wall until she could see in the side window. A brunette was straddling a man with inky black hair and a beard. Something about her was familiar, but Charlie couldn't see her face. The woman moaned for her partner not to stop. Yep, consensual.

No need to continue to watch this intimate moment. Time to go back inside. As she was about to walk away, the woman turned her head toward the window. And time stopped.

"Oh, no." The words slipped out on a whispered prayer that this wasn't happening. But with every blink of Charlie's lids, the woman's face seared into her brain. There was no denying her identity. The former Queen of Zachsville High, Karen Odom, was screwing some man's brains out in the parking lot of Boon's.

Charlie was ashamed at the momentary thrill that all she'd ever wanted could be hers. It was followed closely by a crushing blow to her chest. For that to happen, she'd have to be the one to tell Hank. Would he believe her? She had no idea.

One thing was for sure—she needed to get out of there.

Slick-bottomed cowboy boots and gravel were a dangerous combination. In her hasty retreat, she slipped and fell. She got to her feet, and scrambling, uncoordinated steps had her nearly going down again. Didn't matter. She'd deal with her bloody hands, and the pain shooting up her arms, when she was safely inside the bar with Hailey yelling at her, people staring at her, and her eyeballs not having to see Hank's wife screwing another man.

* * *

What the hell was Charlie doing outside? Hank checked his watch for the third time. She'd been out there longer than she should've been. Had Thomas and Raul intercepted her and taken her off?

Get a hold of yourself, Odom.

He nursed his second beer that was now room temperature. The singer's slurred, off-key voice crawled up his spine like a mountain climber with ice picks on his feet. He stretched his neck from side to side to smooth out the kinks. His unease about Charlie's absence was aggravated by the text he'd received from Agent Sheridan after he told the man about Charlie, Thomas, and Raul Perez. He reread the text, hoping it would say something different this time.

Don't say anything to Ms. Klein. This is very sensitive, and we have jurisdiction on this one.

Translation: They were in charge, and Hank was required by law to do what they said. Damn it.

This situation had the potential to turn into a giant cluster fuck. He had to protect Charlie from this mess. He had no idea how he'd do that, since she didn't listen to a damn thing he said.

It wasn't turning out to be his week. Finding out about Karen's job. The fight with Derek. And knowing beyond a shadow of a doubt that she'd only come back to him because she wanted to settle some stupid high-school rivalry with Charlie, and not because she wanted him as a husband.

His marriage was over. He hadn't pulled the trigger yet. What he was waiting for? Maybe a sign from God. It gnawed at his insides that he'd failed. He'd be walking away from a commitment just like all the other men in his family.

The back door banged open, and Charlie stumbled in with blood dripping from her hands and the glassy gaze of a trauma victim. He was moving before he even registered that he'd put his feet on the floor. "Charlie, what happened?" He took her hands and inspected them. "Did you fall? Are you alright?"

She shook her head, but said, "Yes."

Her white face and red-rimmed eyes told another story, and had the bottom dropping out of his self-control. "Who's out there? Who did this to you?"

"Nobody. I slipped and fell." The words barely gave the air coming from her mouth substance.

"I don't believe you." He grabbed the handle of the back door.

She clasped her hands around his arm. The blood oozing from her cuts seeped into his sleeve. "Please don't, Hank. Help me get cleaned up."

His instinct to take care of her and the need to find out who'd hurt her beat the shit out of each other. Someone hurting her won. He yanked the door open and barreled outside, ready to take whoever had put their hands on her to the ground. Nobody was there. The parking lot was empty of people.

"Hank." She stumbled through the door and took his arm again. "Let's go back inside."

"Charlie, what's going on? You're worrying me." He heard it then. The moans and cries of two people having sex. Was this what she was trying to keep him from seeing? It was most likely teenagers. Did she know them? He glanced around and saw a familiar black SUV swaying back and forth.

His heart skipped and refused to settle into a normal rhythm. Since his pulse had gone off the rails, his breathing decided to follow suit. The muscles in his jaw locked, but he was grateful for the pain. It added to the bonfire of his fury.

He moved slowly and quietly. Each step he took toward Karen's truck was another nail in the coffin of their marriage.

Like the masochist he was, he stood and watched his wife fucking Matt Allen. It was the last bit of evidence he needed to be released from the joke of a commitment where he'd trapped himself.

Rage unfurled through his body, burning and blistering everywhere it touched until his insides were nothing but ash.

He'd seen all he needed to see.

The scrape of his boots on the rocks as he turned to make his way back inside and quiet sobs were all he heard as numbness took him. Who was crying? He locked eyes with Charlie. The tears sliding down her face were the final straw. He didn't want her pity. Why did she have to be here to witness the end of his marriage at the expense of his pride? He strode past her and flung the door open.

Her trembling hand reached for him. "Hank."

"Don't." He might regret that later, but at the moment he only cared about getting as far away from the woman who owned his heart and the one who'd shredded his soul as fast as he could.

Chapter Thirty-Two

SECOND TRIMESTER

Hank grunted and strained, but finally maneuvered his new mattress into place. He'd bought it the day he'd filed for divorce. It was all part of his starting over campaign. Though he couldn't say he was starting over as much as pivoting away from something destructive, and trying to maintain the status quo in the rest of his life.

It wasn't working as well as he'd like. He went to work, followed Thomas Chang, and came home alone. He wasn't really living. He was existing. Since the day he'd filed for divorce, he'd avoided Hailey, Roxanne, and most especially his mom. Anyone who had the power to make him feel better or worse about this fucked-up situation. He didn't deserve their comfort and couldn't handle any disapproval.

That included Charlie. Most especially, Charlie since she'd stood witness to his greatest humiliation, and his pride couldn't take one more hit.

He could accept that what he'd had with Karen hadn't been healthy, probably from the start, but he couldn't put that all on her. He'd used her to try and get over Charlie—that was why their marriage had been screwed from the start. He'd just been too stubborn to see it.

Operation new mattress complete, he went to the kitchen to grab a beer. A knock at the door stopped him in his tracks. If he were very quiet, maybe they'd go away.

Knock. Knock. Knock.

"Hank, I know you're in there. Open this door right this minute." His mother used her don't-give-me-any-shit voice. One he was helpless to disobey. The woman was a pussycat, except when she used that tone.

He opened the front door and stood back to let her pass.

She carried a cookie sheet with several tin-foil covered bowls on it. He would've taken it from her, but she marched past him like a drill sergeant on her way to the front line.

"Hey, Mom."

The cookie sheet hit the table with a clank, and she held onto it for several moments, head down, shoulders stiff, like she was preparing for battle.

Shit.

This didn't bode well for him. He prepared himself for the lecture about commitment and making promises he was sure was coming. She'd pounded those things into his and his brother's heads their whole lives.

When her shoulders began to shake his heart crashed into his gut. He'd disappointed her. "Mom, I'm sorry."

She spun to glare at him. Anger shot from her watery blue eyes. "What exactly are you sorry for, Hank?"

He wasn't sorry he'd kicked Karen out, or about the divorce, but it did hurt him that he hadn't lived up to her expectations. "That I disappointed you."

"I am disappointed in you, Hank. Of all my sons, you're the last one that I thought would do this to me."

If she'd taken a knife and carved the word disappointment in his chest, it would've hurt less. "I know, but Mom, I couldn't stay with Karen. I have my pride. And frankly, I'd swallowed all I could stomach." He raked his fingers through his hair, surprised he didn't yank some of it out by the roots. "I was willing to look like a dumbass to everyone I knew if she and I could turn this around. I owed it to myself and the commitment I made to do that, but I won't be the town pussy who lets his wife screw around with other men."

Her eyes went wide, and her hand flew to her chest. "Hank."

Never in his life had he said something that vulgar in front of his mother. He shrugged. "I'm sorry to offend you, but you need to understand why I finally kicked Karen out and filed for divorce. But I'm sorry it upsets you that I made that decision."

Tears spilled over her lids. "That's what you think? That I wanted you to stay with that lying, cheating witch?"

He blinked and cocked his head. "Didn't you?"

Fresh sobs rattled her body. He couldn't stand it. He wrapped his arms around her until she quieted. Once the crying stopped, she stepped out of his arms and wiped her face with her hands.

"Hank. I'm furious because you cut me out. I haven't seen or heard from you since you told me what happened with Karen, more than six weeks ago. You've dodged my calls and refused to see me. I never thought you'd do that. Though, now that I know you thought I'd be upset because you finally ended things, I guess I can see why you haven't been around." Her forehead rested between his pecs.

He patted her back. "I'm sorry, Mom."

"It's fine. I just..." Her eyes met his. "Why did you think I'd be mad at you?"

His fingers wrapped around her cold hand, and he led her to the sofa. They sat, but he never let go of her. Somehow, he knew she needed the connection. "Mom, all our lives you've preached to us about keeping our commitments, and how important it is to keep a vow, and not too long ago you said that you'd feel like a failure if not for me." He shrugged. "I just figured you'd be disappointed that I was just like Dad and my brothers."

She grabbed a tissue from the dispenser on the coffee table and blew her nose. "That's horseshit, Hank."

He barked a laugh and fell back on the sofa. His mother never cussed. "Don't hold back, Ma. Tell me how you really feel."

"I will. What I meant when I said that was that you were the only one of my sons who even tried to do the right thing. And that's all I can ask of you, that you try." She crumpled the tissue in her hand.

"Now I'm the one who needs to apologize. I shouldn't have put all of that on you."

He wrapped his arm around her and kissed her forehead. "Nothing to be sorry for. I'm the one who was avoiding you. I needed some time to process everything." He drew back and looked into her eyes. "You understand, right?"

Her head shook like she was trying to shake her hair from her face. However, she had it hair sprayed within an inch of its life, and it didn't move at all. "I don't like it, but I do understand." She took his face in between her palms. "I want you to hear me when I say this. You haven't done anything wrong. You gave one hundred percent to your marriage and Karen didn't. End of story."

He loved this woman. But she didn't know about Charlie, or how he'd never really gotten over her and married Karen as a poor substitute. He couldn't tell her. Maybe that made him a bad guy. But he couldn't bring himself to tell his mother how badly he'd failed. He hugged her tight. "Thanks, Mom."

She rose and pointed to the dishes she'd brought. "Heat that on three-fifty for twenty minutes and serve it over the rice. There's also a peach cobbler."

He grinned. "Homemade?"

Hands on her hips, she gave him a death glare. "Yes, it's homemade. What kind of Texas woman do you think I am? I wouldn't bring a store-bought cobbler to make peace with my son."

"Of course you wouldn't." He rose. "Let me walk you out."

"I know the way." She grabbed her purse and keys and headed for the door.

"What kind of Texas son would I be if I didn't make sure my mama got to her car safely?" He opened the door and stood with his forearm resting against it as she made her way out of the house and to her car. "Thanks for coming by."

She stood in the open car door and rested one arm on the roof. "You're a good man, Hank. Don't forget it. Lick your wounds then be happy." She blew him a kiss, then got in the car and headed out of his driveway.

Be happy. The only time he'd honestly been happy in the last eight years was the few hours he'd spent with Charlie in Austin, and that was a one-off thing, never to be repeated. She didn't want to have anything to do with him. Just as well—if she gave him another chance, he'd sure as hell screw it up.

The Odom men were broken, and he wouldn't drag her into that crap.

Chapter Thirty-Three

C harlie made her way through the back door of Boon's. After more than two months of working there, the smell and dim lighting barely registered anymore. She headed to the employee locker room, which was really a broom closet with a few cubbies big enough for a purse and a jacket and not much else.

The bar hadn't been her first choice of places to work. Hell, it hadn't been her thirty-fifth choice of places to work, but she'd grown to like it, as long as it wasn't a night when Chester the ear ripper was performing. Those nights were tough, not just because she had to endure the man's horrible singing, but because the club was virtually deserted. No customers, no money.

While the auditory assault Chester inflicted was terrible, the worst part of her nights at work was that Hank had made Boon's his new hangout since filing for divorce. Yes, she knew about that. She and every other living soul in Zachsville knew about it. She also knew that in the six weeks since he'd filed for divorce, he hadn't spoken to her once. No, he just sat at a corner table and glared at everyone in the place.

So much for thinking that his marriage was what was keeping them apart. If her tender heart had expected him to come to her after his separation, it would've been disappointed. Good thing she hadn't expected it...much.

He didn't want her. That was painfully clear. It was better that she knew now how he felt. It wouldn't be long before she had to tell him about the pregnancy, and she knew he'd try to do the right thing. He'd want them to be together for the little thing they'd created and not because he wanted her. She wouldn't live a lie, not even for Pod.

The guilt of not telling him was keeping her up at night. She knew she needed to quit procrastinating and deal with it. Just when she thought she had conquered adulting, her old tendency of avoidance would rear its ugly snout.

"Dad, I'm doing the best I can." Hailey's voice floated down the hall to where she stood. Charlie wasn't proud that she covertly peeked around the corner to see Hailey and her father sitting in her boss's office. Mr. Lawson looked almost the same, except for the gray head of hair.

"I'm sorry, Hailey. It's not good enough. I've told you what has to happen to keep this place, and you're falling well short of that mark," Hailey's father said.

"It's freakin' Chester. He's horrible, he's a drunk, and he's driving my customers away." She swung her arm toward the door. "He needs to go."

Mr. Lawson stood and placed his hands on top of Hailey's desk. "Unless the man falls down drunk on the stage, he stays. Or we can call off this waste of time and money and sell the place right now."

Hailey's hands went to her hips in obvious defiance. "No. You said you'd give me some time to turn a profit, and I want that time." She rocked back in her chair, insolence written all over her face. "You owe me that."

He shook his head, and something like guilt washed over his features. "Stubborn as your mother was about this place."

"That may be the nicest thing you've ever said to me, Dad."

"It wasn't a compliment." He took a folder from the desk and turned to leave.

Charlie ran back to the lockers and pretended she hadn't just been eavesdropping on a private conversation. She glanced over her shoulder as Hailey's dad went past. "Hello, Mr. Lawson."

"Oh, hello, Charlie."

She pulled her hair into a ponytail. "How have you been?"

He glanced down the hall to Hailey's office. "I've been better. Maybe you can talk some sense into that girl of mine. She's got it in her fool head to keep this place open—"

"Dad." Hailey stood in the doorway of her office with her arms crossed. "Charlie doesn't want to hear our family business."

Like hell Charlie didn't.

"Fine, but you remember what I said."

"Bye, Dad."

He patted Charlie on the shoulder. "Good to see you, Charlie."

"You too, Mr. Lawson."

"He always did like you better than me." Hailey still stood in her office doorway. "Did you get an earful?"

"Ummm... Do you want to talk about it?"

Her boss turned on her heel and closed the office door. Guess not. Mr. Lawson's threats kept playing through Charlie's head while she did the setup for her shift. By the time the first customers began to show up, she had a plan in place.

* * *

"Chester, it's a shame you don't sing every night." Charlie leaned against the bar and chatted up the old guy. The man was at Boon's every night it was open. Mr. Lawson had even set up a cot for him in the back in case he got so drunk he couldn't drive home, which was pretty much every night. He only performed on the weekends. On Wednesdays and Thursdays, the house band played.

"Why, thank ya, darlin'." The alcohol vapors coming from Chester's throat were enough to give her alcohol poisoning. She stepped back so Pod didn't get a contact high.

With a finger point, he ordered another drink.

"Are you sure you need another drink, Chester?" She had a plan, but the man's health was more important than her plan.

He flicked his finger again. "Don't you worry about that. I can handle my liquor."

Not in this life you can't.

Hailey slid his drink across the bar. "Last one, Chester."

He brought his hands under his chin like a praying child. "Awww, Hailey, you can't do that."

"I can and I will, and go ahead and give me your keys." She reached her hand out, palm up, and wiggled her fingers. "You can sleep here tonight."

He grumbled and cussed but handed the keys to Hailey.

Charlie patted the older man's shoulder. "It's alright, Chester." Hailey gave her a squinty-eyed glare, no doubt wondering what she was up to. When Chester did a combo hiccup/burp thing and sloshed his drink into his beard, she had a moment of doubt.

Her scheme was solid, but her conscience was standing in the way of its execution. Then again, the man had no business being on stage, as drunk as he usually was.

She flipped her hair and plastered on her most coquettish Charlie Kay smile. "I love it when you sing *Amarillo By Morning.*"

He threw back his drink, winked, and thanked her, but it came out, "Sank you."

Her elbow went to the bar, and her chin went in her hand. "I do love it when you sing that song." She tried to add as much longing and dreaminess to the statement as she could.

"Charlie, don't you have tables?" Hailey reprimanded.

Dang it. She could see that Chester was almost there. He just needed another nudge. But she didn't want the wrath of her boss coming down on her. "I better get back to work, Chester. I'll talk to you later."

A jaunty salute was his response.

She glanced over her shoulder at Hailey, then put her lips to Chester's ears. "She really should let you sing more." Hopefully, that would be the nudge he needed to get on stage. If not, then she'd have to come up with a plan B.

That blasted guilt hit her again. She honestly liked Chester, he just had no business singing at Boon's Saloon, and he was hurting her friend by doing it. She resolved to try and get him some help when this was over.

Chapter Thirty-Four

Hank didn't know if he could sit through one more night of listening to Chester's drunken wailings or watching Charlie sashay around the club taking orders. If he had to endure her talking and flirting with everyone in the place, men and women alike, then he might tear the club apart with his bare hands.

He wished to hell that Thomas Chang would find another place to hang out. But as long as he was here, then so was Hank. If for no other reason than to try and keep Charlie safe from the man and his drug-smuggling buddy, especially since she was hell-bent on doing business with them. It'd taken all his resolve to not to bust in on the meetings she'd had with them in the last six weeks.

The good news was that with his pending divorce, no one questioned why he was in the bar nearly every time the doors opened.

Well, no one but Hailey. The woman in question sat down next to him. "I'm about to tell Monk at the door to stop letting you in."

"On what grounds?"

"On the grounds that you don't belong here."

"That's discrimination. I'd hate to have to report you."

She snorted. "Try it, and I'll have Lottie bedazzle your uniform."

He laughed. "She does love to bedazzle. All of my dish towels sparkle since I let her loose with that thing when she was over last week."

"What in the hell is she doing?" Hailey growled.

"Lottie?"

She pointed across the bar to Charlie and Chester. "No, your girlfriend. She's flirting with Chester. Sometimes I wonder if Hollywood sucked every bit of common sense from her body."

"She's not my girlfriend."

"That's what you got from what I said?" Charlie flipped her head and giggled, pointed to the stage, then pushed on Chester's shoulder. "If she's trying to get him on stage, I'm goin' to kill her."

"Go easy on her. She's having a bad time."

"Oh, yeah, the poor little starlet has the worst time."

Hank angled his head so no one else could hear him. Not that they could anyway, but just in case. "She's not working here because of researching a role."

"But..."

"She's broke, Hay. Her mother stole all her money, and the money she'd set aside for Wardell. She says she's done with show business." He sat back and took a swig of the beer he was nursing.

Hailey's mouth opened and closed like a baby bird's. "I didn't know."

"Her crazy mother stole from her." He didn't even try to hide his bitterness. His hatred of Shelly Klein went way back.

"I... Her mother?"

"Yeah." He knew why Hailey was having trouble digesting the information. She'd worshipped her own mother, and for good reason. Her mother had been a saint.

Chester laughed and nearly fell from his barstool. "Look at him." Hailey sounded like she was about to blow a gasket.

"Mmhm." He couldn't look at Chester because his gaze was fixed on Charlie.

"This martyr routine is really getting old." Hailey stood, and her hands went to her hips.

"What?"

"It's obvious to anyone with eyes that you want her, but you're denying yourself happiness. For what? Something you didn't even do."

"That's not—"

"Yes. It is." She glanced in the direction that Charlie was heading. "If you'll excuse me, I need to chew my employee's ass."

He followed Hailey's progress as she stormed up to Charlie and said something. He didn't like it, but she wasn't his business. With an eye roll, the only woman in the club for him walked away from Hailey.

Charlie laughed and joked with her customers, then made her way to his table. "You got everything you need?"

No, damn it. He needed her. All he'd ever needed was her. The words stayed trapped in his chest, and he nodded his head. She was better off without him. The Odom men were broken, and until he understood why he was staying far away from her. He wouldn't be responsible for hurting her more than he already had.

Without a word, she made her way back to the bar. He fought the urge to go after her and tell her everything he felt. Instead, he sat mutely and let her go.

* * *

The snick of a door closing reverberated through her heart. She wouldn't be surprised if tears trailed behind her like lackluster unicorn dust as she made her way back to the bar. If she'd had a heart left to break, his indifference would've cracked it.

"Charlie!" Hailey caught her arm and pulled her behind the bar. "What have you done?" She pointed, and they both turned toward the stage where Chester stood. "Look at him. Why would you encourage him to get up and sing?"

"Hailey—"

"Don't lie to me. I know that's what you were doing." Hailey jabbed her fingers into her dark hair. "Oh, for the love of... Look at him." It seemed the old guy was having a hard time getting his guitar strap over his head. One of the guys in the band had to help him put his arm through the hole. "This is my only night to make any money, and now you've convinced him to get on stage and sing. On most nights he's bad, but tonight I'll be surprised if he can stay upright for even one song."

Charlie tapped her chin. "You may be right. He does look like he could fall down drunk at any moment." She extracted her arm from Hailey's grip at the same time Chester swayed several times then headed for the floor. Thankfully, the bass player caught him just before he crashed to the stage. After a quick look around at the other band members, he dragged Chester to the back corner of the stage to let him sleep it off.

Hailey's wide gaze bounced from the stage to Charlie and back. "You..."

She handed Hailey her drink tray and apron. "You're welcome." With purposeful strides, she headed to the stage.

Charlie grabbed the microphone. "Hey, folks. It looks like Chester needs a little break." She glanced at Chester sleeping in the corner. "But if it's okay with you, I'll fill in for him. Hey, boys. You know any Miranda Lambert?"

"*Kerosene*," the lead guitarist said.

"That works. After that, we'll wing it. Sound good?"

"Let's do it." The drummer raised his sticks above his head and counted her in.

Adrenaline and the thrill of performing exploded inside her at the sound of the first note. She sang like she had nothing to lose, which was the most freeing thing she'd done in a long time. She loved performing, but she had no desire to do it beyond this little club and this small town.

By the end of the first song nearly everyone in the place was dancing.

By the end of the second set, she had her best friend back.

And by the end of the night, she was running from the law.

Chapter Thirty-Five

T he applause and whoops were the loudest Hank had ever heard inside Boon's.

Charlie was mesmerizing. Her brilliant smile lit up the dark bar, and the gold of her hair sparkled in the neon lights as she spun and danced on stage. She was a honky-tonk angel. His dead heart rose up and called him the biggest fool around. What was he doing? Hailey was right. He was punishing himself, and for what? Some overgrown sense of duty and pride.

It stopped tonight.

Charlie was the only woman he'd ever loved, and he was pissing his chance away. A sense of rightness melted into his bones. They were meant for each other. He'd get her back, and he wouldn't wait another day. As soon as she got off work, he'd tell her everything.

Her booted foot kicked out and her hand went into the air when the song was over. She turned to say something to the band, the music started, and he lost his damn heart all over again.

"Can you believe it?" Hailey plopped down in the chair she'd just vacated.

"No." He couldn't tear his eyes away from the beauty on stage.

"She planned this. That's why she kept chatting Chester up."

He tore his gaze away from Charlie and stared at Hailey. "What are you talking about?"

Hailey rested both elbows on the table and spoke behind her hands. "She overheard my dad say that Chester had to stay unless he fell down drunk on the stage."

"And she…"

Hailey motioned to the stage and dance floor. "She sure as hell did."

He glanced around the bar. Most everyone was on the dance floor, including Thomas. Those that weren't either had their phones up recording Charlie, or were furiously texting. "I bet she'll be trending by the time the night's over."

"From your lips to God's ears." The words were a prayer from Hailey's mouth as she watched everyone dancing. She turned to him, and after a beat of silence, they both cracked up. "I better get back to the bar. Is it me, or are there more people in here than there were twenty minutes ago?"

"No, I believe it's more crowded than it was."

"Hot damn." She stood to leave.

He grabbed her hand. "Hailey."

"Yeah?"

"You're right. I am being a martyr, but no more." He squeezed her hand. "Thanks."

"Well, now this night just got even better." The current song ended, and Hailey pointed to the stage and yelled, "That crazy chick is my best friend!" Charlie's head jerked in their direction. She made a heart with her hands, and Hailey did the same. It was corny, sappy, and like being in the middle of a sorority party, but he couldn't control the grin that stretched across his face.

The smile slid away, though, when Charlie started the next song and twirled around. Her baby doll top flew away from her body. What the hell? He scrutinized her every move. When she jumped up and down during Jason Aldean's *Hicktown*, he saw it again. There was a distinct rounding to her belly. Wasn't there? Maybe the lighting was off.

Or was she…

No, it couldn't be. He was losing his mind.

The songs kept coming, and so did the people. He kept one eye on Thomas and the other on Charlie. She took a couple of breaks, and he wanted her to come by his table again, but each time she went the other way. He couldn't help the happiness when the two old friends embraced behind the bar, both crying and laughing at the same time.

By the time the third set started he'd convinced himself that what he'd seen was just a play of the light. He spent his time rehearsing the speech he'd give her. It wouldn't be easy. He'd hurt her. Regret for what he'd done was a noose around his neck. He hadn't meant to lie that first night, and even though he'd tried to tell her, it didn't change the fact that it was guilt by omission. But he'd make it up to her.

From the corner of the stage, Chester stirred. The confusion on his face communicated that he had no recollection of what had happened. Hank's concern escalated as Chester's confused look turned to anger. His clumsy attempts to stand went unnoticed by Charlie and the band.

Before he registered that he was moving, Hank was up and heading for the stage. But there were too many bodies between him and the drunk heading for Charlie. He shoved people aside as his anxiety and adrenaline skyrocketed. Cologne, perfume, and body odor curled his stomach that was already on heightened alert. The screams of the people being knocked out of the way got the attention of the band. Unfortunately, that meant they didn't see the pissed-off man marching straight for the woman he loved.

"Hey." Chester grabbed Charlie by the arm and shouted something in her face.

It looked like Charlie was trying to extricate herself from the drunk's grip, but he wasn't having it. The lead guitarist tried to pull him off her. Chester released her long enough to punch the guy. When he turned back to Charlie, she was backing away from him. He tripped and fell into her, and she went flying.

Time stopped.

It was a five-foot drop to the dance floor below, and she was falling backward. Hank pushed the last person out of the way and caught her facing away from him.

She jerked her head around to see who had her. "Oh, Hank. Thank you."

He didn't say anything. Every word he knew jumbled and shredded in his head, because he was holding a definite baby bump in his right hand. His brain tried to make it something else. Too many biscuits, bloating, a beer gut, anything but what he was sure it was.

Betrayal.

Chapter Thirty-Six

Charlie grabbed her purse from the locker and poked her head into Hailey's office. "Do you want me to wait on you?" The tight muscles from her fall loosened when she saw her friend's smile.

Hailey put a bank bag in the safe and locked it. "No, Monk is going to walk me to my car."

Monk was one of the bouncers, so Charlie felt okay about leaving Hailey. "Okay, don't stay too long."

"I won't. I'm exhausted."

She hiked her purse higher on her shoulder. "Goodnight."

"Charlie."

"Yeah."

"I'm sorry."

Shock zipped through her. She knew Hailey, and she never apologized. She'd do anything in her power to make things up to you if she wronged you, but she never apologized. "For what?"

Hailey came to her and took her hand. "For being a bitch to you, for not believing you when you said you didn't know I'd tried to get in touch with you...just for everything."

"Hailey, you don't—"

"Yes, I do. Can I take you to lunch tomorrow?"

Charlie wrapped her friend in a hug. "There's nothing to forgive, and I'd love to go to lunch."

Hailey stiffened in her arms. "Charlie, um...what's that?"

Oh, shit. "Ah..."

Her boss pulled out of her hold and put her hands on either side of her bump. "Charlie."

The saliva in her mouth was so thick she could barely swallow it down. "Can we talk about it tomorrow?" She was bone tired and didn't think she could rehash the whole thing right now.

"Yes, but we *will* talk about it." Hailey gave her a no-nonsense look.

She nodded, but her head barely moved. "Goodnight."

"Do you need Monk to walk you out?"

"No, I parked right outside the door."

The quick hug she got made her feel marginally better about Hailey finding out her secret. "'Night."

The cool, fresh air hit her lungs and refreshed her tired mind. And a good thing too, because a long, tall, pissed-off Texan was leaning against her car with his arms crossed over his chest. "Hank."

"You got something you need to tell me, Charlie?"

Well, damn. This good night had gone to hell in a matter of minutes. "Why don't you tell me what it is that you think I'm keeping from you, Hank?" She didn't know why she was being so cagey. He clearly knew, but for some reason she couldn't bring herself to say it. It wasn't because she wanted to keep it from him anymore, but more that she didn't want to share Pod with anyone else.

His features hardened even more. "Oh, I don't know, maybe that you're pregnant?"

All her bravado seeped away when she heard the words. "Yes."

"Is it mine?"

"No."

Disbelief flashed across his face. "No?"

"I'm growing it. It's taken over my body. I'm the one who dealt with morning sickness, exhaustion, and the terror that I might do something wrong and hurt it, so I've earned the right to claim it as mine alone. Now if you'll excuse me, I'm tired, and I want to go home."

"And whose fault is that? I would've been there if you'd told me." His anger punched the words at her.

She was too tired to be diplomatic. "Uh-huh, and how would your wife have liked that? While I was dealing with an unplanned pregnancy, Hank, you were trying to save your marriage. I didn't think the two things went together very well."

That seemed to take the fire right out of him. His face softened, and he stepped toward her. She was stuck to the spot. The impossibility of moving shocked her, but she couldn't budge, especially when he curled a piece of hair behind her ear. "You're right. I'm so sorry you've had to deal with this alone." He rested his forehead on hers, and the need to throw herself into his arms and let him take care of everything was almost second nature. After all, wasn't that how she'd lived the last eight years?

That sobering thought gave her feet the motivation to move away from him. "I'm doing just fine on my own," she said to his chest. She might be motivated to stand on her own, but her weakness for this man was a danger.

He hunched down some so he could look her in the eye. "But you don't have to anymore. I'm here, and I'm going to do the right thing and take care of you and the baby."

The stab of those words ripped her chest open. Just as she knew he would. He wanted to do the right thing. Her arms went around her middle. It wasn't much, but it was a partial barrier between the two of them and him. "Why?"

"Why, what?"

The adorable crooked grin and cocked head made him look like he used to when they were teenagers. She set her jaw and shoved every bit of strength she had into her resolve to get the answers she needed. This was too important. "Why now?"

He shoved his fingers through his hair. "I know I have some explaining to do."

"Yes, you do. Like why after six weeks of not speaking one word to me do you suddenly want me, but that's only after you found out about this." She placed her hands on her belly. The tightness in her throat strangled her, but she continued. "You know what I think, Hank? I think your over exaggerated sense of duty is why you want me now."

"That's not what this is."

Damn tears. They wouldn't stay where they belonged, and two rolled down her cheeks. "I've spent the last eight years surrounded by people who only wanted something from me. Hell, if you count my mother, then I've spent all my life with people only wanting me for what they could get from me. Now you've decided I'm worth your time because I have something you want." She moved her purse in front of her belly like she could hide Pod's existence.

He took her by the elbows. "No. That's not it. I want you, Charlie, with or without this baby."

More than anything in her life, she wished to believe him. But all the people who'd been so sincere and two-faced at the same time scrolled through her mind. And the way he'd dismissed their night together like it meant nothing, then when they could have been together he'd avoided her, until now—until he knew about Pod. It jacked up her suspicion of his motive.

The promise she'd made herself and the little thing she was growing came back to her. The only people who got to be in their lives were the ones who made an effort to be there. So far, Hank didn't fulfill that criterion. In fact, he'd done nothing but run from her. "I'm sorry, Hank. This thing, whatever it was between us, is over."

That door was locked.

* * *

Desperation clawed at Hank's mind. He had to say something to make her understand. "Charlie, I've screwed up, I know it, but I swear to you that I never stopped wanting to be with you."

A sad smile ghosted across her face. "That's what you say, Hank. It's not what you did. I don't blame you for trying to save your marriage, but after it was over, you treated me like I didn't exist. That's where I'm having trouble reconciling your words and actions."

"What did you want me to? File for divorce then run to your

house?" He splayed his fingers across his hip bones. "I was dealing with some shit."

"No, but you could've at least spoken to me. You certainly had no trouble getting all up in my business before you filed for divorce. You had an opinion about my clothes, choice of places to work, even who I did business with, then you and Karen break up and it's radio silence. What am I supposed to think, Hank?"

He'd honestly lost the ability to hear. The blood in his brain turned to ice at the reminder that she and his child were involved with Thomas Chang and Raul Perez. Dear God, how was he going to protect her if she didn't let him into her life? He needed to regroup. If he knew one thing about Charlie, it was that once she got an idea in her head there was no changing it. She believed he only wanted her because of the baby she carried, so he'd have to prove her wrong. "I understand."

"What?"

"I understand. You're hurt, and I have some things to make right with you before you'll give me a chance. I get it." He moved to open her car door for her.

"Oh." He could see his response took some of the steam out of her tirade. She moved to the open car door, climbed inside, and placed both hands on the steering wheel.

"Charlie."

"Yes?"

Her deer-in-headlights expression made his heart hurt. This was his doing, and he had to fix it. He leaned in and whispered in her ear. "This isn't over."

She didn't say anything, but he didn't miss the goosebumps that popped up on her neck. He closed her door, and she pulled out of the parking lot. He climbed in his truck. He'd follow her home. Hell, he'd follow her anywhere.

Now to get her to believe him.

The streets of Zachsville were empty at this time of night, so it was easy to keep her in view without being right up on her. Somehow, he didn't think she'd appreciate his protectiveness.

The absolute, pure joy pumping through him at the knowledge that he was going to be a father was only dampened by the realization that the DEA had made Charlie a pawn in their case against Raul Perez. A thought occurred to him. Maybe since she was pregnant, they wouldn't want to use her.

He could only hope, because he had no idea how he was going to keep her out of this unless they decided she wasn't useful to them.

After Charlie pulled into her driveway, he drove to the next block and pulled over to send a quick text to Agent Sheridan.

I need to speak with you. Be in Houston at ten.

He prayed it would work.

Chapter Thirty-Seven

"I'm sorry, Hank, but Charlie Klein is still our best chance of nailing Raul Perez." Agent Sheridan rested his butt on the front of his desk, with his legs outstretched and his hands in his pockets.

"She's pregnant, Sheridan." Hank crossed his arms over his chest.

"We know," Agent Murphy said.

What the hell? The DEA knew Charlie was pregnant before he did. There was something seriously wrong with that. "How do you know?"

Murphy pulled a folder out of the satchel she always carried and handed it to him. He was beginning to hate that damn thing. The first thing he saw was a photo of Charlie walking into the Dip N Do with a box in her hands, then another of her in front of Wardell's house watering the flowers. In fact, the folder was full of photos of her at various places in town, including getting out of her car at the Golden Leaf Garden. His heart lodged in his throat. "When…"

"Since you first told us about her having contact with Thomas Chang. She's not involved, by the way," Sheridan said.

Annoyance at these two, but especially Murphy, looped around his vocal chords and made his words ridged. "I could've told you that." He continued to flip through the folder until he saw something about her doctor. Curiosity almost had him flipping through their notes on the pregnancy, but he wanted the information to come from Charlie and not from the fuckin' DEA. He closed the file and handed it back to Murphy.

"Be that as it may, we prefer to do our own investigation."

"Has anyone ever told you that you're fairly unpleasant, Agent Murphy?" There was no controlling the acid in his tone.

She laughed. "A time or two, Sheriff Odom. A time or two."

How the hell did you deal with a person who so blatantly enjoyed her bad reputation? Ignore her. That was his only recourse. "Sheridan, surely there is another way to get what you need on Perez without involving a civilian, let alone a pregnant civilian. What if something happens to her or the baby?" The icicles forming on his spine sent a chill of dread through him.

Sheridan and Murphy shared a look. Apparently, they'd considered the risk to Charlie and decided it was worth it. Damn it.

"Hank, nothing's going to happen to Ms. Klein, because you're going to be there to make sure she's okay." Sheridan's logical demeanor made Hank want to pop him in the mouth.

"How exactly am I supposed to do that?" It was a legit question and one he'd been asking himself since the moment he realized that Charlie intended to do business with Perez and Thomas Chang.

"Zachsville's a small town. You two are old friends. Surely it won't be hard to keep an eye on her?" Murphy said.

He tipped his cowboy hat back. "That's not the problem, Agent Murphy. The problem is that this woman doesn't deserve to be used like this, and that there's every chance this is putting her in danger. I can't get behind that."

Sheridan moved behind his desk, sat, and pulled another folder from his desk drawer. "Take a look at this, Hank."

The file was much thicker than the one on Charlie. It was filled with photos and statistics. "What is this?"

"This is what Raul Perez has done to the small towns in Texas that he's infiltrated just in the last year." Agent Sheridan adjusted his tie. "The incidence of cocaine and heroin use have gone up dramatically. It's like a disease spreading through South Texas."

Hank flipped through the pages. "Some of the statistics are for kids as young as eleven."

"Bastards target kids specifically. Lots of freebies, or cheap drugs, until they're hooked. It's a lifetime client." Disgust dripped from every word that left Murphy's mouth.

He thought of Lottie and the twins. Bile burned a hole in his gut. He glanced up at Sheridan. "You knew this would do it for me, didn't you?"

The agent shrugged. "You're a lawman, Hank, and a damn good one too. You also have an inflated sense of right and wrong. I figured you needed to see the whole picture to make the right decision."

Damn him, and the horrible timing of his life. There was only one thing to do, and it wasn't the right thing for Charlie. He'd have to make sure she was safe. He could do that. He planned to be a permanent part of her life anyway. "You should know that Charlie's baby is mine."

The agents shared a shocked look. Ha! He'd finally managed to get something over on them. But there wasn't any real satisfaction in the bomb he dropped. The whole situation sickened him.

"Hank, I need you to tell me right now if this is going to be an issue," Sheridan said.

"Not at all." The only issue it presented was that it doubled his determination to make her his.

"What?" Agent Murphy shouted. "You're not seriously planning to keep him involved, Jim?" Murphy was fired up. Now, there was some satisfaction in that.

The stern glare that Sheridan gave the other agent stopped whatever she was about to say. "Julie, the way I see it we don't really have a choice. Also, the Sheriff here has an added incentive to run this operation the best he can." His dark eyes cut to Hank. "Isn't that right, Hank?"

That look communicated clearly that Hank's job would be in the shit can if he crossed them. "Absolutely."

Chapter Thirty-Eight

C harlie scanned the menu of El Toro Loco. She'd woken up this morning with a craving for tacos, so she'd asked Hailey if they could have Mexican food for lunch. "Lord, I'm hungry."

"Yeah, being pregnant will do that to a girl." Hailey peeked her green eyes over the top of the daily specials list.

With the prickly sting of heat crawling up her neck, Charlie knew she must look like a bloated tomato. "Yes, well..." The relief of Hank and Hailey knowing relaxed the giant knot that had taken up residence between her shoulder blades.

"How far along are you?"

"Almost seventeen weeks."

"It's Hank's, right?"

The drink of water that Charlie had taken came right back out and into her napkin. "How did you know?"

Hailey sipped her sweet tea. "Hank told me about what happened in Austin." She gave Charlie a devilish grin. "And I'm good at math. I think it's fantastic, by the way." Her friend grabbed a chip and dipped it in a bowl of salsa. "Hank and Charlie back together, just like the old days, only now there's a baby on the way."

Charlie took her own chip and broke it into two pieces. "There's probably not going to be a me and Hank."

"Listen, I know you're not happy with him right now, and I don't blame you. All I'm going to say is, give him a chance."

"Can we not talk about him? I don't know where he fits in mine and Pod's lives."

"That's what you're calling the baby? It's terrible." She laughed.

The chip in Charlie's hand went flying across the table, right in Hailey's face. "Bite your tongue. Pod is adorable. It's short for pea pod."

Hailey sobered. "Honestly, how are you feeling? I was so sick with Lottie that I could barely leave the house."

"I've been pretty sick. Know what the worst smell for me is?"

Another chip went into the salsa, and Hailey shook her head.

"Peanuts. Specifically peanut butter, but any form of peanut is bad."

It was her friend's turn to choke. "Oh, no."

Charlie laughed and set her menu aside. No need to look too hard, it was a taco kind of day. "I understand why you were mad. I wasn't there for you. Haven't been there for you. I'm so sorry."

"I know." Hailey took her hand and gave her a sad smile. "I've missed you too."

Those four little words triggered an explosion of color into the drab interior of her soul. For the last eight years, everything had been about creating, cultivating, and curating Charlie Kay. From her job to her hair color, to the way she behaved and dressed. So much time spent living as a fictional character leached the pigment from real life. Ironic that after so much time in Hollywood, where everything sparkles and is done on a grand scale, her world would've shrunk to something so monotone and small. "I missed you so much."

Hailey placed her elbows on the table and folded her hands under her chin. "So have you thought of a name?"

"No." Charlie shook her head. "You don't realize how many people you hate until you start trying to name a baby."

Hailey laughed. "Isn't that the truth."

"Can I take your order?" their waiter asked.

"Tacos. We want all the tacos." Hailey closed her menu and handed it to the waiter.

A crooked front tooth winked out from his bright smile. "Beef or chicken? Crispy or soft?"

"We'll do it all." In charge, Hailey was taking control.

"Still bossy as ever, I see."

Hailey laughed. "You don't live my life and not be a little bossy. You try wrangling an almost eight-year-old and running a business by yourself."

She chewed on her lower lip. "You better start tutoring me, because I'm going to be doing that very thing. Well, minus the almost eight-year-old. I'm opening a shop to sell my body creams and soaps." She couldn't control her smile. This was what she'd always wanted. Not acting or being a star. Living in her small town and selling the things she made. The dream her grandmother planted years ago was about to come true.

Hailey rested her elbow on the table. "Okay, tell me everything that's going on with you and your career. Hank told me you didn't get the job at the bar to research a role."

The napkin in her lap became very interesting. "No, I didn't."

"Hey." Hailey took her hand. "I'm not mad. Come to think of it, you weren't the one to tell me that anyway—Hank was. He also told me your mom stole from you. What happened?"

"My mom happened." The hollow ache in the center of her body tore open. Would there ever be a time when she could say her mother's name and not experience the sensation of a giant maw swallowing all her emotions? "She stole almost everything I had. Then she took what I'd set aside for Pops."

"How?" Shocked green eyes begged to understand. "I mean how is that even possible?"

That was the multi-million-dollar question. "Because I'm an idiot. She handled all my money. When we first went to LA, I didn't have a choice, but I didn't change things when I turned eighteen."

"Why? I mean, I don't know anything about that kind of thing, but it seems like you'd want to take control of things."

Charlie shrugged. "I should've. But things are so different in the business. I was in control of very few things, and my mom was one of them. When we first got to LA, she was overbearing, meddling, you know, like she always had been. After the money started rolling in, she got worse, but she was my mom. She'd always taken care of me. I had no reason to doubt her. Sure she was unpleasant at times, but that didn't make her a criminal. Then two years ago she got involved with this boxer named Marco, and turned into someone I didn't know. She changed."

Hailey sipped her tea. "Like how?"

"Gambling, drugs, and manic shopping sprees. It looks like that's when the money started disappearing. Then nine months ago she withdrew everything she could get her hands on, and she and Marco fled the country. No one knew where they were until the Italian authorities informed us they'd died in a car accident. Then things really went to hell. The IRS started asking questions."

"She hadn't paid taxes?" Hailey asked the question like she was tiptoeing through a minefield.

"Not in two years. I owe them a lot of money." Charlie tried to wash the bitterness away by pouring iced water down her throat. "They get every penny of my residuals until it's paid off." She raised her glass. "Thanks, Mom."

The side of Hailey's fist came down on the table. "I could wring her neck. How could she do that to you?"

Charlie shook her head. "I don't know."

"I'm so sorry, Charlie."

She flipped her hair over her shoulder. "It's okay. I'm moving on with my life here in Zachsville."

"Won't you miss being a star?" Hailey asked, and spread her fingers into jazz hands by her face.

"No."

Hailey cocked her head. That clearly wasn't the answer she'd expected. "Really?"

"Really." Charlie played with the straw in her drink. "There's no such thing as unconditional anything in show business, Hailey. You know what I mean?"

"Not really."

How to explain it without sounding like a total brat? "In Hollywood, you're only as good as your last role, only as beautiful as your last photograph, only as lovable as the public deems you to be." Elbows on the table, she brought her clasped hands in front of her mouth. Her index finger rubbed against her chin. "It's like...show business drains you of your humanity. I wasn't a person—I was a product. I wasn't a girl—I was a sex symbol. And I didn't have feelings—I had issues. Does that make sense?" She shook her head and picked up her water. "I don't know if I'm explaining it correctly."

Hailey's eyes looked like big green saucers. "It sounds horrible. And to think I was jealous of you for being free and having all the fun." She reached across the table and took Charlie's hand. "I really am sorry."

Her friend's closed fist over hers was a link to the life she wanted, the one she'd fight to have. "Thanks, Hay. I was sorry to hear about your mom."

Tears shimmered over emerald eyes, and she swallowed several times. "Thanks. She was the best mom. I miss her a lot. It's hard to believe she's only been gone a year. It seems like so much longer."

Charlie wondered if Hailey's mom had changed after she left or if Hailey was forgetting all the times her mom wasn't around because of her hours at the bar. They always said if they could combine Charlie's overbearing mom and Hailey's absent mom, then they'd have the perfect mother.

The waiter set their plates on the table. "Can I get you anything else?"

"No, this looks great," Hailey said.

"Honey told me she'd been sick for a while." At Hailey's sad expression she quickly added, "We don't have to talk about it if you don't want to."

Her friend shook her head. "No, it's fine. It helps to talk about her. She had breast cancer." A small smile ghosted across her face. "She fought like a wildcat. You know Mom. Nothing got Peggy Lawson down."

"I remember that time she showed up to our piano recital with a broken arm that hadn't been set yet. She strapped it to her chest with one of your dad's belts and sat in the front row smiling like nothing was wrong." Charlie laughed. "She was a force of nature." What she didn't add was that it was one of the few times Hailey's mom showed up for any of Hailey's activities.

"Yeah, and she made my dad drive through Dairy Bar, so I could get ice cream for playing so pretty, before she let him take her to the hospital. My dad was furious." The loving, nostalgic look she wore bled into a bitter sneer. "He never understood my mom or me."

"What's going on with y'all? That exchange I heard the other night was pretty nasty." The spiciness of the taco was like heaven to her taste buds. She'd probably regret it later, but for now, it was amazing.

"He's getting married." She pushed her plate away from her. "Mom's barely been gone a year, and he's already replaced her. She left the bar to both of us, and he wants to sell it. Can you believe it? That thing's been in my family forever, my mom and grandma both ran it. It's my legacy, and he wants to sell it. Her hand flicked between them. "Forget it. I don't want to talk about my disloyal dad. Tell me about the shop you're going to open."

"Well, you know my grandmother always made body lotions and soaps?"

"Yeah. My mom loved the hand cream."

A bubble of air crawled up her esophagus. Uh-oh. Hopefully Pod wasn't about to have a full-on tantrum about the Mexican food. "I've been making them since I left Zachsville too. When things went south with my finances, I started selling them here in town, and they've sold really well. It's always been my dream to have a little shop. I've taken accounting classes, but I'm nervous. I've never run a business before." She wadded up her napkin and threw it on the table. "Hell, Hailey, up until four months ago I'd never run anything, including my life."

"I'm not gonna lie, it's a lot of work, but I like being my own boss, and I'll help any way I can."

"Thanks. I'm not totally without resources. Pops ran a business forever, so he's already helped with some things."

"See, you're halfway there." Hailey sipped her iced tea.

"The good news is I have a great hookup for getting my essential oils. They can be really expensive, and a lot of the time the quality isn't very good. But Thomas Chang has connected me to his supplier. He's trying to get started in this area, so he's giving me a deal on some of the products."

"See! You're already running your business." Hailey raised her glass. "To badass women running their own lives."

She'd drink to that. She just hoped it would turn out that way.

Chapter Thirty-Nine

Charlie stared at the two documents in her hand. She'd had a busy morning. First, she'd filled out the paperwork that would make her little business a company. Then she'd gotten her Texas driver's license. Her face was a little puffy in the temporary paper ID photo, but otherwise, it wasn't horrible. Both pieces of paper represented one more step in making Zachsville her permanent home. The more she could distance herself from Hollywood the better.

Her cheeks burned when she remembered her first DMV visit in Los Angeles. She'd walked in with her damn entourage while the media swarmed outside the building. Ron and Marci had insisted on having her stylist and makeup artist there with her, then requested several retakes until they got just the right shot. She'd been dubbed the DMV Diva by the media when that little tidbit had gotten out. It was humiliating. Oh, she could be a diva, no doubt—you don't grow up in that environment and not believe you're the center of the whole freakin' world—but in that one instance, it hadn't been her fault. The media hounded her for weeks following that debacle.

The deep breath she filled her lungs with was an automatic reaction to the latent effects of the crushing claustrophobia of those moments. Moments that should've been a private rite of passage, but weren't, moments when she'd been jostled and swarmed until she feared for her safety. Moments where all privacy was violated merely for someone else's entertainment.

"Whatcha got there?" The low, velvety rumble of Hank's voice had an electrifying, two-pronged effect on her. One in the heart and the other in her more intimate places. His sex appeal was so potent that if he hadn't already knocked her up, she was pretty sure his voice alone could do the job.

She shut down her raging second-trimester hormones and raised the shields around her heart. "My Texas driver's license."

He playfully snatched it from her hand. "Lemme see that."

"Give it back." She tried to grab it, but he held it out of her reach. "What are you, in junior high?"

The deep chuckle slid over her. Her skin pebbled, and she ached to rub her body over every inch of his. Now wouldn't that be some juicy gossip for the fine citizens of Zachsville? Hollywood starlet rubs naked body over town sheriff in the county courthouse. Lord, the women at the Dip N Do would eat that information up with a spoon then spread it around like butter.

He handed the license back to her. "I believe you do look like a Texan, Ms. Klein."

She ran her thumb and forefinger down the fold of the paper. "Thanks."

"How's the business?"

That stopped her, and a warm glow of pleasure spread through her belly at his interest. She held up the other piece of paper in her hand. "Great. I just filed an LLC, so The Emporium is now officially a business."

The tightening of his features was weird. "That's excitin'. No problem getting your supplies?"

Maybe the strange look had been a figment of her imagination. He seemed genuinely interested. "None. You know that Thomas Chang connected me to his supplier, and Mr. Perez has been awesome to work with."

"Good." His Adam's apple bobbed. "That's good."

No. She hadn't imagined it—definitely not happy about something. She didn't need his good opinion, no matter how bad she wanted it, which chapped her ass. The only interaction she should have with him was over Pod.

"How are you feeling?"

His question caught her off guard. "I'm well."

One step, then two, and he was right in front of her. "You're not sick anymore?"

The change in position had her looking up at him. "Not so much." Why was her voice so soft and smoky?

Calloused fingers skated up her arms. "Good." The tiny hairs on her skin stood on end and begged for more. The rhythm of her breathing changed. With every rise of her ribs, her tender breasts brushed against his chest, setting off fiery sparks that shot straight between her legs. "You look beautiful."

"Thank you." There was that breathy voice again.

He searched her face and ran his tongue along his bottom lip. "Go out with me tonight, Charlie?"

"Okay." What? No, no, no. She stepped back and put some distance between them. Her body screamed in protest. It physically hurt to pull away from him. "I mean, I can't."

Laughter from a group of people rang down the hall and made her jump. He took her hand and pulled her around the corner and through a stairwell door. "You said yes first." His lips kicked up on one side.

"I'm not dating you, Hank." No way her tender emotions could take another round of heartbreak via Hank Odom. It would crush her, and she needed to be whole for Pod. And besides, she was done with people who only wanted something from her. And Hank only wanted her for Pod.

He scuffed his boots on the concrete floor. "You know, Charlie, I think you can give me one evening, considering the little item you failed to tell me. We have things to discuss."

He played dirty. He knew exactly what to say to get his way. The guilt she'd tried to deny at keeping Pod's existence from him wagged an accusatory finger at her. "Fine. We'll talk. I do owe you that. But this is only about the pregnancy. Any relationship beyond co-parenting is off the table." She didn't like his calculating look. "I mean it, Hank. That door's locked."

The silence and tension emanating from him wasn't a good sign. She knew him, and the only thing Hank couldn't back away from besides doing the right thing was a challenge.

Great. She'd just waved a red flag at an angry bull.

* * *

He was losing her. Hank could see it in the set of her jaw. Unacceptable. Every part of him that belonged to her, which was one hundred percent of his entire being, demanded he do something. But he had to play this right, or he would lose her for sure.

His hands went into the air. "I hear you." The unconvinced expression she wore had him biting the inside of his cheek. She had to know that she'd just thrown down the gauntlet.

Her brilliant eyes narrowed. "I mean it, Hank. I've got more than myself to think about now. I care about you, and I always will. You're one of my oldest friends, and I don't want to lose that. But I'm not going to be your next project."

"That's not what this is." Shit, shit, shit. He cursed the lousy timing that had him finding out about the baby before he'd told her he loved her. She owned him and always had. Couldn't she see that?

How would she see that, dumb ass? You let her down in the worst way.

"Sure it isn't." She slipped the temporary license in her purse along with the other paperwork, then pulled the bag in front of her. Just one more barrier between them.

Fuck that.

He positioned his body close to hers again, took her hand, and placed it on his chest. "Feel that?' The organ beneath his ribs pumped double time. The erratic thumps had started the minute he'd seen her in the hallway and hadn't slowed down since.

"Yes." Her gaze never left where their bodies connected.

"My heart only beats like this for you, Charlie. It always has. I was a fool. I know it. And I'm willing to do whatever I have to do to make it right." He tipped her chin up. "Please, give me a chance." Hope teetered on the edge of his request. One wrong move and it would slip into the divide between them.

Her beautiful features hardened, and she pulled her face from his fingers. "We can go out to discuss the pregnancy, and that's all."

"Charlie—"

"I have to go. I have a meeting with Thomas." She reached in her purse and pulled out her keys.

Shit. "Where?"

"What?"

"Where is the meeting?" He fought the tremor of anger that wanted to wrap itself around every word.

She flipped her hair over her shoulder. "I don't see... Wait. Are you jealous? Really, Hank?"

"No. I'm just trying to..." What was he going to say? Protect you. Keep you safe. He reined in his anxiety and suspicion before he blew the government's entire case. He took his hat off and smoothed his hair back, then chuckled. "No, I'm not jealous. I only want to see if you needed a ride." He pointed to her keys in her hand. "But I can see that you don't. Besides, I need to make sure you and the baby are taken care of."

The suspicious look she gave him communicated loud and clear that his explanation hadn't been convincing. "No need to worry, Hank. We've been doing just fine without you."

His hand went to his chest, fully expecting to feel a gaping wound from the direct hit. He hadn't been there for her. He couldn't blame her for not telling him sooner. He'd like to think that if he'd known, he would've left his failing marriage to be with her. But the truth was, he'd been so invested in saving something that never really existed, that he couldn't swear to what he would've done. Also, he'd made his position perfectly clear to her, so why would she take a chance and tell him about the pregnancy?

He slipped his fingers into his front pants pockets. "Yeah, you have."

That seemed to surprise her. "Thank you."

The emotion in her voice was interesting. "You're welcome. Thank you for taking care of yourself and the baby."

Moisture gathered in her eyes, and she swallowed hard, but only nodded and walked away. He followed her back into the hallway and watched everything he'd ever wanted walk out of the courthouse.

Chapter Forty

Hank's frayed and splintered nerves were hanging by a thread by the time he made it to Wardell's house to pick up Charlie. He'd never been so anxious about a date since the first time he took her out. Of course, back then they'd had to sneak around because her mom didn't approve of the age difference. Strange that it had never been easy with Charlie, and yet he had no doubt that she was the one for him.

Guilt decided to tag along with the anxiety riding him. He'd never gotten over Charlie. He'd taken her with him everywhere, including his marriage. He could see it so clearly now, but at the time he'd been oblivious to the fact that he was still carrying a torch for his first love —his only love.

His phone rang. He answered it through the truck's Bluetooth. "This is Hank."

"Hank, it's Sheridan."

Fuck. Why hadn't he checked the caller ID before he answered the phone? "Yeah, what can I do for you?"

"Murphy and I were talking, and it would be great if you could try to find out from Ms. Klein when her first shipment of product is expected from Perez's company."

What in the hell? "You want me to pump her for information?"

"Well, yes, but you make it sound so crude. If you have a conversation, you could just steer the dialogue that way. Keep your eyes and ears open and be observant."

"You want me to act like a law enforcement officer. Have I got that right?" He didn't even try to conceal the bitterness in his voice. Fuckin' Feds, who did they think he was? He was a cop. He knew how to run an investigation.

Sheridan chuckled. "You don't like us much, do you, Sheriff?"

Hank turned onto Wardell's street. "I don't give you that much thought, Agent Sheridan. We're both just trying to do a difficult job."

"Right you are, Sheriff Odom. We're all trying to do our job. Talk to you in a couple of days."

He punched the disconnect button on the steering wheel. That call was not what he needed right now, not minutes before he was picking Charlie up for what might be the most important night of his life.

He sucked clean country air into his lungs and headed for the door. It opened before he could get there.

"Why, Hank Odom, you good-looking devil, get into this house." Honey Jenkins pushed open the screen door and held it for him.

"Thanks, Honey." The smell of salmon croquettes hit his nose before he made his way over the threshold.

"Sorry 'bout the smell," Honey said sheepishly. "I was on my way to open the door to air it out in here. We had sal-mon croquettes for dinner. They're delicious, but Lord, they smell up the house."

Hank bit the inside of his lip to keep from laughing at Honey's pronunciation of salmon.

Wardell extended his hand. "Honey makes the best sal-mon croquettes in three counties."

"How are you feeling these days, Wardell?"

"Right as rain, Hank. Right as rain. Isn't that right, Honey?" He winked at the older woman and heat shot between the two of them like a laser beam.

Honey chuckled. "That's right, Wardell." The pink tint to the lady's face made Hank shuffle his feet in place. He wasn't sure when he'd been more uncomfortable.

"So, what brings you by?" Wardell asked.

What? Hadn't Charlie told them they were going out? Dual slices of pain and annoyance cut through him. "Charlie and I have a date."

Their reaction would've been hilarious if he hadn't been so irritated. They looked at him, then toward the stairs and back to him.

"Oh, well isn't that nice." Honey's unsure tone was like kindling on the spark of anger inside him.

"It's not a date." The cagey woman he was in love with sauntered down the staircase.

"Don't you look pretty, Charlie." Honey's words were high and a little hysterical, probably due to the tension shoving against the air in the room.

"Thanks, Honey." Charlie made her way to her grandfather and kissed him on the head. "I'm going out for a bit. Will you be alright?" She glanced up at Hank and held his stare. "I shouldn't be long."

Wardell patted her hand resting on his chest. "Don't you worry about me. Honey's here to meet my needs."

Honey snorted.

Charlie shook her head. "Do we need to go over the list of things that are inappropriate for the two of you to say in front of me again?"

Both senior citizens laughed full-on belly laughs. "You're just so easy to bait, Charlie, darlin'," Honey said.

She kissed the older woman's cheek. "Take care of him."

"You know I will."

Hank went to the screen door and opened it. "Shall we?" The statement came out sharper than a Bowie knife.

If she walked any slower, she'd have been going backward. This night wasn't starting the way he'd hoped it would. He'd hoped that by the end of the night they'd have their relationship sorted, but it was obvious that she wasn't ready to forgive him yet. That was fine. She was his, and he could understand her reluctance to accept that, given everything that had happened. And he was prepared to take whatever shit she felt like she had to dole out to even the playing field. He deserved that.

But that baby she carried was his too, and he wouldn't take one ounce of shit when it came to his involvement in that child's life.

Chapter Forty-One

Charlie had considered running back upstairs when she saw the pissed-off look on Hank's face. She might've gone too far with the whole "this isn't a date" thing. But all afternoon she'd been trying to figure out how to draw the appropriate boundaries around their relationship. A relationship that now would last forever due to Pod.

He followed her to her side of the truck and opened her door.

His Hank smell hit her square in the heart. She ignored it. "Thank you." She may be drawing boundaries, but she still had the manners her grandmother had drilled into her head.

Without a word, he closed the door. He made his way to the driver's side of the vehicle, climbed in, and turned the key. They were two blocks away from the house before he spoke. "I'm sorry."

Well, that wasn't what she thought he'd say. With as upset as he seemed, she thought he'd demand an explanation. "For what?"

His thick fingers rubbed across his mouth. "For putting you in a position where you thought you couldn't trust me. Where you'd have to build barriers to keep me out." He glanced at her. "I know I've done that to you, but I want more than anything for you to let me in."

Wow. Her hands shook, and she fiddled with the strap of her purse. She had no idea what to say to that. "Um..."

His chuckle sounded like dry autumn leaves being crunched underfoot. "You don't have to say anything, just know that I'm not giving up, Charlie."

"Hank—"

"Charlie." The sly smile he gave her slipped under her clothes and caressed every sensitive place on her body in the most intimate way.

"You have to..." Her voice ran and hid when she saw where they were. The little piece of land that his family owned just outside town. Butterflies with velvet wings flew back and forth in her belly. This had been their place, where they'd hide from the world all those years ago. Oh, he was playing hardball.

"What were you saying?"

She didn't buy his innocent routine for one minute. "You brought me here on purpose. I said we could talk about Pod, not stroll down memory lane." He was the devil for bringing her here. This was their place. Where they'd dreamed, schemed, and planned for a future that would never happen. Her heart broke for both of those stupid, lovesick kids that had no idea about how hard life really was, or how each of them would eventually hurt the other.

Not anymore. She was a woman with eyes wide open and a baby to consider. Her arms went involuntarily around her womb. A baby. She'd never allowed herself to think of Pod as a baby. It made it too real, too terrifying, too big of a gift for her to wrap her head around. Her heart melted and rearranged into a Pod-shaped form. Even more reason to protect herself from the man sitting next to her.

He didn't want just her. He wanted her because of Pod. And that didn't count. She'd lived too long with people pretending to love her, when what they really wanted was what they could get from her. Not anymore.

"Here." He handed her a black and white polka dot gift bag with yellow tissue paper sticking out of the top.

Her first reaction was to jerk back from the package like it was filled with venomous snakes. "What's this?"

This time his chuckle sounded like hot fudge being drizzled over her nipple.

What. The. Hell.

"Open it."

The crinkle of the tissue paper filled the cab of the truck. She fished out an antique doorknob complete with the plate and a keyhole. "What is this?"

"It's a doorknob."

"I know it's a doorknob, Hank. But why are you giving it to me?"

He reached in his shirt pocket and pulled out a skeleton key with a white bow tied to the end. "I'm hoping this key will open that door that you say is locked." He ran his knuckles down her cheek. "Let me in, Charlie." He watched her like she was a flight risk fugitive. "Tell me what you're thinking."

He'd turned the truck off, but left the radio on. Kenny Chesney sang about some woman and tequila, while every word that would've come out lined up in her throat, ready to be said as soon as her head caught up. She turned to him and decided to be as honest as was possible. Maybe it would prevent any more situations like this.

"I think that you're a dirty rotten manipulator to bring me here. I've spent the last eight years being managed and manipulated, and I won't involve myself in relationships like that anymore."

It broke her heart when his hopeful grin slid from his face. "I swear, that's not what I'm trying to do."

She arched her brow.

He gazed out the front window. "Maybe I was." His eyes found hers again. "But I just wanted you to remember the things we promised each other when we were here." He took her cold hand and rubbed it between his. "Charlie, I've made a lot of mistakes in my life, but the biggest one I've ever made was letting you leave that hotel room in Austin without me. I was a fool...am a fool. But I want you. I want this baby. I want us all to be together. I just want to take care of you like I promised."

The tan line around his fourth finger where his wedding band had been until six weeks ago glowed in the light from the radio. "Because it's the right thing?" She tried to keep her tone as even as possible.

"Yes, that, but there are so many other reasons too." His warm breath fanned across her skin.

Ice crystalized up her spine, and she extracted her hand from his hold. She met his confused stare. "I don't need anyone to take care of me, Hank, and I sure as hell don't need someone taking me on because it's the right thing to do. I want to be the thing you do even though you know it's not the right thing because your heart won't let you do anything else. I deserve that, and I won't settle for anything less than that." She hadn't really known what she wanted until the words started coming, but now that she'd said it, nothing else mattered.

"That is how I feel about you, about us. I swear—"

"Hank, there is no us. This baby is healthy, I'm due in June, and anything else you want to know about him or her, I'm happy to talk to you about it. But there is no us." She shoved the gift bag with the doorknob in it at him. "The door is locked." She swallowed down the bawling tears that wanted to escape. She'd save them for later when she was alone in her room. "Now, could you please take me home?"

"Charlie—"

The ring of his phone cut off anything else he might say. He fished the device from his pocket. "This is Hank."

"Hank! Thank God!"

She could hear Hailey yelling on the other end of the line.

"Hailey, what's wrong?" Hank went into full cop mode and put Hailey on speaker while he started the car.

"It's Lottie! There's been an accident. They've taken her to the hospital." Her voice stuttered on a shaky breath. "Hank, they had to Care Flight her to Austin."

"Where are you?"

"Roxanne is driving me to the hospital." The tears made it hard to understand her. "They wouldn't let me ride in the helicopter with her."

"Have you called Derek?" Hank was doing a three-point turn out of the drive and onto the highway.

"I tried, but he didn't answer. I left a message for him to call me." Her nose was stuffy, making her sound younger than she was. "Will you call Charlie?"

"I'm here Hailey. We're together." She laid her hand on Hank's arm. "We're on our way."

Chapter Forty-Two

Charlie chased Hank through the emergency room doors. The warm air of the lobby did little to thaw the icy dread flushing through her veins. Lottie just had to be okay. She just had to be.

Hank rushed the reception desk with her right behind him. "Can you tell me where Lottie Odom is?"

"Are you family?"

"Yes." Charlie placed her hand on his arm. "This is Lottie's uncle."

"And you are?" the man behind the desk asked.

Hank slid his arm around her shoulder. "Her aunt."

She leaned into him, and his big body offered the comfort that her tattered nerves craved. Considering the conversation they'd just had, she shouldn't take comfort from him, but there was little she could do to stop herself.

"Alright, give me a minute," the receptionist said.

When he disappeared through a door that presumably led to the main ER, Charlie's heart seized. "Why wouldn't they tell us? What if—"

"No." A muscle spasmed in Hank's jaw, and he never took his tortured eyes from the door.

She bit her lip and nodded. For him, she'd hold back the tears that begged to fall freely. "Okay."

"Hank!" Hailey burst through a set of double doors to their right. Tear tracks covered her pale face. She ran into Hank's arms and fell completely apart.

Roxanne followed Hailey out the doors. Her gentle hand went to her sister-in-law's back. "Shhhh, Hailey. It's gonna be alright." Roxanne glanced up at Hank. "She's been like this since I picked her up from the bar," she said on a sob.

Hank wrapped his other arm around Roxanne and held Hailey tighter.

Charlie was on the outside looking in, and was ashamed of the jealous spike piercing her chest observing these three. They had each other, and they all knew that beyond a shadow of a doubt. "I'm going to..." She hitched her thumb over her shoulder toward the waiting room.

"Charlie, oh Charlie." Hailey disentangled herself from Hank and fell into Charlie's arms.

"What happened?" The jagged edge of Hank's question sliced through the air.

Roxanne looked around. "Here, let's sit over here."

"Do you need to get back to Lottie, Hailey?" Hank led them to the empty section of the waiting room.

Hailey only shook her head against Charlie's chest.

"They've taken her back for a CT scan. They wouldn't let Hailey go with her." Roxanne mopped her eyes with a tissue.

Charlie smoothed her best friend's hair and rocked them back and forth. "Can you tell us what happened, Hay?"

Hailey didn't lift her head but motioned for her sister-in-law. "Roxy?"

"I'm here. I'll tell them." She blew her nose and cleared her throat. "Lottie was playing with the neighborhood kids. Tammy, her babysitter, was there along with a couple of the other children's moms. The kids were racing, and according to Tammy and confirmed by the other moms, Lottie said she could beat Sam Fox, even running backward." She chuckled and wiped her nose. "You know how competitive she is.

Anyway, Lottie's feet got tripped up, she fell, and hit the back of her head."

A keening noise came from Hailey. She pulled away from Charlie, grabbed her stomach, and bent forward. The sound was so haunting that gooseflesh broke out on Charlie's skin.

"She was unconscious until she got here, and now she...she can't see, Hank."

Every molecule of air disappeared from the space they occupied. She couldn't have heard Roxanne correctly. By Hank's stark expression, he was feeling the same way.

Hailey grabbed his hand. "My baby's blind, Hank." Body-wracking sobs rolled through her.

"Hailey, don't do this to yourself," Roxanne coaxed. "The doctors said it could be temporary. That's why they've taken her back for a CT." She wiped her face on her shoulder and glanced at them. "The doctor said that she could just have some bruising and that's pushing against Lottie's optic nerve."

"Oh, my Lord." Charlie took Hank's hand. "When will they know?"

The tender kiss Roxanne pressed to Hailey's head was full of devotion. "Pretty soon. In fact, she'll be back in her room shortly. I'll take Hailey back, unless one of you want to go back with her—there can only be two people at a time."

Hank shook his head. It killed Charlie to see tears threatening to spill from his red-rimmed eyes. "I'm..." He swallowed several times. "Give me a minute to catch up. I'll come back when she gets settled back in the room." His fingers tunneled through his hair. "Shit. Mom?"

Roxanne patted his arm. "She knows. She has the twins, and I called her just before y'all got here."

He nodded. "Okay, good."

Roxanne led her sister-in-law to the double doors, but Hailey stopped and looked at Hank. "Can you try to get in touch with Derek? His phone is either off, or he's avoiding my calls. I texted him, but I haven't told him what happened." She wiped her hair from her face. "I didn't want him to hear it in a text."

"I'm on it." The smile he gave Hailey wobbled at the edges but held. "I'll take care of it."

As soon as Hailey was through the doors, Hank headed for the exit without a word.

"Hank." Charlie raced after him.

She found him pacing the sidewalk. After several steps, he placed his hands on his knees and panted through his mouth.

"Hank." His tormented body was a magnet for her hand. She rubbed his back and let him pull himself together.

He stood with his hands on his head. Still he said nothing, just continued dragging air in and out of his lungs.

No matter what was going on between the two of them, this man was a steady and fierce protector, so not being able to do anything for Lottie or Hailey must be killing him. "Can I do anything?"

His arms came down around her. "You're doing it."

As naturally as breathing, her arms encircled his waist. "Good."

She'd worry about the implications of all of this closeness tomorrow, but today they needed each other.

Chapter Forty-Three

Hank's heart thrummed against his ribcage and refused to find a regular rhythm. He glanced around the ER waiting room. Actually, there was nothing regular about this whole evening. Charlie had made him come back inside the hospital, where she'd shoved a cup of coffee with cream and sugar into his hands and forced him to drink it. It'd been horrible, but he did feel somewhat better.

Now his blonde nursemaid was curled in the chair next to him. He glanced at the empty Styrofoam cup and then to her. "How did you know the coffee trick?"

"On an episode of *Charlie Takes the Town*, Charlie had to triage a group of senior citizen women after the police officer she scheduled to speak at their luncheon group about self-defense turned out to be a stripper. They were all in shock, and the staff nurse at the senior home said coffee with cream and sugar would help."

He snorted. "How would that even happen?"

A small smile pushed at the corners of her lips. "Charlie's mischievous best friend gave her the stripper's number. Of course, good, wholesome, Charlie had no idea." Big blue eyes went round as saucers, and her delicate hand went to her chest. "You didn't watch my show?"

Her mock indignation made him chuckle. "Not if I could help it. No offense."

"None taken. I don't blame you. Sometimes it was hard for me to watch. Despite my best efforts, the writing never really improved."

No, he hadn't watched her show, but not for the reasons that she thought. It had nothing to do with the quality of the writing or acting, and everything to do with the beauty currently picking at her nail polish in the chair next to him. Even frazzled and scared, she still glowed. No wonder she'd been the darling of the Carousel Network. He smoothed his thumb over his phone screen. "Do you miss it?"

"Not one little bit." Her sober eyes confirmed the truth.

"Really? There sure seem to be a lot of perks with that lifestyle." He wouldn't have wanted them, but he could see how appealing they would be.

She uncurled her feet from the chair and shrugged. "For every perk, there's an equal or worse drawback."

"Like what?" Talking to her had regulated his jacked-up heart rate, and he just wanted to hear her voice.

The sigh she released clearly said that she was only talking to keep his mind occupied. "There's no privacy at all."

"I can see that, given the paparazzi we had swarming around town."

"It's more than that though. There wasn't one moment of the day that was just mine. There were always people around...until there weren't. I've had my manager and publicist hold a meeting with me from the other side of the bathroom door while I had a stomach virus. There are no secrets. Someone knows where you are at all times, they know what size you are and if you ate a doughnut or not. There's someone to keep track of what's happening to you medically. Your social life is up for public consumption. Nothing is yours, not even your most private moments."

"I had no—"

"And don't get me started on the fans. Don't get me wrong, most of them were great and the best part of the job, but some were just plain scary."

It was like once the damn broke, she couldn't stop talking.

"I had a mom trying to get me to sign an autograph while I was in a bathroom stall. She waved the paper and the pen under the wall. When I asked her to give me a minute, she went into the next stall and stood on the toilet so she could look over the top. And you can't be rude and tell them to fuck off because the media is always one step behind you. So you smile and sign the autograph."

"Shit."

"That was nothing compared to the man who showed up on my front porch with a stack of DVDs he wanted signed. He was at my house. Thankfully, after the bathroom incident, the studio assigned me full-time security or I have no idea what the guy might've done." She grabbed a hair tie from her pocket and pulled her hair back. "I know I sound like an ungrateful jerk. Poor little famous girl..."

His blood pressure had started to rise again when she talked about some asshole showing up at her door. The things she described sounded horrible. "I don't think you're a jerk at all. It doesn't sound like a life I'd want, and certainly not one a kid should have. What about your mom or your manager, the people who were supposed to protect you from all of that? What did they do?"

She laughed, but the bitterness of it could've cut glass. "It's not about protection, Hank. It's about creating a commodity. Something they can sell to the public. Nobody wants the real you. They want who they create. You aren't real, nothing is real, including the fame." She covered her face with her hands. "Ugh. You don't want to hear about my sad Hollywood story."

"Sure I do." He squeezed her knee. "I'm sorry that happened to you."

"It wasn't all bad. I liked that I had enough clout to do some good. I helped raise a lot of money for the Juvenile Diabetes Association with my hairdresser whose niece had the disease, and sometimes I got to visit kids in the hospital. I enjoyed those things." She picked up a tattered magazine and flipped through it. "It's just that that stuff didn't outweigh the other." The tabloid slapped the table when she dropped it.

He didn't know why she was opening up to him this way, but he didn't want her to stop. "Yeah, but I bet the money's nice."

"What money?"

"Oh, shit. I forgot, sorry."

"It's fine. But no, the money wasn't nice. I never really got to enjoy it, and I lost my mother over it." She threw her head back and made a frustrated sound. "I swear to you, Hank, Pod will not have a mother that sells him or her out to the highest bidder."

"Is that how you feel?"

Her beautiful blue eyes landed on his face, and she was as serious as he'd ever seen her. "Yes."

He took her hand. She might rip it off, but he needed to offer her comfort the way she'd offered him comfort. "I'm so sorry, Charlie. Wait...Pod?"

The pink tint on her cheeks made her even more beautiful. "It's what I've been calling the baby. 'Cause it was no bigger than a pea pod when it was little."

He wished he'd been there with her in the beginning. Anger tried to flicker to life, but he squashed it down. He hadn't been there because of his own ignorant self, and nothing else. "I like it. Pod it is."

"Well, just until we find out if it's a boy or a girl. Then we'll have to come up with a name." Her hand covered the place his child grew. The enormity of the happiness and responsibility nearly floored him. How was it possible to love a person you'd never met? But that was the way of it. His heart belonged to the child growing inside the womb of the woman that owned him.

His phone rang, and Derek's name popped up onto the screen. "This is Hank."

"Hank, what the hell is going on? I have multiple messages from Hailey to call, but when I did, she didn't answer."

"Lottie's been in an accident."

"Is she alright?"

Hank tunneled his fingers through his hair. "No."

"No? What does that mean?"

At least his brother seemed to be concerned. "She fell and hit her head. It knocked her out, she regained consciousness, thank God, but right now she..."

"She what?"

"She can't see, Derek."

There was dead silence on the phone.

"Derek?"

"Yeah, I'm here. What do the doctors say?"

He transferred the phone to his other hand. "They just did a CT scan, and they'll let us know if she has any bleeding or if there's just swelling that is pressing on the optic nerve. According to Roxy, there's a good chance that the blindness could only be temporary."

"Fuck." Derek breathed out.

"I know—"

"What shit timing. I'm in Aruba with Ariel. This call is costing me a fortune."

Hank held the phone away from his ear. Surely he'd misunderstood his brother. "So this is an inconvenience?"

"Hell, yeah, it's inconvenient. I mean, we just got here."

"Are you fucking kidding me right now?" Hank tried to keep his voice down, but it was a struggle. "I tell you that your daughter is blind because of a head injury and all you can worry about is how it screws with your schedule. You're unbelievable."

"Fuck you!" Derek made no effort to keep the volume under control. "You have no idea what I'm dealing with."

"Oh, yeah, your life is hard. How can you not care about your daughter?"

"I care, asshole. I just can't be there. Do you know how hard that is for me?"

The guy on the other end of the phone couldn't possibly be related to him. He noticed several people glancing their way, so he lowered his head and spoke through gritted teeth. "You really are a piece of work. You've taken this terrible thing that's happened to your daughter and made it about you. I can't deal with you anymore, and Hailey doesn't need your shit either. If you want any more information, then talk to Mom."

"Fine. I don't want to talk to you self-righteous people anyway."

Hank hung up. He couldn't take one more minute of Derek's bullshit. Maybe it was wrong for him to judge Derek, but he didn't care. What kind of father would abandon his kid when they were so vulnerable?

Would he be the same kind of father? Dread gripped him by the balls. He'd never be able to live with himself if he ended up like the other men in his family. He would not.

"Hank?"

Shit, he'd forgotten about Charlie. She'd witnessed the whole fiasco with his brother. "Yeah?"

"Is there anything I can do?" She kept her hands to herself, probably because he seemed on the edge of exploding.

He had to make her understand that he wasn't going to be like the other men in his family when it came to their child. He grabbed her hand and looked directly into her eyes. "Charlie, I swear that I will never be like my brothers or my father when it comes to this child. I swear it."

She drew back with a confused frown. "Hank, I never... If you think that's why I didn't tell you, then you're wrong."

His head was shaking before she finished her sentence. "I know why you didn't tell me. I don't like it, but I understand."

Her eyes were on their joined hands, and she nodded. "Okay. I don't know what Derek said, but I can tell you that you've never been like him in any way. With all the uncertainty of this baby and our situation, you have to know that the only peace I've had is that you would be this Pod's father because I knew you'd never let it down."

Relief spread through him like ice over a raging fire. The ring of truth relaxed his muscles, and he squeezed her hand. She believed he would be good for this baby. It was a start. Now he just had to convince the baby's mama that he'd be good for her too.

Chapter Forty-Four

Hank drove through the empty streets of Zachsville at one in the morning. The only people out were his deputies or errant teenagers. Hailey had sent him, Charlie, and Roxanne home after Lottie regained her vision, and the doctors came back and said there was no bleeding, thank God. She did have a concussion, though, so they wanted to keep her overnight for observation.

He hadn't bothered calling his brother. A text was all that asshole got from him. His clipped reply indicated he felt the same way about Hank. Whatever. He was tired of trying to redeem his idiot brothers. He had his own redemption to worry about.

Charlie hadn't said two words since they left the hospital. The minute that Roxanne had told them about Lottie, and they'd gotten to see her, the woman next to him retreated behind the guarded wall she'd erected between them.

He couldn't take one more minute of silence. "What a night, huh?"

"Yeah." She gave him a watered-down version of her famous smile.

"Scary to think how something as simple as two kids running could turn into that."

She rubbed her tired eyes. "Yes."

"What happened, Charlie?"

"What are you talking about?" The words were said to the passenger side window.

This was bullshit. "You're a million miles away, but in the hospital, it was like it used to be. I want to know what changed."

A big huffing breath left her small body. "Hank, we were in the middle of a crisis. You were in pain, and so was I. I was only being a decent human being by offering comfort. Don't read any more into it than that."

The woman knew exactly how to filet him, but it was obvious that she'd dug her heels in on this, and for right now he wasn't going to change her mind. Time for a different tactic. "Fine. When's your next doctor's appointment?"

"Next week, why?"

He flipped on his blinker. "Because I want to go with you. I want to make sure my baby is healthy. Text me the date and time, and I'll be sure to be available."

That got her attention. She was passive no more. "There's no need for that, Hank. I'm perfectly capable of getting myself to the doctor and absorbing the information I need."

He shrugged. "I didn't say you weren't. I just want to go with you." He glanced at her. "You owe me."

Oh, she didn't like that, if the fire in her glare and the color creeping into her cheeks were any indication.

He only cocked a brow. She could argue all she wanted, but she knew he was right.

"Fine." She yanked out her phone and started to text, then stopped. "I don't have your number."

"Well, that's embarrassing, isn't it? Here we have a baby together and we haven't exchanged phone numbers." He rattled off his number, and then his phone buzzed in his pocket, indicating a text. "Thank you."

They pulled into Wardell's driveway, and he parked the car.

"There's no need for you to walk me to the door, Hank." She gathered her purse from the floor. "It's late, and I'm sure you need to get home."

Something in her demeanor told him not to argue with her.

"Alright." She opened the door, but just before she exited, he stopped her. "Don't forget your gift." He handed her the decorative bag with the antique door knob and key in it.

She took it with two fingers like it was diseased. The tight-lipped grin she gave him cut him as deep as her statement earlier. The hopefulness he'd experienced in the hospital at her sweetness sifted through his fingers. He was losing her, and he had no idea how to get her back.

Chapter Forty-Five

✿

With a notepad and pencil, Charlie wandered the building where The Emporium would be located. She and Scarlett were making notes before she talked to the contractor. The space was so perfect that the only things she'd have to add were some built-in shelves.

Scarlett moved around the store opening the blinds. "What are you doing Sunday afternoon, Charlie?" Light streamed in and illuminated the dust floating and dancing on the air.

Charlie measured a space next to the counter. "Nothing, why?"

"We're having a party for Jack and Luanne to celebrate their marriage." She must've made a face because Scarlett hurried to say, "Just a few couples and some friends will be there. It'll be fun. Please say you'll come."

This was part of being in a community and having friends. Remember those? "I'd love to come. What can I bring?"

"Only yourself. We're throwing this party on a rock star budget. Of course, you're probably used to that."

She shrugged noncommittally. Her partying life in Hollywood had been pretty much nonexistent due to the death grip her management team and Carousel always had on her. "I think a sink would be good right here, don't you?"

"A sink?" Scarlett asked.

"Yes, I'd love to have a place where people can try some of the exfoliating soaps." She gnawed her lower lip. "Do you think it'll be very expensive to add the plumbing?"

Scarlett shrugged. "I don't know. You should get Marty the plumber over here to give you a bid. I would think if it was situated close to the bathroom, then it shouldn't be too bad."

"Good idea. What's Marty's last name?"

Her friend opened her mouth then closed it. "You know, I have no idea. Everyone's just called him Marty the plumber for as long as I've known him."

Charlie laughed. "You've got to love a small town." She scribbled Marty's name on her pad. "Okay, Marty the plumber it is."

"Speaking of small towns, someone said they saw you and Hank at the hospital the other night."

Oh, for the love...

She wouldn't meet Scarlett's curious stare. "Yes, Lottie had an accident."

"I heard. How is she?" Then sincerity in Scarlett's voice made her less irritated about the Hank thing.

"She's got a pretty bad headache, and she can't go to school for a week, but she should be fine."

Scarlett smoothed her maternity shirt over her baby bump. "That's a relief. Honey and I are taking dinner to Hailey tomorrow night."

Charlie rubbed her lower back. "I'm sure she'll appreciate it."

"Now, let's talk about you and Hank." Scarlett flashed her an innocent smile.

Charlie walked behind the counter just to put some distance between her and the question. "Not much to tell. We aren't a couple." She looked up from her list sheepishly. "But he is Pod's father."

"Shut up!" Scarlett squealed.

A snort escaped Charlie's throat. "It's true."

"How? I know Hank, and there's no way he'd cheat on Karen."

Charlie knew that too and had forgiven him for the bad timing. "They were on a break." She made quotes with her fingers.

"So it happened before they got back together?"

She gave up any pretense of working on her list. "Yes. Just before. Like the night before."

Scarlett's hand went to her mouth. "Oh, no."

"Yep." The mechanical pencil in her hand became very interesting. She twisted the end back and forth. "I saw a text from Karen the next morning stating she was in the lobby waiting for him."

"That must've been such a shock, Charlie. I have no idea what I would've done. Then you found out you were pregnant..."

Charlie glanced up to see Scarlett just staring at her. "What?"

The redheaded beauty shook her head. "You're just so brave."

She laughed. "What? You've got it all wrong, Scarlett. I'm scared all the time. Can I live this life? Can I raise a child? How will I support myself? I'm panicked almost every minute of every day."

"You sure don't show it. From where I'm sitting you're handling your life just right." Scarlett sweet smile lit up the room. "So, what about Hank?"

The knotted muscles in her neck bunched tighter at the question. "Hank will be a great dad."

Her new friend's hands went to her hips. You could tell she was used to not taking any crap. That probably came from living with a rock star. "Let me be more specific. What about you and Hank?"

Her anguish over Hank's behavior tugged on her heart. She quickly fortified the wall that would protect that traitorous organ. She couldn't afford to feel sorry for him, or she would let him in, and then she'd never want him to leave. But what if he left her? What if he broke her? How would she parent this child with only half a heart? Besides, if there were no Pod, then he wouldn't be pursuing her at all.

Another brick, a little more protection.

"There isn't going to be any me and Hank. I couldn't live through him hurting me again." She played with the bracelets on her wrist. "Maybe that makes me weak, but I don't care."

Scarlett's forehead crinkled. "But who says he'd hurt you again? He's free now. There'd be no reason for him to leave you."

Before she could think too much about it, there was a knock on the door. A good-looking teenager with a Houston Rockets t-shirt stood holding a suspiciously familiar gift bag. Scarlett turned to answer the door. Charlie grabbed her wrist. "Don't answer it."

"Why not? That's Brody, he lives at Dad and Honey's house with his mom, Joyce." She examined the death grip Charlie had on her. "He's harmless. I promise."

"No, it's just... I know what he has, and I don't want it. It's from Hank," she hissed.

The traitor's eyes got big as saucers. "Ooooh, a present from Hank." She shook Charlie off and headed for the door. "Hi, Brody, come in."

"Hey, Scarlett." The boy wasn't exactly a boy, but not quite a man either. He was tall with broad shoulders, and black wavy hair with soulful eyes the color of her grandmother's sweet tea. "Um, Charlie?"

"Yeah, that's me." When he flinched at her tone, she changed it. "I'm sorry. It's not you. It's the thing in the bag." She jerked her chin at his offering.

"Oh, well..." Unsure eyes turned to Scarlett then back to Charlie. "I was at the Sheriff's office delivering BBQ from Piggy's, and Sheriff Odom asked if I'd bring this to you." He held it out like it might explode, no doubt because of her reaction to it.

"Give the kid a break, Charlie." Scarlett threw her arm around Brody's waist. "He's just doing what he was asked to do." Out of the corner of her mouth, she said to Brody, "Don't mind her, she's actually very nice."

His nervous laugh made it clear that he didn't know if she was nice or not, but that she was definitely crazy. "Well, I better be going. I need to get back to Piggy's before the lunch rush hits. Y'all have a great day." The sound of his boots clipping on the hardwood floors followed him out the door.

"Charlie, you scared him to death."

Her shoulders slumped. "I know. I'm sorry. I'll make it up to him. It's just..." She motioned at the bag.

"You might as well open it and get it over with." Scarlett was practically vibrating with anticipation.

The trembling in her fingers was ridiculous. She knew that, but it turned out that damn wall she'd built around her heart wasn't as strong as she'd hoped. It shuddered and swayed when she pulled out a skeleton key with a red bow wrapped around it.

"An old key?" The confusion in her meddling friend's tone made her chuckle.

The silk ribbon slipped through her fingers as she played with it. "I told him the door to a relationship between us was locked. He took me out and gave me a key the other night."

"And now he's given you another one. That's so romantic," Scarlett said with a sigh.

A smile snuck onto Charlie's face, unbidden. She quickly wiped it away, but she couldn't do anything about the part of her that agreed with Scarlett, except deny it. "He's only doing it because I'm pregnant." It wasn't romantic. It was manipulative. He was trying to wear her down to clear his conscience. But she wasn't anyone's absolution. And she wouldn't be with a man who only wanted her for what he could get from her.

"Why do you say that?"

"Because he didn't want one thing to do with me until he found out I was pregnant."

"Are you—"

"Let's finish." She dropped the key back in the bag and picked up her pad and pencil. "We both have places to be." Scarlett needed to get back to her family, and she needed to go someplace and fall apart.

Stupid keys.

Chapter Forty-Six

The sweat coating Hank's palms made his hand slip from the top of the steering wheel. He tried to wipe them on his pants leg discreetly, but he noticed Charlie watching him. She, on the other hand, appeared cool as a cucumber. Of course, she'd had longer to get used to the whole baby thing than him.

Once again, it'd been a silent ride from Zachsville to Charlie's doctor in Austin. Sadness and a little desperation hung around his neck. The woman next to him wasn't that lovestruck girl he'd been able to charm and coerce into doing pretty much anything he'd wanted her to do. This fiery lady stood up for herself, had given up everything to live the life she wanted for her child. She didn't need him. And it appeared she didn't want him either.

Maybe he should leave her alone, and just concentrate on his relationship with the baby. But he didn't think that was possible. He'd tried to for six weeks and just couldn't. "So you like your doctor?"

He adored that small, secret smile she used when she really loved something. "Yes. She's fantastic and discreet. I'm so lucky Scarlett told me about her."

He pulled into a parking spot in front of the building that was by the hospital. That made him feel better. "Good. I just want you to be comfortable."

The genuine smile turned into something not so authentic. She nodded and exited the truck before he could get out of the vehicle.

Damn it, what had he said now? It seemed like everything he did was wrong with her. It didn't used to be that way. He missed their easy rapport. Of course, that had been years ago. She may be right. They might not be compatible anymore. Flashes of her willing body crashed into his mind, and he knew that wasn't the case. That night had filled the missing part of his life. The moments before Karen had shown up had been the happiest he'd had since Charlie left town.

"This is it." She pointed to a door that looked like it was the back door of the office. It was unmarked and blended into the wall. She knocked, and it opened, revealing a pretty middle-aged woman with happy eyes.

"Charlie. Good to see you." She caught sight of Hank, and her smile grew wider. She looked him up and down. "You brought the law?"

"I tried to run, but he insisted on coming along. Hank Odom. This is Beth. She's Dr. Shelton's nurse. Beth, Hank's Pod's father." It was all said with zero inflection. She really could care less that he was here.

"Nice to meet you, Hank." If Beth noticed Charlie's apathy, she didn't let on. The nurse pushed a button on a scale. "You know the drill, Charlie."

"Unfortunately, I do." She started to step onto the scale then turned to him. "Do you mind turning around?"

"Oh, sure." He stuck his hands in his pocket and rotated his body away from her. It was stupid to be irritated at her request. What woman wanted to broadcast her weight, but it felt like one more way she was keeping him out of her life.

"You can step off now. Have a seat and I'll get your blood pressure." She led them to an examination room. "Here we go. Dr. Shelton will be here in a few minutes," she said as she shut the door, leaving them alone.

He glanced around the room, and the bottom dropped out of his stomach when he saw a cross-section illustration of a pregnant woman with a baby in her womb. The infant looked full term, and its head was fully engaged in the mother's pelvis. All of a sudden shit got real. His hand traced over the picture, and he stared in awe.

"It's crazy isn't it?" Charlie sat on an exam table with her ankles crossed.

He glanced over his shoulder and couldn't contain his grin. "Yeah. Can you believe you're going to get this big?"

"Ha! You really know how to sweet talk a girl. You might want to take some lessons from Jack on that."

"Oh, wow, sorry. You're right, that wasn't very comforting, but still..." He pointed back to the photo on the wall.

He was saved from the scathing retort that he could see was on her lips when Dr. Shelton came into the room. The woman was breathtaking. If he didn't belong to Charlie, body and soul, then she would've definitely turned his head.

"How is everyone?" Dr. Shelton asked.

Charlie's hand went to her belly. "We're just fine."

"Excellent. And who do we have here?" She extended her hand. "Bree Shelton. I'm the doctor."

"Hank Odom. I'm the father."

White teeth flashed in her ebony face and her eyes crinkled in the corners. She glanced at Charlie and hitched her finger at Hank. "I love it when they play along."

The sullen woman he'd just spent the last hour with laughed like it was the funniest thing she'd ever heard.

"Okay, let's take a look at things. She picked up the tablet she'd brought in with her. "Mmmmm."

"What? Is something wrong with her?" He couldn't control the panic in his voice.

Dr. Shelton grinned up at him. "Everything is fine." She turned her attention to Charlie. "Except I would like to see you gain a little more weight. Don't go crazy, but you need more calories."

"I knew you were going to say that. I just haven't had much of an appetite. I tend to not eat when I'm stressed."

"You've been stressed?" Dr. Shelton asked.

Charlie glanced nervously at him. "Um...well, a little."

Well, shit, now he was causing her not to eat. The last thing he wanted was to be another source of anxiety in her life.

"I suggest lots of foot rubs and warm baths." The doctor made a note on the tablet then swiped her finger. "Blood pressure looks great."

"That's good, right?" He couldn't stop the question from shooting out of his mouth.

Charlie cut him a look, and he held up his hands. "Sorry, carry on."

Dr. Shelton laughed and took Charlie by the hand. "Alright, lay back, Mama, and let's take a look at this baby."

"What does that mean?" That didn't seem right to his nervous brain.

"I'm going to do a sonogram."

"Oh, yeah. Okay."

She smeared some stuff on Charlie's belly. He was in awe because he'd never seen the place where his child lived. The doctor took a plastic thing and rubbed it over Charlie's stomach. All he could make out was a bunch of static. Slowly things came into focus, and he nearly hit the floor. "Is that it?"

The wand moved around and around, and she clicked some buttons on the machine. "It sure is. Say hello to your daughter, Mr. Odom."

And then he hit the floor.

Chapter Forty-Seven

Charlie loved performing. She no longer wanted to do it for a living, but the excitement of the crowd, the freedom of movement in the rhythm of the songs, it all spoke to her. And tonight was no exception. The couples at Boon's danced, and with each step fed her more and more energy. The band was spot on, and she hit every note exactly right. Pod had even gotten into the act, flipping and turning at every up-tempo song.

The night couldn't be better, except for the lawman sitting off to her right. She tried to ignore him, but the intensity of his stare attached to her like a laser beam. Why was he here? Didn't he have a job to do?

Don't lie to yourself, Charlie. You like that he's here.

It was true. Especially after his adorable reaction to finding out he was going to be the father of a girl. A girl. A thrill helped her hit a particularly high note. She couldn't wait to hold her little girl and teach her that she was enough just as she was. The picture of Hank loving on a daughter made her voice crack. It was such a perfect image. Damn it, she just wished she could trust that he wanted her and only her, and that his pursuit had nothing to do with this little girl they'd made.

"Thank you, guys. You've been awesome! The band and I are going to take a break, and we'll be back in thirty minutes." Steve, the drummer, helped her down the steps of the stage. "Thanks."

"No problem, Charlie. You're killin' it tonight."

His goofy grin was one she'd seen before. She had no desire to lead him on or hurt his feelings, so she played it as neutral as possible. "Thanks, Steve. You guys are awesome too. I see someone I need to talk to. Excuse me."

She made her way to Thomas Chang.

He motioned to the empty chair at his table. "Sit, Miss Charlie. Can I get your autograph?"

With a snort, she took her seat. "Yeah, you'll be getting my autograph plenty on all the checks I'll be writing you and Raul."

He raised his beer in a toast. "And we appreciate it." He tipped the beer toward the stage. "You sounded good up there. Why in the world are you going into the soaps and lotions business?"

A tiny stirring of interest in his mischievous teasing flickered and died the second she spied Hank glowering at the two of them. Not because of the glower, but because there'd never been another man who could hold a candle to Hank Odom, glowering or not. She shrugged. "It's just not what I want to do for a living anymore." Not to mention that it wasn't the life she wanted for her daughter. Warmth and love coursed through her and had become her new life's blood.

"I'm not going to pretend to understand that." He laughed. "I don't get how you can just walk away from fame and fortune."

She picked up a peanut and cracked it open. Since her second trimester, she'd been craving the things. Pregnancy was a bitch. "Fame and fortune aren't always what they're cut out to be, Thomas. Sometimes the price to your dignity is too high."

He really laughed then. "I think I'd take my chances."

A little wag of her finger and a lift of her brows. "Don't say I didn't warn you."

"Duly noted. Hey, can you meet with Raul and me on Wednesday? He'll be in town that day, and we wanted to get some delivery logistics nailed down." His thumb and forefinger pinched his lower lip.

Nope, still nothing.

"Sure, text me a time. During the day is best for me." She stood.

During her set, Pod had been tap dancing on her bladder, and she needed a bathroom break before the next set.

"Okay, yeah, for sure. Have a great night."

She squeezed his shoulder. "You too. Stay out of trouble."

He winked. "No promises, Miss Charlie."

That boy was trouble, and she was glad she wasn't attracted to him. She was sure he'd be the downfall of any woman who got involved with him.

Pod made her presence known by drop kicking Charlie's bladder. A quick glance at her phone told her she had time to pee before the next set. Thankfully, there wasn't a line in the bathroom. Business done, she washed her hands. The bathroom door opened and Hank walked in, a look of utter possession on his handsome face.

"Hank?"

His only response was to lock the door.

She knew she shouldn't approve of him locking them in a room together, but her traitorous body was like, *Woohoo!* Really? She and her hormones needed to have a serious talk. "Hailey's going to kill you for locking that door."

"Hailey's not here." He grinned. "I just needed to talk to you for a minute in private. It's so damn loud out there. You sound amazing, by the way."

She wrestled with her twitching lips and lost the fight. "Thank you."

He must've taken her grin as an invitation. In just a few steps he was in front of her. "I'm sorry again for what happened in the doctor's office yesterday. It was just..."

"Yeah, it was."

"So you're still happy?" He searched her face like the answers to the universe were there.

"About Pod being a girl?"

He nodded.

Happiness vibrated through her whole body. "Absolutely. This world needs another kickass woman."

He looped a stray hair behind her ear and cupped her head in his hand.

"Hank, the door…"

"Is locked, I know." He signaled the kiss from a mile away, giving her time to stop him. She didn't. It was wrong, and she knew it, but that thing inside him that called to her took over, and she was helpless against it.

Warm, soft lips brushed against hers. Once, twice, and the third time she opened for him. It seemed to be the only invitation he needed. He claimed her. His big hand went behind her head and tilted it to give him better access. Their tongues slid against each other in long, delicious strokes. Each pass and flick stole more and more of her self-control. She clung to him like his breath was the only air she'd ever need. This was what he did to her. Always had.

The door jiggled, and someone yelled, "What the hell?"

She shoved him back. It had very little effect, but he did break the kiss. The searching look he gave her was the most intimate thing she'd ever experienced. He reached into his pocket and withdrew another key. This one was just a regular key with a thin purple ribbon tied to it. Wordlessly, he took her hand and laid it in her palm then wrapped her fingers around it. He kissed the top of her fingers, still without a word.

Banging on the door drew his attention. He turned, unlocked the door, and slipped past the stunned woman on the other side. She stumbled back with a holy cow look on her face.

You and me both, sister.

Charlie unfurled her fingers and stared at the key.

You and me both.

Chapter Forty-Eight

Hank drove through Zachsville singing along to the country music station. He'd followed Thomas home after the man left the club. And like an overprotective chaperone, watched to make sure he entered his house. Frankly, it was hard to believe Thomas Chang was some international drug smuggler. He was more boring than Hank, who had no life at all unless you counted chasing Charlie Klein. And he'd made that a lifelong pursuit.

His brain called him all kinds of a fool, but his blood and bones knew the truth. She was it for him, and if he couldn't have her, then he wouldn't make the mistake of trying to replace her again.

That door is locked.

Fucking door. He was so sick of hearing that from her. There had to be a way to make her see that it was only her he loved. The baby was a beautiful bonus, but with or without it Charlie was the one he wanted.

He chuckled remembering that she'd played hard to get when they were teenagers. He'd chased her for months before she'd agreed to go out with him, and that had taken him shimmying up the live oak tree outside her house and inching across the rooftop to her window. He'd never forget the look of acceptance on her face when she'd lifted the glass pane. Like she'd just been waiting for him to prove to her that she was worth making the grand gesture.

That was it. She needed a grand gesture. Something to let her know that he was in love with her and only her. He hooked a U-turn and headed to Wardell's house. He parked down the street and made his way to the familiar tree. It had grown quite a bit in eight years, the branches thicker and denser. If she wanted him to prove how much he cared for her, then risking his life to scale this tree to her window should do the trick.

He jumped up and grabbed the lowest branch. With his abdominal muscles, he lifted his leg to loop a foot in the crook of the tree, so he could hoist himself up to sit. Several attempts later, he realized that cowboy boots were the wrong accessory to try and climb a tree.

Finally, he got himself into a sitting position and continued his ascent. As hard as he tried, he didn't remember this much grunting and cursing the first time he made this trip. Limbs and twigs poked and scratched his arms and face, but he persevered. She was worth it. There was antibacterial cream for his skin, but only she could heal his heart. Oh, that was good. He'd have to say that when she tended to his wounds later.

Once at the roof line, he inched his way to the end of the branch, but the thing wasn't prepared to withstand the twenty pounds of muscle that he'd put on since he was a teenager. It creaked, and then there was a crack. He lunged and dug his fingers into the shingles just as the branch broke. The denseness of the foliage kept it from falling to the ground. He'd have to come back tomorrow and remove it, so it didn't fall and hurt anyone. But first, he had to figure out how to get the rest of his body on the roof.

The burning sting of sweat rolling into his cuts was a distraction he didn't need. It was taking all his concentration to leverage the lower half of his body into a position that didn't guarantee a fall. This was the highest point of the house, so it wasn't a place he wanted to lose his grip. Thankfully, he worked out daily and was able to pull himself up into a sitting position.

The sight of the soft glow from her window twenty feet away made him want to beat his chest. She was his woman, and he was coming for her. There was a ledge under her window, so once he got there, he'd be home free. But before that happened, he had to maneuver down the gable carefully to not slip off. A fall from this height would not be good. He began his inching journey, but his foot slipped, and he slid ten feet before he jammed his boot into a recess in the roof. Raspy, sawing pants and old man groans filled the air as he rested and tried to get his pounding heart under control. His shirt stuck to his heaving chest. When the breeze changed there was a distinct aroma of body odor, and he was pretty sure there was a rip in the seat of his jeans. Fabulous. Didn't matter though—all that mattered was getting to her. Besides, this would be a funny story to tell Pod when she was older.

With careful movements, he continued to scoot down the pitch of the roof. Both feet landed on the ledge, and he breathed a sigh of relief. Step by side-step he made his way to her window. Music was playing from the other side of the glass. When he got closer, he could see her sitting on the bed writing in a book of some kind. Her face free of makeup, her hair piled on her head, and her bent knees threw him back in time eight years. It was like replaying the very same scene. They would have a future because he had nostalgia on his side.

Charlie and Hank forever.

Chapter Forty-Nine

C harlie poured her heart onto the pages of her journal. The night had been awesome in so many ways, but that kiss had messed with her head and emotions. All she'd wanted was to fall into Hank's arms and never leave. The problem was that so much sadness was associated with him.

Loving and losing him, missing him to the point of pain. Believing they had a future only to have her stupid hopes crushed by three little text messages. The humiliating realization that his marriage to Karen hadn't been what was keeping them apart, that he could've reached out to her but didn't. Even his pursuit of her now hurt her heart, and made her feel manipulated.

The tap, tap, tap on her window scared the crap out of her.

What in the world? It couldn't be.

Yep, Hank was standing on the ledge outside her window. This was how he'd convinced her to finally give him a chance and go out with him when they were teenagers.

"What a manipulative asshole." She stormed to the locked window, threw the latch, and shoved the thing open.

"Hey." His charming grin only threw gas on the fire of her anger.

Her arms crossed over her chest. "What are you doing here, Hank?"

"Isn't it obvious?" His bravado slipped a bit. "I'm showing you how much you mean to me."

"What happened to your face?"

That goofy grin was back in place. "Don't worry about that. There's ointment for my wounds, but you're the only cure for my soul."

She only arched her brow.

His sheepish expression was adorable and infuriating. "That sounded less cheesy in my head."

"I hope so. Otherwise, you're an idiot. Go away, Hank." Her hands went to the window to close it.

"Wait. Okay, I can see this hasn't worked the way I'd hoped it would, but I want to talk to you, Charlie."

"No."

"At least let me in, so I don't have to climb back down." Disappointment rolled off him like the winds of a thunderstorm.

Not gonna let it affect her. This was for Pod as much as her. Charlie had to know that she couldn't be manipulated. Done with being coerced, bullied, or seduced into doing something she wasn't ready or didn't want to do, she strengthened her resolve. Too much of her life had been lived that way. Not anymore. But she didn't want him to break his neck, so she stepped back so he could crawl through the window. "Fine."

"Thank you." He adjusted his grip and then his stance to maneuver through the window. Time slowed to frames of pictures as he slipped and caught himself at just the right moment.

"Holy crap."

"Don't worry, Charlie. I know what I'm doing." Another adjustment, another twist of his body, and one minute he was there, and the next he wasn't.

"Hank!"

* * *

Hank realized his mistake with Charlie just before he fell. She'd seen what he was doing as handling her, and since hindsight is an excellent teacher, he could now see the error of his ways, especially rolling off her roof. The ground rose up to meet him, and it wasn't happy to see him.

Every particle of air was knocked from his lungs. With his hands resting on his stomach and the stars overhead, he lay there assessing his body and the situation. Had she truly locked him out of her life? His spasming diaphragm screamed yes. He knew his heart would break at the realization, but currently, it was working overtime to keep him alive. Several minutes passed, and he thought she'd left him there to die.

The screen door slammed. "Hank." She dropped to her knees beside him. "Are you hurt?" Shaking fingers fluttered over his body. "What am I saying? Of course you're hurt. You just fell ten feet to the ground."

He wanted to tell her he was probably going to be okay, but he wasn't wholly convinced of that yet. He hadn't figured out how to breathe again.

Her phone appeared in her trembling hands. "Do you need an ambulance?"

Somewhere he found the strength to wrap his hand around hers. "No." It was barely a whisper, but she must've heard him because she put her phone away.

"Are you sure?"

He nodded and hauled in another beautiful breath. "I'm fine. Just knocked the wind out of myself."

"Really?"

He covered her hand that rested on his chest. "Really."

"Are you sure?"

His facial muscles somehow managed to push up the corners of his lips. "Yes."

Her concerned expression evaporated, and anger clouded her features. "What the hell was that, Hank?"

"What?"

"Why were you trying to climb in my window? Who does that? I didn't ask you here, and instead of showing up at the front door like a sane person, you try to crawl into my room via a window. What did you think would happen?"

"Charlie, I..." What did he think would happen? "I don't know. I just want to prove to you that I want you."

"By crawling into my window? That's the stupidest thing I've ever heard."

He carefully pushed himself into a sitting position. "What can I do to persuade you to give us a chance, then? Tell me, and I'll do it." The blood in his veins froze at her stony appearance.

Silence stretched between them like the moments before the drop of the guillotine.

In an instant, he saw it all so clearly. "Oh." There was nothing he could do. The door was indeed locked, and apparently, so was the window.

She didn't blink. She didn't waver. And she was beyond his reach.

Stubbornness was his middle name, especially when it came to getting what he wanted, but even he knew it was time to admit defeat. It just about killed him and went against every fiber of his being, but he officially threw in the towel. "I understand." The slow painful crawl to his feet made his head swim. "You don't need to worry about me bothering you anymore. I'll respect your wishes." The distance to his truck seemed too far to walk, but he'd do it if for no other reason than to regain some of the dignity he'd just lost.

"Hank."

He glanced back at her expressionless face. "Yeah?"

"My lawyer will be in touch with you about a parenting arrangement."

He nodded. There wasn't anything else to say that would change her mind. He could see it in the set of her shoulders, and the way she held her head. He blessedly made it to the truck without fainting. A turn of the key and he headed for the minor emergency center, hoping the doctor could do something for the ribs he was pretty sure he'd broken. Too bad Doc Simpson couldn't do a thing about his broken heart.

Chapter Fifty

The scent of BBQ floated on the air, as did the laughter and chatter from the guests at Scarlett's party for Jack and Luanne. Charlie had hung pretty close to Honey and Wardell's side until Hailey arrived. She wasn't really in the mood to socialize, especially with people she didn't know well. So she was relieved when her friend showed up at the party. "I'm so glad you came." They went to get in line for food.

"I wasn't going to come." Hailey adjusted the Zachsville Raiders ball cap she wore. "But Derek's mom insisted she wanted to stay with Lottie for a while, so here I am."

Charlie picked up a plate and handed one to her friend. "How is Lottie today?"

"Irritated that she can't go outside and play, but otherwise she's fine." The relief in her friend's voice was unmistakable.

Charlie glanced around. "Is Roger with you?"

Hailey plopped a spoonful of potato salad onto her plate. "No. He got called out of town. One of his client's computer systems went offline, and he had to go get them up and running before tomorrow."

"You don't seem very broken up about him not being here." She'd noticed the apathy that Hailey exhibited toward her boyfriend.

She shrugged. "I like Roger's company, but if he can't be around, then that's alright too."

They finished filling their plates and made their way to an empty table. Charlie noticed that she had twice the amount of food that Hailey did. "I keep forgetting I'm only eating for two, and not fifteen."

Hailey laughed. "Thankfully, you're not puking your guts up anymore. I swear, I've never known anyone who's been as sick as you when they were pregnant."

The sweetness of the BBQ sauce burst across Charlie's tongue as she licked it from her finger. "What can I say? I'm an overachiever."

"Yeah. I'd say that." Hailey's fork stopped halfway to her mouth and stared beyond Charlie's shoulder. "Oh, my Lord, I think my ovaries just purred."

"What?" Charlie glance behind her. "Oh, my."

Luanne was making her way to their table with the most gorgeous man Charlie had ever seen, and she'd seen her fair share of gorgeous guys. In fact, two of the hottest men she knew were at this party, but Jack and Gavin didn't have what this man had. Besides his good looks, he practically glowed with...something. It was the "It" factor that everyone in Hollywood wanted.

"Hailey and Charlie, I'd like you to meet Jack's cousin and our newest recording artist, Beau Callan. Beau, this is Hailey Odom and Charlie Klein."

The cowboy tipped his hat. "Ladies."

Luanne placed her hand on Beau's arm. "Hailey owns Boon's Saloon, one of the oldest honky-tonk's in Texas. I'm hoping we can talk her into letting you work on your material and sets at her bar, before you go on the road." She gave Hailey a hopeful look.

Before Hailey could respond, Luanne gasped, "Oh, shit, Aiden is sticking his hands in the apple cobbler Honey made. I'll be right back." The feisty fairy headed toward the pie-stealing preschooler.

Hailey gave Beau an assessing look. "You any good? I mean, you're pretty as they come, but can you sing?"

Beau laughed. "I'm alright." He swung the extra chair out and straddled it with his arms crossed over the back. "This place of yours any good? I mean, you're hot as fire, but does this club live up to the hype?"

Charlie wasn't sure how Hailey remained so unaffected by the cowboy's crooked grin as the two squared off into a staring contest. After several seconds that sizzled with something that made Charlie blush, Hailey chuckled. "Hell yeah, it lives up to the hype."

Beau winked. "Same here."

Charlie had to intervene, or everything around them was about to catch fire. "You're not from Zachsville are you, Beau?"

The friendly smile he gave her wasn't laced with the same challenge and the *I'd like to eat you alive* overtones as the one he'd given Hailey. "No, I'm from West Virginia. I'm actually just visiting Jack and Luanne right now. I have to head back tomorrow. There are a few loose ends to tie up before I move down here. I should probably be back in a couple of months." He said the last part to Hailey.

Hailey shrugged. "I don't know why you're telling me."

He cocked his head. "So you're ready for me, darlin'."

"Pardon me?"

The *gotcha* grin snuck back onto his face. "To book me at the club." His eyes went wide in mock shock. "Get your mind out of the gutter, Miss Hailey."

Charlie snorted sweet tea through her nose. Beau laughed and patted her on the back.

"Har-har." Hailey wasn't amused. "So you're a comedian as well as a singer?"

He cocked his head and met Hailey's dismissive stare. "I can be anything you want me to be." He stood and replaced the chair. "I need to find Jack." He held his hand out to Charlie. "It was nice to meet you, Charlie. Any tips you have about show business are welcomed."

"Nice to meet you, Beau. Watch your money."

"Got it."

He tipped his hat to Hailey. "I look forward to satisfying you—"

Hailey huffed out a laugh. "I seriously doubt you could satisfy me."

"If you'd let me finish." His cocky grin was back in place. "I was going to say I look forward to satisfying you and your customers' entertainment needs." He wagged his finger in her direction. "You've got a dirty mind, Hailey Odom."

She crossed her arms and gave him a stony look.

He glanced at Charlie. "Tough room."

"You may have met your match, pretty boy." Charlie felt he needed to be warned.

"You may be right." He laughed.

Reesa Capland sashayed up to the table. Long legs, perfect blonde hair, and golden, sun-kissed skin, she was five feet, eight inches of Texas bombshell. She ran pink tipped nails over Beau's bicep. "Beau, you promised to show me your guitar." Her pouty tone and big innocent eyes made her look like a wholesome porn star.

"That I did, Reesa, darlin'." He threw his arm around her shoulder. "If you ladies will excuse me—I've got a promise to keep."

"Fine with me," Hailey said, but the two had already turned to leave.

"I don't think *show me your guitar* means the same thing to them as it does to us." Charlie chuckled. She noticed Hailey following Beau's progress through the crowd. "Do I need to douse you with water?"

Hailey pulled a face. "Why?"

"Because the two of you were burning up the air. I think it was insta-lust."

"No way. He's just one of those irritatingly arrogant and shiny men who thinks every woman wants in their pants. I'm not that woman." She scooped up a spoonful of baked beans. "Not my type. Besides, he was all over Reesa. How long could they have known each other? He's only been in town a day or two. Beau Callen is a player. Definitely, not my type."

Charlie decided to eat her dessert first. "If you say so."

"I do."

"So tell me about Roger. Why doesn't he ever come to the club?"

Hailey peered at her over a corn cob she'd just taken a bite of. She lowered it to her plate and wiped her fingers on her napkin. "Not much to tell. He's nice. He's cute. He's kind to Lottie."

"Wow! You're really selling him." Charlie laughed. "No offense, but he sounds very...one-dimensional."

Hailey shrugged. "That's one of his best qualities."

"I don't understand."

Her friend took a long pull on her beer like she was avoiding the question or formulating an answer. "I'm completely off bright and shiny men. I mean, look at Derek. He burned brighter than the sun, so much so that I was blinded to his faults." She poked at the baked beans with her fork. "And look where that got me, pregnant and married at sixteen, a GED instead of graduating from high school, and a husband who resented me for ruining his football career, then used that as an excuse to cheat and lie to me our whole marriage. Now that I'm free of him, I only intend to be with normal, regular, not-shiny men. Roger's a computer geek, no flash in sight."

"And that's enough for you?" Sweet tea slid down Charlie's throat as she thought about how sad Hailey made her life seem.

Her friend snorted without humor. "More than enough. Roger's dependable. He gives me an orgasm a couple of times a week. He doesn't get in my business, and he's nice to my kid. That's all I need."

Charlie cut her chicken with a knife and fork. "I just worry that you'll be bored."

"I hope I'm bored out of my mind. In fact, if I thought he'd say yes, I'd ask him to marry me tomorrow." She laughed. "Trust me, Charlie, living on the roller coaster I've been on for the last seven years was enough excitement and heartache for a lifetime."

The food sliding down Charlie's throat had to squeeze past a lump of sorrow and regret. "I'm sorry I wasn't here."

"It wouldn't have changed anything, except to give me someone to listen to me bitch. I was so blinded by love that I couldn't see my way out of my marriage. It wasn't until I found out for sure he was cheating that my pride wouldn't let me stay." She took a big bite of brisket, then pointed her fork at Charlie. "Never again. I'll never lose myself like that to a man. But enough about me. Let's talk about you and Hank."

Every morsel of food she'd eaten threatened to make a reappearance. "What about us?"

"Let's talk about why he's not here and why I'm going by to check on him on my way home."

Oh no, had he really gotten hurt last night? "Why are you checking on him?"

"Because he has three bruised ribs and a swollen knee from falling off your roof." The tilt of Hailey's head dared Charlie to lie to her.

She played with the condensation on the side of her glass. "Oh, that."

"Yes, that. He told me it was over between you two, something about a locked door and now you'd locked the window too." Hailey lifted her heavy mane of hair from her neck with her hands. "Honestly, I think he was on painkillers because he wasn't making much sense."

"I told him the door between us was locked. Then he tried to get in my window, and it was locked too. But he is right. We're done."

Hailey rested her elbow on the table and covered her mouth. "Why?"

"Because he only wants me now that he knows about Pod. He didn't want to have anything to do with me before that."

Hailey laughed. "Are you kidding me? That's what this is about? Hank told me the night you got up and sang that he was going to tell you how he felt about you."

"Right. That's the night he found out I was pregnant." She crossed her arms over her chest like she'd just made the point of the century.

"He told me before you fell off the stage. He had no idea you were pregnant when he made that decision. Furthermore, the only reason he hadn't done it sooner is because he was punishing himself for what he'd done to you in the first place." Hailey matched her crossed-arm stance.

Really? Her heart jumped with excitement, but her head quickly put the double-crossing body part in its place. "Doesn't matter." She began cleaning up the table. "I can't take the chance that he'd leave me again. It would break me, Hailey. I have a child to raise. I can't do it if I'm broken."

"Are you serious right now?"

Charlie stopped gathering dishes. "Yes, I'm serious."

"Let's review, Charlie." Hailey stuck one finger in the air. "Did you or did you not leave Hank to go to Hollywood?"

"Yes, but I didn't have a choice."

"Just answer the question."

"Yes."

Another of Hailey's fingers went into the air. "And did you or did you not return phone calls from him?"

"I didn't, but my mom never told me either of you called."

Hailey's brow rose in challenge.

"I didn't."

A third finger came up. "Did you or did you not come back for him when you turned eighteen?"

Tears blurred her vision and all she could manage was a shake of her head.

One more finger. One more accusation. "Did you or did you not run from his hotel room without letting him explain about Karen?"

"Seriously? I was supposed to stick around and let him lie to me?"

Hailey stuck up another finger. "That reminds me. Did you or did you not think the absolute worst of him without getting all the facts?"

Defeat sat on her like a thousand-pound elephant. "Yes."

The five fingers stood as evidence against her. "The way I see it, you're the one who's left Hank and not been there for him, not the other way around, and still he's put himself out there to get you back." Hailey took Charlie's hand. "You're throwing up defenses because you're scared. I get that, but if you're honest with yourself, you know that Hank's the one who will always guard your heart."

Was she right? Had all of this been one big excuse because of fear? The answer was a big fat yes. And didn't she owe her daughter more than a mother so scared of life that she refused to live it? She also owed her Pod a mother and father that loved each other and tried to build a life together. The tears burning behind her eyes only confirmed that the place she needed to be was with the only man she'd ever loved, not running from him like she'd committed a crime.

She rose from her seat and hugged Hailey. "You're right. I'm so stupid."

Hailey patted the arm that was slung across her chest. "No, you're just afraid. Go."

She would. There was only one place she wanted to be.

With her man.

Chapter Fifty-One

Hank adjusted the ice pack on his swollen knee. He'd tweaked the old football injury when he fell from Charlie's roof. The burn of humiliation scorched his skin. He'd made a damn fool of himself for the last time with her.

Who was he kidding? He'd do it all again if he thought he had a chance with her.

The irony of the situation wasn't lost on him. Karen had always complained that his pride kept him from truly connecting with her, which was true. But his pride was nowhere to be found when he crawled onto Wardell's roof. All that had mattered was getting to Charlie by any means possible, and look where it had gotten him. Three bruised ribs and a knee that looked like a cantaloupe.

The knock on the door drew him out of his misery. He glanced at the clock. Hailey must've left the party early. "It's open." It'd taken him twenty minutes to get comfortable, and he wasn't moving again until he absolutely had to.

The front door slowly opened, revealing a resolute pair of blue eyes in the loveliest face he'd ever seen. "Charlie? What are you doing here?" He was sprawled on the sofa in a pair of athletic shorts and nothing else but the Ace bandage wrapped around his chest.

She didn't answer, and her tentative steps into the house made him want to scream. The smell of BBQ wafted through his anticipation, and his stomach growled. He pointed to the plates of food she was carrying. "Is that for me?"

A nod and a cautious glance were all he got from her.

Why was she here? A guilty conscience had probably made her come by to check on him. She wasn't a bad person, just a person who didn't want him. "Well, bring it here. I'm starved. Would you grab me some utensils? They're in the first drawer next to the fridge."

Another nod, then she disappeared into the kitchen. She returned with a napkin, knife, and fork, then set the plates on the coffee table.

"Thanks." He swung his leg around, careful to not make any jerky motions. "Have a seat." It didn't matter why she was here. He was just so damn glad to see her. The tangy BBQ exploded over his taste buds, and he nearly moaned. When the first bite of food hit his grateful stomach, he realized he hadn't eaten since the night before.

They sat in silence while he ate. He noticed her examining his house from where she sat. He wiped his hands and mouth on the napkin and pushed his empty plate away.

She pushed the smaller plate toward him. "Dessert?"

His hands went up like he was warding her off. "Oh, no. I'm full as a tick."

A weird look crossed her face before she schooled her features. "You should have dessert. It's carrot cake."

"Stick it in the fridge. I'll have it later."

"You really need to eat this cake." Her eyes had gone a little wild.

"I will, later. I—"

"Eat it!"

What the hell? Maybe she'd made the cake. "Okay, fine. Hand it over." It seemed to upset her that he didn't want the cake, so he dug in with enthusiasm. But his fork clanked against something underneath the cake. He glanced up at her. The tears shimmering in her eyes were so confusing. "What's going on, Charlie?"

She didn't say anything, but one of those tears escaped her lower lid and slid down her face.

He flipped the piece of cake over and found one of the antique keys he'd given her underneath.

"I love you."

"What?" He couldn't tear his gaze from the key covered in frosting.

She dropped to her knees next to him. "I love you, and I want you, and I've been so stupid."

For a second his head spun from the sudden about-face she'd taken, but he quickly caught up. The explosion of joy those three words elicited smacked a giant smile across his face. "Yeah?"

Hands clutched together in front of her chest, she nodded. The lower lip chewing was distracting, but not enough to take his focus off what she'd just said. He cursed his injuries because all he wanted to do was to take her in his arms. "Come here."

She pursed her lips like she was battling her own smile. "Why?"

He pushed himself back so that both of his legs were stretched out on the sofa. He patted the place beside him. "Come here and find out."

Her bottom wedged in next to his hip. Shaking fingers glided over the bandage around his chest. "Hank, I'm so sorry."

"Shhh, it's alright. They'll heal."

Blue eyes jerked up to his. "No, not about your ribs. Though I am sorry about that too. I'm sorry for all the mean things I said." She swiped at another tear. "I'm just so scared of getting hurt, but Hailey helped me see that you're the last person that would purposely hurt me."

Suddenly the lid slammed on the elation bubbling up from his soul. He did have the ability to hurt her by not telling her about the DEA and Raul.

Her brow wrinkled. "What?"

Shit. His face must've reflected his conflict. He couldn't lose her over that. He'd fix it. He'd make sure that didn't happen. His determination shoved at the reservations plaguing him. Her skin was warm in his hands when he cupped her face. "Nothing. So what does this all mean, Charlie? I need the words, baby." The warm kiss she placed in his palm cranked up his anticipation. "Tell me." The whisper was all he could manage with her this close.

"I want us to be together."

She'd barely spoken before he claimed her soft lips. Her taste was familiar and new, something to be savored and devoured, then go back for seconds. He held her in place to drink his fill of her.

Years of need and desire demanded a response. And she gave it to him. Low throaty moans, grasping fingers, and the way her body melted into his were something from a million dreams he'd had of her. A million wishes made in the loneliest times of his life, and a million regrets when he knew he'd hurt her beyond anything she could forgive. She needed to know. He had to tell her everything in his heart, so she'd know that no matter what happened with all the other shit going on between them that this one thing was real. He gripped her head and pulled away from the kiss. "Charlie."

Her eyes were still closed and her swollen, wet lips still pursed. "Huh?"

"Look at me."

Her lids fluttered opened.

"I love you. Have only ever loved you." A kiss to seal things between them. "You know what this means, right?"

She brushed the hair from his forehead. "Charlie and Hank forever?"

The pieces of his life snapped into place. "That's right baby, Charlie and Hank together forever. Now come here." He went back to the place where all the answers of his life were found, and everything that didn't matter fell away. In her embrace, with their lips mating and his body fused to hers.

Home.

* * *

Charlie's knees came up on the sofa to give her better access to Hank's mouth. The swooping dip of her stomach every time their lips touched was a sensation that was quickly becoming her favorite drug. Had she ever been so happy? Only briefly, and that was the night they'd made Pod.

They were together now, and that was the bottom line. A tiny fissure of unease threatened to crack through her happiness. He'd made that weird face when she'd said she knew she could always trust him, probably because he wasn't sure the same thing was true of her. After all, Hailey was right. She'd been the one to leave him.

She'd have to show him that she was committed to him in every way. "Hank."

Big hands smoothed the hair from her face. "Yeah, baby?"

"I want..."

"I want too, but I'm not exactly in the best shape." He chuckled.

She could do this. She was a grown woman, and even though she wasn't very experienced, she could do this. One more deep, soul-wrenching kiss and she stood. His fingers reached for her, but she stepped out of his grasp. "Hang on, greedy."

"I am greedy. I've been deprived of your kisses for too long." The teasing grin slid from his face when she reached up and untied the straps of her sundress. "What are you doing?"

She slid the dress down. The elastic top slipped easily over her rounded belly. "I'd think that was obvious." Self-consciousness tried to worm its way into the situation, but she refused to let it. This was Hank, and he loved her. One arm went around her back, and she unhooked the strapless bra she wore, leaving her only in her panties. Her breasts were larger than when he'd seen them last...hell, all of her was larger than when he'd seen her last.

"Oh. My. God." The reverence in his voice and the dilation of his pupils stoked the fire burning her alive.

Her hands went to his athletic shorts, and she pulled them and his boxers down his legs. The tips of her fingers ran over the part of him begging for her. A low, rumbling moan escaped his throat, and his whole body jerked with awareness. "You like that?"

"You have no idea, but it's not enough. Get rid of that scrap of lace and come here." The tension in his body ran from the corded muscles in his neck to his straining erection. She shimmied out of her panties and straddled his hips, kneeling just above him.

"Like this?" she teased. But her teasing died when the look on Hank's face hit her. Had she done something wrong? "Hank?"

"You are the most gorgeous thing I've ever seen."

The blush started at her toes and bloomed over her body. "Thank you." The strange thing was that she felt beautiful in his eyes. Not since that moment earlier, when she'd had a slight pang of self-consciousness, had she had an ounce of discomfort. This was right and where she belonged.

Warm, strong fingers slid into her hair at the back of her head, and he pulled her to him. This kiss was different than before—long, lazy slides of their lips. His tongue chased hers. Hers chased his. They played and teased, both trying to outdo the other. It was a game where there were no losers, only winners.

An incoherent sound fell from her lips when he began making circles around the tip of her breast with his other hand. He gently tugged on her hair. His teeth captured her lower lip then scraped along the flesh until he released it. He soothed the sting with a velvety lick.

Her body began the climb. Each sensation built on the last, soft, rough, pleasure, pain, until she was hanging on the brink ready to fall. When he brought his mouth to her sensitive nipple and sucked while still toying with the other, she crashed over the edge with his name ripped from her throat.

She collapsed on top of him, but caught herself with her hands on either side of his head, so she didn't hurt his injured chest. Her ragged breaths blew the coarse hair on his chest. A minute. She needed a minute to recover.

"Charlie?"

"Hang on."

He chuckled. "Take your time. I'm here when you're ready."

She glanced up at him through her lashes. "You think this is funny?"

"I think this is heaven." His erection teased her opening...or was she teasing him? It was hard to tell. "You're going to have to do most of the work, Charlie. I'm a little banged up. You alright with that?"

Her response was to lower herself onto him. She moaned low and loud. Sparks flashed before her eyes. This position and the added pressure of the pregnancy changed everything. More intense, more intimate, more everything. She gripped the back of the sofa with one hand to make sure she didn't try to steady herself by placing her hands on his wounded chest. One rock, then two, and she found her rhythm.

"You feel so damn good." He never took his eyes from her. His hands came to her hips and increased her speed. With every rock of her hips, the white-hot glow of release grew higher and hotter. "I'm almost there. Are you close, Charlie?"

She bit her lip and nodded. The delicious friction made speech impossible. He slid his hand between them and found the sensitive bundle of nerves that had the potential to set her off. She closed her eyes and let her head fall back reveling in the deliciousness of the sensation as his fingers rubbed quick circles around the spot.

"Charlie, look at me." The command couldn't be denied.

She did and lost her breath in the process. There was lust and need in his hot gaze, but mostly it overflowed with love. Did she deserve this much love and happiness? She didn't know, but she craved it from him.

They made love to each other with their eyes and their bodies. They didn't speak again, but so many things were said in those moments.

I haven't been whole without you.

You've haunted my dreams.

I've missed you so much.

I'm desperate for more of you.

I love you. I love you. I love you.

Who said what didn't matter, they were bathed in the knowledge that they each felt the same way and it healed something deep inside her.

He increased the movement of his finger. She increased her rhythm. Fire licked between them until her whole body went up in flames. The roll of her orgasm took her. There was no light, no sound, only sensation. She chased every pulsing beat until she was boneless and spent.

He followed close behind. "Charlie." He didn't shout, there weren't any deep moans, he simply whispered her name like a benediction and a prayer.

For a long moment, he didn't say anything else. Didn't move. And she worried that she'd hurt him. "Hank?"

"Mmh."

"Are you alright?" She wasn't. Her entire existence had just been altered.

He opened one eye and grinned at her. "I'm amazing. I was thanking whatever god brought you back to me."

"Oh."

Reverently, he placed his hands on her belly. "You know you're never getting rid of me now. Right?"

"I'm counting on it." He wasn't getting rid of her either, and she'd spend the rest of her life proving it to him.

Chapter Fifty-Two

THIRD TRIMESTER

L ife had never been so good for Charlie. Not when she won her first talent contest. Not when she became a star. Not when she received her first Teen Choice Award. All of those things paled in comparison to her sweet life in her little hometown.

It was common knowledge now that she'd lost all of her money, that she was pregnant by the sheriff, and that they weren't married. The good folks of Zachsville generally regarded her just like everyone else in town. She was gossiped about just like Chelsea Rae when people found out she was making jewelry with her own hair and selling it on the internet. Or Lonnie over at Lonnie's Tires and More, when it was discovered that he and his sister, Loretta used to play lick tongue with each other as kids. Eww.

And she couldn't be happier.

Let 'em talk. With every rumor spread, or tongue that wagged, she became more and more Charlie Klein, resident of Zachsville, Texas, and less and less Charlie Kay, Hollywood star. Which was why when the story broke in the media about her pregnancy, it was nothing more than a trivial footnote in the gossip rags. She guessed Ron and Marci had been right. She was a nobody.

Thank God.

Pod was getting bigger and thriving. Who knew she'd be so good at growing a baby? Some days her ankles swelled, some days her breasts were so sensitive that it hurt to wear a bra, and every day she was so thankful for this little miracle that her heart barely contained her joy.

She was still singing at Boon's a couple of nights a week. While she enjoyed it, she'd be glad when Beau Callen got to town and could take over for her. Performing wasn't something she wanted to keep doing. But she did love being able to help her friend keep her bar in business.

But the most significant source of happiness was her relationship with Hank. Every thump of her heart was for him.

Thump, thump, joy.

Thump, thump, love.

Thump, thump, trust.

She'd laughed more in the last couple of months than she had in the previous eight years. She was safe with Hank, so were her hopes and dreams, and she told him so every chance she got.

Her days were spent making up for lost time with him, growing her baby, and getting her shop ready to open. And they were some of the happiest she'd ever known.

Now she glanced around the little store she'd put together with hard work, sweat, and the help of her friends and family.

"Charlie, do you want the mother and baby care products together?" Her new manager, Roxanne, asked her. It had turned out Roxanne had lots of retail and management experience at a boutique in Austin but wanted to work in Zachsville to be closer to her twins, so it was a win, win for both of them.

"Yes. I have a few things in the back that I'd like to use for the display."

Roxanne set the dusting cloth on the counter. "I'll get them. What am I looking for?"

"A couple of wicker baskets, a few stuffed animals, a blue robe and some slippers. Arrange it however you like. I'm not picky." They were only a week from opening. It was thrilling, but there was still so much to get done, and to make matters trickier, Raul had gone MIA. Thomas had assured her that everything was still a go, but it was unnerving. She had enough product for a month, but she'd need supplies soon. She'd bought all that Thomas had, and not at the whole-sale price she'd agreed upon with Raul, but she'd wanted to make sure she was fully stocked.

Hank had been trying to get her to find a new wholesaler, but the deal with Raul was too good to give up. So she was willing to wait a little longer for him to get back to her before she went with someone else.

Her phone rang, and Hank's name popped up. The butterflies that always came out to play when she was with him did a dive roll in her belly. "Hello."

"Hey, baby." The warm tenor of his sweet voice breathed life to the fire that simmered just beneath the surface of her heart.

"Hey, handsome. What's shakin'?" She broke a dead leaf off a potted plant on the counter.

"Not much. I was wondering if you could take a break and grab an early lunch with me."

She surveyed the stack of work she needed to get done and almost told him no, but one thing she'd learned about running her own busi-ness was that there was always work to be done. This pile of papers would still be here when she got back in a couple of hours. "Sure. Where should I meet you?"

"At the courthouse. I have something to take care of there."

"Alright. Are you headed over now?"

"On my way now. See you there."

She pushed to her feet, an activity that was becoming more and more difficult. Being eight months pregnant was no joke. "Roxanne."

The pretty brunette poked her head out of the storeroom. "Yeah?"

"I'm headed to lunch with Hank. I'll be back in an hour or so."

"Sounds good."

Charlie grabbed her purse just as her phone rang again. She quickly punched the button when she read the screen. "Raul?"

"Hello, chica. How are you?"

"I'm big as a house, but well. How are you?"

"I'm well. I'm sorry my business called me away, but I'm back and will have your first shipment to you tomorrow."

The squeal that escaped her was not professional at all, but she didn't care. "That's fantastic."

"Thomas told me about you and the sheriff. Congratulations." There was the tiniest bit of an edge to his voice.

Maybe Hank had been right, and Raul had wanted more than a professional relationship. "Thank you."

"I think it would be better if we made the delivery at a time when he's not around. I don't think he likes me very much." He chuckled.

That was an understatement. "No problem, but I don't involve him in my business, Raul." She looked both ways at the street before she crossed to the courthouse.

"That's good. I'd hate not to be able to do business because of your boyfriend."

What a weird thing to say. Male pride was ridiculous. "That's not going to happen."

"Good. That's very good."

She nodded and mouthed, "Thank you," to a man that held the courthouse door open for her. "What time should I expect you tomorrow?"

"The delivery will be there around two." The sound of computer keys clacking came through the line. "I'm making this first delivery myself to explain the recyclable crates, the best way to handle them, and the retrieval process."

"Great. I'll see you then." She looked up and down the hall. Hank hadn't told her where to meet him.

"Goodbye." Raul disconnected.

Her already good mood went up about a hundred percent. Things were falling into place.

The goofy smile she'd been wearing got even wider when she saw Hank come out of one of the offices. The sun coming through the high windows shone down on him, making the natural highlights in his light brown hair look like spun gold. He took her breath away, and he was all hers. Her lady bits did high kicks when he caught sight of her and grinned. Lord, he was handsome.

"Hi." She weakly waved, and that was a feat. The man struck her stupid.

He strode toward her. No doubt what his purpose was. His lips came down on her in a kiss that wasn't at all appropriate for the courthouse. He nipped and sucked her bottom lip before he pulled back and smiled down at her. "Hi. I've got a question for you."

"Okay." She hoped he wouldn't ask her to operate heavy machinery, because at the moment that was out of the question.

"Marry me?"

"Okay." That seemed to be the only thing she could say to this man. "Wait, what?"

He laughed and kissed her quick and hard. "Too late to change your mind. You've already agreed."

"Hank, your divorce was only finalized last week." She glanced around the empty hallway. "What will people think?"

The look he gave her communicated clearly that he knew she was full of shit. "You don't give a rat's ass what anybody in this town thinks."

"That's not true." It was pretty much true. "I care what our family and friends think."

"Yeah, and they'll all be thrilled."

The happiness spread across her face until her cheeks hurt. "You're right."

He started dragging her down the hall.

"Where are we going? You cannot drag me into another closet and maul me. The poor janitor hasn't been able to look me in the eye since he caught us in there last time. Besides, I hardly fit in a closet anymore."

He laughed and kissed her hand. "You're perfect just the way you are. But we're not going to find a closet."

"Then where are you dragging me off to?"

"To get the marriage license. I'm not letting you change your mind."

Yeah, like he had to worry about that. It would take a full-on disaster to rip her away from him. "Okay." There she went again, agreeing to everything.

"I want to get married before Pod comes, so I'm thinking in a couple of weeks." He yanked open the door to the marriage license office.

"What's the hurry?"

He glanced around then fake whispered, "Because of what people will say, of course."

She laughed. "Okay." It seemed to be the word of the day.

Chapter Fifty-Three

"Are you going to feed me, or was this all a ploy to get your way?"

Hank hugged Charlie to his side and placed his hand on her belly. "Anything you want, baby."

She tried and failed to keep a put-out look on her face. "Good, because I'd hate to have to hurt you, you being the law and all."

His laughter filled the town square. "Where you from, girl?" He led her to the City Cafe. The familiar smell of home cooking hit him in the face, and he soaked it in.

Her long lashes fluttered. "Why, I'm from the great state of Texas, sir. Why do you ask?"

"Every day your accent gets thicker and thicker. I love it." He pulled her to his side and kissed her head, then led her to an empty booth.

"The regular, Charlie?" Trudy, their waitress, asked.

She'd ordered the same thing for a month—chicken livers with mashed potatoes and fried okra.

A happy sigh passed through her lips. "Yes."

"And for you, Sheriff?"

"I'll take the special, Trudy."

"Iced tea for both of you?"

"Yep." He reached across the table and took Charlie's hand. "Trudy, you can be the first to know. We're getting married."

"What? Oh, my word. How exciting. Congratulations!"

He ignored the stunned look on Charlie's face. Maybe he should've talked to her first, but she'd have to get over it. She was his, and he wanted everyone to know it. He'd decided to ask her to marry him when it had been almost a month since she'd heard from Raul Perez and he'd heard from the DEA.

There was no way he could make this commitment to her with that business between them. Maybe he should've contacted Agent Sheridan, but his philosophy was no news was good news. Also, Pod's birthdate was quickly approaching, and he wasn't lying about wanting to be married before the baby came. Call him old-fashioned, but that's how he felt.

"I can't believe you told Trudy. It'll be all over town by the time the lunch rush is done," Charlie whisper-yelled. "I haven't told Pops or... Oh, my Lord, Honey. If she hears this through the gossip tree, she'll kill us." She yanked out her phone and dialed. "Pops? Is Honey with you? Put me on speaker phone."

As she waited, she gave Hank another fake dirty look and put her phone on speaker too, then turned down the volume.

"Which button is it?" Wardell asked.

"It's the button on the screen that says, speaker." Charlie tried to help without cracking up laughing.

"On the screen? Right here?"

"Yes, that's the one." Honey's voice came over the phone line.

Finally. The clock was ticking on this thing. It was only a matter of time before Honey heard the news now that Trudy knew. "Okay, can y'all hear me?"

"We can hear you, Charlie," Honey said.

"Good." She reached for his hand. "Hank and I are getting married."

"Oh, my word! That's wonderful darlin'!" Honey's squeal rang through the line.

"'Bout time," Wardell grumped.

Hank laughed. "You're right, Wardell."

"Hank?"

"Yes, Wardell. It's me." He winked at Charlie.

"Considering the circumstance, I'm going to forgive you for not asking me first." Charlie's grandfather sounded miffed. He'd never really thought of asking Wardell.

"Don't be such an old fuddy-duddy. She's a grown woman and can make her own decisions," Honey admonished.

Charlie bit her lip, obviously trying to hold in a belly laugh. "Well, I'll let y'all go. I just wanted you to know."

"Bye, darlin'. Congratulations," Honey said.

"Are you happy, Charlie?" Wardell asked.

"Ecstatically happy, Pops." Her blue eyes found Hank's, and the faces of all the other women in the world disappeared.

"Well, then I'm happy too. We'll see y'all later." There were some odd noises on the line. "How do you turn this fool thing off?" her grandfather complained.

"Just push the button, Wardell," Honey said.

"Which one? There are about a hundred on here."

"That one, right there."

"I don't know which one— Oh, this one."

"Yes. You're cute when you're all flustered, you know that?" Honey cooed.

"I'll show you flustered, woman—"

Charlie hung up her phone before her grandfather could complete his sentence. Him showing his girlfriend how flustered he could get was on the list of things she never wanted to hear. Her hands went to her ears. "Make it stop."

Hank squeezed her hand. "Let's just hope we're still as...um...active as they are at that age."

"Are you trying to make me lose my appetite?"

He barked out a laugh. "Not at all, just statin' a fact."

Trudy returned with their drinks, then retreated to check on their order.

"Are you happy?" He hoped he didn't sound insecure, but on some level, he guessed he was. She was a Hollywood star, whether she claimed it or not, and had been exposed to hundreds of handsome, sexy men. Maybe she was regretting her decision to tie her wagon to a small-town sheriff.

Sunlight burst from her smile, and he took an easy breath. "I'm blissfully happy. Why wouldn't I be? I'm marrying the best man I know, I'm about to open the shop my grandma and I dreamed of, and I'm pregnant with that good man's baby."

The muscles in his shoulders unknotted. He wasn't the best man, as evidenced by the fact that he'd not told her anything about Raul and the DEA, but that seemed to be behind them, so he'd spend the rest of his life trying to be the best man she knew. "I'm glad. I've never been happier."

"Oh, gosh!" Her hand went to her mouth. "I almost forgot."

"What?"

"Raul called me this morning." There was that sunshine again. "He's making my first delivery tomorrow."

What. The. Fuck.

She sipped her iced tea. "Isn't that great?"

One terrible scenario after another played out in his head. Each one worse than the other. She'd never forgive him. He knew it. This shop was who she wanted to be, what she'd created for herself and Pod, and he was about to be part of polluting it. In the back of his mind, he knew what had to happen to keep her safe, and she'd hate him for it.

"Hank?"

"That's great." The statement was as hard and rigid as concrete.

"Are you alright?" Her open concern for him was just another slice to his conscience. She'd bared her soul to him, trusted him not only with her heart but with their child, and this was how he was repaying her. With lies and half-truths. But what was he supposed to do?

He plastered on the best smile he had in his devious bag of tricks. "Yes. That's great."

She laughed. "You already said that."

"Sorry, this day is just filled with such good news that I'm having trouble keeping up." He was definitely going to hell for that one. This was the worst news possible.

"Here you go." Trudy set their plates in front of them.

"Thank you, Trudy." Charlie unwrapped her silverware and dug in.

His phone buzzed with a text. Agent Sheridan's name popped up.

Hank, we've got new info. Be there this afternoon.

Charlie pointed with her fork. "Aren't you hungry?"

The chicken fried steak on his plate mocked him. It dared him to take a bite and see if he could hold it down. He couldn't, not with the lining of his stomach spewing acid.

"Anything wrong?"

"Huh? Oh, no." He turned the phone face down but continued to stare at it like it was a ransom note, which it was. Sheridan and Murphy were holding his future with Charlie hostage, and it wasn't going to end well.

Chapter Fifty-Four

Three hours later, Hank was pacing his office and using all his intellect to make sense of what Agent Sheridan was saying. "Say that again."

"We're going to take Perez and Chang at Ms. Klein's store." The man said it like he was reciting the daily weather report.

Hank massaged his temples and tried to think rationally about the situation. But it made no sense. "Why? We can take them at Chang's, or anywhere between there and Charlie's store."

"We want to take both men while they're delivering the product," Murphy said. "And you should calm down, Sheriff. We need cool heads to pull this off."

It was official. He hated Agent Murphy. "She's eight months pregnant, for God's sake!" The last of his professionalism had gone right out the window.

"We're aware," Sheridan said.

The calm demeanor of both agents only ratcheted up the growing turmoil shaking around his insides like a bag of dry bones.

"With my child." Control of his tone was out of the question.

"I told you he couldn't be objective," Murphy said to Sheridan.

Bitch.

He yanked on the tattered restraints of his emotions and hauled them in. They might cut him out of this, and then he'd be completely out of the loop, and no help to Charlie at all. "Fine." He sat behind his desk again. "Tell me."

Sheridan crossed one leg over the other and ran his thumb and forefinger down the crease of his pants. No doubt to give Hank a little more time to calm down. "We want both men, and if we take them at Thomas Chang's place, then his lawyers could claim he didn't know about the drugs Perez was funneling through his business. But if we get the two of them unloading the shipment, we can build a tighter case against both of them."

"Ms. Klein will never be in danger," Murphy supplied.

He only gave her a dead-eyed glare, then turned back to Sheridan. "You can't know that. What if things go south, and she's caught in the crossfire?" He should've gotten Charlie out of this at the start of this nightmare.

"Before you go all caveman," Agent Murphy said, "you need to remember our objectives here. And that's to protect the good citizens of Zachsville, including the children, and to put Perez and Chang behind bars. Isn't that what you want? Those two locked up and away from Charlie?"

"Yes, I want them arrested and put away for the rest of their lives. But..." The thing that had been lurking in the back of his mind, and that he'd prayed wouldn't happen, suddenly became the only way to keep her safe. "You have to take her into custody too."

"What?" Murphy asked.

"Just listen." He stood and began to pace. "If Perez or his associates think Charlie had something to do with his arrest, they could come after her." He couldn't control the barely restrained terror in his voice.

He looked to Agent Sheridan. The man held his eyes without blinking. "It's possible."

The horrible scenarios of what might happen if these people believed Charlie was responsible for bringing down Perez and his oper-ation took over his brain. For her protection, it had to be done. "Then we don't have any choice but to take her into custody too. If they see her being arrested right along with them, then they'll think she wasn't working with the Feds to set them up. If not..." There was no need to finish the sentence. They all knew what these people were capable of doing.

Sheridan exchanged a look with Murphy then turned to Hank and nodded. "Okay. This is probably none of my business, but are you prepared for the fallout from this plan?"

Hell, no. "I'll deal with it. The only thing that matters is that she and the baby are safe."

"Keeping her in a cell should be a joy," Murphy said.

"No."

"No?"

"The only way I will participate in this is if you move her to a safe house as soon as possible after her arrest." He stared down Agent Murphy. "She will not spend the night in a cell." His intensity ticked down a notch when he turned to Sheridan. "I want your word."

The man nodded. "You have it. But if we're doing this, Ms. Klein has to believe she's actually being arrested. If not, then the whole thing will be for nothing. You can't tell her ahead of time. I know she's an actress, so she might be able to pull it off, but for her safety, we can't take any chances. I'm sure you understand."

"I do." He understood alright. He understood that his entire future was going up in a blazing, fucking bonfire.

Chapter Fifty-Five

⚜

Charlie filled the sink in Hank's kitchen with water. She'd made his favorite meal to celebrate and to reassure him that she was thrilled with their decision to get married. The herbs and spices from the dish made the homey house even cozier.

She wasn't living with him—the Zachsville gossip mill could only handle so much scandal—but she stayed here more than at Wardell's.

Her heart grew two sizes at the thought of making this house a home for her little family. The permanency of it all gave her hope that Pod would have what she never did—deep, abiding roots that would help her grow into a strong, confident woman. Her ever-present companion kicked and did a barrel roll in agreement.

Not long now, little Pod.

She couldn't wrap her mind around the fact that in just a few short weeks, she'd be holding a baby. It was incredible how nine short months could change everything.

Warm arms went around her waist, and Hank's big hands rested on her belly. "Dinner was delicious."

His strong and steady body supported her as she melted into the embrace. "I'm glad you liked it. I'm afraid you might get sick of it after we're married. It's all I know how to cook. Well, that and grilled cheese."

"I love grilled cheese." He buried his head into the crook of her neck and inhaled, but he didn't kiss and nuzzle like he usually did. He seemed to be drawing comfort from her. She turned in his arms, and the stricken look in his eyes stole her breath.

She took his face in her hands. "Hey. Are you alright?"

"Fine."

He sure as hell didn't look fine. Her hand went to his forehead. "Are you ill?"

"No, just tired."

It looked like more than fatigue, but if he wasn't ready to tell her, then she'd wait. She gave him her flirtiest grin. "I guess we'll have to go to bed early then."

"Oh, I don't..."

Her hand went to the back of his neck. He melted into the kiss as soon as their lips touched, drinking her in. He deepened the kiss, and she fell a little more in love with him. If she could ease his pain just a little, then she'd give what she could.

He pulled back and rested his forehead on hers. "I love you, Charlie. This life with you is everything to me. You know that, don't you?"

"Hank? What is wrong?"

He shook his head. "Tell me you know it."

She captured his face in her hands again. "I know. You know that I've always loved you too?"

The watered-down version of his brilliant smile when he nodded didn't make her feel any better. "Yes."

She took his hand. "Come with me."

He followed without protest. The lost look in his eyes nearly broke her heart. What was wrong with him? It wasn't her or their relationship, she knew that, but something was definitely wrong. A tiny niggle of unease bumped up against her happy world. She refused to let it in. This was the life she'd built, and she'd protect it with everything she had, including her body. He needed her. She could see it all over his face. He wouldn't use her, but it wasn't using if she offered.

In the dimly lit bedroom, she made him sit on the edge of the bed.

Confidence shot through her when she slid her dress over her head and let it drop to the floor. A passenger no more in her life, she had the authority to direct it and change the course of how things went.

Three steps and she was between his legs, her bare feet next to his. Her hands went to the hem of his shirt. A quick tug and it was over his head and on the floor.

Tears stung her eyes when he leaned forward and placed an open mouth-kiss on the place where Pod grew. "Love you." Another kiss. "Love you both." A shadow of misery lingered behind the adoration shining in his *need you* gaze. A slow blink, then two, and only tenderness remained.

His hands went around her and flipped the clasp of her bra. She held the cups in place, then slowly peeled them away from her breasts. Cool air and his heated gaze teased the sensitive tips. The sensation rippled along her nerve endings, snapping her body to life.

With a slight shove she pushed him back on the bed. His body was ridiculous, but it was the fire blazing from his green irises that caused aching need to pulse between her thighs. "You are...too much, Hank Odom."

He didn't speak, only continued to stare at her like he was memorizing every inch of her body. Like if he blinked, she might disappear. Silly man. Didn't he know she wasn't going anywhere? Not without him, anyway.

* * *

Hank reached for words to express what the sight of her standing before him like this did to him, but they were gone, hidden behind the guilt in his chest. He committed every inch of her body and the love pouring from her to memory.

A strangled gasp was all he could manage when her soft fingers traced the trail of hair that disappeared into the waist of his jeans. A flip of the button, the glide of his zipper, and she slid his pants and briefs down his legs.

All the blood rushed to his erection when she slipped her panties down her legs, crawled onto the bed, and straddled his hips. "This okay?"

"So okay."

She rose to her knees and placed her hands by his head. Her belly made moving awkward for her, so he slowly rolled her to her back, careful to stay on his hands and knees to protect her. Her blonde hair fanned out around her head in a halo. Appropriate. She was the angel that made everything right in his life. And he'd just made plans to blow her world apart.

The impossibility of the situation twisted his gut. The time for deciding a different path had long since passed. He'd made the best decision he could to protect her, but he knew she wouldn't see it that way.

A cold, hard reality settled behind his ribs. This could be the last time he would make love to her. His heart recognized the prickling pressure behind his eyes. He swallowed those emotions down and concentrated on making her feel as good as possible. If this was it for them, then he would hold nothing back. "I love you."

He didn't give her time to respond before his mouth claimed hers. He poured devotion into every stroke of his tongue and slide of his lips. All the things he couldn't tell her, he poured into the kiss.

Please forgive me.

I'm lost without you.

Trust me to make this right.

Desperate love trailed his mouth down her neck, over her chest, to the tip of her breast, finding its mark as he lapped and swirled his tongue around her nipple.

She arched off the bed with a hiss. Her fingers threaded through his hair, and she held him in place. "Hank."

Long sucks, twirling licks, tiny biting nips had her writhing and pleading for release. He slid a hand between her legs and found her wet and wanting. One finger slipped into her body. Her deep, satisfied moan threw kerosene on his desire to bring her pleasure. He circled his thumb over the hidden bundle of nerves and she came in huge wracking shudders, clawing and gripping his shoulders.

Before she stopped trembling, he sank into her on a sigh. This was his heaven.

With her.

In her.

Loving her.

He'd fight the devil himself to keep her. With every stroke and glide, he determined to do whatever he had to do to fix this, to fight for her, for them.

She wrapped her hands around his arms that were still next to her head, anchoring herself to him. "Yes, right there, Hank. Don't stop."

Stop? That was never happening. The deep roll of his hips over and over gave her what she wanted. She found her second orgasm on a loud, sharp cry. His orgasm gathered like the roiling tide of emotions slamming against his ribs and increased his tempo, driving him forward.

The sound of her soft moans and his pounding heart pulsing through his head were all he could hear. The mounting sensation exploded through him. His shaking release slammed into him, desperate and hard. His vision blurred and his arms shook. He rolled them to their sides to keep from collapsing on top of her.

Soft fingers traced over his cheek. "I love you, Hank Odom."

He drew her head to his chest and held her there. "I love you too."

She snuggled in next to him, and they lay wrapped in each other's arms with their baby between them. Long after she fell asleep, and her soft snores were no more than a puff of air, he finally slept, and dreamed of slamming doors.

Chapter Fifty-Six

Hank yanked open his desk drawer. A couple of pain relievers for his throbbing head were necessary if he was going to be able to get through this day. He checked his watch. Agent Sheridan and Agent Murphy would be arriving any minute to discuss coordinating the logistics for the takedown of Raul Perez, Thomas Chang, and Charlotte Klein.

What a nightmare.

Caught between a rock and a fucking awful place. He either took his chances with Charlie's safety and hoped that no one thought she was working with the authorities to bring down Perez and Chang, or protect her by having her arrested and hope like hell she forgave him. Because there was no way she'd see this as anything but the ultimate betrayal and manipulation.

He ran his hand across his forehead. The pain in his head intensified to a constant piercing ache.

"Sheriff, Agents Sheridan and Murphy are here to see you," Barb said through the intercom.

"Send them in."

The agents came through the door wearing their cop faces. Even

Murphy's signature smirk was gone. They were all business today. "Hank, how are you today?" Agent Sheridan asked.

"As well as can be expected." He shook both agents' hands.

"You alright there, Sheriff?" Agent Murphy pulled papers from her leather satchel. He hated that stupid satchel.

He swallowed down any lingering doubt about what he had to do. "I'm fine."

"Good, because we have a lot to talk about, and we're going to need your help." Murphy's grey eyes narrowed under the bill of her DEA ball cap.

"You can count on me." He hardened his heart and put the potential consequences to his relationship with Charlie out of his mind. He was a cop. He'd taken a vow to uphold the law, to protect the community and the children of his town, and that was what he intended to do.

The two agents exchanged a look, then seemed to decide he was indeed on board.

"Alright, later this afternoon, Perez and Chang will bring Ms. Klein her delivery. We'll have agents positioned in the alley behind the shop, but out of sight. You, me, and Agent Sheridan will be in the front. On my signal, we will raid the store and make the arrest. All three will be brought back to Houston, where Perez and Chang will be booked and detained. Ms. Klein will be detained until we can get her to the safe house."

"You still with us, Hank?" Sheridan asked.

"Yeah." He fought like hell to keep his tone steady and professional. "Will we take Perez and Chang in the ally or in the store?"

"In the store," Sheridan said.

"Once we have Chang and Perez booked, we will transport Ms. Klein to our safe house, per your request." Agent Murphy's tone indicated that she believed that was a waste of time. "Where she'll stay for a reasonable amount of time so that it appears she was found to have nothing to do with this. Then she'll be released."

"And her stock?" Hank's vocal chords sounded like they were stuck in a noose.

"Since you've been able to get us samples of her products, and we've had them tested, she will be able to keep her inventory. We're only interested in the drugs."

Hank nodded. At least there was that. The grand opening would be ruined, but she'd still have her products, she and Pod would be safe, and her life could go back to normal.

The big question was, would he be part of that life or not?

Chapter Fifty-Seven

Charlie stepped back from the display she'd just put together featuring her exfoliating soaps that she made with coconut oil and coffee. The white bars with brown flecks popped against the chocolate and blue display shelf. As her gaze drifted around her little store, only one word came to mind.

Perfect.

A quick wave to the paparazzi who were milling around the entrance to the store. She'd called in every favor she knew to get coverage of the Grand Opening. She was surprised some of the media had come to town days before the store opened for business. Probably to get a good look at the pregnant former child star, who was big as a house. Didn't matter. As long as they were here to let the world know about her shop, then she could tolerate them.

She gathered the supplies and put them behind the counter. Her cell rang, and she swiped to answer it. "Hello, Scarlett."

"Hey, girl. Luanne, Hailey, and I want to have a small party for you and Hank after the wedding. I know you guys are only going to do something with the Justice of the Peace, but we want to honor our friends. Please say yes?"

Scarlett's pleading tone made her laugh. "Far be it for me to deny you a chance to throw a party, but you just had a baby. You don't need to be working on a party for me."

"The others will do the work, and I'll supervise. We'll keep it small, just close friends and family. We want to celebrate your new family."

She rubbed little circles on her belly. "Thank you, Scarlett." The words crowded out the tears that seemed to be close to the surface these days. "For everything."

"Oh, no. Don't cry or I'll follow suit. Crying and leaking milk seem to be all I do lately. Anytime Gavin hears me upset in the other room he says, 'Do you need a tissue or a breast pad?' I swear, I'm a hot mess, but I've never been happier."

"You're really selling this post-pregnancy thing."

Scarlett laughed. "Sorry."

"How's baby Molly?"

"Perfect in every way." Molly cooed on the other end of the line, and Charlie's heart melted.

Hard to believe in just a few weeks her baby would be here. Even harder to believe was how far away her old life was from this beautiful existence she'd created here in Zachsville. She had people she loved, people she knew had her back. Nobody had your back in Hollywood unless they were driving a knife into it.

"How are you?" Scarlett asked.

A firming lotion was turned sideways on its display. She straightened it. "I was just thinking that I can't imagine my life being better than it is right now."

"I'm so happy for you. Not that you've done anything the easy way. Getting married, opening a business, and having a baby all within a month of each other."

She chuckled. "Yeah, if it weren't for Hailey and my grandfather I don't know what I'd do."

"Who's going to work for you while you're on maternity leave?"

"My soon to be sister-in-law, Roxanne, is going to manage the store for me. She's awesome and has experience in retail, which is perfect." A knock on the door made her jump. Hank stood on the other side of the glass looking better than a body had a right to. "Scarlett, I need to go. Hank's here." She couldn't help the smile in her voice.

"Okay, we'll talk more about the party later. Bye."

She disconnected and practically skipped to the door, which in her condition was a tricky business. She looked more like a wounded elephant than a graceful gazelle. Thankfully, she knew Hank didn't care. He loved her and believed in her, just like she loved and believed in him. With a flip of the lock the man of her dreams had her in his arms and was kissing her silly.

"Hey." His warm breath fanned across her cheek.

"Hey." She swung the door closed, and they moved farther into the store. "What are you doing here? I didn't think I'd see you until this evening." She smoothed her hands over his shoulders. "Not that I'm complaining. How was your meeting?"

"It was..."

"Are you alright?" He was pale again, and she didn't miss the tremble in his hands as he looped a stray hair behind her ear.

Her phone dinged with an incoming text. She glanced at her phone. "Crap. Raul and Thomas just pulled into the alley." When she glanced back at him, all the color had drained from his face. "Babe, you look awful. Do you want some water?"

He waved her off. "No." He took both of her hands in his. "You know how much I love you and Pod, right?"

"Yes." The pounding of her pulse put her on edge. Something was wrong. "What is it, Hank? You're scaring me."

The back door swung open, and Raul and Thomas walked through, both carrying crates for her delivery. Hank released her hands. She immediately missed his closeness.

"Hello, Miss Charlie—Oh, Sheriff, we didn't expect you to be here." Thomas cut a nervous look at Raul.

"It's fine, guys. You can set those in the back room, and I'll be with you in just a second." She turned to Hank, who'd moved farther away from her. He had the strangest look on his face. "What's wrong?"

Before he could answer, both the back door and the front doors flew open and men and women dressed in black with DEA caps on and guns drawn stormed into the store. "Hands in the air," The woman shouted. The room erupted into chaos as yelling and cussing came from everyone. Everyone but Hank, who also pulled his gun and aimed it at Raul and Thomas.

"You too, Ms. Klein! Hands in the air." A woman, with gun drawn and a vest with DEA printed on the front, rushed her.

Her arms went above her head. "What's going on?" She glanced over to see Raul and Thomas on the ground with their hands cuffed behind their back. Both were staring at her. "What's happening? Raul, Thomas, I don't understand."

The female agent holstered her firearm. She could do that because another agent now had his gun pointed right at her. The female agent took one of Charlie's wrists. "Charlotte Klein, you're under arrest."

"Hank?" It was all that would come out of her mouth. But the man of her dreams did nothing while both of her hands were secured behind her back. Movement from the corner of her eye caught her attention. She turned to see Raul and Thomas being led away by two of the officers. "Why am I being arrested? Hank, do something." She was surprised all the glass around her didn't break with the shrillness of her voice.

"Drug trafficking, Ms. Klein," the male officer said, and began reciting the Miranda rights.

But all she could hear was Hank's whispered, "I'm so sorry."

And that was when she lost her ever-lovin' shit.

* * *

For a second Hank could only stare in disbelief as Charlie kicked out and caught Murphy in the shin, stomped her toe, then brought her head back and clocked the agent in the face.

"Ow, shit!" Murphy tightened her hold on his pregnant fiancée.

"Let go of me!" Charlie's scream pierced his eardrum, and the tears streaming down her face stabbed him square in the heart.

"Charlie, stop struggling." Wrong thing to say—he knew it as soon as he saw murder flash into her blue eyes. She didn't stop fighting, only redirected her fury to him.

"You knew about this."

It wasn't a question, and he wasn't going to lie to her. "Yes. But if you let—"

"Shut up!" It seemed the two words robbed her of all her strength. It looked like she might crumple to the ground. Big, torturous tears rolled down her face. Each one peeled away a piece of his soul. "I don't want to hear one more word from your lying mouth. I trusted you, and you betrayed me."

"Charlie." He stepped toward her.

"Go to hell." She glanced at Murphy. "Get me out of here."

The paparazzi flashed photo after photo of her being led from the front door to the unmarked car parked at the curb. This would be front page news. *Child star arrested for drug trafficking.* Yeah, that's a story that had legs. She'd be ruined.

Sheridan approached, glanced out at the circus on the street, then looked back at Hank. "She'll get over this once she understands why you did what you did."

Hank didn't give two shits about the man's assessment of the situation. "We done here?"

Sheridan stepped out of his way. "Yeah, we're done. Thanks for your help."

Without a backward glance, Hank strode out of the building and didn't stop until he was at his vehicle. He checked his phone and saw fifteen messages from Charlie's friends and family. They used to be his friends and family too, but as soon as they found out what he'd done, they'd tell him to go to hell just like Charlie had. But it was too late.

He was already there.

Chapter Fifty-Eight

The ride to Houston was a blur of misery for Hank. Guilt tried to tag along, but he knew he'd done the right thing. He just wasn't sure he could pay the price for doing the right thing.

She hated him. He didn't blame her. She'd trusted him, and this was how he'd repaid her. She'd never speak to him again.

Think, Odom. Logic this out.

His lungs tried to hyperventilate as he attempted to see his way through this situation. He hadn't intended to deceive her. It was for her own good and protection. Yeah, that would fly, since the mission she'd been on since she climbed out of that bathroom window at the courthouse was to find her way and learn to stand on her own two feet.

He was screwed.

Still, he had to make sure she was alright, that the baby was okay. He whipped his truck into a parking spot for law enforcement officers and jumped out. Each of his steps ate up two stairs at a time. Thank God for his badge. He bypassed security and made his way to the place Charlie was being held.

The room was utilitarian and sparse, with only a few desks and chairs. Agent Murphy sat at one of the desks with an ice pack on her forehead. It looked like Charlie's aim had been true.

"Where is she?"

Murphy pointed down a hallway.

Getting to her was all that mattered. Not the injured agent, or an explanation.

"Sheriff." Murphy held up a key. "You'll need this."

"She's in a cell? What the hell, Murphy?"

The woman shrugged. "She wouldn't cooperate and calm down."

"She's eight months pregnant. I'm pretty sure you could take her, Murphy. You didn't have to throw her in a cell."

She lowered the ice pack and glared at him. "Exactly, Sheriff. She's in there for her protection. I didn't want to hurt her. Contrary to what you believe about Agent Sheridan and myself, we have Ms. Klein's best interests at heart too."

Even though she didn't say it, the statement *this was your idea* polluted the air between them. But he didn't have to explain himself to this woman. He headed down the hallway to the woman he did owe an explanation.

The heavy metal door to the room that housed a cell had a small window in it. He nearly lost the nerve when he saw Charlie curled on the bunk in the cell, crying with her arms around her belly.

The outer door was locked too. He turned the key and moved into the room with the cell. She was singing a lullaby to Pod. The sweetly sung words obliterated his heart. "Charlie?"

She didn't look at him. She didn't stop singing.

He slid the key into the cell lock, but his hands shook so badly that it scraped around the hole. That seemed to get her attention. Faster than a woman in her condition should be able to move, she was at the cell door. He tried again with the key. "Don't worry, baby. I'll get you out."

Her slender fingers wrapped around the bars and yanked the door closed just as he opened it. "No!"

"What? Agent Murphy only put you in here until you calmed down. Let me get you out of this cell. I'll explain everything." He tried to pull the door open, but she held on. Of course, he could've opened it, but he might hurt her.

"No." Her mouth barely moved. The word came from someplace he'd never seen in her. Deep, protective, and absolutely resolute.

His hands went into the air. "Okay, fine. We'll talk like this."

"I don't want to talk to you, Hank."

"Tough. You're going to hear my side of the story." He told her everything. A day late and a dollar short, but he didn't hold anything back. "You're not going to be charged with anything. They had to arrest you too, to protect you."

Her uninterested expression didn't deter him. But he did start talking faster, knowing he was losing her. "I'm sorry. I'm so damn sorry."

"How long?" Her tone was as dead as her eyes.

"What?"

"How long have you known about Thomas and Raul?"

This was the question he was hoping she wouldn't ask him, but he wouldn't lie to her. "Since before you decided to do business with them both."

"And you didn't tell me before I got involved with them." Again, not a question. Just a cold, hard accusation. It hit him like an executioner's decree.

His hands went around hers holding the bar. She slipped hers away. "Charlie, I wanted to, but the DEA has jurisdiction. They ordered me not to."

"And you always do the right thing." She cocked her head. "Except when you don't."

"That's not fair. I was doing my job, but I was still looking out for you."

"You mean using me."

"No."

One blonde brow inched up her forehead. The jagged edge of her silence flayed his skin. He couldn't take it anymore. He had to hold her in his arms, make her understand. He slid the key in the lock again.

She yanked it closed with all her might. "Leave." The fierceness of her actions was in direct contrast to her monotone words. "The door is locked, and there's not a key in the world that will open it."

"You don't mean that. What about Pod?"

"We don't need you." Her chin tilted up, and her spine went straight as a board—clear communication that she did mean it. The tears were gone. Pale tracks and red, swollen eyes were the only evidence they'd been there at all. The woman that stood before him now wasn't weak, or heartbroken. She was a warrior hell-bent on protecting herself and her unborn child from any enemy.

From him.

"Leave." She didn't blink. She didn't hesitate. Her flat stare was the blade that severed their tie.

He nodded. What else was there to say? The heavy metal door clanged shut behind him, and the click of the automatic lock sliding into place rang down the hallway.

How appropriate.

Chapter Fifty-Nine

The safe house they moved Charlie to was an uninteresting suburban ranch on the outskirts of Houston. The modest furnishings were clean and comfortable, so she guessed it could be worse. She could hardly contain her excitement when it was announced that Agent Murphy was the agent assigned to stay with her. The only satisfaction she had was that Murphy didn't seem any more thrilled about the assignment than Charlie did.

She'd been informed that she'd be their guest until the DEA determined it was safe to leave. They'd allowed her to call Pops and let him know she was alright. But it was all so cloak and dagger that it kind of freaked her out. She hadn't been allowed to call him on the house phone or his cell. Evidently, the authorities were worried about his phones being tapped, so he'd been brought to the sheriff's office so they could talk.

Not surprisingly, he was furious with Hank and upset about this whole horrible mess. She missed Pops and Honey. She missed Hank too, but she was sure she'd get over that particular affliction. He was bad for her.

Guilt squeezed her chest. She knew she was being irrational and not even looking at this from anyone's point of view other than her own, but she couldn't help it. He'd lied to her, and used her to get what he wanted, just like her mother and Ron, and everyone else in Hollywood.

"I'm going to make some coffee. Do you want some?" The agent moved to the kitchen after she'd walked through the house to make sure everything was as it should be.

"No. How long am I in your custody?"

"I've already told you that you're not in custody, Ms. Klein. Whether you choose to believe it or not, this is for your protection." She filled the well in the pot with water. "If Raul Perez and Thomas Chang believe that you were arrested and are being investigated right along with them, then the chance that they will think you were involved in their arrest goes away." Murphy scooped coffee into the filter then replaced the lid to the can.

Charlie crossed her arms on top of her belly. "And remind me again why I'm involved in this at all?"

Agent Murphy gave her an exasperated cop stare.

Charlie snapped her fingers. "Oh, that's right. It's because neither the DEA nor the Zachsville Sheriff's department saw fit to warn me away from these two men before I ever started to do business with them. And why was that again?" She tapped her chin with a finger. "I remember now. You needed a mole. Only you forgot to tell me I was the mole. You just used my—Hank Odom to pump me for information."

The law enforcement officer didn't respond, only reached into the cabinet for a coffee cup.

"Thanks for clearing that up for me."

Murphy leaned against the counter, and her fist went to her hip. "Are you always this bratty?"

That shocked a snort from Charlie. "Oh, sister, I haven't even started. I have an advanced degree in brattiness. I was a child star. We're our own brand of bratty." The *well, duh* expression on the woman's face only reinforced that fact that Charlie had zero desire to share a space with her. "I'm going to take a shower." She made her way back to her room.

As soon as the door was closed, her swagger slid away. The tears she'd been crying most of the day leaked from her eyes again. It was all gone. Everything she'd worked for...gone. No way the store would be ready to open, all her work would be for nothing. She'd set up promotions, called in favors from the media. From her years in the spotlight, she knew how to create a buzz, and that was what she'd done for her little store.

Her heart, which she'd forced to keep beating for Pod's sake, gave a sluggish thump. Why she'd thought she could do any of this on her own, she had no idea. Everything Ron and Marci thought of her was true. She wasn't good for much besides being pretty.

Stop it. That's not true.

She'd built this business with her own hands, and she'd done it mostly by herself. Hard work and sweat had gone into every product she'd made. And if not for a certain law enforcement officer betraying her, her Grand Opening would've gone off without a hitch. She'd already made sure of it. But now... There wouldn't be a grand opening. She was ruined.

Charlie moved to the bathroom connected to her room and undressed. The hot water of the shower heated her skin but did little to melt the block of ice in her chest. Within the safety of the shower, she let the tears fall freely. After months of reinventing herself, she was back to square one. Surrounded by people who just wanted to use her for their own benefit.

Too much time hiding in the shower depleted the hot water supply and now the chill of the cold water drove her from the confines of the shower. She flipped off the faucet, carefully stepped from the stall, and grabbed a towel. Trembling fingers smoothed her messy hair from her face. An examination of herself in the mirror revealed dark circles that set off glassy, sad eyes. Sallow, dry skin from all the crying covered her sunken cheeks. Scratch pretty from her short list of accomplishments.

Who the hell even cared. She'd lost everything, and the last thing she cared about was how she looked. All she wanted to do was crawl into bed and hold Pod until she fell asleep. There were a few bags of toiletries, underwear, and clothes on the bed. It must've chapped Agent Murphy's behind to have to shop for her. Good.

She pulled on a nightgown and slid into the surprisingly comfortable bed. Just as she was about to drift off, there was a knock on her bedroom door. "Ms. Klein, Sheriff Odom's on the phone. He'd like to speak with you."

A fresh wave of pain and betrayal smashed into her. "No."

"Alright. I'll tell him. Do you need anything?"

"No." She lay there waiting to see if the agent said anything else. She didn't. Her arms went around her belly. "I'm so sorry, Pod. I've really screwed it all up. I know I promised I'd fix this and take care of you, but I might need a little more time." Yeah, like forever. She was beginning to believe that she might truly be incapable of handling her life.

* * *

Hank chucked his phone onto the coffee table in Hailey's living room. He let his head fall back to the top of the sofa. "She won't talk to me."

"How are she and Pod?" Hailey sat across from him in an oversized chair, her dark hair piled on top of her head, her clean face pinched and worried.

"The Feds had a doctor check them out, and everything is fine." That had been the best news he'd gotten all day. "Agent Murphy says Charlie's fine, except for a bad case of brattiness."

Hailey snorted without humor. "That she can be, especially when she's hurt."

He raised his head and stared at her. "Thanks."

"Oh, my gosh. Sorry. I didn't..."

He waved her off. "It's fine. She is hurt, and it's my fault." His elbows went to his knees, and he dropped his head in his hands.

"How?"

"Excuse me?" He couldn't have heard her correctly.

Hailey crossed her arms over her Shiner Bock beer t-shirt. "I want you to explain how this is your fault. From where I'm sitting, it looks like you had an impossible decision to make. Not to mention, you were doing your job."

"I crushed her, Hailey."

"No. You didn't. You protected her and Pod."

With his elbows still on his knees, he let one hand hang between his legs, and rubbed his mouth with the other. "She's never going to forgive me. It's a miracle that she gave me a second chance after the Karen thing. I don't know why I'm surprised that I screwed this up. We Odom men are cursed when it comes to relationships."

"Oh, for the love... Would you stop with that?" She uncurled from the chair and sat on the edge of the cushion. "I love you like a brother, Hank. But I'm so tired of this Odom chip you carry around on your shoulder. There is no curse. You're not like your brothers or your father. So stop paying for their sins. Live your own life the way you want to live it. If you want Charlie, then talk to her. Don't stop until you've made her understand that you didn't have a choice in what happened today, other than to try and protect her. Which you did."

This conversation wasn't going as he'd expected, and he wasn't enjoying the truth sandwich Hailey was serving up. "I'm—"

"A good man who's sabotaging his own happiness." She rose and came to stand before him. She smoothed her hand over his hair like he'd seen her do to Lottie a million times. "Stop it."

He reached up and caught her hand. "How?"

She squeezed his fingers. "I have no idea, but you'll figure it out. Lock the door when you leave. I'm going to check on Lottie. Good night."

Was that what he was doing? Sabotaging his happiness because he didn't believe he deserved it? Was that why he never went to find Charlie after she turned eighteen? And why he married a woman knowing they could never really be happy together? Was he catastrophizing this situation and preparing for the worst because he thought he didn't deserve the love of his life and their child? The answer was as clear as Hailey's glass coffee table.

Yes.

"Hailey, you're—" He glanced around, but she'd already gone upstairs and turned off all the lights except for a small lamp. The more time he spent in the dimly lit room, the more he could plainly see all the ways he'd denied himself true happiness, and how the unachievable high standards that ruled his life only fueled his conviction that because he wasn't perfect, he was just like his brothers and father.

He thought of Charlie and their child. This was the time to choose. Believe the negative shit in his head telling him he'd ruined everything, or fight against it and go after the life he wanted with the woman he loved, no matter how hard or messy it was going to be.

He rose and headed for the door. There was no question in his mind what he'd do. Charlie and Pod were everything to him, and he'd fight like hell, even if that meant fighting against himself until they were a family.

Chapter Sixty

The smell of bacon and something sweet lured Charlie from a deep, fitful sleep. She pushed her mess of hair from her face and glanced at the clock on the nightstand.

It was 9 a.m. on her fourth morning as a guest in the safe house. So far she'd managed to avoid Agent Murphy as much as possible, choosing to take her meals in the bedroom in front of the TV set up there, not leaving her room unless she knew her babysitter was in the shower, or in the middle of the night when the good agent was asleep. She didn't need or want the woman's attitude.

A pang of misery crashed through her chest. Tomorrow was supposed to be the grand opening of her shop, her beautiful emporium. The thing she'd put together with her own two hands. She didn't know why she was being so dramatic about the whole thing. No one had taken the store away from her, it would still open, but now it would be tainted by this situation.

Ugh, she was sick of her own company. Agent Murphy was preferable to spending another minute alone with her thoughts. She climbed out of bed, that and any other movement she made was becoming increasingly difficult. "No offense, Pod, but you're about to be evicted. It's been fun and all, but I want my body back."

Pod gave her a hitch-kick to the sternum.

"Ow." She rubbed where Pod's foot had connected. "Sorry. I take it back."

A pretty pink robe that she'd found in the bag of clothes went over her pajamas, and she made her way to the kitchen. She needed to thank her warden for the clothes. Having clean underwear and clothes had been the one thing to make this time bearable. It'd kill her, but she'd express her appreciation.

"She lives." Agent Murphy was at the stove wearing leggings and an oversized tee. The smart ass never turned to face her.

"Yes, she does, and she's hungry." Charlie grabbed a mug and poured herself a cup of coffee. "Would you like a refill?"

A blue mug was shoved in her face. "Yes, three sugars and cream."

"Wow, that's pretty sugary for someone so acerbic."

Murphy pulled out the cop glare, but it lost some of its punch when Charlie noticed the unicorn with a rainbow shooting out of its butt on the front of her shirt, under the words *I poop rainbows*. "Sit down and zip it before I decide not to feed you."

Charlie snorted. "I'm pretty sure that's against the Geneva Convention."

"And that would matter if this was an international incident and not a federal situation. But good try."

Heat pricked Charlie's cheeks. She hated being the dumbest person in the room. Or at least feeling like the dumbest person in the room. She'd discovered over the last several months that she was good at some things, and that she was pretty smart. So instead of being defensive, she decided to learn something new. "Oh, really? I didn't know that. Can you explain the difference?" Again, anything was preferable to her own company. She almost doubled over laughing at the look on Murphy's face. Well, double over was a bit ambitious in her condition, but the point was still true.

"Mostly it applies if we're at war, and it's boring as hell. I'd rather talk about something else. Like how the pity party you've been throwing yourself has stunk up the whole house." She transferred the bacon and French toast to a plate and brought them to the table.

"I'm not having a pity party. I have a lot of things on my mind."

Now that did make her defensive, mostly because the woman was right.

Murphy passed the platter of food to her before she filled her own plate. "Oh, please. You've practically got poor me stamped across your forehead."

"Why are you trying to make me mad? I came out here to thank you for the clothes and toiletries you bought me. They've helped to make this less horrible. But if you don't stop baiting me, then I'm not going to say it." The agent's confused expression baffled her. "What?"

"I didn't get those things for you."

Charlie took a bite of perfectly cooked bacon. "Oh, well please pass along my gratitude to whoever did."

"You should probably thank him yourself. It was Sheriff Odom."

The bacon lodged in Charlie's throat, and then the coughing began. She grabbed her coffee and tried to wash it down, but all that did was burn her esophagus. "What?"

"Hank's responsible for those things. We have some clothing we keep for our...guests, but he wouldn't have it. He went and got them after you sent him away on the day you were arrested." She sawed through her French toast. "He's a real bastard, that fiancé of yours," she said around a mouthful of syrupy bread.

The room took a dive with her in it. "He's not..."

"Your fiancé? Oh, that's right. You tossed him aside for doing his job." She waved her fork in the air. "I forgot."

Charlie shoved her full plate away from her. "He lied to me. He not only let me be arrested, but he came up with the idea. If that's his job, then it sucks."

Agent Murphy dropped the sarcasm and looked her straight in the eye. "Sometimes it does. But in the Sheriff's case, he had no choice but to follow orders, unless he wanted to lose his job. Is that what you would've wanted?"

Did she? She hadn't considered that he might've lost his job if he'd warned her. "I don't—"

"And the man did everything he could to ensure your safety and comfort. This," she flung her arm out to indicate the house, "isn't something we do for everyone. He insisted on this for his cooperation.

Maybe we would've eventually come around to bringing you here, since you're pregnant. But he made it part of the deal. And as far as him coming up with the idea to arrest you along with Perez and Chang? Can you imagine how hard that was for him to watch? But he did it to protect you, knowing you might react exactly the way you have. Like I said, he's a real bastard."

Charlie fiddled with the tie to her robe. The robe Hank bought her. "I didn't know."

The messy bun on top of Murphy's head wobbled back and forth as the agent shook her head. "You didn't know. And why is that? Because you turned him away even after he explained things to you. Listen, Princess—"

"Don't call me that."

"Listen, *Charlie*, I've seen a lot of bad shit, a lot of bad men." She shrugged. "It's the job. But Hank Odom isn't a bad man. He's one of the good guys, and if you're too stupid to see that, then there are plenty of women out there who will appreciate him." The chair scraped when she pushed to her feet. "Your turn to do the dishes. I'm going to shower."

Charlie examined the officer's beautiful face, smooth skin, and rock-hard body as she exited the kitchen. "Agent Murphy."

She stopped and glanced over her shoulder. "Yeah?"

"Are you one of those women who would appreciate Hank?"

The woman's cop stare had a flirty edge to it. "In a heartbeat. But he's so in love with you that he wouldn't see another woman if she danced naked in front of him with hundred-dollar bills hanging from her ears."

"What's your first name, Agent Murphy?"

"Julie."

"Stay away from Hank, Julie."

Murphy snorted. "Like you care."

She did care. She cared very much.

* * *

"Good news! We're getting out of here."

Charlie glanced up from her book to see Murphy in her bedroom doorway, phone in hand.

"Really, when?" After their conversation that morning, there'd been an uneasy peace between them.

"Right now. Grab your things, and I'll drive you back to Zachsville."

Charlie glanced at the bedside clock. It was ten at night. But it didn't matter—she just wanted to go home.

Murphy tapped the door jamb. "I'll meet you at the front door."

Charlie flung back the covers and stood. The moment her feet hit the ground a pain low in her belly sliced through her. Sometimes she forgot her big-as-a-house size, and that sudden movements weren't a good idea.

The ride to Zachsville was quiet. That was one of the things she appreciated about Agent Murphy—she only spoke when she had something to say. Her hard truths from this morning hadn't gone unnoticed. Her words had pounded on the door to Charlie's heart all day and made her do some serious soul-searching.

For the last eight years, and probably even before then, she'd let other people do her heavy lifting. It was easier to avoid conflict and not have to deal with overbearing personalities, but mostly it was just easier. She'd liked easy. It kept you deaf, dumb, and blind to the challenges of life, but it also made you a bystander in your life.

When she'd decided she was going to start making some of her own decisions, her solution had been to run in the face of difficult circumstances. She'd run from Hank in his hotel room, from her wedding, and she'd been relieved to run away from Hollywood due to her Pops' accident. But that wasn't her anymore. Over the last eight months, she'd learned to face her problems and not run from them.

Not letting Hank explain when he'd come to get her out of that cell was a classic example of the old Charlie. She'd done the same thing after their night in Austin, and when he and Karen broke up for good. Shame washed over her. Once again, she'd assumed the worst of him instead of letting him explain.

Her grandfather's house was dark except for a lamp in the living room. She'd called Pops once Murphy had returned her phone to tell him she was on her way home. He'd wanted to wait up for her, but she'd made him promise that he'd go to bed.

The car rolled to a stop and Agent Murphy put it in park. "You'll understand if I don't walk you to the door."

She laughed. This woman was a piece of work. "I understand." She gathered her belongings and opened the door. Her lower back ached like crazy and was beginning to seize up on her. "It kills me to say this, but thank you."

Julie Murphy cocked a grin at her. "Hank and I will be sure to wave to you when we see you around."

With a hand on the door for support, Charlie hoisted herself from the car, then poked her head back in. "Not unless you want me to smack you in the face again. He's mine."

Murphy laughed. "Bring it, sister."

One thing had become abundantly clear throughout the day. She couldn't live one more day without Hank in her life. Murphy was right, he was one of the good ones, and she'd be a fool to let him go. They'd work it out. She was unsure how at the moment, but she still had faith in them, and that was all that mattered.

Chapter Sixty-One

Charlie stared at the ceiling. Between the pain in her back and Pod sticking summersault landings on her bladder she'd hardly slept at all. If the back pain didn't improve today, then she'd have to call the doctor and see if there was anything she could take. If she was going to figure out her life she needed to do it with as little pain as possible.

First thing on her list was find Hank, give him a chance to explain, then forgive him. She wasn't wasting one more minute without him.

The second thing was to reschedule the opening of the store. Yes, not opening when she'd planned was a setback, and being arrested had caused a bit of a scandal. She'd watched the entertainment reports during her stay at the safe house, and it was all they could talk about. Child star arrested on suspicion of drug smuggling. As they say, there's no such thing as bad publicity. Sometimes being notorious was just as good as being famous. Bottom line, nothing was ruined, she'd figure it out, and it would all be okay because she wouldn't stop until it was.

Her phone rang. She checked the screen—it was Honey. "Hello."

"Charlie?" Honey shouted over the noise in the background.

"Yes, Honey. It's me. Where are you?"

"I can't hear you over all this racket."

She raised her voice so the older woman could hear her. "I said, it's me, Honey."

"Darlin', there's no need to yell."

"Oh, sorry."

Honey seemed to move to a quieter place because the chatter died down some. "Don't be sorry, just get your heinie down here right now. We're swamped."

Confusion clouded Charlie's brain. What in the world was Honey talking about? "Where are you?"

"I'm at The Emporium, and there's a line out the door. We need your help." The line went dead. Charlie stared at her phone like it might give her the answers to all the questions rolling around in her head. It didn't.

As fast as she could, she crawled out of bed and dressed. Some concealer, mascara, a quick braid of her hair, and she was out the door. Pops wasn't at home, but the Buick was in the garage. When she pulled up to The Emporium, there was indeed a line out the door. A big pink and black *Grand Opening* sign hung suspended over the front door, and the media was bunched together snapping photos. "What in the world?" When she'd been hauled off in handcuffs five days ago, the store wasn't ready for the grand opening.

One of the paparazzi caught sight of her as soon as she exited the car. The rapid-fire questions and the sound of cameras clicking barely fazed her as she elbowed her way from the car to the front door. "Excuse me. I need to get in."

"So do we, wait your turn," a woman wearing a pink tee that read, *Free Charlie* said. Her dark hair made the hot pink of the shirt pop.

"I'm the owner."

"Oh, my Lord, it's you." She gestured to several women with her who were sporting their own pink *Free Charlie* shirts. "We're here to support you. You go, girl."

Charlie noticed then that all the women in line were wearing *Free Charlie* t-shirts. "Where did you get the tees?" she asked the woman with the dark hair.

"Oh, they handed them out to the first two hundred people in line. Great idea, by the way." She held her fist in the air. "Girl power!"

Charlie was so stunned that she barely noticed when the lady shoved her to the front of the line.

Her little store was packed with pink-shirt-clad women. It was the most beautiful thing she'd ever seen. She scanned the crowd and saw all of her friends pitching in and helping. Scarlett and Luanne were seeing to customers on the floor, Hailey and Roxanne were running the two registers, and Honey and Wardell were allowing people into the shop as others left. Even Gavin and Jack were helping. Tears floated behind her lids.

A familiar blonde with cat-eye glasses hurried up to her. "Marci?"

Her former publicist threw her arms around Charlie and hugged her tight. "Charlie. I've missed you."

She disentangled herself from the woman's grip. "What are you doing here?" A horrible thought occurred to her. "Is Ron here?"

"I'm here to help. When your fiancé contacted me—"

"Hank contacted you?"

Marci nodded. "He had some questions for me about Ron, and when he found out I'd quit working for Gaylord Entertainment, he asked if I'd like to help with your grand opening. The shirts were my idea. What do you think?"

"They're... Marci, I can't afford you." Her brain hadn't caught up with what was going on around her.

Sadness clouded Marci's eyes. "I'm not charging you. I'm doing this for a friend, if she'll still have me? Especially after I let Ron bully me into abandoning you. I'm so sorry."

Charlie would have to sort out her feelings about all of this later, but right now she was glad to see Marci. "Of course I'll still have you. And the shirts are brilliant. But what did Hank want to ask you about Ron?"

Marci glanced over Charlie's shoulder and smiled. "I'll let him explain." She squeezed Charlie's hand then disappeared into the crowd.

She followed Marci's gaze and her heart about burst from her chest. Hank was making a beeline for her. "Hey." His tentative greeting spiked her guilt. She'd behaved so badly by not letting him explain.

"Hey."

"I'm sorry," they both said together. Then they laughed. He guided her through the crowd to the backroom.

"You did all of this?" Her voice was as watery as Honey's oatmeal.

"Yes. I've also got a list of other suppliers who sell top-of-the-line products, for when you're ready."

The tears that had pooled in her eyes at the sight of her friends spilled over and ran down her face.

"Aw, baby, don't cry." He gently wiped the moisture from her cheeks.

She stepped as close as she could get to him with Pod between them, and raised up onto her toes. Her lips slid over his in an all-too-brief kiss. "Thank you...for everything."

His arms went around her, and his smile was brilliant. "You're welcome."

They stood like they were the only ones in the whole store, just holding each other. "I mean, for everything. For trying to protect me, and for the clothes at the safe house, and for being such a good man."

"How did you know about the clothes?"

Her fingers toyed with the hair at the back of his neck. "Agent Murphy. She's a real gem, by the way."

He snorted. "Tell me about it."

"Honestly, she helped me see what an idiot I was being. Of course, she was her ultra-charming self when she did it, but I got the message. I am so sorry for the terrible things I said to you." The regret in her throat chewed up the words and spit them out of her mouth.

"I'm the one who's sorry—"

"You don't have to be."

"I love you, Charlie. I want to tell you the whole story."

"And I'll let you, but not right now. Tell me why Marci is here. She said you called her."

A huge grin spread across his face. "I did. I've had a suspicion since you found out about your credit and all the accounts that were opened. So I did a little digging, and turns out that Ron used one of those credit cards to pay for your marriage license here in Blister County."

"What?"

"Yep."

"So Ron opened all those credit cards?" The bomb he'd just dropped made the room swim.

"Some of them. But you were right about your mom opening the majority of them. I'm sorry about that, Charlie."

She waved off his concern. Her mother had no place in this amazing day. "Just tell me how this involves Ron."

"Well, since I'm the law here in Blister County, I can issue a warrant for his arrest, which I've done." He checked his watch. "The authorities in LA should be picking him up right about now."

Talk about needing time to unpack these emotions. "I... I don't know what to say."

He kissed her forehead. "Say you love me."

She readjusted her position against him. "I love you, Hank. Um... Will you marry me?"

He laughed, then took her face in his hands and crushed his lips to hers. "Of course I'll marry you. We'll do it tomorrow if you like."

She shook her head. "Tomorrow's too late. Marry me now." She could hear the panic ruffling her voice.

"Why?"

"Because my water just broke."

Epilogue

Charlie swiped at the gauzy material stuck to her sweaty face. "Honey, if you don't get that veil off my face, I'm going to climb down off this bed and strangle you with it."

Honey laughed. "You and what army?" She readjusted the piece of white fluff and slid the attached comb into Charlie's bun. "You're hardly in any shape for hand-to-hand combat. Even with my bunion, I could take you. Now hush and concentrate on your breathing, and not what I'm doing."

The murderous look she shot Honey would've crushed the emotions of a weaker person.

But it had zero effect on Honey, who stepped back and observed her handiwork. "Be careful, darlin', or your eyes will get stuck like that."

"Breathe with me, Charlie," Hank crooned softly to her. He was freaking out a little. She couldn't blame him. Pod wasn't due for several more weeks, but the doctor had assured them this was perfectly normal.

Pain slid from her body like it had never been there, and guilt took its place. "Oh, my gosh, Honey. I'm so sorry."

Honey waved her off. "Nothing to be sorry for. You worry about getting that baby here safely. Hank, Wardell, and I will worry about everything else." She pulled a bouquet of flowers from her bag and set it on the table next to Charlie's bed.

Pops tied a bunch of balloons to the back of the rocking chair in the corner. "Hank, when is JP Norris going to get here?"

"He's here." Larry Norris strolled into the room in his fishing vest and hat. "Sorry it took me so long to get here, but I was on the lake when Hank called."

Oh, thank God. She hadn't told any of them, but she was pretty sure Pod was very close to crashing this wedding.

Hank extended his hand to Larry. "Not a problem. You're here now, and that's all that matters."

The JP went to the sink and washed his hands. "Do you have the marriage license?"

Hank looked at her, wild-eyed. She pointed to her bag. "In the inside pocket." Oh, shit, another contraction wracked her body. Her eyes closed, and she sucked in a pained breath through her nose. Crap, this one was barely three minutes from the last.

"I'll get it, Hank." Honey began rifling through Charlie's bag. "You just take care of her."

"I'm right here, baby. You're doing great." She leaned to the side, and he pressed the heel of his hand into her lower back. "That's right, slow and steady." As her breathing eased, he took the washcloth the nurse had given him and wiped her forehead. "That's it. One more deep breath in and out."

She relaxed against the bed then smiled up at him. "You're pretty good at this." She smoothed the worry line between his eyes with her finger. "How are you doing?"

He chuckled and lowered his brow to hers. "I'm about to lose my shit. How are you?"

"I'm fantastic. There's no place I'd rather be and no one I'd rather be doing this with." He went a little blurry when tears washed across her vision. "I love you."

He placed a kiss as soft as a baby's skin on her dry lips. "I love you."

Larry made his way to the other side of the bed. "Are you sure you want to do this now, Charlie?"

Was she sure? She'd been waiting half her life for this moment. "Nothing's going to stop me, Larry."

He glanced at Hank. "Is she on any medication? She needs to be able to make a clear-headed decision."

Hank squeezed her hand. "Why don't you ask her? She knows her own mind."

If it was possible to fall more in love with him, then she just did. *She knows her own mind.* If she weren't already about to marry him, then she'd throw herself at him and beg him to never leave. "Larry, I'm not on any medication, and I'd really like to be, so can we move this along?"

Hank laughed. "You heard the lady."

"Alright, then let's get this done." Larry pulled a laminated card from his back pocket.

"We're here today—"

Another contraction ripped into her like a wolf with its next meal. Pressure moved along her tailbone inch by excruciating inch. She gasped and made a move-it-along motion with her hand. Little puffs of air swooshed in and out of her nose. Yep, this was definitely about to happen. "Honey, call my nurse," she ground out between rhythmic respirations.

"On it." The woman who'd become so important to her grabbed the bouquet of flowers and shoved it into Charlie's hands, then dialed the number on the nurse's station.

"Charlie?" Hank's eyes communicated that he knew they were running out of time.

Her hand went over his. "I'm okay."

Larry looked a little shell-shocked. "I think we should wait until you're more...comfortable, Charlie."

"No!" Pant.

"I'm fine." Pant.

"Let's do this." Pant.

"A...alright. If you're sure." Larry rubbed the back of his neck. "Do you, Hank, take Charlie to be your wife?"

"Yes." His brilliant smile eased some of the pain slicing through her.

"Do you, Charlie, take Hank to be your husband?"

A short respite from the pain eased through her, and she took full advantage of it. "Yes! One million times, yes!" The tears streamed down her face like a joyful river.

Dual sniffles sounded from the sofa where Honey and Wardell sat cuddled together.

"By the power vested in me by the state of Texas, I pronounce you husband and wife."

The door opened and in walked Dr. Shelton and the nurse. "Looks like we missed the party." Dr. Shelton scrubbed her hands in the sink.

Charlie huffed through another contraction. "No, I think you're just in time."

"That's my cue to leave, but first you each have to sign the marriage certificate." He handed them both a pen and they each signed their names. "That'll do it." Larry made his way to the door. "Congratulations, you two."

"Hang on, we'll go with you," Honey said, and came to stand by the bed.

Charlie took Honey's hand. "You don't have to go."

"I believe that if you weren't there for the conception, then you shouldn't be there for the birth. Besides, look at your grandfather. He's about to faint."

Wardell blew her a wobbly kiss from the door.

Honey kissed her cheek, then they were alone. Well, except for Dr. Shelton and the nurse.

The physician took a seat at the end of the bed and flipped back the sheet. "Let's see what we've got going on here. Oh, my. We're about to have a baby."

"What? Now?" Hank looked from Charlie to the doctor. "I thought first babies were supposed to take a long time."

"Most do, but this little gal is ready to be born," Dr. Shelton said.

There was some scrambling, some pushing, a bit of swearing, and a lot of encouragement, and then Phoebe Patrice Odom, Pod for short made her way into the world, screaming like her hair was on fire.

When the nurse laid the baby on Charlie's chest, her sense of unbelief intensified ten-fold. A new, fierce kind of love infused her at the first sight of her daughter. She would live and die for this little girl. Hank's expression communicated the very same thing.

"Charlie, look at her." The velvety reverence in his voice cuddled the three of them in a cocoon of tenderness and adoration. He placed one hand on the baby's back and the other behind Charlie's head. "I love you...both, so much." He rested his forehead against hers. "Charlie and Hank forever."

She kissed his sweet lips. "Forever."

Hello!

Sign up for my **Reader Group**! That's the best way to find out about special giveaways, contest, and new releases.
Click to join the fun

Did you enjoy ***Running From the Law***?
If you did, it would mean the world to me if you left a review on Amazon for me. Reviews are like gold to an author, and they go a long way to giving a book social credit.

Also, I'd love to have you in my Facebook reader group, Jami Albright's Brightens.
Join Now!

A note from Jami

Every time I sit down to write a note for another book, I'm blown away by how unbelievably lucky I am to get to write books for a living. And that's all because of you, sweet readers. Thank you from the very bottom of my heart.

So, Charlie and Hank. I hope you love them as much as I love them. They were the most real characters I've ever written. I wanted to write a second chance romance where the couple had to really fight to be together. And how do they come together again when they're both having to start their lives over.

Charlie was never hard to write. I took every strong single mom I knew and rolled her into one person who would do anything to create the best life possible for her child. I wanted to show a woman who came into her own, and I believe I did that with Charlie.

Hank, was a different story. I wanted to write a hero who was concerned about being a good and ethical man. A man who followed through on his commitments and treated women with respect, no matter what. I'm ashamed to say that it took me a while before I could write him authentically. I had to examine my own biases and prejudices to get to the heart of who he was. I think as women we sometimes say we want a man one way when really we're willing to accept and even expect them to act another way. It was very eye-opening for me to say the least.

In the end, I wrote two characters that I love and respect, and I hope you did too.

Thanks again, for always supporting me and for reading my books.

Jami

Acknowledgments

As always there are many people to thank at the end of the writing process. It seems the list gets longer with every book.

First, I have to thank my husband for being so great and patient with me as I stumbled through this book. He listened to me cry, he encouraged me when I thought I couldn't finish it, and celebrated with me when I had a finished manuscript. Thank you, honey. I love you.

My kids, Zach, Alexa, Julie, and my son-in-law Dillon have been so encouraging and helpful to me. They're busy people with lives of their own, but they never failed to ask me about the book and to encourage me all along the way.

I have to thank my critique partners, Stacey A. Purcell and Carla Rossi for helping plot and form the ideas and characters for this book. Their input and expertise in storytelling was invaluable.

H. Claire Taylor and her **The Story Alignment** for helping me get unstuck when my plot came to a grinding halt. She is a story ninja and pulled me back onto the right path.

During the writing of this book, there were moments when I wasn't sure I could tell the story the way it needed to be told. I needed someone else's eyes and opinions. I want to thank Cristi Duvall, Ruby Dodson, Viper Spaulding, and Kirsten Oliphant for Beta reading and for sharing their honest and sometimes difficult feelings with me. They helped make this book one-thousand times better. Thank you, thank you, thank you.

I also want to thank my proofreaders, Dana Luniewski and Christina Montminy for helping make this book as clean and professional looking as possible.

Thanks again to the talented Najla Qamber of **Najla Qamber Designs** for the beautiful cover and for making my Brides on the Run series memorable.

Of course, I could never deliver a book to you without the expertise of my fantastic editor Serena Clarke of **Free Bird Editing**. She helped me mold this book into something I'm incredibly proud of. I have to thank her too for always being patient with me and for being one of my biggest cheerleaders.

Speaking of cheerleaders, a huge thanks go to my besties Danielle and Sarah for listening to me as I took over our lunch dates to talk about this book. Your friendship, love, and solidarity means the world to me.

I could never write a thank you note without including my mother. She is the absolute best and is always, always in my corner. Thank you, mom. You are my heart.

Y'all I have the best online writer friends that have become like family to me. A gigantic thank you to Maria Luis who walked beside me every step of this book. She picked me up when I was discouraged and celebrated every victory with me. If you haven't read her books, then you totally should. You will also notice that I used her hero from her book

Body Check in my book. Jackson Carter is mentioned as one of Zachsville's hometown heroes.

To all the members of Indie AF, Rom Com Authors Network, DND Author Group, and Writepro Mastermind thank you for being in the trenches with me, for allowing me to celebrate and cry with you and for being the absolute best examples of professionalism and excellence. I love you all.

Lastly, to you the reader. I can never thank you enough for spending your hard-earned money and your precious time reading my books. You make every day special for me. Thank you so very much.

Preview Running From a Rock Star, Brides on the Run Book One

Chapter One

Light seared through Scarlett Kelly's eyelids. She buried her face in the cool pillow to block the glare, but even that slight movement caused an explosion of agony. Pain and nausea crashed into her like a train on fire.

After several minutes of panting through her symptoms, the misery subsided long enough for her to peel open her dry, sticky eyes.

Her conservative dress and equally unadventurous bra stared at her from a condemning puddle on the floor.

Stomach tight, she slid her gaze slightly farther to the right to identify the black pile in her peripheral vision. A motorcycle jacket. Combat boots. Black jeans. And...a guitar? Yes, a beat-up guitar leaned against the wall on the far side of the room. And poker chips littered the carpet like crushed confetti after a wild party.

What the—

Suddenly, something warm cupped her naked breast. She peered down at the large hand connected to a tattooed arm, connected to a...

Oh. My. Lord.

She rotated her head, and a stifled gasp jammed in her throat as she stared into the sleeping face of the man who shared the bed.

Gavin Bain? A thrill skittered through her. The sunlight shone on his raven hair. His smooth bronze skin. Fascinating tattoos. Bam! A memory surfaced through her muddled brain. She'd traced the lines of one of those tattoos, the ninja star on his chest. She'd touched and then kissed her way... Oh, heavens, had she done *that* with this rock god?

She, Scarlett Kelly, children's author and poster girl for responsible living, had sex with Gavin Bain. Gavin Bain, the rock star, AKA *The Delinquent*.

Her brain tried to piece together the previous night. She rarely drank and certainly not to excess. Even during the worst time in her life, alcohol hadn't been involved.

An acute case of bed-head made pushing her red curls from her face a painful challenge. Why had she drunk so much? It all came back in flashes of utter dismay. The Children's Writer's Conference in Las Vegas. Nervous anticipation of signing the contract that would save her family financially. That dream blowing up in her face. Then the added humiliation of overhearing herself described as a No-Fun-Nun.

She'd shown them. Look at her now, naked in a strange man's bed, the absolute picture of wholesomeness.

I've got to get out of here.

She held her breath as she removed his hand and slid from the bed. Moving unsteadily, due to her pounding head and sour stomach, she searched for her clothes, careful to be as quiet as possible.

The purse, bra, dress, and boots were easy. But where were her panties?

A panic attack threatened, and her whole body trembled. Could she have removed her underwear before she got to the room? If so, she hoped that memory stayed hidden. She gave up on the lost undies and headed for the bathroom.

Lord, she needed to pee, but after a prolonged study of the toilet, decided it would be too loud and leaving an unflushed toilet was just bad manners. Even though she'd become, by all appearances, Slutty

McSlut Slut, she couldn't bring herself to be impolite. So she dressed as fast as her shaking hands allowed.

The reflection in the mirror caught her eye, and the blood pounding through her veins turned to ice. Her head jerked toward her image so fast her brain vibrated. For the briefest of seconds, she saw her mother. A tiny whimper cut through the silence, and she ran trembling fingers over her face. People always said she looked like her mother, but now, while making the walk of shame, the resemblance was uncanny. The mental mantra she'd been repeating her whole life reverberated in her head. *I am not my mother. I am not my mother. I am not my mother.* She grabbed her purse and fled the pristine bathroom.

A cool breeze from the air conditioner drifted up her dress and skimmed her bare bottom. She didn't ever go commando—too much freedom. Restrictions were safe. Without restraint, a girl could find herself hung over, panty-less, and on the verge of a nervous breakdown while covertly fleeing a rock star's hotel room.

Oh, wait. That already happened.

She glanced at the door. Nine feet, and she'd be free of this disaster. Logic screamed escape. Compulsion kept her rooted to the spot, and it became imperative that she find her underwear.

I cannot leave without them.

Where could one pair of basic white panties hide? The chandelier was blessedly free of them. Nothing on the drapery rod. But a photo on the desk made life as she knew it come to a screeching halt.

A gaudy cardboard frame held a picture of her and Gavin under a red neon heart. *The Valentine Wedding Chapel of Love* spelled out in rhinestones around the frame's border.

It couldn't possibly mean what she thought it did.

Nooooo.

Next to the picture, the condemning proof—a marriage license issued by the State of Nevada, signed by Gavin Michael Bain and Scarlett Rose Kelly. Her vision blurred, causing the letters on the certificate to dance like cartoon characters.

She wrapped her arms around her middle and glanced back to the gorgeous sleeping man in the bed. A wave of vertigo slammed into her, along with the memory.

She'd told him she'd only have sex with her husband.

With shaking hands, she grabbed the evidence of their reckless night and shoved it into her purse.

While her hard-won reputation exploded into a million pieces, her inner wild child made a victory lap around the room. If that hussy had been driving the bus last night, then she was the reason for this catastrophe.

How could she have been so irresponsible? What was she going to do? No good answer for the first question, but she knew the response to the second. Find the panties and get the heck out of Las Vegas.

She dug through the comforter at the foot of the bed. She kicked at his pile of clothes. She checked behind his guitar.

Nothing.

Nothing.

Nothing.

They had to be under the bed.

Crap.

Not interested in waking The Delinquent, she cautiously made her way to his side and quietly lowered herself to the floor, ignoring the sweet smile he had on his face while he slept. The white material peeked out between the headboard and the mattress. Hallelujah. She reached in and yanked them free.

All the extra movement pounded dizzying pain into her skull. She bent forward and

rested her head on the soft carpet, and waited for the room to stop spinning.

"Are you praying?" asked a sleepy male voice.

She squeaked, then slowly turned her head without lifting it from the carpet. Amusement sparkled in Gavin's smoky gray eyes.

"Yes, I'm praying you're a very bad dream."

He rolled his eyes as if that couldn't possibly be true. "Good one. Why are you really on the floor?"

"I, uh, I..." The marriage certificate hidden in her purse and the cacophony of self-condemning thoughts made it hard to focus.

Suspicion darkened his handsome face. "What are you hiding under the bed? Is there a recording device under there?"

"Are you serious?"

He leveled her with a deadly serious glare. There was no trace of the formerly amused man.

"Actually, there's a reporter from TMZ under here, would you like to say hello?"

When his features went from dark to thunderous, she knew she'd made a critical error with the sarcasm.

"I was just...um...looking for something." She forced herself to meet his eyes.

"Looking for what?" Titanium coated every word and drilled into her hungover brain.

Time to go.

She scrambled to her feet. An increased heart rate, combined with residual alcohol pumping through her system, made the room spin. She swayed and toppled cheek first into the side of the dresser, dropping the panties in the process.

"Ouch!" She covered her face with her hands.

Sheets rustled, and suddenly, he was in front of her. "Shit, are you okay?"

She slowly lowered her hands and...hot mother of a freakin' cow. A very naked Gavin squatted in front of her with all his dangly bits...well, dangling.

"Fine, thanks." That's it? That's the best she could come up with a gorgeous naked guy in front of her. So much for clever repartee.

She honestly did try to keep her eyes above his shoulders, but—come on. This was her last chance to see a rock god in all his tattooed, naked glory. One quick peek, then she rose unsteadily to her feet.

"It was nice to...um...meet you, but I should go." She inched toward the door.

"Wait. You're not going anywhere until I have some answers." He made a grab for her arm. Fear and adrenaline lit her up like a rocket. She forgot her injury, made an evasive move, and sprinted to get away.

When she got to the door, she glanced over her shoulder. Gavin hopped on one foot trying to yank on his jeans. The last thing she saw was her husband as he fell, legs tangled in the fabric of the jeans.

She bolted down the hallway toward the elevator. "Come on, come on, come on." She jabbed the down button repeatedly. A small, logical part of her brain, not currently recovering from near alcohol poisoning, wondered what she hoped to accomplish by running. But the larger, wholly irrational, part of her psyche screamed, Married? I'm freakin' married? I've got to get out of here.

Gavin stumbled from the room and into the hall, still struggling with his jeans. They were over his hips but not buttoned. He strode down the hall toward her.

The indicator bell dinged.

"Stop. Do not get on that elevator."

The sight of him stole the air from her body. Magnificent—scary as hell—but totally, completely magnificent. For a crazy instant, she almost complied, but then the doors slid open and broke the spell. She lunged forward, but relief made her clumsy. She tumbled head over heels into the elevator, dress flying over her head as the doors slid shut.

Great, she'd just mooned her husband.

Continue reading

RUNNING FROM A ROCK STAR

Preview Body Check, Blades Hockey
Book Four

We authors are always up to shenanigans, and that's definitely true of my friend Maria Luis and me. She used my town of Zachsville and Honey in her book Body Check. Here's a sneak peek of Body Check. If you like smokin' hot hockey players, sassy heroines, and steamy scenes that make you want to slap your mama, then you'll love Maria's books.

Chapter One

Holly

The groom is sporting hard wood.

And I'm not referring to the hockey stick he wields around TD Garden for the Boston Blades. No, I'm talking about the metaphorical type of wood—the one that sprang to life in his black tuxedo pants the minute his bride, Zoe, began the walk of all walks down the center aisle of Boston's historical Trinity Church.

My knees burn against the scratchy red rug as I angle my camera to snap a photo of the groom's awestruck expression. While Andre Beaumont—King Sin Bin to hockey fans across the country—may have hired me as his wedding photographer, I'm pretty sure he's not interested in having his erection memorialized in between pictures of Zoe's gorgeous, ivory lace gown and the flower girl prancing down the aisle like a cotton ball made of tulle.

Then again, it's the ball-busting kind of photo that his teammates and brothers-in-hockey-gear would kill to get their hands on, and Andre should have known better than to rope me into this gig.

Swallowing an ill-timed laugh, my fingers slide over the camera's familiar black, plastic frame.

Click.

One inappropriate photo down. Only one hundred-plus elegant ones to go.

Wedding photography isn't my thing. And, sure, maybe it's because I lived the Happily Ever After fairytale and came out on the other side with my gold band tucked away in my dresser and my newly signed divorce papers doused in wine, sweet-and-sour sauce, and dried tears.

It was a rough night.

Scratch that—it's been a rough three years.

Like a moth to a flame, I lower the camera and slide my gaze to the second groomsman standing to the right of Andre. My grandmother once called him "strapping." Accurate, I'll admit, albeit begrudgingly. He's built like a linebacker: tall and broad with muscular thighs that strain the fabric of his tuxedo pants. Dark brown hair that's casually tousled in the same style he's worn for years now. Even when he graced the glossy front page of *Sports Illustrated* last February, he looked exactly the same.

Some things change . . . he hasn't.

Hard, square jaw. Formidable body. Shrewd brown eyes that I imagine terrify his opponents on the ice when he comes barreling toward them.

Jackson Carter.

Captain of the Boston Blades.

Otherwise known as my ex-husband.

Those astute dark eyes meet mine now, and I wait for the rush of familiar emotions to hit me like a freight train. Only, before I have the chance to do my usual shushing of my heart, Jackson's full lips part and he mouths something that looks *suspiciously* like, "Did you just take a picture of his dick?"

And that right there, *that's* the reason why I've felt so lost for the last three years.

Our marriage didn't crumble because one of us cheated. Jackson isn't that sort of guy, and I've always been a one-man kind of woman.

It didn't combust in a ball of fiery flames because we fought like we were prepping our audition tapes for that trashy reality TV show *Marriage Boot Camp*.

No, we simply . . . grew apart.

He passed out on the couch.

I slept in the bed.

He ate meals with his teammates.

I chowed down on mine alone at my desk, late into the evening hours after my employees had already gone home to their families.

He reached out to Andre or the Blades goalie, Duke Harrison, when he needed to talk.

I acted like smothering my emotions was as easy as breathing.

Eleven years ago, I married the man who swept me off my feet during my first semester at Cornell University.

A year ago, we sat opposite each other at a wooden table, our feet locked on our respective sides instead of tangling together the way we'd always done, nothing but our signatures standing in the way of a divorce.

The cry fest with the Chinese food and wine came later that night. No matter how alone I'd felt prior to finalizing our divorce, spending that first night in our house—empty but for the select furniture I'd kept—had been a hard pill to swallow.

Accepting the fact that we'd failed at the *till death do us* part of our vows was even more difficult.

Camera feeling heavy in my hands, I lift my gaze from Jackson's mouth and return silently: "Blackmail."

His eyes crinkle at the corners, and my pathetic heart dives into an incessant *thud-thud-thud* that could rival the quick-paced tempo of an EDM song. *Dammit.* Those creasing laugh lines are more attractive than they have any right to be. Hell, the fact that I still find Jackson attractive at all feels like unjust punishment, doled out for some unknown bad misdeed I've committed in life. Considering my worst transgression of late is accidentally tossing half a burger into a recycling bin, the unyielding attraction seems a bit unfair.

He drags his thumb across his bottom lip, in that revealing way of his that tells me he's trying to wrestle back a grin, and I nearly hurl my camera at his head in retribution.

I can just imagine the newspaper headlines now: *Ex-wife of Famous NHL Player Interrupts Wedding of the Season by Flying Camera—Updates to Follow.*

Once upon a time, I'd made it my mission to make Jackson's infamous steel resolve disintegrate in inappropriate places. He always got me back—generally in bed with me fisting the sheets and his tight body powering into mine.

Now, I swallow hard at the memories and divert my attention to the bride.

Zoe radiates warmth and happiness. When her lips turn up behind the gossamer fabric of her veil, I readjust my grip on the camera and rise to my haunches. Knees cracking, I scoot back to avoid blocking someone's view. The five bridesmaids to my left all smile, as if on cue, and I catch a shot of them, too.

The light streaming in through the stained-glass windows paints them in a mural of jeweled tones, and I know—even if I make my living taking photos of professional athletes—that the picture will be one that's kept on their walls for years to come.

I get Zoe next, just as she steps up to meet Andre and her father gives her away.

Whether or not Andre is still sporting wood, I've got no idea. I keep my gaze above the belt, so to speak, as I step into the dance that's become as familiar to me as breathing over the last number of years: finding the best angles for the best photos.

Beaumont looks down at his bride like she's his greatest gift, and then he throws tradition out the window by lifting the veil and smoothing it back over her head with a mammoth-sized hand.

The Blades' toughest son of a bitch grins, looks at the priest, and announces, "Sorry, Father, I'll always be the worst kind of sinner."

"Andre—" Zoe's hands flutter upward.

He promptly cradles her face with one hand, binds an arm around her back, and, without giving anyone the chance to object, drops a heady kiss onto her mouth.

"Hell fucking yeah!" shouts one of the guys from the groom's side. "Get it, man. Get. It!"

Someone in the pews follows up with an equally boisterous, "Don't get her pregnant in the church, dude!"

The guests roar with laughter, palms kissing with thunderous applause.

I capture it all on camera:

Zoe's wide gaze as her fiancé steals a kiss before the ceremony officially begins.

The top of Andre's dark head as he glides his mouth over his bride's, his hand flexing at the small of her back, as though he's desperate to strip her out of the gown and touch her bare skin.

The bridesmaids whistling.

Father Christopher's red face and twitching lips.

My lens finds Jackson.

Click.

His hands dive into the pockets of his well-tailored pants.

Click.

He grazes his teeth over his lower lip.

Click.

Familiar brown eyes land on my face, startling in their intensity.

Click.

Long ago, he'd look at me just like he is now and whisper in that rough, endearing Texas drawl of his, "Always you."

The sentiment used to send my heart soaring.

Now he only averts his gaze, stubbled cheeks hollowing with a heavy breath, and turns back to the bride and groom.

Click.

The final shutter of the camera mimics the steady rhythm of my heart.

One inappropriate photo down.

Five too many pictures of my ex-husband already catalogued.

Father Christopher clears his throat. "Perhaps we can hold off on the impregnating until after we exchange vows?"

I snort.

And then the four-year-old ring bearer seals Andre Beaumont's sinner status for good. Thrusting one little arm up in the air as Andre releases Zoe and steps back, the kid shouts, "Mommy! Mommy, Mr. Beaumont has a sword in his pants! *I* want one that big!"

I find Andre's shocked expression with my lens.

Click.

I may not have the husband or the white picket fence or the two-point-five kids, but goddamn it, I love my job.

Some days, it feels like enough.

Continue reading ***Body Check***

About the Author

Jami Albright is a born and raised Texas girl and is the multiple award-winning author of The Brides on the Run series--a fun, sexy, snarky, laugh-out-loud good time. If you don't snort with laughter, then she hasn't done her job.

She is also a wife, mother, and an actress/comedian. She used to think she could sing until someone paid her to stop. She took their money and kept on singing.

Jami loves her family, all things Outlander, and puppies make her stupid happy. She can be found on Sundays during football season watching her beloved Houston Texans and trying not to let them break her heart.

Jami loves to hear from readers. You can reach her at

www.jamialbright.com

Made in the USA
Middletown, DE
02 March 2019